The stone c
downward. Th
artisans had ca
had witnessed had not been sufficient, Aryx gaped as each
and every unliving champion roared out a victory cry, followed by the name of him they saluted.

The name "Sargonnas" echoed throughout the Great
Circus. . . .

## CHAOS WAR SERIES

*The Doom Brigade*
**Margaret Weis and Don Perrin**

*The Last Thane*
**Douglas Niles**

*Tears of the Night Sky*
**Linda P. Baker and Nancy Varian Berberick**

*The Puppet King*
**Douglas Niles**

*Reavers of the Blood Sea*
**Richard A. Knaak**

# Reavers
## of the
# Blood Sea

Richard A. Knaak

To my family, both near and far, including
that very young new author,
my nephew Alex.

# REAVERS OF THE BLOOD SEA

Cover art by Jeff Easley
Interior art by Sam Wood
First Printing: May 1999
Library of Congress Catalog Card Number: 98-88139

9 8 7 6 5 4 3 2 1

ISBN: 0-7869-1345-2

T21345-620

U.S., CANADA,                           EUROPEAN HEADQUARTERS
ASIA, PACIFIC, & LATIN AMERICA          Wizards of the Coast, Belgium
Wizards of the Coast, Inc.                                P.B. 2031
P.O. Box 707                                           2600 Berchem
Renton, WA 98057-0707                                       Belgium
+1-800-324-6496                                     +32-70-23-32-77

Visit our website at **www.tsr.com**

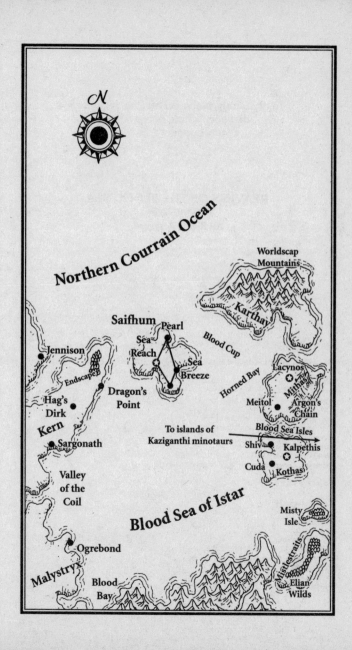

# Adrift in the Blood Sea

## Chapter One

Even though he was barely conscious, Aryx could not help but think how aptly named the Blood Sea was at this moment. The life fluids of his companions had already been spilled into the sea, and soon his own would join theirs, darkening the waters further and no doubt attracting still more hungry denizens of the deep. The minotaur did not fear death at the hands of such creatures, but he wished he could go down fighting, not floating helplessly like some damned gift to the sea goddess Zeboim's pets.

Waves rocked the dusky gray minotaur about like a rag doll. Fog—the same cursed fog that had led to the slaughter aboard the *Kraken's Eye*—cut off all but the faintest light of the pale white moon. None of the constellations, not even those of the gods Sargas or Kiri-Jolith, were visible. In Aryx's jumbled mind, that could only mean that the gods themselves had turned against him.

As he coughed up seawater, flashes of memory returned to haunt Aryx. The screams, the fighting, the flames, the dying, and the fog-enshrouded monstrosities swarming over the ship, dragging what remained of his companions under the surface of the sea after they had finished with their butchery. Brave though the minotaur crew had been, they had stood no chance against their attackers.

Aryx was almost willing to drown rather than recall the images, but in the end, he could do nothing. They swarmed through his mind, and once more the wounded minotaur lived the final minutes of the condemned ship.

1

\* \* \* \* \*

"Damn this fog! Where could it have sprung from?" Graying Jasi stalked the deck of her beloved *Kraken's Eye*, glaring at the thick mist that blanketed everything. She sniffed. "And what's that peculiar scent? Like something musky . . ." Torches provided some light aboard the ship, but they barely penetrated the dense haze. Most of the minotaurs clustered together so they could see one another.

During her years as a captain, Jasi had sailed over much of Krynn, overcoming countless dangers. That she now showed such anxiety over this thick fog greatly disturbed her crew, who respected both her skills and her experience.

"Maybe her sea majesty's displeased with something," the first mate, a black male, muttered. Hugar had sailed with Jasi for more than half the captain's career, and together they had raised three children, one of them now a captain himself. Shorter than many minotaurs, Hugar made up for his lack of height with strength so great that at one time he had been a top contender in the arenas. However, knowing that the arena would keep him separated from his beloved Jasi, he had abandoned the competitions, preferring to be at her side on the high seas. "Maybe it's us she's angry with."

Jasi shook her head. "No, this doesn't feel like one of Zeboim's moods. This is . . . different."

The two dozen members of the ship's crew, including Aryx, listened intently. This was his first voyage on the *Kraken's Eye*, a proud old twin-masted vessel, although it was his fifth year as a ranked crewman. Both in the arena and aboard two previous minotaur vessels, Aryx had proven his worth. Many other captains had offered him positions. Many of his tutors had predicted that even if he did not rise high in the arena, he would command his own vessel some day soon. He had chosen the *Kraken's Eye* with a future command in mind, knowing he could learn much from its mistress. In fact, in the thirteen months since they had sailed from home, the young minotaur had gained more experience and knowledge than he had during all his previous voyages.

Slimmer than most, Aryx compensated for his relatively slight build by being quicker, more determined than most other minotaurs. He had a good eye and a swift hand with both axe and sword. His features were more angular than usual, but among the minotaurs, this made him a bit exotic. Narrow of snout and with attentive, deep brown eyes, Aryx had never lacked for female companionship, even if none of those relationships had lasted very long. Too often he found himself anxious to return to the sea to visit new lands. While this wanderlust was common among his kind, in him it had become almost an obsession. Even his family was hard-pressed to understand Aryx's desires at times.

A slight bumping sound against the ship set his senses on edge, but after seeing no reaction from any of his crew mates, Aryx tried to settle down again. Although he lacked Jasi's experience, he, too, felt something was amiss with this strange weather. Perhaps the dead calm that accompanied the infernal fog had something to do with it. The fog seemed to push in on them, as if it had some dire purpose in mind. Worse, the thicker the fog became, the stronger the musky odor grew. The smell had begun to give Aryx a headache.

Trust in the gods to interfere in your life any way they can. He thought of the ancient family motto, somewhat mangled through the centuries. It was said to have been first mouthed by one of the most famous of Aryx's ancestors. Of the clan Orilg by blood, Aryx could claim direct descent from the legendary renegade Kaziganthi, known also as Kaz of the Axe and Kaz Dragonslayer. In truth, his lineage had both served and worked against him, but in the end, he had always felt stronger because of his birthright.

Once again he heard a slight thumping sound, as if something hard had bumped against the ship. Aryx wanted to go to the rail to see what it might be, but Captain Jasi chose that moment to break the silence.

"Well, we'll never make port if we don't get moving!" Jasi drew herself up, looking every inch the able sailor and commander she was. "If the sails have failed us, then we'll just have to row back." Like many minotaur vessels, the *Kraken's Eye* had been designed for both wind and calm. If nothing else, minotaurs always knew that they could rely on their strength. "Gods or no gods, we're headed home!"

Hugar took the cue. "All right, all of you! Man the oars! It's time to earn your pay! Get moving!"

No one questioned how the captain intended to navigate through the thick haze. Jasi seemed to have a sixth sense about the location of Mithas, or so Aryx had been told. One of the elder crew members had regaled him with stories of the captain finding her way home from halfway around the world even though storms and hostile natives plagued her ship nearly the entire journey. From what little he already knew of her, the young minotaur believed those stories.

The moment Hugar began barking his orders, the crew started to their posts. Everyone save those needed on deck would take to the oars, including Aryx.

No sooner had he taken a step toward the hold, however, than the *Kraken's Eye* began to rock back and forth violently as if it were being slapped around by some great pair of invisible hands. Several crew members lost their footing, and one tumbled into the bowels of the ship. Jasi barely kept her balance. Only the handrail prevented her mate from falling overboard. The fog quickly intensified to the point where Aryx could barely see the minotaur next to him.

"By the horns of Sargas, what's happening?" one of the crew called out. Everyone gathered on deck, trying his best to maintain his balance.

"Have we run aground?" someone asked. "Can't see anything in this blasted mist!"

"This is no natural mist," another sailor muttered.

"Belay that talk!" the captain, barely a shadow, roared.

Hugar had made his way back to Jasi, his concern more for her than the thick fog. One of the other minotaurs, a brawny male called Hercal, cautiously made his way to the side and peered down into the murky sea. Aryx had to squint to make out the outline of the muscular sailor's form.

"Can't see a cursed thing," Hercal muttered. Aryx thought he saw the vague shape of the sailor stiffen. "What by the wrath of the Sea Queen is—"

He never had the chance to finish. As Aryx stared, wide-eyed, a long shadow thrust itself up through the other minotaur's back, then just as quickly sank back out of sight.

Hercal rolled backward onto the deck, at last coming into sight. A gaping hole in his chest spouted crimson, and the minotaur's eyes stared sightlessly up to the hidden heavens. Underneath him, more blood pooled.

The nightmares began swarming over every rail.

Aryx had faced elves, dwarves, and draconians in combat, and none of those races had ever sent so much as the slightest chill of fear through him. Yet now, staring at the vague, horrific shapes climbing onto the *Kraken's Eye*, he felt such foreboding that he could only watch at first, doing nothing to repel the monstrous boarders.

Tall they were, at least half a foot taller than the largest of the crew. These creatures were no minotaurs. Aryx made out shells that seemed to encompass their entire forms, almost giving the appearance of huge lobsters standing upright. Instead of heads, the creatures had knoblike growths where the eyes should be and long, impossibly flexible snouts. The young minotaur knew immediately that nothing like these invaders had ever been reported in the annals of his people's history.

Then one of the horrors raised a wicked, curved weapon, much like a sword-length scythe, with angled and edged teeth, and sliced down the nearest crew member.

The brutal act broke the spell over the rest of the crew. Captain Jasi drew a massive broadsword from her back harness. Hugar, proficient with an axe, appeared at her side, already swinging his heavy weapon down on the nearest of the monstrous invaders. Aryx reached for his own axe, his every thought consumed by the upcoming battle.

Hugar's axe struck the creature's dark armor, bouncing off harmlessly. Jasi barely deflected a multibarbed lance with three heads that threatened to skewer her mate. Then she brought the blade up from underneath, striking not the armored hide, but the general area where the face and possibly throat should have been. The blade buried itself in the murky invader. The fog-enshrouded monster hissed horribly, and then a fount of bright, yellowish liquid splattered both the captain and the first mate.

"Sargas take me!" Jasi cried. "Their blood burns!"

Her warning came too late for one minotaur. Cutting an arc with her battle-axe, the female crew member had nearly severed the squat head of her foe, only to have a shower of acidic fluid drench her face. She dropped her weapon and cried out, the monster's blood having burned her eyes and much of her snout. Before anyone could come to her aid, a second attacker impaled her, twisting the barbed tip of its lance into her midsection. The dead minotaur vanished into the fog, dragged away on the head of the lance.

"Form a square!" Jasi called. The crew tried to obey, but their monstrous adversaries had already moved to cut them off from each other, leaving the minotaurs to fight in small pockets or, worse, by themselves. These were no simple beasts they faced, Aryx realized, but trained warriors.

Another behemoth sought to slice Aryx in half, but he ducked back, receiving a stinging but shallow cut across his midsection. He brought the axe around and managed to sever a three-digited, clawed hand from his shadowy adversary. The attacker emitted a hissing shriek that hurt Aryx's ears, then tried again to cut him down. This time, however, the minotaur took advantage of the creature's slowed reflexes, deflecting the blow and countering with a deadly strike of his own at the horror's unprotected throat.

When the shower of acid came, he had already moved aside to face a second foe. Aryx beat back the barbed lance but could not break his new adversary's defenses. Another of the armored monsters joined the fray, pressing him back. Now facing both lance and scythelike sword, Aryx found his skills with the axe wanting. The armored creatures fought with styles that differed greatly from what he was familiar with. All around him, he saw that the rest of his companions were in similar straits, facing both unfamiliar styles and opposing numbers that continued to grow. Wave after wave of armored terror clambered over the rails, their collective fury focused on the small group trapped on the deck.

At last the monsters' superior numbers exacted their toll. Belac, an elder sailor who had taught Aryx some tricks with the axe, fell, pinned to the deck by three lances in his torso. Krym, on his first voyage aboard the *Kraken's Eye*, called out for help from Aryx just before a scythe-bladed sword decapitated him. Somewhere deep in the fog, Aryx heard another crew member scream, a scream cut mercifully short.

The battle turned into a slaughter. For every watery invader the crew killed, three more took its place. Aryx downed one of his attackers, receiving a stinging shower of acid across his chest, then stumbled away as the other sought to spit him on its lance. He whirled around just in time to witness Hugar fall to his knees, the first mate's axe—and his arm—lying in a bloody pool beside him. A scythe sword came down, cutting a swath through Hugar's chest. With a mournful cry, Captain Jasi rammed the point of her acid-scorched blade through the head of the monster, but too late to save her beloved.

A minotaur named Feresi seized one of the torches and tried to drive several of the creatures back. Her desperate gamble worked at first, the flickering flames seeming to frighten the armored attackers. Several scrambled back to the rail, enabling many of the surviving minotaurs to gather into a group. Aryx and the captain joined Feresi and six others, their combined might stemming the tide for a time.

Unfortunately the minotaurs could not maintain their momentum. Fresh marauders pressed forward. A barbed lance broke through Aryx's defenses, catching Feresi in the stomach. She gasped and dropped the torch. It rolled along the deck, passing between two crew members and leaving in its wake a smoldering trail.

"Hold them!" Jasi cried, blood seeping from a shoulder wound. The armored reaver who had wounded her fell at her feet, its fluids searing the already damaged deck. Aryx gritted his teeth as he stepped into a shallow puddle of the acidic liquid, but he held his place. Everyone's lives depended on holding fast against their attackers.

The minotaurs' strength gradually ebbed. A husky male to Aryx's right fell prey to both scythe sword and lance, his body pulled forward into the mass of monstrous creatures. Aryx watched the corpse disappear into the mist, knowing that he could very well be next.

Warmth suddenly bathed his back, a warmth that swiftly increased. Someone shouted. Aryx heard a crackle of flame and realized, to his horror, that fire now threatened the *Kraken's Eye,* fire likely caused by Feresi's loose torch.

The bright flames slowed the monsters from the deep, but not enough to give any hope. Even if the attackers did retreat, it didn't seem likely the crew would be able to put out the fire in time to save themselves and the ship. Yet still they fought on, for fighting was all that remained for them.

And then Captain Jasi fell.

A scythe sword caught her in the throat. The captain's neck exploded, her chest drenched in crimson. Clutching at the gaping wound, she nonetheless managed to push forward, thrusting her blade at her killer's head. The sword sank in where Aryx guessed the eyes to be. The shadowy invader gave a hissing squeal and fell into her. Minotaur and monster collapsed together.

"Captain!" Aryx cut a path toward Jasi, killing the nearest attacker and pushing several others back. Even before he reached her, the young minotaur could see that she had already died. Snarling, he took his axe and brought it down on another of the armored boarders, managing to cleave through the damnable hide that protected its chest. Pulling back before its life fluids could scar him, Aryx sought out another foe. Desperation and rage controlled him now. He knew that soon he and the others would share the captain's fate, but he would see to it they were accompanied by as many of their attackers as possible.

The small knot of defenders had shrunk to no more than a handful. Aryx cut down one foe in an attempt to save a companion, only to watch helplessly as two other reavers impaled the same minotaur on their lances. Aryx shattered one of the lances but could not prevent the remaining attacker from flinging the dying minotaur aside.

Kiri-Jolith, he thought, if you watch over me, may you and not the Horned One take my spirit when I perish. He had never had much time for gods, be it Sargas, father of the minotaurs, or Kiri-Jolith, God of Just Causes, whose worshipers among Aryx's race had been grudgingly accepted only a century ago by the rulers in Nethosak. Now he hoped his family's long history of following the way of the bison-headed god would give him some benefit in the afterlife.

The flames pressed on one side, the monstrous warriors on the other. Somehow Aryx found himself nearly flattened against a rail. With him stood only three other crew members, although two or three more still fought futilely elsewhere on the deck.

A fog-enshrouded form so immense that it loomed over the rest raised a scythe sword, its attention clearly fixed on the minotaur nearest Aryx. Aryx moved to deflect the attack. Only too late did he realize that the attack had been merely a ploy; the scythe sword cut a twisting arc back toward *him*. Unable to bring the head of his axe back in time, Aryx tried to defend himself with the handle.

Powered by the great strength of its wielder, the scythe sword cut easily through the thick axe handle and, barely slowed, across the chest and stomach of the hapless fighter. Aryx roared in agony but refused to topple. He grabbed the upper half of his axe and threw his entire weight into one last blow. The axe head sank deep into white flesh just below the creature's wriggling snout.

Foul, burning blood spewed over him, blinding Aryx in one eye and sending the rest of his senses into turmoil. He felt part of the edge of the shelled horror's sword pass into his side as the pair grappled.

They fell against the rail, shattering it. Both combatants plummeted into the Blood Sea, still clutching one another.

He broke free from the creature's grasp before they bobbed to the surface. Through his good eye, Aryx caught a glimpse of the murky shape of his adversary rolling onto its back, its arms floating limply at its side. A moment later, the still form slowly sank out of sight.

Aryx tried one feeble stroke, then dropped his arm. He could feel his life slowly ebbing from him. The waves began to push him away from the blazing inferno that had once been the *Kraken's Eye*. He heard another cry and knew that there could be only one or two defenders left.

Something bumped against his legs. His first thought was of sharks, but then the new outline of one of the aquatic attackers rose from the water next to him.

A three-digited claw reached out toward him. Aryx wanted desperately to reach out and try to choke the monstrous reaver, but he couldn't even raise a finger. Even when the sinister figure raked his open wound with its claw, Aryx could do nothing to defend himself.

He watched as the creature turned and swam away from him. Rather than at least give him an honorable death, it had decided he was too far gone to be worth the effort. Aryx was left to die a slow, ignominious death in the water.

The *Kraken's Eye* was little more than a blazing shadow in the fog. The sounds of combat had ceased. Aryx heard a series of splashing sounds. The attackers had begun to abandon the ruined vessel. Moments later the ship itself began to list to the stern.

Mercifully, Aryx passed out before he could witness the *Kraken's Eye*—and his hopes—vanish beneath the dark waters.

\* \* \* \* \*

At first it amazed him that he still lived, but Aryx knew the state might be only a temporary one. Even as his mind relived the death of his friends and fellow crew members, the wounded minotaur noted that he could no longer feel either his legs or his left arm. At least the pain had lessened.

Not long now, he thought dimly. The fog had thinned slightly, but somehow it seemed even more oppressive. Aryx could see no sign of life. He heard only the lapping of the waves and the distant roar of the Maelstrom. Eventually, if the sharks didn't get to him first, he would drift inexorably toward the Maelstrom, then be sucked down into the Abyss.

"Kiri . . . Kiri-Jolith," he gasped, his voice barely more than a whisper. "I'm no coward, but I ask again that you take me before . . . before . . ." Aryx's voice failed him. His head dipped beneath the water, and he had to fight to force it up again. Soon it would be over.

The familiar sound of oars in the water startled him. At first the wounded minotaur believed he had imagined the sound, but then he heard it again. A booming voice, a voice that could not have come from one of his kind, called out unintelligible orders. Human, perhaps, or maybe that of an elf or dwarf, although it seemed unlikely either of the latter two would be out here. Only the humans even came close to matching the minotaurs' love of sailing and exploration.

But what was a human ship doing out in such treacherous waters?

It didn't matter. In this fog, they'd sail right past him. Even if they did spot him, he had bled too much to survive. Only a cleric could save him now, and any vessel daring to sail in these parts wasn't likely to have a cleric on board. These newcomers were probably marauders or pirates.

An ominous shape took form in the mist, growing larger by the second. Through his good eye, Aryx judged it to be several times the size of his own proud vessel. A warship, in all likelihood. A human warship.

Closer and closer it came. Torchlight on the deck created an eerie halo in the fog. He spotted figures on deck and heard the clank of metal against metal.

The ship would pass within a few yards of him. Vague hopes sprang in Aryx's breast. He tried to call out, but all that escaped his mouth was a gasp. His head began to swim, and the minotaur fought to stay conscious.

Aryx could hear the well-synchronized oars dipping into the water as the immense ship neared him, but he no longer fought to gain the crew's attention. The numbness had spread throughout his entire body. Aryx just wanted to sleep, to forget the pain, the horror, the shame.

In his last moments of consciousness, the minotaur dreamed that the ominous vessel sighted his limp body. They lowered a small boat, manned by humans clad in dark clothing. The sole exception seemed to be a tall figure in flowing, light-colored robes, who appeared to be guiding the small boat toward Aryx. He imagined that, despite his condition, they pulled him from the water and returned to the great ship, where the crew carefully hoisted him aboard.

The dream faded for a time, and when it returned, Aryx thought he saw several figures, mostly human, standing over him, including a young man in the robes of a cleric and an older, scowling warrior in ebony armor. They drifted from his view, to be replaced by a tall, blood-colored minotaur whose face bore the scars of many years of battle and who stared at Aryx curiously. Although he seemed old enough to be Aryx's father, the other minotaur looked capable of besting even the strongest of the champions of the Great Circus. Curiously, however, instead of a kilt and harness, the crimson minotaur wore an immense dark cloak that seemed to flutter despite there being no wind.

His image filled Aryx's world, becoming more distorted with each passing moment. The crimson minotaur leaned forward, as if still uncertain of what he saw. Deep within, Aryx knew that the moment the dream ended, his own life would end with it. He accepted that fact, knowing that if Kiri-Jolith took him, it would be all he could ask for.

The image of the other minotaur twisted first into fog, then faded into darkness. As the dream came to an end and consciousness slipped away, Aryx heard a human voice mutter, "I would say welcome aboard the *Vengeance*, warrior, but by the time you recover, you may wish the Maelstrom had taken you instead. . . ."

# Dread Companions

## Chapter Two

The realization that he still lived struck Aryx when brief but intense pain jolted him to consciousness. He opened his eyes and tried to focus on his surroundings. Instead of endless miles of the fog-enshrouded Blood Sea, Aryx saw that he lay upon a bunk in the bowels of a ship. A single oil lamp on one wall illuminated his surroundings. Other than the bunk, a simple wooden table, one chair, and a good-sized chest, little else decorated the spartan chamber. The room in which he lay could hold a dozen warriors or more if they did not mind being crowded, but Aryx suspected it instead served some other purpose, perhaps as some officer's quarters. On the wall opposite him stood the only exit, a strong, wooden door. Gradually bits and pieces of what he had thought to be a dream came back to him, along with the knowledge that the dream had been reality.

He tried to rise, but stiffness and pain prevented him. Yet the pain proved far less terrible than what he had suffered aboard the *Kraken's Eye*. Cautiously Aryx touched his chest, moving his hand down to his stomach. The wounds that should have been fatal had been healed. Only long scars remained. Stunned, Aryx forced himself to a sitting position. This time he found he could fight the pain.

A detailed examination confirmed his suspicions. All of his wounds had been healed, even the burns from the monsters' acidic blood. The vague image of a human in clerical robes returned to him. With it came the other images, especially the faces of the cleric's companions: the knight in ebony, a foreboding presence; the older minotaur, the one with the disturbing, questioning gaze.

What had one of the humans uttered? *I would say welcome aboard the* Vengeance, *warrior, but by the time you recover, you may wish the Maelstrom had taken you instead.* So this warship, carrying both humans and minotaurs, bore the name *Vengeance*. A name of strength, of determination. Aryx had no quibbles with the choice, but the rest of the other's words made little sense. Why might he regret being rescued?

He would find out nothing by remaining in bed. The answers lay without, and he determined to go above deck. Carefully the minotaur lowered his legs from the bunk. They ached, but the pain he had experienced earlier did not return. Greatly encouraged, Aryx placed his feet on the floor, then, adjusting to the ship's rocking motions, the once-injured warrior stood. At first his legs seemed ready to buckle, but with effort, he kept them straight.

He looked around for a weapon. Despite the fact that their cleric had healed him, Aryx did not assume that his rescuers were his friends. If marauders, they might want him as a slave or as a source of information. Aryx also wanted a weapon simply because of his own uncertainty. Memories of the monsters that had slaughtered his companions still burned in his mind. What if the creatures attacked this vessel as well? Would even the *Vengeance*, with its possibly larger crew, be immune from such danger?

On teetering legs, Aryx began to search. However, he had only just begun when he heard someone at the door. Moving as quietly as he could, the minotaur tried to hide behind it in order to ambush any potential foe.

The door opened a crack. A voice Aryx had heard once before called out, "If you try to jump me, warrior, you are only going to splatter your dinner over the floor. After a day without food, I would imagine you have a hole in you as big as the Abyss, so you might not want to do that."

The gray minotaur stepped to the center of the room and faced the entrance. "All right. I won't try anything."

The door swung open, pushed aside by the same tall, robed human Aryx recalled from his dreams. Pale and blond, he had the solid, earthy features one might have found on a farmer. Blue eyes watched the minotaur with some slight amusement, but the thin mouth remained set in a neutral expression. Aryx wondered if this was the one who had healed him, for the young human wore a cowled robe colored

13

brown and white, and from his neck hung a medallion with the profile of a bison upon it.

A cleric of Kiri-Jolith! Aryx had met a few such clerics, for they were scarce among his own people. He wondered if he should kneel in the other's presence, but he held back. This might be a cleric, but he was also a human.

In one hand, the newcomer held a bowl that contained a concoction that looked like a mixture of fish and seaweed. The handle of a wooden spoon thrust upward from the center of the unsightly contents. The food repelled him, but nevertheless the minotaur's stomach grumbled loudly. His visitor chuckled. "I hope you still feel that way about it after the fourth or fifth mouthful. It tastes as awful as it looks."

At the moment, Aryx didn't care. Once he had hold of the bowl, he quickly began devouring the contents, not even bothering to sit back down on the bunk until well into his meal. The cleric stood over him, watching.

As the first mouthfuls reached his stomach, Aryx began to calm down. He looked up to study the cleric. Not much older than he, if Aryx reckoned human years correctly. Faint lines under the eyes, though, as if this cleric had lived through some troubles. For a human, the nose seemed a little on the majestic side, although compared to a minotaur's, it looked like a mere knob. The blond hair hung shoulder-length and seemed well groomed. Perhaps there was a hint of a well-to-do background after all.

The robed figure handed him a water sack, and Aryx drank thirstily. After the young warrior had returned the sack to him, the stranger asked, "Do you have a name?"

"Aryx."

"What clan?"

The younger warrior hesitated only briefly. "I am Aryximaraki de-Orilg. My father, Marak, fought in the War of the Lance. My grandfather slew seven ogres in one battle." With a hint of defiance, he added, "I trace my ancestry directly to Kaziganthi de-Orilg, also known as Kaz of the Axe, Kaz Dragonslayer, Kaz the—"

"Say no more! Say no more!" His rescuer laughed. "I know all the names. He is spoken of even amongst us humans, although not so openly! It is said he fought side by side with the hero Huma of the Lance. Very impressive, although I know that being one of his descendants cannot have always made it easy for you. His reputation for defiance against the powers-that-be in your kingdoms was well known." He sobered, pointing at his medallion. "Well, I certainly cannot claim such illustrious ancestry, and my calling is plain to see. You will need a friend aboard, though, and I hope to be one. You may call me Rand."

"Well met, Rand." With some hesitation, they briefly clasped hands. Aryx felt he could trust the cleric . . . to an extent. "You saved me, didn't you?"

"I had that humble honor. In truth, I did not know if I could. Such things are more the field of followers of Mishakal, but Kiri-Jolith granted me such talent."

"Thank you." Aryx took a breath, then asked the questions that had been haunting him since he had awakened. "What is this ship, cleric? A human one, I know, but why is it in these waters? I remember a warrior in black, an older human . . ."

"Broedius." Rand did not speak the name with fondness. "The knight is Lord Broedius. You'll be meeting him soon."

"Why are they here? I also saw another minotaur, a cleric of the state, I think. Where—"

"Listen to me, Aryx." When the cleric had Aryx's full attention, he shook his head and continued. "You will know soon enough what is happening, warrior. As soon as you go up on deck, in fact. Broedius said that as soon as you recovered enough, I was to bring you to him immediately."

"Bring me to him?" Aryx tensed, suspecting some sort of inquisition. Humans and minotaurs had never been on very good terms, and a warship meant humans with a mission of conquest . . . a mission that had, perhaps not so coincidentally, led them deep into minotaur waters. . . .

"Don't jump to conclusions." Rand stared deep into Aryx's eyes. "Forget everything you know, warrior!" The cleric seemed to force the next words out. "Forget that your people have been free since the War of the Lance. Forget everything about Krynn you ever thought had to be. It will be better in the long run if you do." Before Aryx could protest, Rand shook his head. "I know you don't want to listen, but I have to try. I must take you now to Lord Broedius. There is no choice. You definitely look stronger, and it would not be wise to delay. When you are before him, answer any questions as honestly as you can. Ask no questions of your own." When

Aryx sought to interrupt, the cleric cut him off. "Ask no questions of your own, I said . . . but listen. If you listen, you will learn. That is all I can say."

"Cleric—"

Rand rose. "Come. I suspect Lord Broedius is already growing impatient. He wanted to question you even as I worked to save your life, minotaur."

Curiosity mingled with anxiety. Aryx bit back the questions he wanted to ask. In silence, he followed the human outside, where a faint trace of the musky scent greeted him. Aryx hesitated, recalling the attack, but the trace seemed so weak that he finally decided to push aside his anxiety rather than shame himself before his rescuers.

Their journey proved a short one, but by the time Aryx stood on deck, he had already learned a great deal. The *Vengeance*, a great, black-sailed, three-masted vessel, bristled with humans, all clad in dark armor adorned by a skull and death lily pattern. The eyes of each warrior bore an intensity that unsettled him. He had never seen, much less heard of, humans so dedicated to war, save perhaps the Knights of Solamnia, but he knew that these were not the fabled knights. This force had some more dire purpose in mind, something they intended to back up with an impressive show of arms. How many there were on the vast ebony ship he could not estimate, but it was a sizable force indeed.

Yet if the warriors disturbed him, those who commanded them made him pause. Rand had to urge him on, or else Aryx would have remained where he was, staring at Lord Broedius and the two who stood near him. The knight himself, although not quite as tall as a minotaur, was as broad as one, even without the armor. Broedius had eyes of the darkest black, even darker than his garments, and a heavy, furred brow that shadowed those dark, wary orbs. Below the wide, flat human nose hung a thick, ebony mustache that draped down the edges of his tightly set mouth. Lord Broedius wore armor akin to that of his men, save that the patterns were more elaborate. Attached at his shoulders was a long, draping cloak of dark red.

Beside him, clad in similar armor, stood a smaller, wiry figure whom Aryx did not recall. Although, among his own race, female warriors had always been as common as males, the only female knights among humans that Aryx had ever heard of had been some of the dragon highlords during the War of the Lance. While she was certainly too young to have been one of them, this female appeared to have been struck from the same mold. She stood as if poised to attack at any moment. Like Broedius, she wore her visor open, but while her features were a much softer version of his, possibly even attractive by human standards, she had the exact same deep black eyes and an even more determined expression. Her delicate upturned nose and soft, full lips did nothing to detract from her combative image.

"Well, Rand," Broedius rumbled, sounding almost like a minotaur. "You spoke true after all."

"I do not make promises I cannot keep." The pale, blond human looked almost as out of place as Aryx felt among so many black-armored figures, and no wonder. The knights did not seem to be worshipers of the bison-headed god. Judging by their garments, any god they followed had to be of a nature as dark as Lord Broedius's eyes.

"Yet I thought only a cleric of Mishakal could have saved this one from so near death."

Rand showed no trace of pride, only acceptance. Despite his relative youth, the thin cleric did not seem at all fearful of the knight. "It came to me in a sudden vision that I could keep him from dying. You, of all people, should understand visions, Lord Broedius. I would not be here otherwise."

The knight seemed ready to argue the point, but at that moment, another figure spoke. This human should have been the one Aryx noticed most, and yet until the cloaked figure had broken his silence, the young minotaur had completely forgotten him. "You have questions to ask this one. Ask them and be done with it."

The deep, commanding voice left a trail of silence in its wake. Before Aryx stood the cloaked minotaur from his dreams, the tallest of his own kind that the prisoner had ever seen. He had thought the blood-red color of the other's fur a creation of his delusions, but Aryx saw now that the stranger's fur bore a deep crimson tint the likes of which the young warrior had never seen among minotaurs. The cloaked stranger stood off to the side, looking around absently, as if only partially interested in the matter at hand. Indeed, since he had spoken, the mysterious minotaur's gaze had already turned elsewhere.

Broedius appeared ready to reply, but then he simply nodded toward the female, who suddenly called out, "The minotaur will step forward and identify himself!"

"Answer . . . don't ask," Rand whispered.

Head high, Aryx walked toward Broedius until the latter indicated he should stop. Two more knights abruptly flanked the minotaur. Broedius and the female knight studied him closely. Rand tried to give him a reassuring nod, but Aryx felt no better.

"Your name, minotaur?" Broedius's aide demanded.

"Aryximaraki—"

"Shortened form only."

"Aryx."

"Your vessel?"

"I sailed aboard the *Kraken's Eye*." He felt no concern about revealing such information, not with the ship now lying at the bottom of the Blood Sea.

"How long since you've berthed at home port?"

"Just over thirteen months."

The woman paused briefly, as if mulling over his answer. Then, more carefully, she asked, "What contact have you had with other minotaur vessels in that time?"

Aryx had to think. Jasi had been an adventurer, seeking out regions rarely frequented. "We saw three, maybe four vessels." What could these knights possibly do with such useless information? "The last one was probably six or seven months ago. They'd been out even longer than we had."

Broedius nodded to himself, an action that sent an unsettling sensation through Aryx's stomach. What had he said that so satisfied the human?

The aide continued the questioning. "How many crew aboard your ship?"

So far, all questions had come from the woman, but Aryx saw that her commander observed very closely how the minotaur answered. Aryx wondered how well the human could read a minotaur's expression. "Just over twenty."

This response made the woman glance at her commander. Broedius nodded slightly and the other knight went on. "Tell us what happened. Omit no detail, however fantastic you might think it. Your life may depend upon it."

Aryx longed to look to Rand for some support, but to do so would have been to show weakness, however slight. He

18

stared back into the black eyes of the knight, daring Broedius to find fault with the story he would relate.

Once more Aryx relived the horrible fate of the *Kraken's Eye* and its crew, but at no time did he reveal any of his pain to the humans questioning him. They listened intently as he described Hercal's surprising death, then the swarming of the monstrous marauders. Only when Aryx failed to describe the creatures in enough detail did the woman interrupt, asking for things that the minotaur could never recall because the fog had shielded them from his gaze. The weary minotaur found himself grateful when she finally allowed him to go on with the rest of the story. As the only survivor, Aryx experienced each death acutely, in great part because of the shame he felt for not having perished with his fellow crew members. Delving so long and so deep made those deaths painful all over again.

Not once did Lord Broedius himself interrupt, although occasionally a questioning expression briefly crossed his features. Only when Aryx grew silent did the knight at last speak. "So. A tale of exceptional interest . . . if it's true."

The minotaur bristled. "I do not lie."

"No, I suppose you don't. I suppose you tell as much as you can recall. . . ." Broedius turned, as if he were about to say something to the cloaked minotaur, but to Aryx's surprise, the tall figure had moved. Instead, he now stood by the rail, staring out into the fog as if searching for something. The knight grunted, again eyeing the shipwreck survivor. "My respects for the loss of your comrades."

"A horrifying end," muttered Rand. Only Aryx seemed to notice him glance surreptitiously at the female knight, although the reason escaped the survivor. As for Broedius's words of sympathy, the minotaur found them wanting. The knight's tone indicated that he found the crew's death only mildly disturbing; the monsters who had slaughtered the crew of the *Kraken's Eye* interested him much more.

"Shadowy, shelled monsters with clawed hands, swords, and lances . . . that sums up your description, yes? Not much to go on."

"Imagine a fog ten times as thick as what you see now," Aryx returned, angered. The knight had not been there; he had not been fighting for his life. Aryx had not had time to try to study the attackers close up. To do so, he would have had to practically climb into the deadly behemoths' arms.

Dissatisfied, Broedius forced Aryx to go over every detail he could recall about the creatures. Had he ever seen or heard of such beasts before? Could they have been armored sea elves? What were the dimensions of their weapons, and did it seem they preferred one over another? What tactics did they use? What tactics proved most effective against them? His memory still very hazy, the minotaur could only give vague answers at best, none of which seemed to satisfy the Dark Knight's appetite for information.

The questions went on for more than an hour, and by the time the human had finished with him, Aryx almost teetered from exhaustion. Although he had been healed by the cleric and then had been given food and drink, he had not yet had the opportunity to completely recover his strength. Nonetheless, the young warrior kept as straight as he could, refusing to let a human see any frailty.

The commander stared at him. "You've nothing more to add?"

"Nothing," Aryx returned, some of his exasperation evident in his tone.

"Then this interview is at an end," Broedius abruptly announced. He rose. "Knight-Warrior Carnelia." The female beside him snapped to attention. "Take charge of this one."

"Yes, sir."

Without another word, Broedius turned on his heels and strode away, disappearing a moment later through a cabin door guarded by two visored knights. Carnelia marched over to Aryx, blandly stating, "You are now a member of the crew of the *Vengeance*. You will obey all orders at all times or you will be punished. Since the wind refuses to blow, you will be assigned to the oars."

"He needs more time to recover, Carnelia. A day at least."

The knight jumped at the sound of the cleric's voice so near her. Aryx fought back a grin, having watched Rand silently join them. A flush of red filled the woman's cheeks. However, her gaze remained fixed on the minotaur. "What do you say? Are you still weak?"

The last question stirred up Aryx's blood. Although his body ached and he yearned for sleep, he could not bring himself to admit it to this human. "I can row."

Carnelia looked up at Rand. "He has made his decision."

"Just because he is as stubborn as your uncle does not make his decision—"

"Take care, Rand. My uncle suffers your presence aboard this ship, but only because you're protected."

"And he has need of my abilities. Let us not forget that." The cleric eyed Aryx. "If you insist on killing yourself at the oars, minotaur, at least let me give you something to ease the pain you will soon be—"

"Cleric." This time it was Rand's turn to jump. Aryx twitched but managed to hide his own surprise. The cloaked minotaur had joined the group without anyone noticing him.

Like Broedius, the crimson minotaur had asked no questions. In fact, he had seemed entirely oblivious to the inquisition, instead staring out at the sea or the shrouded heavens. That he now took interest in Aryx seemed to confuse not only the prisoner, but the others as well.

The cloaked figure towered over all of them. For the first time, Aryx noticed the stranger's eyes. No minotaur he had ever met had eyes so crimson, even when under a berserker rage. The eyes belied the calm, almost chill attitude the mysterious newcomer conveyed. In them, Aryx saw fury barely held in check, fury and a hint of tremendous frustration.

The cleric's pale countenance grew paler. Even Carnelia seemed put off by the newcomer. Both humans gave the minotaur respectful berth. Aryx felt an intense, almost primal, urge to kneel, but fought it, not at all understanding why he should want to give this stranger fealty.

"Cleric," the cloaked figure repeated. "Have you had another vision concerning this warrior?"

Recovering, Rand shook his head. "No, but—"

"Then let all proceed about our business." With that one sentence, the mysterious figure ended all protest by the human. However, to Aryx's secret dismay, he now became the subject of the other minotaur's attention. "Aryximaraki de-Orilg. You fought. You remain true. I accept that . . . and you. Your patron chose well."

With those enigmatic words, he turned from the party, heading once more for the rail. For several seconds, no one spoke, all eyes still fixed upon the receding figure. Then, without thinking, Aryx blurted out the questions that had been preying on his mind since he had been brought before Broedius. "Who is he? What's happening here? Why does a cleric of the state sail aboard a human warship?"

The moment he finished asking, regrets engulfed him. Aboard the *Vengeance*, he had no rights. The humans had saved him, but only to toil for them as a slave. By demanding answers, he could encourage them to throw him back over the side rather than deal with his mutinous behavior. The young minotaur tensed; if they tried, he would see to it that he did not go overboard alone.

"Calm yourself, Aryx." Rand put a comforting hand on his shoulder. Aryx shrugged it off. Carnelia began to reach for her blade, but Rand intervened. "A few simple answers would not hurt and would certainly go a long way toward easing present tensions." He steepled his fingers. "Although I am human and you are minotaur, I believe we follow the same god, Aryx. You follow the ways of Kiri-Jolith, do you not?"

"I may, but that does not make us comrades in arms, human. We're still of two races, with little love between them."

"Fair enough, but I hope you will at least believe me when I say I now speak to you the truth."

The female knight's face grew flush. "Enough of this politeness, Rand! The minotaur wants the truth? Then he'll hear it plainest from me!" She thrust a gauntleted finger into Aryx's chest, a riskier action than she knew. "Here's what all minotaurs will know soon enough! This ship is the *Vengeance*, flagship of the Knights of Takhisis! And though you can't see them in this fog, behind her sail *Predator* and the *Queen's Veil*, equally as commanding in size and strength. Each vessel carries a full contingent of knights dedicated to our lady's cause. Over the past few years, we have taken control of most of your outer settlements, and now we sail for your capital in order to take full command of your race in the name of her glorious majesty!"

"Humans?" Anger rose. Aryx knew too well the story of his race, how although superior in so many ways to the others, it had nonetheless been enslaved time and time again. The Orilg clan had a long tradition of fighting against such masters, legend stating that Kaziganthi had even slain a great red dragon who had manipulated the minotaurs' lives for years. Now, only a generation after they had regained their freedom from the dragon highlords, the humans again sought them for slave soldiers. "Not this time! Never again will we follow the madness of humans. Not even a score of warships twice the size of this one would be sufficient to bring us under heel! Fight your own wars; we'll have none of them!"

Some of the humans on deck looked up at this outburst, but Aryx didn't care. He would fight here and now if need be.

Rand kept a hand on Carnelia's sword arm, preventing her from drawing her weapon. Curiously, she did not attempt to remove the cleric's hand, although he certainly had no right to stop her from acting against Aryx. Fighting down her fury, the knight leaned forward. "Stupid bull! There's a war barely started that's already ravaged good portions of Ansalon and will engulf the rest of it before long! This is no longer one race against another! This is for the future of all Krynn, and we, the Knights of Takhisis, are that future!"

He couldn't believe her audacity. Did these humans think that his people would sit idly by? "And how will you convince my people of your destiny? How, with only these three ships, do you plan to become our masters? Your ships will be sunk before they enter the harbor, and even if that doesn't happen, once the emperor hears your demands, he'll merely laugh! By the gods—"

Rand intervened, but not as Aryx might have expected. "Let it pass, warrior. This is a battle you cannot win. Come with me."

The furious minotaur pulled away from the other human. "What sort of cleric of Kiri-Jolith are you? Where's your spine? Surely you cannot condone—"

Rand kept his calm. "Only a fool fights a futile battle, Aryx. You do not understand everything that has happened or will happen. Come with me and cool off, or you will be dead where you stand. Look about you if you do not yet see that."

Rand took hold of Aryx and forced the minotaur to see what his outburst had caused. Nearly a dozen knights had come to reinforce Carnelia, every one of them with his weapon drawn. Aryx might stop one or two of them, but without his axe, he would be cut to ribbons in seconds.

"Let not anger rule," Rand uttered, possibly speaking to both minotaur and woman. "The true warrior follows reason and care. So says Kiri-Jolith."

The knights stood ready, awaiting Carnelia's command. Aryx took a deep breath, surveying those surrounding him. He desperately desired to strike back, but Rand was right.

Any action he took would only result in his useless death. Yet to back down seemed so cowardly, so dishonorable. . . .

It took the greatest of efforts, but Aryx managed to smother his fury. The cleric relaxed, but Carnelia remained poised for attack. It took Rand some time to assuage her, finally succeeding only when he promised to take full responsibility for the minotaur.

The knight glared at Aryx. "Learn your place, bull, or even the cleric's promise won't be enough to save you. Now, since you seem so full of vigor after all, I think even Rand can't argue about your manning the oars."

"I'll row."

The cleric stepped around her. "I'll take him there, Carnelia."

"Perhaps that might be better." She gave Aryx one last dark look, and as he turned to follow the cleric, the Knight of Takhisis called out, "You asked how we'll become masters of your kind, minotaur? Turn your gaze to the robed one by the rail. Do you see him?"

Aryx stared at the strange minotaur with the crimson eyes. The other paid him no mind, apparently still transfixed by something beyond the fog. Unsettling as the mysterious minotaur might be, he surely could not take on the legions of the emperor by himself. "That's your answer? One cleric will not turn an entire people into willing slaves!"

"Carnelia!" Rand shook his head. "We have been sworn! Not until landfall."

She gave the other human a peculiar smile, as if the two of them shared something that no one else could understand. "I wasn't going to tell him everything, but he can know this much. Believe what you like, minotaur, but know this: When we dock, all we've got to do is wait for the robed one. He'll deliver your people to us, make no mistake about it, and none will be able to stand against him when he does."

The woman turned and stalked off. The other knights returned to their duties. Aryx inhaled deeply, trying not to lose control of himself. Finally he whirled on the cleric. "What does she mean, human? Who is that? What can he do to make my people bend their knee to Broedius and his ilk?"

Despite the difference in size, Rand took hold of the minotaur by the arm and turned him away. "We are sworn, she and I. She said too much as it is. You will learn all in good time, Aryximaraki, as will your people. Trust me at least when I say that if there were another choice, I would not have matters follow this path."

"I don't understand."

"You will, in time. Leave the matter at that. The best thing now would be to do as she said. Go to the oars," Rand urged. "The Knights of Takhisis are not a patient lot."

"How do you come to be with them, cleric? How does one who follows the God of Just Causes come to be with Takhisis's soldiers?"

Rand ushered Aryx to the hold. "As with all else, you will know that when the time comes. However, if it gives you some comfort, know that Kiri-Jolith, too, watches over his children. He will not forget us."

The young minotaur snorted. So far, Kiri-Jolith had not shown all that much interest in his fate, not if having him rescued by the Knights of Takhisis could be used as an example. However, as they descended into the hold, Aryx did give thanks for one thing. If Kiri-Jolith did not have time to watch over him, then certainly the Horned One, Sargas, had even less interest in following the warrior's tribulations. Aryx hoped it would remain that way, for it had been said in the Orilg clan that when Sargas—or Sargonnas, as the humans knew him—took interest in one of his so-called children, that interest had a quick and bloody way of shortening the chosen one's life.

# Nethosak

## Chapter Three

At times Aryx thought his arms might wrench free at the shoulders, but still he worked. When he rowed he did not have to think. Aryx already had too much to think about, and not only what he had learned on deck that first night. In the days that had followed, he had learned much, much more, yet at the same time, the number of questions clogging his mind had grown a thousandfold.

Most of what he had learned had come to him from Rand. From the cleric had come the shocking revelation that hundreds, perhaps even thousands, of minotaurs already worked in the service of the Knights of Takhisis. He hadn't believed what he had been told during his first encounter, but Rand spoke with such a sense of truth that Aryx could no longer deny it. The dark-armored humans had once more enslaved his kind, once more forced them to fight for a cause that meant nothing to them.

It did not end there, though. Rand would not say why, but it seemed that something drastic had changed the war, that now the humans needed to step up their efforts. Perhaps the war against their rival human factions had turned sour; the human did not say for certain. Rand said only that more than ever the Knights of Takhisis needed the strength and courage of the minotaurs. They had seen it in some vision they all shared, some perverse dream come down from their barbaric goddess.

A hand fell upon his shoulder, causing Aryx to miss a stroke. "Aryx. Stop. You have gone two shifts. You will kill yourself and not do anyone any good."

He shrugged off both Rand's hand and concern. "I'm fine! Let me row!"

"A warrior does not shirk from battle," the cleric reprimanded. "Even if that battle is in his head. Besides, come the morrow, you will not have this to help you hide from your thoughts. Tomorrow we will reach Nethosak."

"Tomorrow?"

"Yes, tomorrow . . . and since you have not been on deck for some time, I have other news for you. We left the fog behind a short while back. The wind is finally starting to pick up as well."

Aryx eyed the other rowers, for the most part unarmored knights. When he had first entered the hold, he had expected to find slaves or prisoners, but such was not the case on the ships commanded by Lord Broedius. Instead, Broedius had his officers assign each man to different shifts whenever the oars were needed. This he apparently saw as a way of keeping his soldiers fit while aboard ship. On days when the wind sufficed, other forms of exercise were used.

Utilizing his men served another purpose as well. Carrying slaves or prisoners meant unnecessary mouths to feed and, more importantly, the possibility of insurrection. Broedius had too much on his mind already without adding potential problems.

As he joined Rand, Aryx wondered about his own status. He did not exactly seem to be a prisoner, but neither did the Knights of Takhisis treat him as a comrade. Yet he had been tolerated in many ways, which further confused the young minotaur. For reasons not apparent, the humans were forcing themselves to show at least a modicum of respect to Aryx, although Carnelia had trouble doing even that. If not for Rand, whom Aryx had decided she must for some reason favor, the female might have tried to run through the young minotaur on two separate occasions. The woman hated minotaurs with more passion than most of her race.

"Aryx?"

He blinked, realizing that Rand had been staring at him. "My apologies, cleric. My mind wandered."

"Nothing good rest will not help, but first you had better come up top with me and get some fresh air. You will need your senses sharp in the days to come, mark my words."

A refreshing sea breeze greeted them as they stepped out

on deck. The sky remained overcast, but one could at least see to the far horizon. Aryx felt a sudden release of tension and realized that until this moment he had been constantly poised for an attack by the monstrosities. Now that the fog had lifted, the likelihood of that appeared greatly reduced. The release forced him to lean against the rail and recuperate for a time.

The grim sailors of the *Vengeance* continued their tasks, showing scant interest in the pair. The knights' commander remained secluded in his quarters, and fortunately for Aryx, Carnelia did not seem to be about, either.

"Wonder of wonders," Rand murmured. "It's the first time I have seen you relaxed since we fished you aboard."

"I can't help it, Rand. I can't forget those creatures. We stood no chance. After seeing my shipmates slaughtered, I expected them to do the same to this vessel, no matter how many armored humans there are on it. Rand, what were those things? I never saw such horrors in my life! We're trained from birth to face any foe, but if I'd fought those creatures on land, I'm ashamed to admit I might have run!"

"Under the circumstances, I would say the shame would have been a slight one, Aryx." The blond human rubbed his jaw. "I have seen nothing like you described to Broedius, although he knows something, I think. I have watched him and the robed one arguing about secret matters . . . well, Broedius argued, and the robed one ignored his protests. What it concerned, even I am not privy to." He shook his head. "But that does not matter. You fought as bravely as any from the sounds of it, Aryx, and you should be proud. That is what is important."

"Captain Jasi and the others are dead. I should have died with them!"

"Yes, a great, noble, and *useless* death! There will be better battles in which to perish, if that is what your destiny is to be, warrior. In the meantime, make what you can of life and do not go burying yourself under regrets."

"Sometimes honor and duty leave one nothing but regrets with which to live," a somber voice intoned.

Aryx took some small comfort in the fact that Rand also flinched. The cloaked minotaur moved as silent as a shadow. The crimson orbs studied both of them, and Aryx had the uncomfortable sensation that the stranger could see into his very soul. Having kept to the oars or his bunk for much of the journey, the young minotaur had managed for the most part to avoid the dark figure. Only once had they crossed paths, but Aryx had managed to avoid a conversation then. He still didn't even know the other's name, although from what he had discerned, it seemed to him that only Broedius, his niece, and, possibly Rand knew. The few times he had heard the other humans refer to the stranger, it had been in such terms as "that one" or "the red bull," the latter never said within earshot.

"Maybe so, maybe not," Rand countered, recovering first. "All a matter of perspective."

Something flickered in the stranger's daunting gaze, and his eyes shifted from Rand to Aryx. "And what is your perspective, Aryximaraki?"

"I . . . I don't know."

The cloaked figure swept past them, taking a position at the rail and staring ahead. After a moment of contemplation, he commented, "Perhaps that is the best answer of all. When one chooses a particular path, a particular perspective, it often means that many other viable possibilities remain forever unrealized."

The other two looked at one another, seeking enlightenment but finding none. Their unsettling companion eyed the sea for a short time more before turning back to them. "Tomorrow this vessel docks. Tomorrow begins a time of turbulence, a time that will make even skirting the edge of the Maelstrom seem like a child's pastime. The knights' original mission has become a tattered shadow, although only their commanders know some of this yet. They have a newer, more important task at hand. They will demand from your people much that the minotaurs may not find to their liking, yet must accept for the sake of all." The eyes bored into Aryx's own. "In times such as this, the need for honor and duty become paramount. Aryximaraki, are you one to whom honor and duty come before all?"

The question made Aryx bristle, perhaps because in these past few days, he had begun to doubt himself. Could the fear he felt belong to a warrior in whom honor should be foremost? If the creatures from the deep had fought him on land, would he have stood his ground? He prayed so. "Yes, I . . . I think I am."

"A truthful answer . . . perhaps better than the one I might give right now. Tomorrow you will stand at my side. Only there will you be guaranteed safety." The cloaked minotaur reached out and touched Aryx on the chest.

Aryx nearly pulled back, feeling a tingle where the other's fingers grazed his skin, but he forced himself to stand his ground. He would not shame his ancestors and clan any more than he felt he had already.

The crimson stranger removed his hand. "I ask nothing but that you remain true to what you have been taught. Honor and duty, regardless of the cost. Sometimes one must sacrifice the present so that the future will survive. Only by remaining true will the minotaur race perhaps live through what is to come." He glanced briefly at the heavens. "I have been away too long. Dire matters press on, whether I will them to or not. You will remember what I said. My blessing upon you, Aryx-imaraki . . . for whatever worth you take it."

The tall figure moved off, as silently as ever. The paralysis that seemed to have struck Aryx vanished, and he started after the cleric, intent on dragging some answers out of him. However, Rand blocked his way.

"Do not follow, warrior. That is asking for trouble."

"What does he mean by all that, Rand? Who is he to think that I . . . that my people . . . will follow him so blindly?"

For the briefest of moments, Aryx thought the cleric had an answer for him, but then Rand frowned in frustration. "Tomorrow you will find out just that, Aryx, and this I must tell you: If Lord Broedius believes in him, you had better believe yourself that he is more than just a mad fool."

Tomorrow. Aryx both yearned and feared the day to come. Tomorrow he would be home, but with what mystery did he sail to Nethosak? The minotaur suddenly wondered if they would let him arm himself in preparation for their arrival. He hoped so. Aryx had the feeling that arriving home without a weapon at his side just might prove to be a fatal mistake.

\* \* \* \* \*

"Six ships. Closing fast," Aryx muttered to himself as he leaned back from the rail, his expression grim. "A welcome with sharp horns to it." The minotaur snorted. "They'll sink us as soon as they see the humans."

Sleeker than the human warships, the minotaur vessels coursed through the waters with ease, clearly able to outsail and outmaneuver the *Vengeance* and her sisters should that be required. Despite their swiftness, however, the minotaur ships were not tiny. While smaller than any of the warships, each bristled with crew and weapons, all ready to be brought against the invaders at a moment's notice.

"They will not," came Rand's voice. "Whatever you think of him, Lord Broedius is not a fool. He has put up flags signaling for a parley." The pair watched the minotaur fleet shift formation, creating a pincer with the black vessels in the midst. "They will let them land, which is all that Broedius needs."

Aboard the *Vengeance*, the Knights of Takhisis had formed an honor guard around their leader. Row upon row of knights stood at attention, eyes straight ahead. For humans, they were an impressive sight to behold, but Aryx did not think they stood much hope of survival once those in Nethosak discovered the reason for which they had come. Brave they were, but foolish as well.

"It's time," growled a newcomer, a knight wearing the insignia of one of Broedius's subcommanders. Although the man had his visor down, Aryx knew that behind it hid a lupine face with brown, crafty eyes, long narrow nose, and a tiny, trimmed mustache. The minotaur had met the knight, Drejjen, only once during the journey, but once had been enough. Drejjen did not hide his distaste for minotaurs, his belief that they were best suited for pulling plows in the fields. Of course, Drejjen always kept such opinions to himself whenever the tall, crimson minotaur walked by.

Drejjen did not come alone this time. The subcommander stood flanked by two lesser knights, one bearing a massive war axe of dwarven design. Rand indicated the weapon. "The cloaked one said it would be remiss for a warrior to stand unarmed at this juncture. Aryx, I hope this will do for you."

Drejjen raised his hand, and the knight to his right thrust the single-edged axe toward the young minotaur. Aryx took it, admiring the craftsmanship. For all their faults, the dwarves forged excellent weapons, especially axes. He hefted the weapon, noting its superb lines and the way it fit his hand. Some of his anxieties vanished. "My thanks."

"It is only your due," Rand replied.

"Lord Broedius expects both of you in your positions immediately," the visored officer said, a hint of disdain in his voice. "We should not delay."

Aryx hefted his axe again, eyeing the assembled knights and knowing what they intended for his people. "I don't know if I want to do this after all."

"Too late," Rand murmured. "Here he comes."

The cloaked minotaur glided into view, taking up a place to the side of Lord Broedius. He studied the fleet with what Aryx thought was a mixture of pride and regret, and then, to the warrior's surprise, turned to look at the pair over his shoulder. Crimson eyes locked briefly with Aryx's own before returning to the spectacle of the oncoming fleet.

Drejjen stirred with growing impatience, clearing his throat. Aryx reluctantly swung his axe over his shoulder and started forward.

"It is the chosen course," the human cleric uttered as he passed. "Remember, Kiri-Jolith watches over you."

Aryx refrained from any outward sign of disbelief, trying to keep his expression as formal as those of the humans around him. With Drejjen in the lead, they made their way to where the others waited. With the exception of Broedius and his niece, Carnelia, the knights gave the cloaked stranger wide berth, whether out of respect, loathing, or fear, Aryx couldn't say. Rand pointed to the stranger's right, indicating where the minotaur should stand. Aryx obeyed. The minotaur cleric paid his arrival scant attention. His gaze was fixed on the nearest of the opposing ships.

Aryx had expected the fleet to close in on the newcomers, but to his surprise, they began to turn. Slowly it dawned on him that they intended to lead the human vessels into port. Not a normal procedure, from what he recalled, especially considering that the *Vengeance* and its sisters were clearly warships.

"They did as you said they would," Broedius remarked to the stranger with a modicum of respect.

"My servants have prepared the way. There could be no doubt."

As the stranger spoke, Aryx caught sight of an unfamiliar form on the deck of the nearest minotaur ship. With effort, he made out the dread gray robes of a cleric of the state. The tall, thin figure faced Aryx's ship and seemed to be wearing a medallion, no doubt with the symbol of Sargas upon it. His head was bowed, as if in prayer or respect. The dusky minotaur glanced at his unsettling companion, realizing that the other cleric must in part be paying some sort of homage to him. However, the stranger seemed unaware of the respect, almost as if he found it so natural a thing as to be of no consequence.

With the other vessels escorting them, the humans' three black ships sailed into port. Aryx's anxiety gave way for a time to excitement as he drank in the panoramic view of his homeland.

Immense marble structures filled the city of Nethosak, tribute to the minotaurs' hard labor and pride in their home. The imperial capital boasted some of the tallest structures in all of Ansalon, including the Great Circus, the upper edge of which could be seen from the deck of the *Vengeance*. Aryx heard a faint roar, a sure sign that even now the vast arena welcomed a full house.

His gaze shifted to the port again. Even here the pride of the minotaurs revealed itself. Elaborate stone structures, some of them part of the thriving shipbuilding industry, rose high. Minotaurs by the score rushed into and out of these buildings, most carrying some object or another. Beyond those, a haze of smoke ever above them, stood other examples of the seafaring nation's industrial might, smithies and ironworks that belched smoke without pause. A little farther inland, Aryx could see more elegant buildings whose sculpted facades included columns carved into the forms of minotaur heroes, a long-standing tradition among the native artisans and clan houses. Many of the great clans had holdings near the port. Aryx's own clan, the House of Orilg, being one of the greatest and longest-standing houses, lay much deeper in Nethosak, among other great powers of the nation.

In the months since he had set sail, activity had increased greatly, from what he could see. New shops, smithies, and other trade buildings stood side by side with structures that were centuries old. A fastidious race, the minotaurs kept the streets and the older structures in as excellent shape as possible.

The port had expanded, a tremendous feat considering that only a generation earlier, the minotaurs had been forced to rebuild after the wreckage of the War of the Lance. More than a score of large ships stood docked at the moment, all of them vessels at least as massive as those that escorted Broedius's trio. Countless other ships of varying size clustered around the port, not all of them minotaur in design. Nethosak saw no need not to trade with the lesser races if such trade favored Mithas and Kothas.

Lord Broedius, on the other hand, did not appear pleased to see the foreign ships. "When the islands are secured, those ships must be confiscated."

"That is no concern of mine," the stranger returned.

Under the guidance of minotaurs, the *Vengeance* and her sister ships docked. Once the crew finished their work, Broedius and the others descended down a wide plank to the shore. By the time they reached actual ground, a legion of warriors and a swarm of curious onlookers had assembled. In the front stood two figures in gray robes and a third wearing the trappings of the Supreme Circle, the governing body under the emperor. The clerics looked awed, almost feverish in their respect; the official, in turn, appeared suspicious and more than a little at a loss.

Aryx continued to keep his expression neutral even though he suspected that among the crowd had to be at least one or two who would recognize him and wonder why he traveled in such bizarre and forbidding company. When the unknown cleric descended, Aryx and Rand kept to either side of him. Why Aryx did so instead of running to join the onlookers, he could not say. A sense of pride and honor, perhaps. To abandon his position went against what his parents had taught him. He only hoped that the councillor and the others would understand his lack of choice should matters come to a head.

"That'll be far enough," bellowed the circle member. "Another step and you place yourselves at risk."

It turned out to be the mysterious minotaur and not Broedius who made the decision as to whether or not to obey. The cloaked figure paused, but only after an additional step beyond what the councillor had ordered. The other minotaur, a black and brown, short-snouted elder, snorted but did not order the guards forward.

Seeing the councillor hesitate, Broedius chose to take advantage of the situation. "I am Lord Broedius, servant of her wondrous majesty Takhisis! In her name and that of her most loyal commander, Lord Ariakan, these islands are hereby claimed! All resources, including all able warriors, are now under my control as the new provisional governor."

At this point the councillor, who had been struggling between fury and amusement, gave way to the latter. He laughed out loud. Soon those with him, save for the clerics, joined in the laughter. Among the knights, several bristled, especially Drejjen, who could barely restrain himself. However, Aryx knew that behind the show of humor lay the fact that the humans' lives now hung by a very thin thread.

"Such a sorry band of conquerors! With but three ships, you think you'll take over? Even for humans, you must be fools! Do you think that we'll simply give over our lives to you?" The councillor's hand rested on the hilt of his sword. "Fools or not, however, you might just be the very pirates responsible for so many missing ships. Yes, the more I think it, the more that sounds likely. If you're mad enough to invade our islands, then you're mad enough to attack our ships at sea, . . ."

A dangerous rumble rose from the minotaurs. Aryx tightened his grip on his axe, not at all certain what he would do if it came to battling his own kind. He owed Broedius and the stranger his life, but did he owe them enough to fight those protecting his homeland?

Then the crimson minotaur took another step forward, his gaze sweeping across the gathering. Aryx couldn't see the dark figure's eyes clearly from his angle, but something in them silenced the crowd, even the member of the Supreme Circle. Apparently satisfied with the reaction, the cloaked stranger turned to the clerics.

"I have commanded an audience with the present emperor. He is not among you."

The clerics fell to one knee, the older of the two whispering, "Blessed One, we have followed your orders to the letter!"

"You informed the emperor and he did not come?"

"We have sent word to the palace many times, but to no avail! Only today did we receive word that he would not deign to come himself."

"And so this one here is to speak in his place?" The gaze with which Aryx's unsettling companion graced the councillor made the latter stumble back a step. Only when he realized how cowardly he might appear did the circle member recover.

"I'm General Hojak of the Clan Sorjian, eighth member of the Supreme Circle. The emperor has more than enough weighty matters to deal with. If you have claims, I'll deal with them." The tone of his voice made his distaste quite evident. Aryx did not recall Hojak and so suspected him to be the newest and therefore most junior of the eight councillors. The insult could not have been more blatant.

"The emperor would not hear the truth, Blessed One," one of the clerics, whose high rank startled the young warrior, apologized. "Even now, instead of kneeling before you, Chot Es-Kalin watches over the games in the Great Circus."

The cloaked stranger's crimson orbs burned. "Then he and those who do not believe must be made to see the truth. If he will not come to me, I will go to him . . . this once and *only* this once."

With no warning, he raised his arms, and as he did, the flowing cloak spread out in all directions, as if caught up by a great wind. The crowd, including Hojak and the clerics, stepped back warily. Even the knights stirred uneasily. Lord Broedius gritted his teeth, but to his credit, the commander did not give ground. Aryx willed himself to remain where he was, although every fiber in his being screamed for him to run.

The cloak fluttered and expanded, growing so great it could have enveloped a full squadron of minotaur warriors. However, much to Aryx's dismay, the sorcerous cloak sought to enshroud him and Lord Broedius. Surprisingly, the living folds avoided both Carnelia and Rand, almost with intent. The female sought to join her uncle, but the blond cleric held her back, shaking his head.

They were the last sight Aryx beheld before darkness enveloped him.

A chill passed through him, a chill that burned. He could see no one else. The dusky gray minotaur felt as if he stood at the end of a vast chasm and that one more step would send him hurtling into space. The sensation passed swiftly, but it was all Aryx could do to remain standing.

Then the darkness gave way to the bright sun, and Aryx found himself and his party standing in the midst of one of the most honored places in Nethosak, the Great Circus.

More than anything else, the Great Circus, also known as the Great Arena, represented minotaur society. True, there were countless other stadiums spread throughout both kingdoms, but they were for lesser competitions, preliminary combats. To truly rise in rank, to truly become a name among the minotaur race, one had to compete in the Great Arena. Here the champions of the other stadiums fought, seeking both status and power. Generals were created here, as were councillors. Even Chot Es-Kalin fought here, not only to gain the crown of the emperor but to defend it against all worthy adversaries.

The Great Circus had been destroyed and rebuilt time and time again throughout the centuries, but the design rarely changed. More circular than oval, with tiers of simple stone seats surrounding a vast field where combats of all sorts could be played out, the immense structure had been noted even by the other races as the largest of its kind. Sand covered much of the floor, but at times, wooden platforms or even small towers had been placed within the area of the field.

One more recent change had been the addition, along the upper rim, of a legion of tall, lifelike statues representing the greatest of all champions ever to fight in the arena. Only those whose careers marked the highest standards by which the minotaurs measured themselves had been so honored. Although Aryx could not see it from where he stood, he knew that even Kaziganthi de-Orilg had received his place of honor here, for despite his renegade status, his legend had grown too great for any emperor to ignore. In fact, the tale of his epic struggle against the red dragon in one of the earlier Great Arenas had remained so fixed in the minds of Aryx's people that when this present version of the massive structure had been completed, a stylized dragon's head ten feet high had been set to adorn the roof of the booth of the emperor himself.

In that grand booth, Emperor Chot Es-Kalin, one of the youngest warriors ever to lead his people, stared in disbelief at the party that had appeared in the midst of the games.

A hush fell over the crowd. Two minotaurs locked in combat stood frozen, both aware of the intruders in their midst and the fact that their opponent just might use the moment to seek advantage. A row of archers on the walls, set there more for precaution than need, suddenly grew alert.

"Not exactly the grand entrance I would have chosen," muttered Lord Broedius.

The cloaked stranger waved him to silence. That the human obeyed without hesitation did not slip past Aryx. All their lives now depended on this mysterious cleric, and even the knight knew it.

Emperor Chot recovered quickly. He looked as if he had just stepped out of the games himself. Aryx had no doubt that Chot had readily made his way up the ranks, handily defeating his opponents. Some previous emperors had been rumored to have had aid of one sort or another, but not Chot.

"I have come to you, Chot Es-Kalin, this once. It will not happen again."

He spoke quietly, yet his words echoed throughout the stadium. A murmur rose in the audience; most in the throng did not know what conflict existed between the emperor and this cleric, but already anticipation had arisen that it might lead to an unscheduled duel between the pair.

"And who might you be?"

Aryx's eyes narrowed. He studied the face of the emperor and found no guile there. Chot truly did not know who confronted him. However, a dark, shaggy figure to the emperor's side did not look so innocent. He eyed the newcomers with loathing.

"Who he is means nothing, my lord. He's mad, is what he is, and no consequence to you. It was deemed a matter of the circle . . . nothing to bother you with."

Chot leaned back. "There were clerics needing to speak to me some time ago. Something urgent . . ."

"And the circle dealt with it accordingly, my lord."

The cloaked minotaur shook his head. "No, Garith Es-Istian, *you* dealt with it. *You* chose to reject the entreaties of my servants. The responsibility, the failure, is yours . . . and so must be the penalty."

The shaggy warrior rose from his seat, red rage flaring in his eyes. "And who are you to speak so to me?"

"I am your god."

The councillor's mouth snapped shut as he absorbed the audacious statement. Chot stiffened, but still he did not commit himself. As for Aryx, he could only think now how he had condemned himself by standing beside one who must surely be insane.

The voluminous cloak shifted, and as it did, a chilling transformation began. The stranger's features softened, flattened, and he shrank a hand's width. Beside Aryx, there suddenly stood a towering human with angular features and pale skin. He wore a form-fitting suit of ebony armor marked by a stylized bird, a condor, with outstretched wings and savage talons.

"I am Argon." As he spoke, the human metamorphosed, growing slimmer, more elfin in appearance, although an elf of such evident disposition had to be a dark one indeed. "I am Kinthalas and Kinis." The elf shrank, growing squat and muscular, becoming a devious dwarf with an unsettling smile. "I am Sargonaxethe Bender."

Only Broedius seemed unaffected by the transformations. Even Chot moved uneasily in his chair. Garith crossed his arms, snorting in derision.

There came then the worst change of all, as far as Aryx and many other minotaurs were concerned, for the dwarf had shifted into a slight, nimble-fingered kender with hands that moved so quickly they seemed to leave traces of smoke behind. "I am the Firebringer."

Aryx recognized none of the names, but he saw that some others did. Through the minotaurs in attendance spread a myriad display of emotions: curiosity, disbelief, anger, uncertainty . . . even fear.

And then a crimson minotaur, clad in a long, flowing black cloak, once more stood with Aryx and the others. He eyed all, clearly gauging their reactions, then added, "I am the Horned One, Sargonnas, he who has been called Sargas by his children."

Now a roar erupted from the crowd, one led foremost by Garith Es-Istian. Only a sense of duty kept Aryx from abandoning his position. Never had he heard such absolute madness. How could Lord Broedius remain steady? How could even a human believe that the minotaurs would accept this self-proclaimed god?

Yet the clerics he had seen earlier had all seemed swept up in the very same madness.

"A very impressive display of illusion, cleric!" Garith roared. "But we all know how skilled your kind can be at such manipulation and how you'd like nothing more than to return to the days when the priesthood ruled behind the scenes! This council and this emperor are stronger, though, than those in the past! Your tricks will not work here!"

"Do you challenge my claims, then?" The would-be god seemed to take the entire matter too calmly.

The shaggy warrior snorted. "More than that! I challenge you!"

Something in the way the mad stranger moved suggested to Aryx that the councillor had acted exactly as desired. He raised his hands slightly, indicating that both Aryx and the knight should step away. With great relief, the young warrior did just that, shifting over to the human's side.

"He orchestrated that well," the veteran knight muttered, mostly to himself. "He knew this Garith would be the type to immediately challenge him."

Self-proclaimed deity faced outraged member of the Supreme Circle. "I await you here," the self-proclaimed god declared.

Garith rose, and as he did, two other minotaurs came to his aid. One took the cloak of office from him, while the other handed the burly leader a massive axe that Aryx would have found difficult to wield. Although, for countless generations, it had been forbidden for spectators to carry weapons inside the circus—wagers over duels often resulted in hot tempers— those seated in the emperor's box apparently did not have to follow the same rules. As the councillor hefted his weapon, the second of his aides placed a medallion around his neck. Garith then turned to the emperor. "With your permission."

"You have challenged; he has accepted. The law is the law. Let the Great Circus judge."

The shaggy minotaur joined the others on the field. He took up a place some distance from his intended adversary, who had not moved since the challenge had been issued. Garith eyed the taller figure, no doubt deciding that, despite the other's height, he had the weight advantage. "You need a weapon."

"I have one." From beneath his cloak, the crimson minotaur drew a long jeweled blade. Aryx's eyes widened. Although the cloak hid much, he had never so much as noticed the slightest lump that might have indicated a weapon lurked underneath. Long and light, with a great green stone in the hilt, it looked worthy of an emperor . . . and perhaps even a god. Still, against the great war axe, it seemed insufficient. True, a bellguard protected its bearer's hand, but how sturdy would it prove when Garith began to wield his axe?

"A pretty thorn," the councillor snarled, "but not a weapon for a true warrior."

"It will do." The cloak fluttered to the ground as if it had never been attached. The crimson minotaur stepped forward, his lean, smooth form a contrast to the heavily muscled Garith. Aryx now recalled the name Garith Es-Istian. A champion of champions, a mere step or two from the throne himself. He had chosen instead to join the Supreme Circle, which did not mean that he might not someday choose to challenge the emperor. Perhaps Chot knew that, which might explain why he watched all with a veiled expression. It would serve him well if somehow the mad cleric with the sword defeated the councillor.

"I'll make short work of you and end this priesthood plot once and for all." Garith indicated the medallion. "Know that your cleric's tricks will not work on me, fool. I am protected. The mark of the *true* god is on me."

The crimson figure raised his pitifully inadequate weapon and saluted. "A shame you never believed in me."

Garith laughed . . . then charged, his war axe a whirling fury that brought gasps from the audience in the arena.

The stranger's head should have rolled at his feet, but the crimson minotaur somehow remained out of reach without seeming to move. Then his blade came up, and although it barely touched the edge of the councillor's weapon, Garith's axe turned, sending the shaggy warrior off-balance. Aryx found himself silently urging the stranger forward in order to take advantage of his fortune, but the latter did nothing. His foe recovered quickly, now more furious than ever.

Again the axe became a whirlwind, spinning so fast that few likely could keep track of its path. Garith brought the weapon around and down, again and again, never along the same route. Any opponent trying to decipher the pattern of his attack would leave himself open to a sudden change.

Yet his adversary did not even attempt to follow the axe. Rather, he simply stared directly at the councillor. When Garith's axe abruptly shifted direction, cutting a killing arc toward the chest of the outsider, the crimson minotaur raised his jeweled sword in an absurd attempt to deflect it. Aryx braced himself, knowing that the heavy axe would shatter the sword and, barely slowed, bury itself deep in the stranger.

The sword moved. Instead of meeting the edge of the axe,

its wielder brought the blade under it, then up. He caught Garith's weapon beneath the head, twisted his wrist . . . and tore the axe free. As the massive weapon went flying into the air, the self-proclaimed god brought the blade down.

It had to be his imagination, but Aryx thought he heard the sword wail briefly just before it dug deep into the chest of the councillor. At first, Garith did not even seem to realize that he had been slain. He looked around, puzzled, as if wondering where his weapon had gone. Then the shaggy warrior's eyes rolled up, and he collapsed on the arena floor, blood already drenching him.

A movement caught Aryx's eye. He reacted without thinking, throwing himself toward the crimson victor and raising his axe high in the air. He heard something ricochet off the side of the axe head. A gasp came from several onlookers within the emperor's box.

Rising to his feet, Aryx looked toward the sound. One of Garith's aides lay dying, a slim dagger embedded in his throat. From what someone else shouted, it appeared he had tried to avenge his superior's death, but Aryx's quick act had caused the blade to deflect back to its owner. The gray minotaur eyed his weapon, then glanced at the one whose life he had just protected. A brief confrontation with those scarlet orbs left him wondering if luck had been the only force behind the dagger's miraculous turn.

All thought concerning the dagger vanished as a rumbling noise rose from every side of the coliseum, a noise that did not originate from the crowd. Chot and every other minotaur, Aryx included, turned about, trying to discover the cause. The long, low rumble reminded Aryx of a great landslide he had once witnessed while part of an expedition sent by Captain Jasi to search an island. Hundreds of tons of rock had come cascading down just a short distance from the crew's encampment. The sound had remained burned into his mind, for until the slaughter of those aboard the *Kraken's Eye*, it had been the most momentous event in his young life.

A commotion far above caught his attention. Minotaurs in the topmost sections had scattered from their seats, looking back as if something were following them. Aryx saw nothing at first save a line of gray-furred warriors moving slowly forward. Then, as he squinted, he realized that *they* were the source of the din.

The statues of every champion had come to life.

Aryx turned around, surveying the stunning spectacle. The marble figures moved slowly, but with purpose, forming a long row that circled the top of the circus. Stone groaned against stone as they marched into position. Aryx glanced at the emperor and saw that Chot watched, as stunned as the rest.

The stone champions paused, their empty gazes focused downward. Then, as one, they raised the weapons that the artisans had carved for them in salute. As if the marvels he had witnessed had not been sufficient, Aryx gaped as each and every unliving champion roared out a victory cry, followed by the name of him they saluted.

The name "Sargonnas" echoed throughout the Great Circus, and even well beyond. In fact, not all the cries came from within the arena. It dawned on Aryx that likely every such statue in the capital repeated the god's name. The young warrior wondered what those outside the arena must be thinking of the moving figures and the shouts of "Sargonnas" issuing from their stone throats. He doubted that anyone in Nethosak could have avoided hearing the great cries. Again and again the stone figures roared the Horned One's name: "Sargonnas! Sargonnas!"

Fire burst from all around the tall figure on the arena floor, sending both Aryx and Lord Broedius back several steps. A blazing corona surrounded the self-proclaimed god, a corona that crackled and sent brief, jagged shocks of lightning shooting out in all directions. Aryx had never witnessed anything like it and sincerely doubted that any mortal could have wielded the power to do all of this, not even the legendary human mage Raistlin.

With the simple wave of a hand, the crimson minotaur silenced his unliving worshipers. At the same moment, the blazing corona extinguished itself, leaving not even a whiff of smoke behind.

Sargonnas turned his baleful gaze on Emperor Chot. Without hesitation, Chot fell to one knee. The others within the box immediately followed. Row after row of minotaurs in the stands sank to the same position. Caught between his own worship of Kiri-Jolith and the fact that a god now stood next to him, Aryx reluctantly knelt. Only two living figures still stood: Sargonnas and the Knight of Takhisis.

43

That the Horned One did not strike down the unbeliever made no sense, but Sargonnas did not even seem to notice the human's blasphemy. He held up the jeweled blade, turned once more to survey his children, then faced Chot again.

"Rise, Chot Es-Kalin."

The emperor obeyed. Aryx noticed he did not face the living god like some defeated warrior. "My throne is yours, Blessed One. There can be no emperor in the presence of a god."

"I have no concern about mortal thrones . . . only about the welfare of my chosen." The crimson minotaur looked up at the stricken crowd, his voice carrying to each. "I have come in this hour to my children to let them know that their time of destiny is at hand! The war of wars has come to Ansalon, to all Krynn, and the minotaur race must be prepared to play its most vital part! The balance of the world has shifted, and if you, my children, will not be integral to its future, you will be of its unlamented past!"

The statues cheered again, and as they did, the audience began to cheer also, possibly without fully understanding why. They knew only that Sargas—or Sargonnas, as the god himself seemed to prefer—had a duty for them to fulfill . . . and had that not always been the basis for their existence? Even those who worshiped Kiri-Jolith or Paladine himself could not help but feel some pride. Aryx's chest swelled. He had dreamed of rising high among his kind, earning a captaincy or better, and this grand adventure the Horned One spoke of sounded like a return to the days of true champions, true heroes. Aryx had missed the War of the Lance, but now he had the opportunity to prove himself in what would be one of the few wars in which the minotaurs fought for their own glory, not that of a master.

Sargonnas had come to lead his children to their destiny.

The dusky gray minotaur found himself cheering. Even the emperor cheered, although with a bit less enthusiasm. Chot no doubt felt some disappointment at no longer being needed, but he would come to accept it.

*We have been enslaved, but we have always thrown off our shackles. We have been driven back, but always returned to the fray stronger than before. We have risen to new heights when all other races have fallen into decay. We are the future of Krynn, the fated masters of the entire world. We are the children of destiny.*

The day of destiny had finally come.

Suddenly Sargonnas brought the jeweled blade down hard, cutting a swath in the air. The baneful sword wailed, a shuddering sound that silenced the crowd in the Great Circus in midcry. Even the animated statues ceased chanting, as if they, too, had been caught by surprise.

"The greatest force that has ever been raised by you, my children, must be ready within weeks, even days, for a foe more terrible than any ever known has already struck! From beyond has come a horror that calls itself the Chaos, and it would lay waste to Mithas and Kothas, Ansalon, all of Krynn! The Knights of Solamnia will be helpless, despite their courage and honor. The dwarves of Thorbardin will find no protection behind their gates. The elves will discover that no forest can hide them for long. Only one race has the will to stand against the Chaos! The elves, knights, dwarves, and the rest of the lesser races will find that, in the end, it is the minotaurs who will be their saviors!"

As the crimson minotaur finished, Broedius stepped up beside him, as if he somehow deserved to stand on equal terms beside the chief god of Aryx's people. It seemed a wonder that Sargonnas did not simply swat him aside.

Only then did Aryx recall what he had been told while aboard the *Vengeance*.

"By honor's face!" Aryx muttered to himself. "He would not do that!"

"Chot Es-Kalin." Fiery orbs stared down the emperor. "You will have all generals, all commanders, all ship captains gathered immediately. Plans must be finalized."

Chot quickly recovered his wits. "Yes, Blessed One! They shall be gathered as quickly as can be, ready to hear and obey your every command."

"No. Not mine."

The emperor tried to hide his confusion. "Blessed One, I do not under—"

Lord Broedius took a step forward. "Your people will report to me, Chot. In the name of my lady and queen, Takhisis, and by her pact with her consort and your god, Sargonnas, I take charge of these islands and all who live on them!"

"A hu—" With great effort, Chot smothered his horror. "That is—"

"That is the way of things," Sargonnas interjected, his tone brooking no rebellion. He still spoke so that all could hear, whether they now desired to or not. "Before a fortnight passes, the minotaur legions will ready themselves, sail to the mainland, and fight . . . under the command of my queen's knights."

Roars of protest arose, too many elder warriors recalling the yoke of slavery the minotaurs had worn in the last war. Now their own god had decreed that they return to the yoke willingly. Had there been weapons allowed in the audience, a riot such as none had ever witnessed would have surely taken place then, god or not.

Sargonnas eyed them. The words that he spoke next were surprisingly tender, yet still struck like an axe. "The gods have decreed that all of this will be so . . . and so it will be."

He turned away then and as he did, he transformed one last time. No longer did he appear as a tall, imposing minotaur warrior, but with each step away from his children, he looked more and more like a human. . . .

# The Temple of Sargonnas

## Chapter Four

As Sargonnas stalked past, his gaze briefly settled on Aryx. Even in human form, his eyes disturbed Aryx so much that the minotaur had to tear his gaze away.

"Come" was all the god said and all he really needed to say. Aryx obeyed immediately, despite misgivings. Behind him, the young warrior could hear Broedius giving commands to Emperor Chot—the beginning of a new age of slavery, this time sanctioned by the gods themselves.

"All minotaurs of fighting age will begin to gather at designated points to be set by the morrow. Runners will be sent from Lacynos to all points on Mithas. Messengers will then be sent by ship to Kothas."

Aboard the *Vengeance*, Aryx had learned that the knights called Nethosak by another, typically human sort of name: Lacynos. It served now as a reminder that minotaurs no longer ruled their own home.

The cloak Sargonnas had worn in minotaur form leapt from the ground to fasten itself around his neck, all the while fluttering as if blown by some mad wind. The sallow figure in black armor reached out, spreading the cloak even wider. Aryx didn't notice until too late that it was once more about to envelop him. He had time only to take a deep breath before the Great Circus vanished and the unsettling darkness devoured everything.

The folds of the cloak reopened almost immediately, but not to the sight the dusky gray minotaur had expected. Instead, he now stood beside the god in the midst of a great temple, where massive figures of Sargonnas, the Horned One, looked down upon them. Torches lit the interior, revealing the vastness of the chamber. Tapestries commemorated the deeds of the chief god of the minotaurs, including battles against sea serpents, raising high Argon's Chain—the string of volcanoes that dotted Mithas—and bringing the first minotaurs to the safety of the land they would call home.

Great condors of gold perched over the inner entrance to the chamber, sculpted with such care Aryx almost thought them alive. In their talons, they clutched struggling figures, metallic dragons cast in what seemed to be platinum.

Two acolytes in gray robes let out gasps and scurried away. Sargonnas, still in human form, paid them no mind, instead staring up at his carved images as if not entirely recognizing them. The avian cast of his present features made him seem more akin to the condors than to his own statues. Under dark, narrow brows, his crimson orbs, the only features unchanged, took in everything with what seemed self-mockery. The thin, bloodless lips curled slightly downward. Sargonnas said not a word, although Aryx would have dearly loved to know why he had been given the honor of becoming the traveling companion to a deity. Other than the fact that he had ended up on the *Vengeance,* he saw no reason why Sargonnas should honor him so. In fact, Aryx would have been pleased if the Horned One—a title something of a misnomer at the moment—had completely forgotten him.

The acolytes returned with a full legion of robed figures, foremost among them one clad in the robes of the high priest himself. Tall and thin of fur atop his head, the elderly high priest made a sorry contrast to the stern figure he approached, but at least he was a minotaur. Aryx found it both curious and disturbing that Sargonnas had elected to retain his human shape rather than that of one of his children.

"Blessed One! Forgive us for not making your welcome a proper one! We knew you first to be at the docks, then in the arena! We've made preparations, but they're up front, not here in the central chamber! Please forgive us!" As if he had not abased himself enough, the high priest fell to his knees. A wave of robed forms followed his action.

While Aryx could not blame the clerics for showing their obedience, he found their actions a bit revolting. Perhaps because he was not a follower of Sargonas, he did not see their intensity as quite appropriate. Minotaurs believed in dignity and honor. The clerics fairly fawned over their master.

"You have made ready all I ordered, Xarav?"

"Yes, Great Sargas."

"You will call me Sargonnas." Thinner and more angular than minotaurs, the god nonetheless looked easily capable of taking any of the robed figures and crushing the life out of him with one hand.

"Yes, my Lord Sargonnas!"

"This chamber will serve as my domain."

"This?" the high priest looked around. "Great Sargonnas, I've set aside my very own chambers for your pleasure! While you grace us with your earthly visitation, you must have nothing but the best."

"This chamber will be mine." Sargonnas eyed the looming statues. "The better to remember myself," he added cryptically.

"As you command! These humble priests and acolytes will remain here at all hours to serve your needs."

"I need no one. No one will enter this chamber unless I summon him."

Xerav swallowed hard. "As you command."

"I do. You will all leave me now . . . all save you." The last referred to Aryx. Xerav glanced jealously at the young warrior, wondering, no doubt, as Aryx did, why this one should be so blessed. Unwilling to question his god, the elderly minotaur rose and, bowing, backed out of the chamber. Aryx found the departure almost humorous, the many robed figures occasionally colliding with one another as they backed up. The last of the group respectfully shut the huge bronze doors.

When they were alone, Sargonnas faced him. Suddenly the god sat on an ornate, high-backed throne that had not existed prior to the priests' departure. The sinister blade he had used on Councillor Garith now hung from a sheath at his side, the green stone seeming to wink at the minotaur. The god closed his eyes for a moment, as if gathering his strength. For a deity of such power, Aryx thought Sargonnas looked rather weary.

"At one hour before dawn, you will come to me. Listen for the bell marking the fifth hour. Knock then. No sooner, no later. If I do not summon you immediately, you will stand before the doors and try thrice more." He did not ask if Aryx understood, only acted as if what he commanded made perfect sense. "You will also find quarters in my house."

"The priests won't be happy with my company," Aryx pointed out.

"They will make do. You are permitted to leave now. I must think . . . and plan." As he finished speaking, Sargonnas raised his left arm. A flutter of massive wings echoed throughout the immense chamber. The minotaur looked up, spotting the huge form as it descended.

A condor alighted onto the arm of the god, but this was no ordinary bird. The condor shared the same burning eyes as its master, and streaks of fire offset its otherwise ebony plumage. It eyed the mortal as if trying to decide whether to make him its next meal. Sargonnas stroked it, treating it almost like a beloved child. He no longer paid the slightest attention to Aryx.

Recalling that he had been dismissed, Aryx turned away, leaving the god to his pet. The uneasy minotaur wondered where the bird had come from; he could see no openings in the top of the room. Of course, a pet of Sargonnas's did not necessarily arrive by mortal means.

As he departed from the chamber, Aryx heard the dark deity quietly command, "Tell me what she does now. . . ."

Another voice, almost a whisper, spoke, but fortunately for Aryx's nerves, once he shut the bronze doors behind him, the warrior could not make out what it said.

The entire encounter had left the warrior confused and anxious. Sargonnas had hardly turned out to be what the minotaur had expected, but he supposed gods were well beyond mortal comprehension. He had heard that the god Paladine sometimes walked the world, wearing the most outlandish forms. The same had been said about some of the other deities, but Aryx had assumed that Sargonnas would be different, that the Horned One would have remained ever in the form recognized by his chosen.

More than the dark god's choice of shapes, Sargonnas's mood and actions disturbed him. Much had been left unsaid, much that Aryx suspected touched the minotaur race heavily. He wondered what those things were, then wondered if he really wanted to know.

Suddenly the high priest and several tall, muscular acolytes blocked his path. The senior cleric looked down his especially long muzzle at Aryx. "The Blessed One is satisfied with his surroundings?"

"I think so."

"You are most fortunate to have been granted his company for a time. Truly an experience to cherish for one's entire life. Now that you return to your mundane existence, you would do best to remember that."

The priest's attitude nearly made Aryx bristle. He did not like being dismissed as inconsequential. "I'm not leaving just yet. The Blessed One wants me to stick around for the foreseeable time."

"Oh?" Xerav did not seem at all amused. "You may have been mistaken."

"'You will find quarters in my house,'" Aryx added. "He said so himself."

The high priest steepled his fingers. "I see. One would certainly not mistake such words, would one? Not without fearing his wrath."

The young warrior nodded. "Exactly."

"Then we shall see if we can find you most suitable quarters." Xerav pulled himself together. "Will you come this way?"

Although from then on the priesthood outwardly treated him with respect, Aryx readily noted the sour attitude hidden behind the polite words and conscientious expressions. The high priest soon presented him with a small but suitable chamber, clean and proper, but much farther from Sargonnas than Aryx believed necessary. Moreover, the clerics seemed to be watching for any action or word that they might take for sacrilege. Casually asked questions about his faith ended with raised eyebrows when Aryx did not denounce the worship of Kiri-Jolith and Paladine. While the official face of the state clerics reflected tolerance for the minorities following the ways of the latter gods, especially Kiri-Jolith, Aryx quickly came to realize that the high priest had hoped Sargonnas's coming would put an end to the other religious factions.

With great relief, the young minotaur watched as the last acolyte departed. Alone now, he unharnessed his ax, then threw himself on the simple cot. While not the most comfortable, compared to his berth on the *Kraken's Eye* the cot felt like soft down. In seconds, Aryx found himself struggling to stay awake. He welcomed the thought of sleep; for a time, he could forget the madness of which he had become a part. Still, disturbing questions played in his mind even now. Aryx could not help wondering what tomorrow would bring.

"We're his chosen," he muttered to the ceiling. "He wouldn't want to endanger us."

Aryx tried hard to believe that . . . and was still trying when sleep at last claimed him.

\* \* \* \* \*

Gods do not sleep, not in the mortal sense. They may blanket their thoughts for a time, but rest as humans or elves or minotaurs know it is beyond them.

Secretly, Sargonnas had always envied mortals for this.

He sat in the grand throne he had created, seeing many things, doing many things, appearing many places. Most mortals did not understand that what they often saw was only part of the god, that at any time he or she might be in three or four other places at the same time. When events grew particularly dire, this meant that the gods could not concentrate on any one thing with the effort that they might desire. Considering also how each had to protect himself against the personal machinations of his own brethren, it seemed a wonder sometimes that they managed to accomplish anything at all.

Plots, counterplots, plans, dreams . . . and all for very little in the end. Sargonnas brooded. She plotted again, twisting what should have been a working plan into one of her campaigns for personal victory. All she ever thought about was getting the upper hand over Paladine. Even what they had once shared no longer truly existed. She plotted against him, too.

Of course, he did the same.

The minotaurs, his chosen, were to have been the great power after the War of the Lance. Even with the factions split between their worship of him, oh-so-noble Kiri-Jolith, and the Platinum Dragon himself, Sargonnas had been certain of his children's eventual ascension to glory. Now, once more, he had bowed to her whims, turning the minotaurs once more into slave soldiers.

Of course, she did not know that this time he had formulated plans of his own. Although he hated her, he also adored her, but too long had she ignored his desires and entreaties. She would have the minotaurs, but not necessarily the way she wanted them.

He stiffened in the throne. Already the strain took more out of him than he had thought. Fighting on more than one level of existence drained him too much, especially with the plans he had to put into motion at the same time. None of them, not even Paladine nor her, knew just how thin he had spread himself. True, he had help now, help from the only one he trusted to some extent, but would that be sufficient if the veil he had cast over his activities thinned too much? It had proven difficult enough to keep the ships and his work on the islands hidden.

Sargonnas feared that the veil had already been pierced. He could sense that something lurked in and around the dark, churning waters of the Blood Sea, something beyond the macabre beasts the minotaur had spoken about. Not for a minute had Sargonnas disbelieved Aryximaraki de-Orilg's fanciful tale, even though such creatures had never been created by either the gods or the cursed Greygem. Perhaps they had other origins, but he doubted that, or else why could he not sense more than a shadow of their presence? They had to have been sent by the Father of All and of Nothing.

Damn you, Reorx! You should have told us the truth about the Greygem from the start! He stiffened again. Gods do not feel pain as mortals do, not generally, and when they do feel pain, it is on a threshold far beyond that which any mortal could tolerate even for a second. The battle that Sargonnas fought now, a battle that she had only hinted at to her loyal puppets, Ariakan and Broedius, grew more fierce, and the Horned One had few worthy allies, especially among his own band. He already entertained suspicions about some of them, more suspicions than usual.

Yes, he grew more and more certain that her announced plan had already floundered, that the minotaurs had already been discovered. The knight might believe her absurd Vision, but Sargonnas believed only in reality. The Father of All and of Nothing surely knew that they planned to reinforce those on the main continent, to force him to expend more and more energy on the mortal plane, thereby draining him on all others. A combined, coordinated effort would have struck him a terrible blow, whereas confusion only served his cause. Damn you, Father Chaos!

Something else, something massive, stirred all around his islands, something shielded even from his piercing gaze. He could protect the islands some, but not as he might once have. She knew that he had spread himself along too many places, not that she would trouble to do so. As much as he desired her in all respects, he hated her for this and other things. Someday he would teach the temptress a lesson for all her tricks and half-truths . . . that is, if they all survived this.

Again he felt movement in and around the Blood Sea. At the same time, the battle on those other planes intensified, demanding more of him. Sargonnas braced for the pain, shifting more of his presence from the world of mortals to the beyond. Time to fight back with the intensity that had earned him the title of Lord of Vengeance not only among the mortals but also his own kind.

Sargonnas's eyes flickered shut. His body shimmered, growing transparent, as if he had somehow turned into colored glass.

The battle of the gods raged on.

* * * * *

In a vast undersea cavern at the edge of the Blood Sea, dark forms, serpentine in shape, slithered and swarmed about one another, endless forms without head or tail, only body. They moved as one, for in fact they *were* one. Scaled, green-gold in color, and with segments as thin as reeds or as thick as two full-grown ogres, the swarming mass moved with much agitation, much excitement.

The time had nearly come to strike. The Magori had gathered, had been told what they must do if they desired to exist. The Lord of All and of Nothing had given permission.

The Coil could hardly wait.

* * * * *

The shadowy outline loomed over him. Aryx's pathetic little axe bounced off the hard armor of the mist-enshrouded creature. In each three-digited hand, it held a scythe sword. Aryx tried to back away, but the deck was too slippery, awash with the blood of his fellow crew members, who cried out for his aid.

The monster swung its weapons, cleanly cutting off first one, then the other arm. Aryx cried out and tried to reach for his fallen arms. His horrific foe waded forward, both swords raised high. The shadowy form filled his view.

The minotaur screamed as the jagged blades crossed. . . .

Aryx woke, gasping. He inhaled deeply, trying to pull himself together. A dream . . . only a dream. Yet it had played over and over in his head. Each time he relived the battle on his ship, each time the attack growing more brutal, more hopeless. Aryx saw each of them die . . . Jasi, Hugar, Feresi, Krym, Hercal, and the rest. He saw the murky shapes of the abominations again and again, slaughtering everything that moved. . . .

The weary minotaur doubted that he would ever forget the deaths, but he prayed that at least he could live with the nightmares. Aryx wondered how others survived such dreams, or if perhaps only he suffered them. Somehow he doubted that.

Perhaps if he tried thinking of his family—his brothers, sister, and parents. He had meant to see them when he returned from his voyage aboard the *Kraken's Eye*, but the extraordinary circumstances of his arrival had kept him from even thinking much of them. Somehow he would make contact with them, providing that they, too, were home.

Aryx exhaled, feeling a little better. The phantoms of his shame retreated. He now became aware of a distant noise. The Knights of Takhisis at work already? Lord Broedius seemed adamant about getting matters moving ahead regardless of how hard this would all be for the minotaurs to accept. To surrender their freedom, especially to servants of the Dark Queen, was unthinkable.

The world under Takhisis. Not something to appeal to any minotaur, since the Dark Queen had generally seen fit to utilize the minotaurs as fodder. Even the fact that Sargonnas, her reputed consort, saw the minotaurs as his people had never seemed to hold sway with Takhisis . . . and now the Horned One himself had given them over to her minions. Why?

Thinking of Sargonnas, Aryx recalled the god's command. Sargonnas had made it very clear that he wanted the young warrior to come to him at a certain hour, the reason for which the Lord of Vengeance had not bothered to elaborate. However, when a god commanded, it generally improved one's chances of survival to obey without question.

Despite being without a method by which to tell the time, Aryx felt certain that he had not missed the hour. He quickly readied himself, deciding to leave his axe ready in his back harness. No sense going about unarmed, even here. He did not expect attacks by the priesthood, but also did not know what Sargonnas might have in mind for him.

Acolytes were already hard at work in the temple, the high priest no doubt wanting his god's place of worship in good order since Sargonnas had taken up residence. Some looked up at him as he passed, and Aryx could sense both their curiosity and distrust. The priests had been trained in the belief that, since they were the most dedicated of the Horned One's children, they were the ones he would most appreciate. To see an outsider so honored—not that Aryx thought of it that way—had to grate them.

He would have gladly given up the dubious distinction if only he knew how.

Although torches and oil lamps illuminated most of the temple, the area around the great doors leading to Sargonnas's chamber remained dark. Aryx wondered whether that was by the god's choice.

He reached up to knock, then paused. From the acolytes, he had learned that a few minutes still remained. Sargonnas had specifically commanded him to knock when the hour struck, and Aryx suspected the god had a particular reason for that command. The minotaur doubted that Sargonnas simply wanted to be awakened.

Minutes passed, minutes in which Aryx wondered whether the clerics had forgotten to ring the bell. Then, just as he grew particularly edgy, the hour struck.

He reached up and knocked.

At first there was no response, but then the tall bronze doors shuddered, as if an immense wind within tried to shake them loose. The shuddering increased, growing to such intensity that several acolytes and priests came to see what had happened. Aryx stood back, not at all certain that the doors would not fly off toward him.

The shuddering abruptly ceased. Then, from within, came a sound, at first like a hiss, but almost immediately more resembling a groan like that a ship would make on the high seas as the waves tossed it about. The priests backed away, but Aryx refused to step back.

The groaning ended.

The doors slowly creaked open.

"Enter."

Aryx obeyed. The priests started to follow, but the doors

shut behind the lone warrior before the others could step inside. Aryx looked around at the massive chamber, somewhat disappointed to find that it had not dramatically altered despite the ominous actions. He had also thought that Sargonnas might have redecorated the entire interior in some fashion suitable to his station, but the shadowy deity had made few, if any, changes. The same high-backed throne perched in the midst of the great chamber, although now it seemed decorated with scrollwork and two fanciful avian figures resembling birds of prey. Upon the intricate chair sat the Horned One, still in human form. Aryx began to wonder whether Sargonnas had even budged from the throne since the night before.

Suddenly the wary minotaur blinked. For the briefest of moments, he thought that Sargonnas faded slightly. The stylized condor pattern on the back of the chair appeared and disappeared, as if he who sat upon it had vanished, however briefly. The warrior blinked again, but now Sargonnas did indeed sit before him, every bit as solid as any normal person. Had Aryx been mistaken?

"I am not your god," Sargonnas quietly uttered.

His words startled the dusky gray minotaur, for he did not know how to take them. Had the shadowy figure confessed to some great hoax? Surely not. No mage could have done what he had.

"Corij lays claim to you . . . far more claim than I could ever make."

At first Aryx did not recognize the name, but then he recalled it from an encounter with an Ergothian trader. The Ergothians called Kiri-Jolith by that title, among others.

The crimson orbs flashed as Sargonnas continued. "But Corij is not here and I am, and so foremost you are of my chosen, a warrior dedicated to honor and duty . . . concepts that some might claim at odds with who I am." The god stared at him, and not for the first time, Aryx felt he looked into the minotaur's soul. "You have done as you were bid. Now you may go, but you will return at this time tomorrow and each morning after without fail until I tell you otherwise."

With that said, Sargonnas closed his eyes as if resting. Aryx did not move immediately, the abruptness of his dismissal momentarily catching him off guard. He had only just arrived, and now Sargonnas had commanded him to depart. Aryx stared at the ominous figure on the throne, trying to decipher him. Then, still more than a little disgruntled, the minotaur finally backed out of the chamber. However, long after the doors shut behind him he continued to seethe within, feeling like a puppet.

"Gods," muttered Aryx, seeing no one would hear him. "They're all mad!" Yet he also wondered if there had been more to Sargonnas's short ramblings than simply madness. Sargonnas had many secrets he no doubt did not feel he needed to share with mortals, and some of those secrets clearly pressed on him. What would bother a god so?

Suddenly he noticed a band of priests, Xerav in the lead, headed toward him. The high priest regarded the warrior with a veiled expression. "You have spoken with him?"

Aryx nodded. "I have."

"We must see him about important matters. We have been waiting."

The warrior pointed at the great doors. "Try knocking, then. It seems to work. Excuse me now. I must be going."

He made his way through the hostile throng, never looking back. Aryx marveled at his own behavior. A year ago he would have never dared to speak to the high priest in such a flippant tone.

It would probably be prudent if he left the temple for a time, returning to the outside world. Sargonnas had told him when to come back.

Outside, the first traces of light had just appeared on the horizon, casting a peculiar tone over the entire city. A thin mist also filled the air, not an uncommon sight this close to the sea, but one that reminded Aryx too much of the events surrounding the slaughter aboard the *Kraken's Eye*. He shivered, but fortunately there were few around to notice.

The slim minotaur looked around, for the first time drinking in some of the details around him. Foremost, Aryx noticed the exterior of the temple itself, which he had not had the opportunity to see, considering the unusual circumstances of his arrival the night before. Utilitarian in many ways, as often was the case with government structures, the central temple of the Holy Order of Stars resembled an oval ball half-buried in the earth. A pair of towers offset the effect to some extent, but not enough to erase the image from Aryx's mind. There were, of course, the obligatory statues of Sargonnas in his minotaur form, mighty titans guarding the entrance with crossed axes. Bas-reliefs of the god's head had also been carved into the front walls near the great doors. Seeing them now after having spent so much time in the company of the actual deity, Aryx found them somewhat deficient in their rendering.

Some distance from the temple stood a tall, wide edifice with an arched roof, marble columns, and a long series of wide steps in front. What at first seemed a sculpted park surrounded the building, a park patrolled by legions of wary sentries ready to strike down any and all unauthorized intruders. Although impressive in its size, like the temple, it also lacked personality. A few windows equipped with small balconies dotted the upper levels of the structure, which stood some five stories high, but otherwise it appeared even more subdued than the building from which Aryx had emerged. In so many ways, the minotaurs tended toward the functional, and the palace of the emperor served to reflect that attitude as well.

Aryx wondered what Chot did now. Once the emperor had ruled two kingdoms, but now . . . now who needed him when a god walked the streets and barbarians from the mainland had control of the capital?

Beyond the palace lay the boxlike building housing the central quarters of the Supreme Circle, the administrators of the empire. It was slightly more elaborate than the previous two structures. The front entrance, a steep set of wide steps rising to twin pairs of tall, iron doors, bore the emblems of the great houses of the empire, from which the administrators tended to come. Banners representing those and the lesser houses hung above. Minotaurs clad in gray kilts, part of the State Guard, protected this place, their eyes most often turned toward the temple. In times past, they had served the priests almost as the acolytes did, but since long before Aryx's time, their loyalties had shifted. The guard was now as wary of the temple as the Supreme Circle was.

Remembering the late, unlamented Garith, Aryx wondered how the Supreme Circle fared. Like Chot, the surviving members were probably at a loss as to exactly what function they served just now.

Pushing aside such thoughts, Aryx finished orienting himself, then began wending his way through Nethosak toward distant House Orilg. It would be good to return to those who knew him, especially if one or more of his family were there. Some of his brothers, Aryx knew, were either training in the wilds or aboard ship themselves, but a few, like his youngest brother Seph, surely had to be somewhere in the capital.

He had made only slight progress when the thunder of hoofbeats made him pause. Aryx moved to the side mere seconds before a quartet of riders passed swiftly. The riders paid little attention to those in their path, nearly running down an elderly woman who happened to step outside a building at the wrong time. She cursed quietly at the vanishing forms, then continued on her way, but others stood and glared after the foursome long after they had disappeared.

Knights of Takhisis. He knew that they were here, that they now commanded the capital, but to actually see them riding arrogantly through the streets shook him to the core.

Aryx started to step out into the street, then quickly pulled back again as two more riders appeared. However, not only did this pair ride more slowly, but they were accompanied by a full squadron of minotaurs, all armed and carrying packs. Aryx recognized one, a brown youth with a short snout who had been an acquaintance of his younger brother. The warriors stared ahead, somber, unflinching. At the rear of the marching column rode two more knights, their human faces hidden behind black visors.

The Knights of Takhisis had already begun gathering able-bodied warriors for their mission. Aryx had assumed that it would take the humans a few more days before they began that part of their plan. The swiftness of Lord Broedius surprised him. He only hoped the commander would know what to do with them. Too often, past masters had wasted minotaur lives as freely as they breathed the air.

With the column gone, Aryx tried to move on, but his progress quickly slowed. The streets were growing more and more crowded by the minute. Massive carts rumbled back and forth, those headed toward the dock filled with supplies of all sorts, clearly intended for a long-term journey. Now and then a knight on horseback moved through the crowds shouting orders or rushing to some unknown destination. Many of the faces Aryx studied eyed the humans with loathing, although never when one of the knights turned toward them.

More squads marched by, heading, no doubt, for different parts of the port. Several times Aryx spotted familiar faces, some of them from his own clan, yet none from his family. Again it amazed him that so much activity already took place. The minotaurs prided themselves on their efficiency, but so far the knights had proven themselves at least their equals. Yet despite that efficiency, the knights lacked one important trait, one that became more evident each time one of them passed or gave a command. There seemed little if any respect in their tones; they commanded as one commanded cattle, not soldiers.

"Broedius must want the first ships off by tomorrow morning," Aryx muttered to himself. "It'll be interesting to see if everything goes as planned."

He forgot all about knights and missions as a familiar and very welcome face passed by in the crowd. Aryx abandoned his position, rushing out to greet a slim, young, light brown figure carrying a sack over his shoulder. "Seph!"

The other minotaur looked around, saw him, and nearly dropped his sack. "Aryx! When did you get back?"

They clasped one another briefly, joy blotting out even the nearby presence of a pair of knights. Of all the familiar faces he could have run across in Nethosak, this one was one of the dearest to Aryx.

Seph grinned at his older brother. "Aryx! We've all wondered what happened to you! Your ship's been gone over a year, with no word for six months at least! We knew you'd be gone a long time, but not that long. When did you arrive home? What did you see? Did you get into any battles?"

Another human rode by. Aryx snorted, not liking so many so nearby. "Maybe we should find a better place to talk. Is there a good inn nearby? It's been too long since I was home and I don't recall which were best."

"There is, but don't expect much right now. These . . . these humans are closing most places down, claiming all supplies for their grand mission! Did you see them arrive, Aryx? It's said that Sargas himself came with them. It must be true, because even the emperor and the Supreme Circle back the humans' efforts."

Aryx sobered. "I know all that. Let's find that inn first, and then I'll tell you what's happened with me. I promise."

His young brother led the way, soon bringing them to an inn called Champion's Roost. The duo entered, finding only two other customers seated. They located a table, and a moment later a heavy elder minotaur came to see them.

Although much muscle had given way to fat, the tarnished medallion he wore about his neck proudly proclaimed him a former champion of the arenas. His pronounced limp explained why he no longer fought.

"I'm Jol. Won't be too much since those humans came, but I can offer you good soup and some ale for now."

They settled quickly on that, the better to return to their conversation. Seph still bubbled over with enthusiasm at the return of his brother. The nearest in age to him, his younger brother had spent most of his time growing up with Aryx. "Kaz's axe! I still can't believe I ran into you in the midst of all this! So tell me, Aryx, when did the *Kraken's Eye* make it in to port? How's Captain Jasi for a commander? I heard she's tough but fair."

"The *Kraken's Eye* sank, Seph. I'm the only survivor."

Seph stared, wide-eyed. Aryx pretended not to notice. For now, he didn't want to tell his brother the entire truth. Instead, he added, "The enemy took us in the fog. We fought. I fell overboard. The waves swept me away. The last I saw, the top half of the *Kraken's Eye* was on fire and the ship itself had begun to list."

"Gods! Was it a terrible battle? How'd you survive?"

"Yes, it was terrible." Aryx felt every muscle in his body tense at the bloody memories. "If not for the *Vengeance*, I'd probably have drowned."

"The *Vengeance?*"

"One of the three black ships. The humans found me, Seph."

His brother's eyes widened more. "You sailed in with the Knights of Takhisis?" Instead of horror, Seph's expression revealed only excitement. "Did you see him? Did you see Sargas?"

"I saw him," Aryx returned somewhat vaguely. "He likes to call himself Sargonnas these days. He likes to look human these days, too."

Jol approached, bringing their soup and ale. He set them down. Aryx realized he had no money with him, but Seph reached into a pouch and paid. When the innkeeper left, Seph continued his questioning.

"What do you know about all this, Aryx? A lot of folk are rumbling about the humans taking over, but Sargonnas must have a good reason. We're his chosen, aren't we?"

Aryx had begun to hate that word. If the minotaurs were the god's chosen, he had a peculiar way of showing it. Likely a lot of others were thinking the same thing. Wanting not to speak of it, at least for a while, he changed subjects. "How are our parents, Seph? Are they in Nethosak? What about Kylo and the others?"

"Father and Mother are on Kothas, dealing with clan business. Kylo's on a voyage somewhere . . . left three months ago. None of the others, including Oreta, are in Nethosak, although I think Hecar's supposed to be back from his voyage in a week . . . though that might've changed." Seph leaned forward, eagerness spreading across his face. "I would have gone along with Mother and Father, but I've just received my first posting!"

This was news to Aryx. He knew his younger brother had grown old enough to take his own place in the forces of the empire, but not that he had already been posted. A minotaur's first posting had always been considered a rite of passage, marking him as a true warrior. "Congratulations!"

"I was supposed to join them in three days, but I received word this morning to put all plans on standby. Looks now like we all might be shipping out. I've heard rumors that the Knights of Takhisis are taking everyone who can fight."

"They'd be mad to strip the islands of every capable fighter," Aryx snarled, suddenly having too much of the humans' arrogance. The bitterness he had felt aboard the *Vengeance* came bubbling to the surface. "If they keep this up, they'll destroy us for the sake of their war!"

Seph straightened, giving him a look of warning. Aryx quieted, then casually glanced at the doorway. Two Knights of Takhisis, faces covered by visors, had entered, and their stance indicated that they had not come to dine. One of them looked at the two minotaurs seated on the other side, then at the brothers. The knights marched toward the first pair, questioning them. One of the minotaurs snorted, but both replied to the humans' words, also showing them certain papers. Seemingly satisfied, the knights then proceeded to Aryx and Seph's table.

The taller of the two raised his visor, revealing a thin, lightly bearded face. Aryx had not had much opportunity to judge humans by age, but he suspected that this knight had only just earned his rank. The man could be no older than Aryx, if that much.

"All minotaurs of fighting age are to present themselves to their clan houses for listing so that they may be organized into units and prepared to be shipped out as soon as possible. Those not yet scheduled are permitted free travel throughout Lacynos until their assigned time. Have you your posting papers?"

Aryx had no idea what the man meant. "I've been busy in the Temple of Sargonnas. Lord Broedius knows why."

"Have you a record of this?"

"You'll just have to take my word."

The knight's expression darkened. "Lord Broedius, in conjunction with the orders set down by the glorious Lord Ariakan, has arranged with your leaders for this system to be put into place, the better to accurately organize island forces. You will come with us now and rectify your error."

A dangerous rumble rose from the Seph's throat. Aryx glared at the human. "Are you suggesting that I'd be so dishonorable as to lie to you?"

The other knight put a hand on the hilt of his sword. "Those who dare disobey the edicts face severe punishment."

"I was aboard the *Vengeance*, human," Aryx growled, rising. "I accompanied Sargonnas himself!"

His words fell on disbelieving ears. The two knights started to pull their weapons free.

"They are not yours, good knights."

Rand stood by the doorway, the picture of calm. The blond cleric walked between the two parties, putting himself in the path of any weapon.

"We've our orders, cleric," the second knight muttered, clearly recognizing Rand but refusing to give in.

"And they apply to all but these. What this one said is true. He is favored by Sargonnas, who is your own mistress's consort, as you know."

The cleric of Kiri-Jolith stared at both men, his straightforward expression daring them to contradict him. At last the two knights quieted. The first one eyed the brothers with some lingering anger. "Very well, then. We shall be on our way."

Still glaring, the ebony-clad warriors departed the inn. The group watched them leave, Aryx not at all certain that they would not suddenly change their minds.

"So here you are," Rand continued as if nothing had

occurred. "When Sargonnas took you with him yesterday, I must say I feared for you a little. Carnelia said she was glad to be rid of you, but she only spoke from frustration at being left behind."

"Did you come looking for me?"

"In a sense. That was why I happened to be here at so opportune a time. To be honest, I have been trying to locate you since yesterday, but until shortly after the fifth hour, I was unable to tell if you even remained in Nethosak."

So despite his powers, the cleric had not been able to find him before now? Aryx had remained in the temple almost all that time. Being in the Temple of Sargonnas had evidently shielded him from the human's skills.

"The Blessed One decided to keep me nearby for a time," Aryx finally informed Rand.

"So I should have guessed. You are marked by him. I can see it. Marked as well by Kiri-Jolith. You could say that you are doubly blessed."

"Or doubly cursed," Aryx blurted.

"One could see it that way, too, yes."

Seph had remained silent during the entire exchange but had been unable to keep his eyes from the human. Aryx realized that his brother had never seen a human this close, at least not one that acted as a friend rather than a potential foe. "Seph, this is the cleric, Rand. Cleric, this is my youngest brother."

"Yes, he has the same look about him as you do."

"What look is that?" Aryx's brother asked.

"The one Kaz Dragonslayer is said to have had. Courage, determination, and a tendency to leap headfirst into the fray."

This evoked a laugh from Aryx, his first true laugh since the ravaging of the *Kraken's Eye*. "That could apply to all young minotaurs, human! Certainly Kaz didn't remain that way as he grew older. Those that do tend not to grow too old."

Rand only smiled in response. Then the smile faded a bit. "A word of advice. It might be best to keep your brother around you for a time, Aryx, or else he might be shipped out soon. I thought you two might prefer to stay together."

Aryx thanked the human for his concern. At least this way he could watch over his brother should danger rear its head.

Seph studied the human's robes. "Cleric, would you be willing to give me your blessing?"

"I would be remiss if I did not." Rand touched Seph first on the forehead, then the chest. "Head and heart. If we do not heed both, we fail as warriors. If we do not heed both, we are not whole."

The two minotaurs who had been seated on the other side of the room rose, clearly not at ease around the cleric. As they abandoned the inn, one started to cough, as if something had suddenly filled his lungs. He continued to cough for as long as he was in range of their hearing.

"I wish Broedius would give me the authority to look over some of your people. That is not the first of those peculiar coughs I have heard. Could it be this continual mist?"

Aryx tensed at mention of mist. "Why do you say that?"

"Today the fog does not seem willing to lift, despite the sun. In fact, the farther out at sea one looks, the thicker it seems to be getting. Almost as bad as it was when we found you." The human gave Aryx a pointed look. "Is this normal for your islands?"

Flickering images of the *Kraken's Eye* and its destruction coursed through the gray minotaur's mind. Suddenly both food and ale lost all taste. "Thicker, you say?"

"Yes, very thick, I'd say."

"Did you notice any sort of odor or scent when you stood near the sea? Especially from the direction of the mist?"

"Other than fish?" Rand chuckled. Then, seeing the minotaur's concerned visage, he grew serious again. "Yes, now that you mention it, there was a scent of sorts. Something I had smelled recently, I think."

"Aboard the *Vengeance*? A sort of musky smell?"

The cleric pondered. "Musky? I do not think it . . . well, perhaps you are right. Just faint, but, yes, I would say that it was somewhat musky. Why do you—"

Rand had no chance to complete his question, for suddenly there burst through the doorway more than a dozen armed knights, with weapons drawn. Aryx rose, reaching instinctively for his axe. Seph followed suit. However, the cleric quickly stepped before the pair, preventing them from charging the oncoming figures.

An officer, his face veiled by his visor, slowly walked in, clearly expecting to discover the two parties in combat. Upon learning otherwise, though, the Knight of Takhisis quickly recovered. He glanced first at Aryx, then Rand.

"Cleric." It was Drejjen's voice. "I hadn't expected to find you here."

"I go where I must, where I am needed."

Drejjen ignored him. Opening his visor, the human peered at Aryx. "Open arms against her majesty's servants? Treason, I would—"

"No treason," the cleric of Kiri-Jolith interrupted politely. "Simply the reflexes of well-trained warriors when a force of black-armored figures come charging in with swords drawn."

Drejjen's eyes narrowed, making him look like a wolf who had just seen his prey escape. However, his expression shifted almost immediately thereafter, becoming almost apologetic. Stroking his short, well-groomed mustache with one gauntleted hand, he considered Aryx. "You're correct, of course. I knew only that some minotaur defied the orders of Lord Broedius. Had I known it was this one, I'd have understood." He performed a sweeping and quite mocking bow for the minotaur. "My most humble apologies."

Rand stared at Aryx. Not at all pleased, the minotaur slowly lowered his weapon back in place. Seph did likewise. Drejjen watched carefully, as if hoping for some excuse to unleash his men.

"You see?" the cleric said to all. "No harm done." To the arrogant officer, Rand added, "Forgive us for distracting you from your work, Drejjen. I hope we will not keep you from it any longer."

Now the knight smiled, an expression that raised Aryx's hackles. "Oh, you've not wasted my time! In fact, you've made my job easier."

"What do you mean?"

Drejjen's hand remained near the hilt of his sword. "As a matter of fact, I've orders to find this one. I thought I'd have to search all over this stinking city for him, but the Lady's favored me today."

"Me?" Aryx now regretted putting away the axe. "Why do you want me?"

"Oh, I don't want you at all, bull," the Knight of Takhisis returned smoothly. "But Lord Broedius does . . . quite urgently, too. He said to bring you in." Drejjen clamped his hand on the hilt. "Do you have any objections?"

The minotaur cursed and started to reach for his axe again, then saw something in the officer's eyes that made him pause.

Drejjen baited him, wanted Aryx to create a conflict. The knight could not have lied about Lord Broedius wanting him, though, Aryx suspected. If that were the case, then it served the minotaur better to choose a path other than battle.

Aryx lowered his hand again, briefly glimpsing disappointment in Drejjen's face. "Very well. If Lord Broedius needs me, I'll come."

"As will we," Rand added, saving Seph from making a protest that would have only served the knight's hidden cause.

Drejjen clearly did not want them along, but also knew better than to protest. With more than a little venom in his voice, he turned away from them, taking his anger out on his men. "What are you waiting for? Form ranks and get moving!"

The Knights of Takhisis immediately filed out of the inn. Drejjen waited until the last had left, then glanced at the trio. "We'll await you outside."

"We had best follow him quickly," the cleric suggested after the officer had departed. "He will seek every opportunity to stir you into some terrible mistake."

"It wouldn't take much from him," Aryx growled. Still, he saw the blond human's point. "All right. Let's go, Seph."

They marched out to find Drejjen and his men waiting. The knights formed a square around them, making it look more as if the minotaurs were prisoners rather than allies.

*Were* they prisoners? Aryx realized he had no idea what Broedius wanted from him. He had originally assumed his part in this to be over once he had left the ship, yet still Aryx had been drawn back in, first by Sargonnas and now by the knight. What did the dark-eyed commander want with a simple warrior?

The gray minotaur grunted. He would find out soon enough, whether he wanted to or not.

# The House of Orilg

## Chapter Five

The *Obsidian Axe* had been at sea for some time, but soon, Krag knew, they would reach their destination. The husky black minotaur could hardly wait to see the homeland . . . or anything else, for that matter. The fog they had come upon the other day refused to lift, making day almost as dark as night and certainly murkier.

With the wind so quiet, the crew had taken to the oars, which meant only a few hands on deck. One of those, First Mate Belso, a barrel-chested brawler with eyes like a hawk, stood in the crow's nest, trying to make out anything through the murky fog.

"Well?" Krag called.

"Like starin' into the woolly side of a sheep!" the tawny first mate replied. "And about as bad a stench, too!"

There the captain had to agree with him. The peculiar musky smell had increased over the past few hours. Krag had peered over the side more than once, trying to see if some huge sea mammal or something swam nearby, but the Blood Sea revealed nothing.

"Captain, I"m doin' no good up— Hold on!" Belso leaned to the port side, peering out into the fog. Krag turned in the same direction, but only thick mist greeted him. He looked up at the first mate.

"Thought I saw somethin', but no. . . ."

For some reason, the black minotaur did not like that hesitation. "What did you think you saw?"

After a moment of consideration, the other sailor called, "I thought . . . I thought I saw a serpent . . . a huge one!"

The Blood Sea held many mysteries, but Krag had never come across a sea serpent. He began to wonder if his first mate had been dipping into the rum rations before coming on duty. "A serpent, Belso?"

"Probably not, Captain. It looked like a long tubular form as big as me . . . but my eyes're probably playin' tricks. This damned fog is gettin' to me, I'm not too proud to say, sir."

It had been getting to all of them. Captain Krag leaned on the rail, studying the murky water. Minotaurs did not spook easily, but the veteran sailor knew his nerves were on edge, and so were the nerves of every other member of the crew.

He tried to calm himself by listening to the rhythmic stroking of the oars. Something good and solid about the oars. They made him think of the strength and skill needed to keep the ship on course rather than moving in circles. Better a good arm and a sturdy oar than some cleric's or mage's contrary spells. Krag had heard of human vessels that had made use of such, often to their misfortune. Not minotaurs, though. Krag would never have relied on . . .

The water just beyond bubbled slightly.

The captain leaned over. For a moment, he thought he saw a massive tubular form much as Belso had described. Stuff and nonsense! He'd sailed these waters long enough to know that if he avoided the blasted Maelstrom, he had little to fear. Any minotaur with an ounce of brains learned early how to avoid the hazards of the treacherous sea, and those who did not lay at the bottom of it, food for the fish.

A dark shape swelled momentarily above the water, a dark shape of gargantuan proportions.

"Sargas preserve us . . ." The captain backed away from the rail.

"Captain Krag!" Belso called out, clearly having sighted the same shape.

Krag turned. "All remaining hands to the oars! Double-time strokes! All remaining hands to—"

His mouth hung open as an arch rose from the sea and quickly towered over the ship. Even in the fog, Krag could see that it had scales like a snake, a vast serpent, green-gold in color. Yet if this was a serpent, it kept its head and tail beneath the surface, an awkward position for such a titan.

Unable to turn or halt its progress in time, the *Obsidian Axe* sailed beneath the monstrous arch. A torrent of seawater dripping off the massive shape drenched the crew.

"Get those oars moving!" Krag had an uneasy feeling about the way the living arch patiently waited. He could see the pulsing of the great body, almost feel the rhythm of its movements. It *waited*, waited for the correct moment.

The minotaur ship moved directly beneath it.

"Sargas save us . . ." the black minotaur whispered. He waited for the inevitable, knowing he could do nothing.

The serpentine form came crashing down.

The *Obsidian Axe* splintered. Minotaurs screamed as fragments of the ship flew in every direction. Those below had no chance of survival. Krag saw his first mate go flying from the crow's nest. Another sailor screamed as one of the masts crashed down on him. A heavy plank struck the captain in his midsection, cracking ribs and throwing him off what remained of the deck. He struck the water hard.

Krag rolled in the water, wondering what he had done to upset Zeboim so. Surely only she could be responsible for such a catastrophe.

The waves tossed him about. Someone cried out, but the cry cut off abruptly. Krag tried to make out other survivors, but the fog hindered him.

Suddenly he saw a form swimming in his direction. Krag gradually recognized it as none other than First Mate Belso. The monster's attack had thrown him clear, and, as ever, the huge first mate's prime duty remained his captain. Krag tried to wave to him, but his injuries slowed any efforts.

Suddenly Belso stopped short. He gazed down into the water, his eyes widening. He had time only to gasp before something pulled him under. Blood stained the dark sea. Krag searched desperately, but his second never resurfaced.

Sharks? The captain found that hard to believe. It generally took several minutes for them to arrive. A horrific thought occurred to him. Had the serpent returned?

The water around him began to bubble . . . and then a hideous shadowed form like that of no creature Krag had seen on the face of Krynn rose out of the Blood Sea. Eyes, too *many* eyes, stared unblinking at the stunned mariner. A sinewy maw snapped open, revealing row upon row of teeth. In the back of his mind, Krag knew somehow that this could be no creature of the sea goddess. This monstrosity had no right to even exist on this world.

71

The barbed lance that the horror wielded skewered him through the chest with such speed that the captain's expression remained one of astonishment even after he died. Krag's body twitched several times before finally growing limp. The minotaur's killer shook the lance once more for good measure, testing for any sign of life.

A moment later, victor and victim vanished beneath the waves. The fog continued to thicken, burying any last traces of the *Obsidian Axe* from sight.

\* \* \* \* \*

Aryx marched defiantly toward the headquarters of the Knights of Takhisis, a lesser clan house near the port now usurped by the human invaders. Young though he was, even Aryx knew the insult that the knights had heaped not only upon that clan, but the rest as well. If the humans would take from the lesser, they would soon grow bold enough to demand from the great houses as well.

Orilg, for one, would never stand for that.

A full legion, or talon, if Aryx recalled the proper term, of knights lined the grounds of the clan house. The dusky gray warrior noted others—archers, watching from the top of the three-story structure. Broedius had chosen well. The house, belonging to Clan Skalas, was of recent origin, which enabled that clan to fortify it with the latest and strongest materials. They had also lined the roof with battlements, creating a miniature castle much like those of the humans. Perhaps that made the knights feel more at home here.

Messengers and soldiers continually entered and exited from Lord Broedius's stronghold, many of them clearly emissaries from Aryx's people. One wore the insignia of an imperial aide, which meant that the commanding knight had forced Chot to deal on Broedius's terms. Aryx doubted that many human aides rushed to the palace.

Drejjen led them past the guards and into the tall edifice. The wary minotaur marveled at so many knights; he had never really discovered just how many there had been aboard the *Vengeance*, much less her sister ships. Carnelia's brief mention had only given him a vague idea, which he already saw had been a severe underestimation.

As if hearing her name in his thoughts, Carnelia herself

appeared at the iron doors that no doubt led into what had once been the clan elder's hall. She returned Drejjen's perfunctory salute, but not before glancing at Rand. Again Aryx suspected that the cleric and the female knight had some secret—or perhaps not so secret—understanding.

"As commanded," Drejjen announced. "The minotaur Aryximaraki de-Orilg."

Carnelia nodded, then eyed Seph. "And the other?"

"Aryx's brother," Rand interjected. "He is with me."

Her eyes widened briefly at that, but she seemed to accept it. To Drejjen, she said, "Well done. You will now take your command and supervise the fitting of *Ariakan's Victory*, the three-masted ship still labeled *The Hand of Orilg*."

Aryx's eyes narrowed and he barely contained himself. *The Hand of Orilg* had still been under construction when he left Nethosak aboard the *Kraken's Eye*. Now, if he understood her correctly, the knights had not only taken her for their use, but they had also stripped her of her proper title.

Drejjen nodded, but with a surreptitious glance at Aryx, he added, "I know the vessel. A scow unworthy of the name. I thought these minotaurs were supposed to be exceptional shipwrights. I've not seen a decent vessel in this port."

"That'll be enough of that," Carnelia snapped, seeming not so upset over his remarks as his hesitation to obey. "You have your orders."

"As you command." The officer saluted, then, with his men, departed.

Aryx watched Drejjen leave, his ire still dangerously near to erupting. Rand put a hand on his shoulder, a warning. Belatedly Aryx realized that Carnelia was watching him, possibly waiting for his reaction.

The minotaur exhaled. "All right! I'm here. Why?"

"Lord Broedius will answer that," was all she would say. Carnelia indicated the doors.

"You must go alone from here," Rand whispered.

Snorting, the wary warrior marched forward. He expected the sentries at the doors to demand his axe, but to his mild astonishment, they simply opened the way for him. Bracing himself, Aryx continued on, noting the great hall that had been stripped of all clan markings and the few bits of furniture, around which several angry minotaurs and humans eyed one another. Chief among the humans stood Broedius himself, his black, penetrating eyes sweeping up to the new-comer from a chart on the vast oak table before him.

"And here he is," the commander remarked blandly. "As I said he would be."

A score of minotaur faces turned to inspect him, their insignia and cloaks enough to mark them as high-ranking generals. Aryx recognized Hojak of the Supreme Circle, but no one else. As a fairly young warrior, Aryx had not had close contact with any of the senior commanders, although he recognized one as a distant clan member.

"This is the Blessed One's favored?" that one asked, looking somewhat incredulous.

"You saw him in the circus," Broedius replied.

"Aryximaraki," the unknown general pronounced. "Do you know who I am?"

Aryx tried to remain stalwart, although suddenly he wished that he could return to the safety of his quarters in the temple. To be of interest to these senior commanders could not be a good thing. "No . . . no, sir. I've been away for well over a year, and—"

"The *Kraken's Eye*, yes . . ." Several of the other generals muttered, as if somehow the ship meant much to them. "A pity, that." He straightened. Although graying, especially around the muzzle, the broad-shouldered general reminded Aryx of his father, Marak. Several scars along the side of the elder warrior's face attested to years of battle experience. The scars also served to jog Aryx's memory. This general not only stood as a clan member, but he was also a distant cousin of sorts. "I am General Geryl of House Orilg, member of the Supreme Circle and speaker for this delegation."

General Geryl. Aryx immediately knelt, recognizing the tall, stately warrior as one of the champions of the realm. "I am your servant, Geryl."

"On the contrary, we are more likely yours, lad."

Aryx only barely caught the irony in Geryl's tone, so stunned had he been by the actual words. "Sir?"

Geryl frowned. "Up off the floor, blast you!" He glared at Broedius, who, for the first time that Aryx could recall, wore the ghost of a smile. "You enjoy this, don't you?"

"He was your choice, too," the knight replied simply.

"We had no choice." The general approached Aryx. "It seems, warrior, that there must be someone to coordinate matters between our allies, the humans here, and our own people. This one here"—Geryl indicated Broedius—"would have none of us, but rather the one with whom the Blessed One himself chose to travel. As it turns out, word has already spread of this mysterious warrior who walks with gods, a warrior whom some few in the crowd recognized as being of my own clan." Tired but still capable brown eyes studied Aryx. "One who must be more than he seems."

The assembled generals and knights all stared at Aryx as if marking him for target practice. "I don't understand, sir."

"Don't call me 'sir.' I am General Geryl to you, or if you choose, simply Geryl. I . . . *we* . . . will be addressing you as Administrator General and will, it seems, be taking our lead from you in all matters concerning the eventual shipping out of our warriors to the mainland."

*A nightmare.* It had to be a nightmare. Otherwise how could such madness actually exist? "You can't be serious!"

"You walked with the Blessed One. Many saw that. You leapt to save his life as if he were any comrade-in-arms. We've been told of your rescue, the luck of the gods surely playing a hand in that as well. You are a symbol already to many of those who attended the Great Circus yesterday, the champion of Sargas . . . Sargonnas." Again Geryl looked at Broedius. Aryx read little love in the general's expression. "And this one's chosen you, too, for his *own* reasons."

Aryx still refused to accept the outrageous announcement. *He* had been chosen to be some sort of representative between his people and the god-sanctioned invaders? Broedius's reasons for doing so Aryx might have understood. The appointment of a low-ranking warrior such as himself was just another example of the menial position the minotaurs would play in the chain of command. Yet surely his own people would not accept him in such a role. Surely someone like Geryl would have been better suited.

The general apparently read his expression. "There is no choice in this matter. The emperor has decreed this, and more significantly, our illustrious allies will have no other."

"Now that this matter is settled," Broedius interrupted, not concerned about anyone else's opinion on the matter, "we may return to the task at hand. Aryx, step forward."

At Geryl's silent coaxing, the warrior obeyed. Broedius had him come around to where he stood. In one hand, the knight held a badge with the skull and lily symbol of the knighthood etched into it. This he pinned on the front of the minotaur's weapon harness. Aryx glanced down at the horrific badge, feeling more disgust than honor. Such a badge would earn him no respect from his own kind.

"You are appointed. You will act as an in-between for both sides in all matters. Is that understood?"

Aryx understood very little, but he nodded nonetheless. It occurred to him suddenly that perhaps he could use the unwanted position to benefit his people. How he might manage that, the gray warrior did not know, but given time, perhaps . . ."I understand."

Aryx heard a voice very similar to General Hojak's mutter something about puppets, but someone else hushed him. Broedius had the unwilling administrator turn to face the senior officers, who, led by Geryl, saluted him.

"Your business with me is at an end, generals and councillors," the ebony-eyed knight announced. "You've been given your instructions. Anything else I require . . . or that you think you might need to know . . . will be addressed through this warrior from now on. I trust I'm understood."

The assembled minotaurs nodded. At a signal from Geryl, they left, with much rumbling accompanying their departure. Hojak again seemed the most vocal, although not once did Aryx hear anything Broedius might take as treason. Still, the knight surely had to know that at some point there would be physical defiance of his demands.

"You'll see to it that trouble remains minimal, won't you, Administrator General?"

Aryx suddenly realized that other than the commander's personal guard, he stood alone with Broedius. He turned on the human, ever aware that any wrong move might result in his death. "What do you really gain from this? Why me?"

The massive, armored figure gazed almost blankly at him. "You heard the reasons."

"What do you expect me to do?"

"Whatever it was that made your god take such an interest in you . . . and that touches upon the other portion of your duties."

Aryx blinked. "What do you mean?"

"Sargonnas has marked you." The thick black brow furrowed, the first sign that not all went as Broedius would have preferred. "More than I think your simply being aboard the *Vengeance* warranted. There is something about you, minotaur, and perhaps by throwing you into the thick of matters, I'll discover what it is . . . and how it is linked to my Lady's oft-treacherous consort."

He would have liked to shout at Broedius that there were no mysteries, that the only reason Aryx seemed marked had been because others kept marking *him*. Aryx was a warrior striving to live up to the codes of honor and duty by which he had been raised, nothing more. Now, because he had survived where none of his fellow crew members had, a cascading chain of events had thrown him into this insanity.

"What would you have of me now?" the new administrator general asked.

The black eyes bore into Aryx's own. "For now, I'd like very much if you kept an eye on your patron."

"My . . . you mean Sargonnas?"

The commander leaned over the charts he had been studying. "More than the rifts between your kind and mine, the state of mind of your Blessed One concerns me, minotaur. Were he not a god, I might suspect his stability. I would be very suspicious of his loyalties. Were I in your place, I would also find those matters of great import."

Aryx snorted, at last unable to hold back at least some of his frustration. "That's it, then, human? You want me to keep an eye on a god? With all my other overwhelming tasks, I should also watch over the Horned One?"

Broedius stared at his charts, effectively dismissing his visitor. "Yes, that about sums it up."

It took much strength for Aryx to hold back, but he knew that arguing with the knight would only bring more trouble. Still, the unwilling administrator general decided he at least had to broach another subject before agreeing to be dismissed. "About the ship now called *Ariakan's Victory* . . ."

"What about it?"

"You seized it from my clan, House Orilg. Even changed its name."

"To one more suitable." Broedius remained fixed on his charts, which Aryx at last saw were the latest showing the eastern and northeastern coasts of Ansalon. "It is to become the command ship for one of my officers, Pries Avondale. I've appointed him officer-in-charge of the mobilization of forces on Kothas. The ship leaves in two days. That is the end of this discussion and, I think, all others for now. Good day, Administrator General."

This time, two of the commander's personal guards stepped forward, Broedius's farewell apparently a signal. Aryx waved them off, turning brusquely and marching out of the chamber without any glance back at the knight commander. The human's immediate dismissal of the subject of the former *Hand of Orilg* had given Aryx a clear picture of his true position. Broedius had set him up to be a shield, a puppet. Just as he had suspected, the hapless warrior's main purpose was to deflect the anger of his people.

There *would* be anger, too. Much of it. The Knights of Takhisis moved with as little regard as past masters had done, taking whatever they chose without thinking of the consequences. Orilg and the other great houses would not long stand for that.

And what about Sargonnas? Did Broedius truly think that Aryx would be able to keep an eye on the dark god? What *did* the human think was wrong with the Horned One? True, Sargonnas acted enigmatically at the best of times, but was that not the way with gods?

Seph awaited him outside. "What happened in there, Aryx? I saw generals and councillors come out muttering, some of them saying your name! Then, when you didn't come out immediately, I started to worry!"

"I've been appointed a living target," Aryx snarled. When his brother looked perplexed, the older minotaur exhaled. "I'll explain later." He finally noticed Seph stood alone. "Where's the human?"

"The cleric? He left with that female knight. One of the other knights rushed in, saying that some workers on the dock were refusing to obey their orders. The female . . . she exploded. She said she would bring a talon of knights down on the workers!"

Images of full-scale rioting shook Aryx. "She did that?"

"She might have, but the cleric calmed her. He offered to go with her to see that matters were settled peacefully." Seph's eyes narrowed as he glared at a passing knight. "They don't care for us very much, do they?"

"Not much, no. . . ." Aryx hoped that Rand would be able to bring matters under control, but even if he did, the fact that the minotaurs already protested their treatment did not bode well. The Knights of Takhisis could not treat his people like cattle and expect them to take it.

Rand's words aboard the *Vengeance* came back to him. *You may wish the Maelstrom had taken you instead. . . .*

Aryx began to believe that the cleric just might have been right after all.

\* \* \* \* \*

As he had feared, tensions only grew over the next two days, the newly christened *Ariakan's Victory* finally causing some of that tension to boil over. Aryx had avoided becoming embroiled in matters up to this point, but now, with clan Orilg involved, he had no choice but to try to play the role Broedius had thrust upon him.

It began as the ship prepared to sail off for Kothas, the tall, aristocratic human Pries Avondale commanding. Aryx had seen the pale avian man only once and, of all of Broedius's officers, found him the most competent, but that did not mean that Avondale treated or understood the minotaurs much better than his commander. Raising the banner of the knighthood over the ship a day earlier had not gone over well with many of the nearby minotaur captains, especially those with ties to Aryx's clan, who wondered if their vessels would be next. Then, in response to the growing crowd of frustrated minotaurs watching the pride of Orilg make ready to depart under a human name, Avondale ordered a squadron of mounted knights to drive the throng back to a more acceptable distance.

Perhaps such arrogant methods of crowd control worked among his own kind, but Avondale had seriously underestimated Aryx's people. Instead of simply allowing themselves to be pushed around, they pushed back, forcing the riders to struggle with their mounts while fending them off. Fortunately, the matter had ended with no loss of life, but since then, many minotaurs had either slowed down in their tasks or refused to aid the knights at all. Broedius issued threats, threats Aryx knew he would carry out, but still the minotaurs did not acquiesce, becoming more and more militant in their refusal with each passing hour.

Worse, at the head of that dissension stood clan Orilg.

From the temple, there came no word. Sargonnas surely had to know what occurred beyond the walls of his sanctum, but not since Aryx had again knocked on the great doors that morning had anyone seen or heard the God of Vengeance. To Aryx, he had said nothing other than to remind him to return the next morning. The minotaur had never been tempted to interrupt Sargonnas at other times, but this day he made an exception. The moment the news reached him, Aryx returned to the temple, assuming that Sargonnas would keep things from turning disastrous. Behind him came Seph, who now shared with his brother the quarters the priests had grudgingly given him. Seph had never come with him when Aryx had entered the god's chamber, and the thought of doing so now kept the younger minotaur talking constantly.

"Do you think he'll be upset? Don't you suppose he must know by now? What if—"

"Be still, Seph." Aryx barged past two burly acolytes, heading straight for the massive doors to Sargonnas's sanctum. He nearly shoved them open, then thought better of it and simply knocked.

Nothing happened.

The anxious warrior pounded the doors again, this time with so much force that they shook. Still nothing. Aryx glanced around and saw a priest watching with barely veiled amusement. His patience worn thin, the slim minotaur finally tried pushing the doors open. If Sargonnas chose to strike him down, then so be it, but he would not be left standing here.

Emptiness greeted him. Although the throne remained, the God of Vengeance no longer sat upon it, nor did he seem to have left any trace of his whereabouts. Aryx swiftly scanned the vast room, finding nothing. He charged back out into the hall, followed by a somewhat disappointed Seph, and accosted the priest who had been watching.

"You there! Have you seen the Blessed One? Is he somewhere about?"

A slight smirk crossed the elder's features. "You would know better than I, wouldn't you?"

Aryx muttered an epithet that the priest surely could not hear clearly but nonetheless understood well enough. The two brothers abandoned the temple, Aryx's mind racing. Sargonnas would be no help. No word had come from the palace, but then Chot had been absent often of late, choosing to let the knights do what they would.

Something had to be done. Aryx didn't like the role Lord Broedius and the minotaur leaders had thrust upon him, but unless he chose to do something, it seemed everyone else was willing to let Nethosak crumble into disaster.

Aryx had not yet had the opportunity to return to his clan house and likely would not have done so today if not for the potential catastrophe. However, going there appeared the only hope of resolving this matter without useless bloodshed. As to whether any there would listen to him, the young warrior could not say.

Seph and he had gone only a few yards from Sargonnas's house of worship when Rand and Carnelia, both on horseback, appeared without warning. With them rode a full squad of knights, all armed for combat. To Aryx's surprise, they did not head toward the temple, but rather sought *him*.

"You're to come with us," Carnelia snapped irritably. "Rand thinks you might be of help in sorting things out with your clan, and he's convinced Broedius of it."

"The other choice might have been the knights having to deal with an armed insurrection," the cleric added.

"It may still end that way. We can't afford this right now."

"Which is why we are dealing with it . . . and need I remind you that Aryx was made administrator general by your own uncle in order to deal with such matters."

Carnelia grimaced. "And you think he actually expects something from this bull?"

Aryx held back his anger. "I'll go with you to the clan house. I was already on my way there, in fact." He stared pointedly at the female knight. "Whatever you or your uncle believe, I'll do whatever I can to preserve my homeland . . . with or without your support."

"Oh, I'll support you, bull." The black eyes so much like those of Broedius met his gaze squarely. "Until I see that I'm wasting my time."

Snorting, Aryx did not deign to continue the useless conversation. With Seph in tow, he led the riders through the inner recesses of Nethosak, seeking his clan. It did not take too long to reach his former home. House Orilg commanded a great expanse of property in the middle of the imperial capital. In fact, as Aryx neared, he realized that it now commanded even more land than he recalled from before his long and tragic journey aboard the *Kraken's Eye*.

In recent times, portions of the House of Orilg had been rebuilt, in part because of the past war but also because the clan itself had outgrown the older building. The imposing structure, five stories tall and not much smaller than the imperial palace, in many ways resembled a great ship sailing the sea of civilization. The eastern edge narrowed, creating a shape reminiscent of a ship's bow. Row upon row of massive marble columns, each with the blunt-nosed, broken horned profile of the great Orilg himself carved into the center, lined the lower floor of the edifice like oars. The marble, like the rest of the clan house, had an almost iron shading to it, a trick of Orilg's artisans. Iron symbolized durability and strength among the minotaurs, especially Aryx's people.

Above the building fluttered the great banners proclaiming the clan, Orilg's brown silhouetted profile, with its broken left horn, dominant. Two twin-edged axes crossing one another stood below the profile, a symbol of the house's strength and of one of its other champions, Kaz Dragonslayer. Orilg and the axes stood stark in a field of white—no accident, for the two colors also represented Kiri-Jolith. It had been this banner that the knights had so carelessly removed from the minotaur ship, not thinking of the clan's pride and honor.

It did not surprise Aryx that his house might be at the root of rebellion, not given its history. Since the time of his august ancestor, Kaziganthi, the worship of Kiri-Jolith—and, to a lesser extent, Paladine—had taken preeminence over all others. Sargonnas might be a god, but to Orilg, he was not the preeminent god, and after the humans' wretched behavior, this clan had had enough.

These days, wherever clan Orilg went, many of the other houses generally followed.

"I can't believe old Torvak would go this far," Seph whispered as the brothers and their escort approached the vicinity of the structure.

Aryx had to agree with Seph. Torvak did not strike him as a great rebel, but even the monetary-minded patriarch could have limits. "There are guards around the building."

Indeed there were. Warriors of the clan kept a wary watch from points surrounding the great house, axes, lances, and long swords ready. Minotaurs from some allied clans, badges on their weapon harnesses marking their loyalties, stood ready, as if prepared to lend a hand should trouble result. Such a danger clearly existed, for a fighting talon of the Knights of Takhisis under the command of a scarred veteran filled one end of the street. The knights looked eager for action, as did the minotaurs. Aryx had vast confidence in his clan, but he had to admit that the humans would inflict heavy casualties if it came to a fight.

"They refuse to follow the dictates of our Lady," Carnelia reminded him, "and even those of your god."

"Sargonnas isn't their god," the gray minotaur countered. "Do all humans follow Takhisis?"

"They will eventually."

He saw no more point in bandying with Carnelia. If Aryx could not convince his clan to deal with the humans, he feared for not only Nethosak, but the twin kingdoms as well. Sargonnas had spoken of a threat to all Krynn, and Aryx, with ever-fresh memories of the fog-enshrouded horrors that had slaughtered his friends, suspected that he had already confronted the fringes of that threat.

"It would be better if Seph and I entered alone," he informed the knight.

"Out of the question. I'll accompany you."

"*We* will accompany you," Rand corrected. "If I read the banner's colors correctly, I might be of some good in there."

While it was not a choice to his liking, Aryx did not argue. If Carnelia chose to put her life in the hands of his clan, so be it. As for Rand, the cleric likely wanted to come along in order to see that the knight did nothing foolish.

The others behind him, Aryx walked up to the guards standing near the front gate. Distrustful eyes scoured over the group.

"This is clan Orilg ground," one called. "Only those of the blood may enter."

"You know the blood flows in my veins, Kamax," Aryx called. "You tried to spill enough of it during our training together."

"Aryx?" The massive brown male took a step forward. "By the Horns of Orilg, it *is* you!"

"I'm here to speak with Torvak. You know Seph, too."

Kamax peered at the others accompanying Aryx. "I know

you and your brother, Aryx. I don't know these two others, but the fact that they're both humans eliminates them as clan. They stay here. You and your brother can enter."

"Out of the question!" Carnelia blurted. If not for Rand's hand, she might have charged the guard. Kamax and the others readied their axes. The knights who had ridden in with Carnelia drew their swords and the fighting talon poised for the command to attack.

"Kamax!" Aryx strode forward until he stood no more than an arm's length from his old sparring mate. "Kamax, they have to come in with us."

"I have orders, Aryx."

"Kamax, we may not care for the knights, but this isn't the time to fight them, not if, as Sargonnas himself said, a threat exists that may engulf Mithas and Kothas eventually! I'll vouch for these two. The male is a cleric of Kiri-Jolith, Kamax! Do you think he can't be trusted?"

The other minotaur eyed the humans. "And I suppose she's a cleric of Kiri-Jolith, too? I might be able to let him pass, but Torvak'll have my horns if I let one of those knights through!"

Aryx forced a smile. "You mean the whole of the House of Orilg can't take on a single human knight? What do you think she'll do, Kamax?" He indicated the massive long swords many of the guards wielded, then Carnelia's smaller blade. "Cut us all down with her little toothpick?"

The appeal to minotaur pride and superiority worked to ease some of the tension. Kamax actually chuckled. "She's a terror, Aryx, but I doubt that big of a terror."

"I'll take responsibility. So will the cleric, if you like. You have to let us through, though."

"Kiri-Jolith guide me!" Kamax muttered, with a look to the sky.

Not for the first time, Aryx wished that it had indeed been the bison-headed god and not Sargonnas who had come down to the mortal plane. Where had Kiri-Jolith gone? If Sargonnas found it of necessity to be here, why not his rival? Did not the other god care about those who followed him?

A grim look stole over the brown minotaur. "All right, Aryx. I've known you for a long time. I'll take it on my head to let you all pass, but if some treachery befalls the clan while she's in there, I'll be the one to finish the job before I face my punishment in the arena. As it is, Torvak'll probably have me assigned to mucking out the stables!"

"Nothing will happen." So Aryx hoped. He turned back to the others, signaling them to come with him.

Carnelia turned back to her escort. "You know your orders if I'm not back out before the allotted time."

One of the men nodded gravely. The knights made no attempt to sheathe their swords, an ominous sign. Aryx understood then that if he did not talk fast and get Torvak to agree even faster, the fatal incident that sent the two races to war would be on his head. He wondered just how much time the female had allotted for this meeting. Not nearly enough, the anxious minotaur suspected.

Kamax waved two other guards aside, allowing just enough gap for the small party. "Move quick, Aryx, before I recover my wits."

Beyond Kamax, they passed a gauntlet of sentries, none of whom looked on them with favor. Aryx understood that his own position had become suspect. Why would a warrior of Orilg come in such company during this crisis? Even those who recognized and knew him well could not necessarily be counted as comrades. He had hoped that some of his immediate family might be in attendance, especially his parents, but only a few cousins seemed to be present, and they stared back at him as if they did not recognize him.

Burly warriors lined the halls, the walls behind them filled with relics and symbols of Orilg champions past. Axes, swords, shields, most of them dented to near uselessness, spoke volumes of the adventurous history of the descendants of Orilg. Busts of some of the most famous—or infamous, as many of those outside the clan thought them—warriors stared down at the intruders. Most unnerving was the bust of Kaz Dragonslayer, which, when Aryx was young, had seemed as much a god to him as Kiri-Jolith. Broad of face, stern, and yet with a rebellious look in his eyes, the heroic visage seemed to demand great things of the dusky gray warrior.

The legacy of Orilg did not go unnoticed by the humans, even Carnelia sensing the history and strength. She eyed the relics with something near respect, a warrior perhaps at last recognizing those as dedicated as she.

A pair of intricately adorned doors opened for them, reminding Aryx of his entry into Sargonnas's chamber. In truth, there were similarities between the two great rooms, especially their vast dimensions, but whereas the sanctum of the God of Vengeance echoed an emptiness that Aryx felt whenever he was in Sargonnas's presence, the hall of the clan patriarch remained ever the center of activity.

At last they stood before the assembled elders and the patriarch, barrel-chested, battle-scarred Torvak, who, by this time, had learned of their coming. The patriarch looked a bit unwell, the rims of his eyes slightly redder than normal, and every now and then he coughed. The hair atop his head had thinned to almost nothing, a rare thing among Aryx's kind. Torvak's generally round features sagged, and even his lengthy muzzle seemed to droop. His rich robe of evening blue and ivory had been soiled by his incessant coughing, which the patriarch only managed to get under control after sighting the party. Several of the elders in attendance also coughed, but not with the intensity of the clan leader.

"Well, well," Torvak rumbled. "I think I spy young Aryximaraki . . . and his shadow, Sephimaraki. Too old for stealing food from the kitchens now, so why are you here?" Attentive eyes looked over both humans. "Hostages, perhaps? Doubtful, doubtful, knowing your tendencies. When I saw your father but weeks ago, I asked Marak if you'd returned from your voyage aboard Jasi's old vessel." Another cough. "I hear old Jasi's died a warrior's death and you've new shipmates. I hear a lot."

Torvak's rambling manner did not put Aryx at ease one bit. He knew that behind the almost fatherly tones dwelt a cunning and occasionally unpredictable mind. Torvak preferred to keep the clan coffers filled and business as usual, but Aryx recalled that his method for maintaining business as usual sometimes involved the ruination and frustration of rival clans. Once in a while it even became necessary to sacrifice a clan member . . . for purely honorable reasons, of course.

Aryx hoped now would not be such a case. "Patriarch, I come to you to speak about this protest that Orilg has made against Lord Broedius."

"Speak, then, lad." He coughed again. "I never refuse to listen."

Nor promise to consider the words, either. Nonetheless, Aryx pushed on. "Patriarch, clan Orilg must end this protest. It's essential that we all work hand in hand, not fight one another when a threat exists that seeks to engulf all of Krynn."

"We have only a few stray words on that."

"The words of the God of Vengeance, who is much a part of our lives even if our eyes do turn to Kiri-Jolith."

Torvak leaned forward, coughing. "Before you go any further, Aryx, I would like to ask you if you would continue to argue for these humans if you knew that one of the ships we believe they recently sank carried your brother Hecar?"

The words so stunned him that the gray minotaur could not answer at first. Aryx's hands folded into tight fists. Behind him, he heard Seph choke back a sob.

It had to be a lie.

A look of compassion spread across Torvak's wide features, a look shattered by a brief spell of coughing. "I am so sorry, Aryx, Seph! I had thought you heard! Hecar sailed off on the *Crimson Blade* a week ago. Word reached me yesterday that wreckage identified as coming from the *Blade* floated ashore. Three others of our clan perished on that ship"—he stared intently at Carnelia—"a vessel that vanished under very suspicious circumstances."

The young minotaur held back his anger. Despite his claims to the contrary, the patriarch had surely known of Aryx's ignorance and chosen to play on it. Trust Torvak to find a way to set him off course. Aryx stood there, feeling as if he had just sailed into the heart of the Maelstrom.

Rand broke the silence. "Patriarch, may I offer both the condolences of myself and the blessings of Kiri-Jolith for the fighting spirits of your revered dead."

"I am very touched, cleric, very touched indeed. An honor and pleasure it is to have one of our own among us for a change instead of the state robes. For too long have we endured the temple when it does not even speak for our hearts. Now, in his black name, in his *human* name and form, Sargonnas would have us march to the slaughter for these knights." The barrel-chested figure snorted. "After Hecar and so many others, why should we who do not even acknowledge him obey? We can defend the empire without these humans."

The blond man seemed unperturbed. "I should tell you that this mission is sanctioned by not only Sargonnas, but also the other gods as well, including Kiri-Jolith."

A buzzing of conversation rose up among the elders.

Torvak slammed his fist against the arm of his chair, nearly cracking the wood. Silence reigned again.

"I've only your word of this, cleric, however august your station."

"Very true, but if you know me to be what I claim, then you must also consider the fact that I would willingly travel in the company of those who would follow the Dragon Queen. Just as important, you should wonder why they would suffer me to live."

"Many games require pawns, human." Another short fit of coughs prevented Torvak from adding anything more.

Rand started to say something else, but Aryx cut him off. "Patriarch, if I may speak again."

"Please feel free."

He looked long and hard at the elders, meeting the gazes of as many as he could. Among them, Aryx recognized several of his teachers, minotaurs who had turned their long experience to the benefit of the clan and its future. "Clan Orilg, the heavy news that the patriarch passed on to me only urges me more to press for a peaceful end to this impasse. I've little love for the Knights of Takhisis, but I fear that we may truly face far worse than their arrogance and insults very soon. My ship, the *Kraken's Eye,* went down with all hands save myself, the crew slaughtered by creatures who, though I cannot swear to what they were, I feel must be precursors to this Chaos of which Sargonnas spoke. What little glimpses I had were of no beast born of Krynn."

"In the darkness and fog, armor can resemble nightmares, young Aryx."

"These were nightmares, but no knights!" The frustrated survivor looked around at the mostly disbelieving faces. But one thing might convince them of the truth of what he spoke. Straightening, Aryx met Torvak's gaze. "Perhaps if you had lived through what I did, patriarch, elders, you would understand better. . . ."

He related to them then the story of the ship's tragic fate, leaving out no detail, however bloody. Small things that he hadn't even recalled when speaking before Broedius surfaced, adding to the depth of his terrible tale. Torvak sought to interrupt him at the start, but perhaps the ailing patriarch saw something in Aryx's darkening expression, for the elder minotaur held his peace from then on. The rest of the clan leaders listened with varying looks of disbelief, growing astonishment, and, more often, bitter frustration as the hopeless cause of the ill-fated crew unfolded.

As he spoke, Aryx saw each of his crew mates as if they stood before him: Captain Jasi, Hugar, Hercal, Feresi, and all the others. The ghosts stood and listened, as if hoping that by telling their story, Aryx would at last let them rest. He could not, though, because so long as he lived, as long as he felt responsible for failing them, they would haunt Aryx.

Torvak leaned back as he finished, the patriarch having stifled his coughing as best as possible throughout the retelling. "A tragic tale. Very tragic. Very disturbing, too."

Aryx pressed on. He had to make his final plea before he lost the sympathies of the crowd. "Patriarch, elders . . . although Sargonnas may not be our patron, I believe his tale. Surely Kiri-Jolith would have intervened if this expedition did not have merit. The Horned One himself has said that we're needed to help save the rest of Krynn; if we fight among ourselves here and now, we'll be of no help at all. Ansalon, all of Krynn, may fall to worse than what took the *Kraken's Eye*, and by our own actions, we'll have dishonored ourselves beyond all redemption."

Honor . . . it always came down to honor, the cornerstone of minotaur society. Sargonnas himself was said to have been the one to instill the trait within his children. A warrior who did not live with honor did not live. Even those who followed the God of Just Causes acknowledged what history said about Sargonnas's influence in the early days. The minotaurs might not even exist if not for the Horned One.

"Can we trust the word of the God of Vengeance?" one of the elders asked. "We have abandoned him. He may now be living up to his name."

"Even Kaz Dragonslayer found times to trust the Horned One," Aryx added, a hint of black amusement in his voice, "and no one trusted Sargonnas less than he."

The patriarch opened his mouth to speak, but before he could, a sentry barged in.

"Patriarch, the humans without are preparing for an assault!"

"What?" Fury overtook Carnelia. "Someone's disobeying orders! I gave them a specific timetable to follow. My men would not disobey!"

"These are not the ones who came with you," the guard replied curtly. "These are the ones who were already stationed in the street."

"That would be Dumarik. Let me talk to him. I'll see to it that he's kept under control."

Torvak shook his head. "If this is a sign of your trust, the time for talk is past."

She met his gaze. "Only if you let it be. I mean what I say. I want no battle between us. It goes against fulfilling the Vision."

"Ah, yes, this Vision I've heard so much about." Torvak scratched his chin in thought. "Your goddess shows each of you your place in an overall vision of the world beneath her boot, if I understand correctly."

"We know our place in the future of Krynn, yes."

Aryx knew something of the Vision from his time spent aboard the *Vengeance,* but he found it as hard to comprehend as the patriarch apparently did. Still, the Knights of Takhisis seemed, for the most part, very dedicated to it.

The patriarch coughed. His eyes shifted to Aryx, then back to the knight. At last he inclined his head. "Go and speak to them, but know that we'll be ready for whatever the outcome."

"I'd expect no less, but the outcome will be as I promised."

"I will join you," Rand said. Carnelia nodded and the pair started out.

Torvak gestured. A pair of tall warriors flanked the humans, escorting them. The patriarch's trust went only so far.

He turned to Aryx. "I believe she will keep that promise . . . but only because it serves her now. So you still think we should trust them, young Aryx? You think we should also trust this humanized Sargas?"

Aryx took a deep breath. "I think we've no choice but to work with them. I think the fate of the empire and our people depends on it."

"I note the word 'trust' didn't enter your response, young warrior."

"I say what I think."

The massive patriarch roared with laughter, which ended in yet more coughing. He looked even worse than when Aryx had first come in, but still Torvak's energy did not flag. "A tendency of your lineage, Aryximaraki, and one that will both serve you and continue to make your life an adventure, to say the least! Try not to seek my position too soon, will you?"

"I've no desire to be patriarch."

"Neither did I when I was as hot-blooded a warrior as you, boy . . . neither did I." Torvak looked around at the elders, and Aryx realized that he sought a vote from them through their expressions. Aryx studied the worn and scarred visages but could not read their decision. However, Torvak apparently could with ease. "Settled, then. We will, at least for the time, rejoin the humans' efforts." He stared at the two brothers. "Make certain that Lord Broedius understands, though, that Orilg and those aligned with it will not long brook the arrogance and disregard with which he has treated our people so far. We will be slaves no more, regardless of what Emperor Chot and the circle have agreed. You'll relay this to the lord knight himself, of course, Aryx. In addition, since I already have a recommendation of you from young Geryl, you are hereby chosen as our representative in these matters and any future ones that may pop up. You'll come speak directly to me if necessary." Torvak ignored Aryx's suddenly stricken expression. "Congratulations . . . and watch your neck, lad."

He snapped his fingers, and four well-armed warriors immediately formed a guard around Aryx and Seph.

"Patriarch—" the dusky gray minotaur began.

"You're"—a cough—"honored, of course." Torvak coughed long, his eyes watering.

Aryx suddenly realized that the patriarch had been fighting back such a fit through most of the audience, and now his resistance had at last slipped. The exasperated warrior gave up, knowing that he could not argue with the stricken elder now.

Another collar had been hung around his neck. Aryx felt some relief that the present crisis had been averted, but knew that this victory would not alter the minotaurs' precarious situation much in the long run. Something else would have to be done, something, unfortunately, that would probably fall on his head.

Resigned to his fate, Aryx saluted the stricken elder, then turned around in order to depart. He needed to relate the news to Carnelia as soon as possible.

A loud crash, followed by several shouts of consternation, made Aryx whirl back.

Patriarch Torvak lay in a heap at the foot of his chair, unmoving. Two robed minotaurs knelt by his side, trying to check his condition. One of them muttered, "He pushed himself too far. . . ."

Aryx barged passed the sentries, Seph close behind him. Torvak's bodyguards kept most of the crowd at bay, but Aryx managed to get near enough to see the patriarch's face. He had thought Torvak ill, but not this bad. "What's happened to him?"

"The same thing that has happened to many others," one of the robed figures replied. "A strange new illness spread by means we do not understand. We only know it starts with the cough."

The cough. Rand had mentioned seeing minotaurs coughing, but at the time, Aryx had not thought much about it. Even minotaurs caught colds.

"The cleric!" Perhaps Rand could help. Turning on the nearest guard, Aryx ordered, "Find the human cleric! Tell him he's needed here urgently!"

The robed figure who had spoken took umbrage. "A human? What can he do for our patriarch?"

"Possibly nothing, but there's a good chance he can help."

The guard reluctantly left, to return a few minutes later with Rand in tow. The look of concern on the cleric's visage indicated that he had been informed about what had happened.

"How is he?"

"Trouble breathing," one of the robed ones, clearly a physician, reported. "The red around his eyes is stronger. He lost all control as he started to seat himself. We had warned him not to put up so strong a front, but Torvak will be Torvak."

"They said it started with that cough you mentioned," Aryx added.

"Did it?" Rand looked grim. "I should have known." He bent down. "I promise nothing but to give the utmost available to me through my patron."

The cleric put one hand on the fallen patriarch's chest, the other on his forehead. Rand closed his eyes and started whispering. Try as he might, Aryx could not understand one word.

A minute passed. Two. Five. Still the human continued to whisper. Aryx saw no change in Torvak, and from the hard expressions of the others, neither did they.

At last the cleric removed his hands. Looking at the crowd, he shook his head. "I can do nothing . . . and that is curious."

"And why is that curious, human?" the first robed one asked, very skeptical.

"Because the power of Kiri-Jolith should flow through me and into this one, and no mere illness should be strong enough to block such power. Perhaps a healer of Mishakal would do better, since that is her sphere, but I know what I can do. No, I find this curious, just as I found it curious when I examined one or two others who had the cough. I could not discern a way to aid them either."

A sense of foreboding struck Aryx. "What does that mean?"

Rand frowned. "That this disease may be more than we think. There may be a force behind it . . . the same force, I think, that Sargonnas fears will eventually encompass all of Krynn."

# The Encroaching Darkness

## Chapter Six

Since their realm had been invaded so many times, the minotaurs had attempted to stem some assaults by creating a complex series of sentry posts situated around the perimeter of each island. Each post depended upon the terrain, the defenders believing that an attacker should not have advance notice that he had been spotted. Because of this, most posts consisted of carefully camouflaged blinds or holes dug deep into the earth. Other times, the minotaurs made use of natural formations, such as overhangs, ridges, or boulders . . . anything natural behind which one could hide. In times past, this natural series of sentry posts had indeed preserved the islanders' independence. It was other faults, such as overconfidence, that were more likely to bring about the race's downfall.

With the coming of the Knights of Takhisis, the posts had suffered. Lord Broedius did not trust minotaur sentries to report to his commanders. In addition, he wanted as many of the able warriors as possible to be prepared to depart for Ansalon the moment he gave the order. Therefore, the knight commander had immediately begun stripping the more distant posts, gradually replacing them with a series of roving patrols consisting of his own warriors. Only key points retained sentries, and those posts were generally reduced to no more than two or three men. Aryx's people had, of course, protested this stripping of their right to secure their own domain, but Lord Broedius had been adamant. The fragile sense of cooperation that the gray minotaur had managed to put together threatened again to come apart. Lord Broedius had made a mild concession, allowing the possibility of some of the inhabitants rejoining in the defense of those regions near and surrounding Nethosak, but he had left to his sub-commanders the decision as to how those minotaur sentries would be used.

Sir Brock, a broad-shouldered, heavily mustached subcom-mander in charge of several miles of shoreline southwest of Nethosak, cared little for the minotaurs' protests or, for that matter, their very manner. In his eyes, they had shown none of the efficiency or training for which they were reputed, and as far as he was concerned, they were little better than the brutes Lord Ariakan had recruited. Not trusting them at all, he main-tained his own patrols, all knights, and personally rode to each checkpoint to see that security remained high. So far he had come across no major incidents, but he felt certain that eventually the minotaurs would reveal their hand, sabotaging Lord Broedius's efforts.

Accompanied by ten men, Sir Brock rode toward the most remote of the checkpoints. This night, all had been in order, something of a minor disappointment. The only annoyance had been the damnable fog, which had finally crept in to the edge of the island. The patrol leader could do nothing about the weather. He yearned for action or the discovery of some plot against his commander. Brock dearly wanted *something* he could hang on the minotaurs other than their slow pace and constant grumbling.

"How much farther?" he asked of his second.

"Just a short distance, sir. Even with the growing fog, we should see their torchlight any—"

Brock cut him off with the wave of one massive hand. He saw a torch flickering just over a tall ridge. The figure of one armored man stood nearby. The subcommander frowned. He could see that this night would bring nothing of interest. The other two men stationed here were probably resting, so bored that they would dare disobey orders. While he could not blame them for that, they would still have to pay for their insubordinate behavior.

In order to reach the others, the band had to ride along the very edge of the shoreline, in this case a sandy beach. The horses had to move slowly, but Sir Brock had no intention of dismounting and leading them. After he reprimanded these men for their lack of discipline, the subcommander planned to return to headquarters as soon as possible. Perhaps he would at last be able to convince Lord Broedius to assign him to something more active.

Two figures lying near the hill showed him that his suspicions were true; the sentries were asleep at their post. Such negligence would require harsh punishment indeed. As his party neared, Brock called out to them. "Ho there! Look alive, you sluggards!"

None of the three moved. The lone knight standing remained by the torch, uncaring.

"Sir Tristyn, ride up there and drag that one down while I deal with these other miscreants!"

"Aye, sir! Gladly, sir!" Eagerly Brock's second urged his mount around the side of the hill. Tristyn was an excellent second, a young blade who brooked no fault in his fellows. Someday he would be leading his own fighting talon.

"Probably drunk, all of them," Brock muttered. The other knights exchanged glances. Drunkenness on duty was punishable by death. He sniffed the air, a peculiar odor prevalent everywhere. "What's causing that stench?"

The patrol leader rode up until his steed nearly stood hoof to toe with the dark, slumbering figures. Disgusted, the huge knight finally dismounted. If they did not wake up soon, he would kick them awake.

The sandy soil proved very moist, caking his boots. He decided to clean them off on the nearest of the insubordinate pair.

"Wake up, damn you! Wake up or I'll have your head!" He kicked the man in the side as hard as he could.

The body rolled with the kick, but the helm—and the head within—rolled to his feet.

"Great Takhisis!" Brock reached for his sword.

From above, Tristyn called, "Sir! The man up here's been gutted and hung like a fish!"

"Get down here quick!" Sword free, the commanding knight mounted. This had to be the work of minotaurs, and with any luck, they would still be nearby. Brock would track them down and—

A scream from the top of the hill made him pause. In the dim torchlight, he saw Tristyn come tumbling down the hill . . . in three different directions. Something had not only beheaded him, but cut off his legs as well.

The beach erupted with sand-covered forms, monstrous, shadowy figures that Brock could not have envisioned in his worst nightmares. Horrific, armored creatures, with savage weapons in their inhuman appendages.

A sicklelike blade severed the arm of one of his men. The injured knight screamed, and as he did, another of the monsters dragged him from his suddenly fearful charger and buried a wicked, barbed lance in his throat.

The knights were surrounded. Brock tried to turn his mount, but everywhere he looked the hellish creatures loomed in the fog, which seemed to grow thicker by the second. He struck at one with his blade but watched with horror as it bounced off the armor . . . or, rather, *shell*.

Two more men went down, one with a lance through him, the other minus his hand and head. Even the horses were not spared, sometimes man and mount dying together. Stunned, many of Brock's knights perished while they were still trying to draw their weapons. The few that did manage found their adversaries as difficult to kill as Sir Brock had.

Managing to fend off the creature nearest him, the sub-commander glanced around, intending to rally those still with him. To his horror, though, nearly all of his knights had already been slaughtered. One of his remaining men tried to flee, but a flurry of scythe swords cut both horse and rider to ribbons.

"Sir Brock—" The cry for help ended abruptly, along with the last of his warriors.

His horse screamed, its front legs cut out from under it. Brock swore as he fell with the dying animal. One of the shadowy behemoths loomed over him, slashing with the wicked sword through the metal protecting his shoulder. Blood—Brock's blood—spilled over the disbelieving subcommander. He was a Knight of Takhisis, one of her majesty's chosen! He wore her mark; he wore the armor that she had promised would make him nigh invincible!

His enchanted armor did nothing to stop the seven lances that pinned his twitching body to the ground.

\* \* \* \* \*

The morning brought with it many things, few good as far as Aryx was concerned. The fog, which had previously remained some distance offshore, now covered most of the edges of Mithas. Aryx sniffed the air but detected no noticeable increase in the faint musky odor. Still, he tried to alert Lord Broedius of the possible danger, certain that the commander of the occupation force would understand his great fear. To his astonishment, however, Broedius refused to even see him, allowing the minotaur only to pass his concerns on through a disinterested aide who seemed unlikely to disturb his superior.

Frustrated, Aryx headed back to the temple, for once alone. Seph had returned to the clan house, seeking news of the rest of their family, especially their parents. The death of Hecar still haunted both, but Aryx most of all. He could not help but link his brother's mysterious disappearance with the destruction of the *Kraken's Eye*. He wondered how many others might also be dead. Minotaurs lived with death, it being part of the way of the warrior, but the monstrous shadows who struck from beneath the waves were unlike any foe that they had ever faced.

His gaze happened to drift toward his destination, the looming, ever staid Temple of Sargonnas. His so-called chosen had perished, or at least vanished under sinister circumstances, and yet the god did little. Where did he disappear to each day? Why did Broedius and not the great Horned One oversee the grand expedition? Surely the mood of the minotaurs would be much higher under the leadership of the god. With Sargonnas leading the way, Aryx suspected that even followers of the other gods would take up arms for the crusade. Instead, the minotaurs cursed the Knights of Takhisis and threatened insurrection, a course leading to nothing but useless bloodshed.

The ground beneath him suddenly shook. Caught up in his thoughts, Aryx did not immediately realize the seriousness of the situation, not until a large chunk of marble from the top of the building next to him fell, coming within a foot of his head.

He immediately abandoned the walkway, stumbling toward the center of the street even as the shaking intensified. Aryx's instinctive reaction proved fortuitous, for the building by which he had been standing already had severe cracks running through it. More pieces of loosened stone, some quite larger than the first, dropped from its high roof. Another minotaur who had moved a bit slower than Aryx fell, bleeding, struck down by a jagged stone.

No minotaur born and raised on either Mithas or Kothas could have reached adulthood without having experienced at least one tremor a year. Aryx's homeland reflected those who peopled it, volatile, unpredictable, powerful. Most prominent of all features were the volcanoes of Argon's Chain. If one did not rumble, another soon would. Situated far to the north, the four largest stood like angry sentinels, gods even, watching over their domain. Some called them the Horns of Sargas, for the Lord of Vengeance also went by the title of God of Volcanoes, and they often seemed to reflect his dark mood.

As the tremor increased, Aryx looked to the temple, wondering if indeed Sargonnas grew angry over something. He knew that the volcanoes most often rumbled of their own accord, but with the deity here in Nethosak, the thought that Sargonnas's ire might be the stimulus could not be ignored. The unsteady warrior tried to make his way toward the temple, which seemed to stand strangely still, despite the shaking. The going proved maddening, however, as even the street began to turn treacherous.

Aryx recalled tremors of the past, but none that, within his memory, had grown so violent so quickly. He managed two more steps toward the distant temple before a new shock wave sent him tumbling.

No longer could this simply be called a tremor. It was a full-fledged earthquake.

Someone screamed. A bell tower atop one building began to tip, the bell ringing madly. A fault developed in the street, running across the entire width. Even as Aryx watched, the widening fault reached an inn, tearing the front in two. Mortar, brick, and stone crumbled, while minotaurs still inside fought desperately to escape the deadly rain. On one of the nearby clan houses, spider-web cracks spread across the foundation, then upward. The statue of a minotaur near the gate of the clan house toppled over, scattering the already harried guards trying to maintain their positions throughout the crisis.

A great, slow groan filled the air, and a shadow covered Aryx. He looked up and saw that, above him, the face of one building had broken away and now slowly fell in his direction. Scrambling as best as he could over the increasingly unpredictable surface of the battered street, the minotaur dodged massive fragments presaging the complete collapse of the wall. The shadow continued to keep pace with him, dire warning that he needed to move even swifter.

A tawny figure collided with him, a slim female fleeing from one of the buildings to his left. She paid him no mind as she pushed away, but in doing so, she fled directly toward the path of the crumbling wall. Aryx cursed, reaching out at the last minute to keep her from a fatal mistake. Caught off guard, she struggled little, enabling Aryx to drag her along.

The shadow moved ahead. He cursed again, wondering if it were even possible to escape. In the end, his unwilling companion still in tow, Aryx had to throw himself forward, praying to Kiri-Jolith that both of them would at last be out of range.

The wall crashed to the ground, chunks flying everywhere. Aryx grunted in pain as one struck his shoulder, another his left leg. Beside him, the female also cried out. Uncertain as to whether the downpour had finished, they remained still, waiting.

And then, as quickly as it had begun, the quake ended.

For several minutes, an eerie silence reigned. Then, from around the city, cries rose up, some of them in pain, some in anger, and others from those trying to help.

Aryx at last arose, the agony in his leg and shoulder beginning to subside. He inhaled, trying to regain his breath, only to cough violently as he swallowed dust.

"Let me help you," a feminine voice insisted. Strong hands pulled him around. "It's the least I can do after you saved my life."

He waved off her aid, the coughing already slowing. For the first time, Aryx had a good look at his companion. Near his age but more lithe of form, she looked as formidable a warrior as she did an attractive one. Deep brown eyes stared out over a short, graceful muzzle. A streak of white ran down from between her eyes to her nose. Her horns were slightly curved inward and no more than half the length of Aryx's. She stood a few inches shorter than he, but not for one second did he think her less than his match in skill.

Under his gaze, she lowered her eyes momentarily. Then, recovering quickly, she said, "My thanks for saving me from my own foolishness. I was so eager to escape from inside I never considered the dangers outside."

"In a quake, it's hard to find anywhere safe." He saw blood on her arm. "Are you badly injured?"

"This?" she shook her head. "More surprise than pain . . . but you have two terrible bruises."

"They'll heal." Aryx looked around. "We were lucky."

"Thanks to you. I am Delara Es-Hestos, and I pledge that I'll repay you for what you've done for me."

"I am Aryximaraki de-Orilg, and you owe me nothing." He stopped as a peculiar look came over her. "Are you all right?"

"Aryximaraki de-Orilg? The Blessed One's companion?" Delara's eyes shone. "He who walks with Sargonnas?"

To his horror, she started to go down onto one knee, apparently to pay him homage. Angered more than he should have been, Aryx seized her by the shoulders, pulling her up. "Stop that! You owe me none of that! I'm a warrior like you, Delara, nothing more! The humans' ship, the *Vengeance,* found me adrift after my own vessel had been attacked. Sargonnas happened to be aboard. Nothing more! No godly connection, no divine intervention! I am no more chosen than—" He stopped, having been about to say "no more chosen than any other minotaur," but clearly Delara belonged to those who followed closely the worship of the Horned One. "I am no chosen of the gods."

"As you say," she finally returned, although the light did not completely vanish from her eyes.

"What matters more," he persisted, "is seeing to the injured."

Even as he spoke, cries rose anew. To her credit, Delara immediately agreed with him, and the two began to work in earnest to help wherever they could. The building from which she had emerged was their first destination, since many of those behind her had failed to escape. Aryx, Delara, and soon a host of others fought to free those they could and to gather for burial those for whom the quake had proven fatal. Fortunately, the loss of lives turned out to be less than Aryx had feared, but even those few hurt, for somehow he felt responsible.

Despite the quake's brevity, some parts of the city had been struck hard. The worst damage had been near the imperial capital. In addition, the storehouses where the knights had put many of the supplies intended for the fleet had suffered badly. Some had been completely leveled. The region around the headquarters of the Knights of Takhisis had also been ravaged, but the reinforced clan house Lord Broedius had usurped still stood, albeit now with a few cracks. Many of the other clan houses nearby had also suffered at least minor damage. On the other hand, regions of the capital where past quakes had proven prevalent had hardly faced more than a slight tremor.

The quake had been very focused, but only Aryx seemed to find this so. He chose to say nothing, not at all certain of his suspicions.

Hours after the quake, the weary minotaur paused, his gaze sweeping past the temple. He felt his blood race as he stared at the sanctum of Sargonnas, which had not suffered so much as a single tiny crack. Little if any help had emerged from the temple, least of all the Blessed One himself. Once a few priests had made their way around the perimeter of the area, but they seemed more interested in avoiding those in need than in reaching out to them.

At last he could stand it no longer. Weary but fueled by his increasing bitterness, Aryx abandoned his work the moment circumstance permitted him. He had to try to see Sargonnas. Even after the quake, surely the god could do something for his people. They had already sacrificed too much not to deserve at least that.

He realized belatedly that someone followed him. Turning, he saw Delara at his heels.

"I saw you run off. You had such a look on your face, I . . . I feared for you."

"You've no reason to worry about me, Delara, and where I head, you may not wish to follow."

She glanced past him to the temple. "You're going to see the Blessed One, aren't you, Aryx? You're going to ask him for help!"

At this point, Aryx planned to *demand* help, whatever the consequences. True, he would probably fail, but at least he, of all people, might stand a chance. Certainly no one else seemed to be willing to speak with the dark deity.

Delara's face lit up. "I want to go with you. May I?"

Aryx started to tell her that she could not, then realized he had no right. Besides, as one of Sargonnas's truly faithful, perhaps her presence would aid him in gaining help from the dark one. Even if the God of Vengeance chose to strike him down for his audacity, Delara would probably be safe.

"All right, you can come. But if we do see him, and he seems a little angry with me, be sure to keep your distance."

He moved on, ignoring her puzzled look. Aryx's mind raced ahead, wondering how he would confront the god. The entire notion seemed insane, but he could not back down. Sargonnas had to be made to see that he had a responsibility.

As he neared his destination, anger again overrode his uncertainty. Many buildings in the vicinity of the temple either lay in ruins or showed some visible sign of damage, but the sanctum of Sargonnas stood untouched. A good sign, in some respects, but if the god could preserve his house of worship, then why did he not preserve the houses of his worshipers as well?

"Halt there!" A temple guard, big and brawny, blocked their path. "The high priest orders—"

He got no further, for Aryx charged him without warning, pushing the guard against a marble column. Stunned, the other minotaur collapsed long enough for the duo to enter the temple, Delara with some sudden nervousness. Several acolytes, eyes wary, stood within, but none approached them.

"Aryx," Delara dared. "Perhaps a little caution and respect would be advisable here."

Aryx would not hear her. He felt he had been too passive in this matter. Since the death of his crew mates, his shame had secretly held him back. No more. What point was there for a god to come to his people if the god did nothing?

"Sargonnas!" He pulled his axe out and prepared to hammer the great doors with the base of the handle. "Sargonnas! Your people need you! Sargon—"

Aryx paused, suddenly aware of voices within. Sargonnas's he recognized, but in addition, a female spoke. Her very tone, her every word, seduced and beguiled him, and yet for reasons he could not explain, Aryx did not feel lust so much as distaste and suspicion.

Beside him, Delara whispered, "What is it? Why have you stopped?"

"Don't you hear them?"

She leaned close. "I hear nothing. Is—is this where he stays?"

She heard nothing? Aryx almost questioned her, but then the beguiling voice filled his ears once more.

". . . could I ever be disappointed in you, my dearest Sargonnas? You, who have been my shield, my warrior, my true one?"

"I have played many roles to suit you, from sycophant and coward to reluctant avenger. Whatever your whims desired. I choose no longer to play roles. We are beyond that point. We are beyond the plotting, beyond the tricks, beyond the betrayals. We agreed to this pact, but I am feeling as if you have forgotten that, and so I have had to ask you."

"Ah, my sweet Sargonnas! You wound me! With Father Chaos prepared to strike all around us, do you think that I would jeopardize all? Surely you know me better than that."

"Which is why I dare ask."

"I do not think I like this present incarnation of yours. It's too arrogant even for you. Too much the warrior, with little of the labyrinthian mind I cherish so much. Where has my sweet, dark Sargonnas gone?"

"To war. We have made a pact—Paladine, you, and all the rest—and I, for one, will honor that pact."

The mysterious female might have said something in reply, but a sudden urge drove Aryx forward, almost as if his body had decided to act without his mind. Axe in one hand, the gray minotaur shoved the doors open, using every bit of strength at his command. The great bronze doors swung back hard, rocking on their hinges. Unable to prevent himself, the young warrior charged inside.

Shadows surrounded Sargonnas, who, for a change, did not sit upon his throne. As Aryx's eyes adjusted to the unexpected gloom, he thought he saw a face and form in those shadows, a human or possibly elfin woman of such remarkable dark beauty that even the minotaur wished for a second glance. She seemed to smile knowingly—whether at Sargonnas or himself, Aryx could not say—then all trace of her faded. The mortal blinked, wondering if he had imagined her. One look at Sargonnas, though, made him suspect not.

"Aryximaraki . . ." the armored figure whispered, his tone very cold. "You have some reason for disturbing me now?"

The horned warrior snorted. "Other than the fact that Nethosak's suffered a tremendous quake and many of your people were either killed or injured? Or that you've done nothing but sit here safely ensconced in your little temple, oblivious to all?"

"My children have suffered worse. It is their lot . . . and you do not understand the game now unfolding, a most terrible game."

"Games such as your kind play, we mortals can do without," Aryx snarled. "Perhaps if we had a god or two acting *with* us, it might be different."

"You are my children, my chosen." Eyes like embers swept over the pair. Aryx glanced to the side, in the heat of anger, having forgotten Delara. She had fallen to one knee, her awe of the Horned One clear. Sargonnas seemed to consider her before finally asking, "Do you think I do not fight beside you, fight for you?"

"We've seen damn little—" Aryx began.

"I know what you have seen, Aryximaraki, and I know very much how you think. You were chosen for that reason, among others."

Taken aback by the god's enigmatic statement, Aryx could only blurt, "What do you mean by that?"

Sargonnas went on as if the minotaur had not spoken. "I fight on more levels than mortal minds can comprehend. This battle began long before the minotaur race became involved, and it may continue long beyond the last minotaur is laid to rest."

This did not sit at all well with the young warrior. "Vague riddles and evasive talk! So far, the only thing I know is that you do nothing for your so-called children, while the knights prepare to use us as fodder in some war we don't understand!"

"You will be used as necessary, or else none of us may see the end of this terrible trial."

"Spoken like a god . . ." Aryx took a threatening step toward Sargonnas, heedless of the possible consequences. "Will you at least help—"

The pale, gaunt figure suddenly clutched the side of his head, as if struck by a great ache. Ember eyes blazed hotly. He glared at the defiant minotaur with such intensity that Aryx at last faltered. "This audience is at an end, Aryximaraki. Do not presume upon your position again. You will come when summoned and no sooner. Nethosak and my children have suffered other quakes, other wars. They will do so again and be the stronger for it."

"Stronger, or all dead? I've lost a brother already, his fate as murky as your damned words, and—"

The dark god straightened, looking impossibly thin. At Sargonnas's side, the gem in the hilt of his sword seemed almost to wink at Aryx. Sargonnas momentarily shimmered, the vague outline of the throne briefly visible through him. "I said that this audience was at an end."

Aryx abruptly found himself standing outside the great temple. Beside him, Delara, still in a kneeling position, leapt quickly to her feet, stunned by the shift in location.

"Blasted gods . . ." muttered Aryx. He almost regretted having talked his clan out of their struggle against the Knights of Takhisis. Sargonnas claimed to care for the minotaurs, but when confronted, the god rejected his children's entreaties. Of what use was he, then?

Of what use am *I?* the frustrated young warrior asked himself. He had failed in his most important quest. Sargonnas turned a blind eye to events, claiming godly struggles more important. That was the way with gods; their own bickering took precedence over all, even the very existence of the little mortal creatures they claimed to cherish.

"You might have been killed in there," Delara whispered, interrupting his dark thoughts.

"I should have been dead like the rest of my crew mates," he snapped back. "Perhaps that would have been better."

She chose to ignore his outburst. "He seemed . . . not at all what I would have expected."

"Are the gods ever what we expect . . . or hope them to be?"

"That's not—that isn't what I mean. He looked . . . weaker."

"Looks can be deceiving." If the dark deity could send them away with but a word, Aryx refused to believe he could not help those who had suffered from the quake.

She prepared to refute his words, but Seph came along at that moment. Nearly out of breath, Aryx's younger brother stumbled into his arms. Seph looked greatly relieved at having found his elder sibling.

"Aryx! Praise Kiri-Jolith that you're all right! When I couldn't find you, I grew worried! Then someone said he saw you heading toward the temple."

"Save your breath, Seph. I'm fine. What about you?" Aryx felt a little guilty. Between aiding victims and venting his fury over Sargonnas's lack of assistance, he had all but forgotten his young brother.

"I'm okay. I was at the clan house when it happened. The building shook a little, but nothing more!"

"Good. Any news of the rest of our family?"

Here Seph exhibited disappointment. "I only know that our parents are still supposed to be on Kothas. As for the rest, only rumors, but all have been seen of late somewhere, so . . ."

His brother trailed off. Aryx, though, understood what had gone unsaid. As far as they knew, the rest of their family remained alive. Kiri-Jolith and Paladine smiled over them so far, if they watched at all. If Sargonnas spoke some truth, then perhaps they, too, no longer listened to the entreaties of their followers. It would certainly explain why the God of Just Causes allowed the grand plans of the Knights of Takhisis to proceed as they did.

Seph suddenly grew alert again. "Kaz's axe! I almost forgot! I did hear some other news . . . news about you!"

He felt the hair on the nape of his neck crawl. "News?"

"About an hour ago—" Seph broke off as a storm of thundering hooves made all three minotaurs look off to the right. A full talon of the Knights of Takhisis rode toward the temple, at their head, Carnelia and a rather dour Rand. Aryx knew immediately that once again they sought not the god but him. He suspected that Seph's unspoken news had concerned this very fact.

This time he chose to meet them head-on, striding toward the massive party as if unconcerned. Inside, his mind raced, wondering what they sought of him. Had Orilg turned once more against the knights? Did they now want him to confront Sargonnas with some wrong? If so, Aryx would have to disappoint them. He doubted that, today at least, the God of Vengeance would even allow him back into the temple, much less grant him an audience.

Carnelia raised a hand, calling a halt. Rand looked ready to say something to Aryx, but a glance from the knight silenced him. Clearly the matter was of some great import, enough to drive a wedge between the pair.

"We've been scouring the capital for you, bull," Carnelia called. "You should have left some word where to find you!"

"I am not one of your uncle's servants," the minotaur snapped back. "And you seem to find me readily enough. My people suffered a catastrophe and I helped. Would you have expected otherwise from me?"

She calmed a little. "I suppose not, but your constant moving about made my task all the more difficult. You're to come with us immediately!"

"What have I done?"

"It's not what you might have done, bull. It's what you might be able to do!"

Aryx tensed, not at all liking the sound of what she had said. "What I might be able to do?"

"Some sentries and a patrol are missing," Rand interjected, ignoring Carnelia's expression. "They must have vanished last night. Lord Broedius thought you might know what happened."

"Does the human think I kidnapped them?" Had Broedius gone mad? "I've no time for this. The city is still trying to recover."

"Lacynos will recover without your help," the female knight retorted, seizing control of the conversation again. "As for the sentries, no, Broedius doesn't think you kidnapped them. He thinks instead that they're all dead, and that others of your race, perhaps even your own clan, are responsible." She leaned forward, making certain he heard every word. "And unless you can prove otherwise, you and your kind will pay for each life with one of your own."

# The Storm
## Chapter Seven

Aryx dismounted and began inspecting the moist, sandy shore. Superficially there were no signs of the missing knights save the remains of their campfire, but the knights who were investigating the site had already found some small traces they claimed were bloodstains, and Carnelia herself had located a black dagger she said that the missing subcommander, Brock, had owned.

Try as he might, Aryx could find no clue as to what had befallen the humans. However, like the others, he, too, suspected that they had been killed. That his own people might have done this made some sense, but the attack had clearly not been an honorable one. Some trap had to have been set, one to which the knights had readily fallen prey. As most of them had been riding together in a patrol and not even their mounts had been located, that bespoke a large, coordinated group responsible.

With Torvak ill, nearly dying, had Aryx's own clan rejected the stricken patriarch's pledge to cooperate? No doubt Lord Broedius saw it that way, which might have been why he specifically had chosen to include Aryx in this hunt. Perhaps he used the warrior to draw out the clan or even believed that Aryx, too, might be a part of the murderous plot.

"How many men were stationed here?" he asked an impatient Carnelia, stalling for time.

"Three. Brock probably had at least half a dozen men with him; we're not sure yet exactly how many. They were last seen at a post beyond that high ridge." She pointed to her left.

Aryx studied the ridge. By rights, the post there should

have been able to at least see the fire, however dimly. "What did they say?"

"The fire stayed lit, but they couldn't see anything else because of the growing fog. The sea and wind made it impossible to hear anything softer than a horn blast."

"Fog?" Aryx stiffened. "Thick fog?"

She shrugged. "Thick enough. Not like that soup still out there.

"Don't even think it, bull," the knight went on. "Lord Broedius has eliminated that possibility. The sentries at the other post said that not once had they noticed that musky smell you harped about when we were aboard the *Vengeance*." From her tone, Aryx suspected that Carnelia doubted great parts of Aryx's earlier story of disaster. So, too, it seemed, did her uncle, who clearly preferred standard foes, such as rebellious minotaurs, to aquatic reavers whom no one alive other than one injured survivor claimed existed.

Aryx, however, knew they existed, but proving it here and now seemed unlikely. Nonetheless, he clamped his mouth shut and continued his search, his mind churning over the possibility. Shadow monsters, tall, armored, and clawed, haunted him as he crawled over rocks, inspected the camp remains on the ridge, and even dug in the sandy soil as the waves rolled in.

"Do you really think you'll find anything?" Delara asked as she helped him with the last of the three tasks. Although strangers to one another, she and Seph had united together, insisting on accompanying him. Possibly they feared for his life in the company of so many hostile knights, although Aryx trusted Rand's presence enough to believe himself safe. That the humans might arrest him was still a risk, but Aryx wanted to see the evidence. If his clan had done this . . .

The kneeling minotaur shifted away more sand. The deeper he went, the more moist it grew. The ground seemed terribly loose, too. Aryx had noticed that upon first riding over it, his mount sinking in more than it should have. The knights, unfamiliar with the terrain, had appeared to notice nothing amiss, but Aryx wondered what could have turned the land so soft, even taking into account its link to the sea. It almost seemed as if the ground had been churned up.

"This is futile," Carnelia remarked, clearly bored by Aryx's absurd-looking activities. "We should move on."

Aryx had come to the same conclusion, but something urged him to dig a little deeper. Did he expect to find some tunnel, some hidden underground passage that might . . .

He pulled back as fingers from below grazed his own.

"What is it?" Seph called, leaping from his horse. "Aryx! do you need—"

"Get back!" Carnelia roared. She, too, had dismounted and now stood at Aryx's side, peering down at his grisly find.

It proved to be a hand, one still wearing a gauntlet, but when Aryx dug deeper, he found the hand no longer remained attached to any arm. The appendage had been neatly severed at the wrist, the blade that had been used having cut through metal, bone, and flesh with the same ease. Carnelia swore, then commanded some of her men to dig in the vicinity of the find.

They worked for half an hour but found nothing more. Carnelia at last waved the men back, eyeing the moist gaps they had created. She looked at Rand, but the cleric shook his head, which to Aryx meant that the blond human sensed nothing. Neither looked at the minotaurs, not a good sign at all. Aryx belatedly realized that what he had found not only failed to prove his people were innocent, but also had possibly incriminated them in a deed much darker than first imagined.

Carnelia confirmed his fears. "This won't go over well with my uncle, bull. I don't think you had anything to do with this, but some of your kind will have to pay. Mark me on that."

"No minotaur did this," Aryx insisted. He sniffed the air. Could that be a faint hint of musk in the air, or did he simply imagine it? "Something else took them."

"Your sea monsters?" She briefly took off her helm, brushing back hair that had fallen loose. Aryx noted Rand's gaze drift to her hair. "No one's seen them but you, and your description's as murky as the fog you keep mentioning. I'm inclined to think maybe sea elves in armor took your crew, but I doubt they could have done this. No, Aryx, your people are to blame, and Broedius will see it that way, too, I'm afraid. He'll think, as I do, that they killed the patrol and the sentries, then dragged the bodies away to either be buried elsewhere or tossed into the sea. It was just luck they missed the hand. You know it as well as I do."

He sensed some sympathy from her, a change from Carnelia's generally dismissive attitude of minotaurs. However, even her changing emotions would do nothing for Aryx's kind. Lord Broedius held sway over the empire, and he would clearly demand his brand of justice once Carnelia reported what they had found.

The subcommander removed a pouch from her belt, cautiously placing the severed hand within it. Giving the pouch to one of her men, she faced Aryx again. "It might be best if you came along when I present this evidence to Broedius. You'll have the opportunity to speak for mercy for your people. That's all I can do, Aryx."

"Speak for mercy?" Delara snarled. "No minotaur would have done such a dishonorable deed!"

"I'm afraid my uncle won't see it that way."

Aryx cut off Delara and his brother before they could protest further. Carnelia had given him an opening he had sought for some time. An audience with Broedius, whatever the reason for it, would give him the opportunity to impress upon the commanding knight the danger Aryx felt certain lurked around the islands.

"I'll go. I want to see him."

"You may regret it after he's made his decision," Carnelia returned.

The party mounted up, the holes the only testament to their visit. Aryx eyed the holes, already filling in with loose sand and seawater. Then his eyes drifted away from shore to the fog. Did it seem nearer to shore? Could it have drifted in during one of Sargonnas's mysterious absences, then retreated? He stared at it, trying to judge distances. It *did* appear nearer than previous days.

"Aryx?" Rand called.

He turned, discovering that the others had already started off. Urging his mount on, the worried minotaur tried not to think of the soft ground, ground that he suspected held more secrets than any of them realized. He only hoped that he could convince Lord Broedius of that.

\* \* \* \* \*

The ebony eyes narrowed under the thick, furrowed brow. The broad-shouldered knight leaned over the table covered in charts, hands clenched in barely checked anger. He had listened in silence as Carnelia had reported their findings, his set expression growing more tight with each passing moment. His silence more than his manner disturbed Aryx, for he knew that Broedius had probably already made up his mind as to how the minotaurs would pay for this transgression.

"So . . ." the knight commander finally uttered, his voice so quiet that Aryx had to concentrate to hear him. "So . . . all dead. Each one of them slaughtered."

Carnelia had presented him with the most gruesome piece of evidence immediately. Broedius had picked up the hand with curious gentleness, almost as if afraid he might break it. He had stared at it for some time before finally placing it on one of his charts. Now he stared at it again, coming to a final determination.

Aryx could not allow him to do that without speaking in turn. Only he and Carnelia had been allowed to see Broedius. Not even the cleric was permitted to speak in the minotaurs' defense. Saving his people had once again been thrust upon the young warrior, and he dared not fail.

"Lord Broedius, by my ancestors, this act couldn't have been committed by my people! So dishonorable, so heinous a slaughter is not how minotaurs—"

"I know very well the depths to which the minotaurs may stoop," the commander interjected too calmly. "As does my niece Carnelia."

Aryx glanced at the female knight, who had grown pale at her uncle's words. She shook her head at the senior knight, but Broedius ignored her.

"As you may or may not know, minotaur, my brother—her father—was slain by your kind, killed with the rest of his companions by marauders on the Blood Sea. Minotaurs, Aryx. Minotaurs who proved they have no greater sense of honor than anyone else!" He touched the severed hand gently. "So do not seek to sway me by fanciful tales of your kind's noble aspects. I won't believe them."

"Then what of my own past? What of the creatures from the sea who attacked my own ship, human? For some time, I've tried to see you, tried to warn you that the same fog that encroached upon the *Kraken's Eye* now creeps nearer and nearer to shore! I believe that in its wake will come, perhaps has already come—"

"Nothing will come with the fog." Broedius held up a piece of parchment. "Since our arrival, fourteen vessels have docked in the imperial capital, not one of them reporting so much as wild water! True, we also have reports of two ships wrecked, but no proof that weather or pirates or any threat of a more mundane nature might not have been at work!"

Aryx found it amazing that the human could deny what to him seemed so obvious. "How can you—"

Broedius turned away from him. "Carnelia!" The female knight snapped to attention. "Place the emperor, his staff, and every member of the Supreme Circle under house arrest. Locate the leading elders of House Orilg and do the same . . . the patriarch, too, if he's fit enough."

"Sir . . . Uncle—"

"That is an order, Carnelia! See to it now!"

"Yes, sir." Despite her obvious feelings concerning minotaurs, she did not look at all happy about obeying her uncle. Nonetheless, she saluted, turned, and stalked out of Lord Broedius's chamber.

"As for you, minotaur . . ." Broedius stepped around the table, meeting Aryx's glare with his own unsettling eyes. "I allow you to go free for now because I've no proof you were part of this. However, know that if your kind thought their situation distasteful before, they're about to find out how easy they had it. Your clan especially will see changes from here on."

Fighting against his own temper, Aryx rumbled, "Human, you'll bring down everything if you try to keep the emperor and elders under guard without proof that they did the deed! We will not stand—"

"Then you will kneel. Consider the choices, minotaur, and consider them wisely. Your god has given you to us; you will obey one way or the other. Those who will not, those who would dare strike at us, will suffer the consequences of their ignorance."

"Your troops are already thinly spread," the furious minotaur pointed out. "If you do the emperor and the others such dishonor, do you think you'll be able to stand against the tide of rage you're creating? I do not threaten when I say that the Knights of Takhisis would be washed away by such a tide."

"We shall not be so thinly spread. I already intend to pull the sentries in to the higher ground, thereby requiring fewer of them."

"A few paltry warriors—"

Broedius gave him a grim smile. "And, of course, the *Queen's Champion* and the *Dragonwing* will be here soon, too." In response to Aryx's puzzled look, the commander explained. "Did I fail to mention that others were on the way? Yes, bull, two more ships, reinforcements, will be arriving. They'll help with the second phase of this expedition. My Lord Ariakan leaves nothing to chance."

"You never said anything about more troops."

"I found no need. Your god knew that they were coming; didn't he tell you? Of course not. Knights of the Lily and Knights of the Thorn, bull. You know the Knights of the Thorn, don't you?"

There had been but a small handful aboard, yet Aryx recalled them well. The Knights of the Thorn had differed greatly from the Knights of the Lily. In fact, they were not knights at all. They were mages, once black-robed spellcasters following Nuitari, but now loyal only to the dread queen. The other warriors aboard ship clearly cared little for them, but that did not mean that they did not understand how useful the cloaked, secretive figures could be in battle.

Broedius nodded. "You do. You see, Aryx, I intend to maintain order and command here, and if your kind won't see the necessity of that, I'll simply have to show them."

"Sargonnas will not permit it." Aryx uttered the words without much conviction. The God of Vengeance appeared not to care one whit.

"In this, he has no choice, I promise you." The knight turned away. "Dismissed."

Aryx started forward, refusing to end the argument. However, Broedius's personal guards immediately stepped toward him, weapons drawn. Despite his fury, the minotaur knew better than to face such odds. He showed the knights his empty palms and moved back.

"I have an offer for you, Aryx," Lord Broedius announced, his back still to the minotaur. He seemed to be contemplating the far wall, upon which hung the banner of the knighthood. "One that just occurred to me. Bring me those who are responsible for the deaths of my men, and I'll recall the guard from the emperor and the rest. That's all I ask. Bring me those who will confess so that I may execute them for their crimes and end the matter. A simple, straightforward offer, I think."

"Damn you, human, there's no one to bring before you! Your men weren't killed by my kind!" Aryx could not prove that, but in his heart, he knew it. "We're all in danger! You should be fortifying the shoreline with more men, even minotaurs, not relying on fewer sentries located far from land's edge!"

Still gazing at the banner, Broedius casually signaled with one hand. The guards moved in on Aryx.

He backed to the door, but he made no move for his axe. The wary eyes of the guards watched him carefully. Any suspicious move on his part would be the only excuse they would need to attack. Broedius turned as Aryx exited the room, the human's broad face expressionless.

"The *Queen's Champion* and the *Dragonwing* will arrive in two, three days at most," he repeated. "I'll expect the murderers by then, bull, or I may have to begin taking more absolute measures . . . beginning with your clan."

\* \* \* \* \*

Lord Broedius proved true to his word. The commander's elite talons spread out through the capital, surrounding and seizing the palace and the citadel of the Supreme Circle. Those members of the latter who were not immediately taken into custody the knights began to hunt down, General Geryl at the top of that list. Orilg's elders were also placed under arrest, but nothing could be done to Torvak, for the patriarch had died from his illness that very day.

The minotaurs, in turn, did nothing but further foment trouble. True, Aryx could not blame them for being furious over the knights' dishonorable conduct, but he had hoped that they at least would recall the threat of which Sargonnas had spoken. Both sides seemed concerned only with bending the other until one of them broke.

It did not help that the next day rumors began to circulate concerning minotaurs who were missing. These spread swiftly, growing in proportion until some claimed entire clans had been dragged off in chains by the knights. Aryx knew few of the stories to be true, but those with some merit disturbed him. Three of the missing warriors had last been sighted near some part of the island's vast shoreline, always when the fog seemed just a little thicker, the air just a little musky. No one could tell him whether the fog had ever touched land's edge, but Aryx felt certain that it had.

He abandoned all attempts at mediating, his short term as Broedius's administrator general and even shorter one as clan representative of little use now. Of the knights, only Carnelia listened at all to him. Most of the others tended to share the attitudes of Drejjen or Lord Broedius. On the other side, the minotaurs, especially those few left in charge of clan Orilg, could not decide what to make of him. Many still saw him as Sargonnas's servant and so treated him with awe, but others looked at Aryx as if he had betrayed his own race. In truth, he could not argue with those who thought the latter.

Perhaps because he could find no way by which to resolve the growing tensions between the two races, Aryx chose late the next day to saddle his horse with the intention of riding out to investigate the site from which the knights had disappeared. Although Carnelia's men had rather thoroughly searched the area, Aryx could not help but hope that perhaps they had missed something, some clue that would reveal the minotaurs were not to blame. True, such clues would raise new and possibly more frightening specters, but he could not leave matters as they were.

Seph found him just as he mounted. Aryx swore under his breath, wanting to leave his brother out of this.

"Where are you going in this weather, Aryx? I thought you'd be staying nearby today. Those gathering clouds look like a possible storm."

"Nowhere you need to worry about, Seph. Go back to our quarters. I'll watch out for the storm."

"And have just the priests for company?" The younger minotaur snorted at the thought. "Maybe I'll be lucky enough to have dinner with the high priest himself!" Xarav ever loomed in the vicinity of Sargonnas's chamber, hoping, it seemed, to be summoned by his god. Each time Aryx came and knocked on the god's doors, the high priest materialized, ready to enter at a moment's notice. Sargonnas, though, never invited his chief servant inside, and Aryx's audiences, however short and unenlightening they were to the warrior, clearly drove Xarav to jealousy.

"You're going somewhere important, aren't you?" Seph's face took on an eager expression Aryx did not like. "I'm coming with you!"

"You're not!" He tugged the reins of his mount. "I'm leaving now. It's a long ride, and you'll never find me, so give up now."

"If you leave now I'll follow your trail and even if I lose it, I'll keep riding. You know I will, Aryx."

The gray minotaur gritted his teeth. He knew Seph would keep his word. The stubborn streak that they could trace back to Kaz Dragonslayer and, before him, Orilg, ran true in both brothers. Aryx did not like the thought of Seph being with him, but better under his eye than running loose.

"All right . . . but stick close. You have your axe?"

His brother's eyes narrowed. "Where are we going, Aryx?"

"Just get your horse."

The ride to the spot was uneventful. As eager as Aryx had been to reach it, he did not look forward to having any of his fears confirmed. Staring down at the sandy shore from where the signal fire had been located, Aryx could not help wondering whether his decision to come here had been a foolish mistake. But, no, he could not leave matters where they stood. Someone had to keep the two factions from each other's throats lest the empire crumble from within.

"I thought this was where you wanted to go," Seph whispered. "I almost wish I hadn't come."

"I almost wish I'd stayed with you." He peered down at the seemingly innocent beach. Just looking at it made every nerve tingle, as if something even now awaited them below. The cloud cover had darkened more, turning the threat of a storm into a promise. A chill sea breeze coursed around them even now. For that matter, the fog looked ominously close, much closer than during his previous visit. All in all, it felt more like dusk than late afternoon.

"Do we go down, Aryx?"

He nodded. They would have to go down to the shore. The rocky ground up here would reveal little in the way of clues. Urging his horse on, he let the animal slowly make its way down the ridge. Had they come from the opposite direction, their route would have been simpler. But that also would have meant the pair would spend much too much time riding over the sandy shoreline, a danger Aryx had wanted to avoid. An entire armed patrol and three sentries had vanished in this region, and based on what he knew so far, the sand seemed the most likely place of ambush.

The horses struggled a bit for footing but made the descent without incident. Aryx immediately dismounted, studying his surroundings. The holes dug by Carnelia's men had already almost filled in. The spot where he had discovered the armored hand seemed almost pristine, as if the minotaur had never dug there. He frowned as he moved nearer. For so much of the area to have been reclaimed already pointed at a violent sea, but last night had been relatively calm.

Seph dismounted. "What do you hope to find?"

"Anything that would prove our people had nothing to do with the disappearances." He wondered why he continued to call them disappearances. The severed hand proved that the humans had probably been slaughtered to a man. "Preferably something small and easily carried away from here."

They began to comb the area. Aryx reminded Seph to remain close. The quiet lapping of the tide did little to relax him, for each time he looked up, the fog seemed to have edged a little nearer to shore. At last, giving in to the urge, Aryx pulled free his axe, the weight in his hand a comfort. It made his search a little more cumbersome but eased his thoughts somewhat. If anything came at them, he would ready for it.

More than an hour passed, an hour in which the pair discovered nothing, not even a single bit of armor. The few traces of blood Carnelia had discovered previously had been all but washed away by the tide. Had he not known what had happened here, Aryx would have thought this the most peaceful location on Mithas.

Then Seph summoned him to his side, the younger warrior's voice filled with excitement. "Come see this, Aryx! It might be what you're looking for!"

Aryx's brother had worked his way to some of the larger rocks at the bottom of the ridge, climbing over one particularly large rock to reach his present location. Aryx saw nothing at first, but Seph pointed behind the rock. As slim as he was compared to many minotaurs, Aryx still had to struggle to see properly into the narrow area his smaller brother had uncovered.

There, hidden from normal sight, lay what only Aryx truly recognized. His sudden intake of breath, though, immediately warned Seph that they had discovered a prize.

"What are they, Aryx? They almost look like . . . like *fingers* of some sort."

They were. Two, to be exact. Thick and long, curved like claws, and covered in the same sort of skin as the appendages of a crab or lobster . . . possibly the one lucky strike the hapless knights had garnered against their monstrous foes.

"This might do it," Aryx muttered. He extended his arm, but the fingers remained out of reach. Cursing, he stretched down as best he could, straining the muscles in his arm and shoulder to the point where he nearly felt like screaming . . . and still they remained a few inches beyond his grasp.

"Let me try," Seph finally insisted.

Aryx did not want to surrender his position, feeling somehow he could stretch still farther. Yet Seph, not completely grown, did have a slightly better chance of reaching them. Snorting in frustration, Aryx pulled back and let his brother try.

Even for Seph, the distance proved almost insurmountable. On his second try, he nearly snagged the severed appendages with his fingers, but halfway up his tentative grip faltered. Aryx bit back a curse. He tried to guide his brother's hands with his eyes, silently commanding Seph to shift position or turn his hand in a different direction. Still the horrific prizes escaped them, although with effort, Seph gradually pushed them to the side of a rock, where he then managed to prop them up.

"I think . . . I can . . . get them now, Aryx."

"Be careful, Seph. Take one at a time if you have to."

The younger minotaur grunted. "Don't . . . worry . . . I won't fail you. . . ."

Aryx nodded, then leaned forward to get a better look. He blinked, trying to clear his eyes. He had been staring so intently, his vision had begun to blur. Pulling away, Aryx straightened up and looked around, hoping that by doing so his eyes might refocus.

Tendrils of fog drifted out over the shoreline.

His eyes hadn't been at fault. Aryx instinctively clutched his axe tightly as he scanned the region. Nothing had changed other than the encroaching mist. No massive forms rose from the sea. No overwhelming stench of wet musk assailed his nostrils.

"I . . . I think I have one, Aryx!"

"Seph—"

"I do! If I bring it up slowly, I should keep a hold on it!"

Despite the lack of any sign of danger, Aryx felt an overwhelming urge to leave . . . now. "Seph, forget it. Let's go."

"Just a few seconds more. . . ."

Aryx blinked. He could swear that the sand beyond them had stirred in one spot. Taking a step toward the questionable region, he studied it. The sand did not shift again, but Aryx felt certain that it had the first time. Perhaps some small crustacean had been disturbed by the incoming waves . . . .

Seph straightened. "Look! I've got one!"

As if reacting to his brother's loud call, the sand everywhere began to swirl.

"Seph! Onto the rocks! Climb up!"

He had no time to heed his own warning, for suddenly the ground beneath him grew soft. Aryx's feet sank in up to the ankles, and it was all he could do to pull one free.

"Aryx! Give me your hand!" His brother perched atop the massive rock, trying to reach him.

Aryx tried to seize the proffered hand, but the sandy ground shifted again, dragging him away and causing him to sink to his knees. Behind him, he heard the horses struggling. Aryx glanced over his shoulder and saw one animal pull itself up to safety, but his own mount, a brown male, fell back onto the sand.

A miniature maelstrom formed beneath the helpless animal, pulling it down. The horse managed to right itself, but all four limbs sank up to its torso. At the same time, a powerful, musky stench permeated the air, nearly causing the trapped minotaur to choke.

The frantic horse continued to struggle, but rapidly the sand swallowed it. Aryx could do nothing, his own life in question. He saw the body of the beast sink below the sand, the head still trying to keep above it . . . but all for naught. With one last gasp, Aryx's mount disappeared into the horrific maelstrom. The sand shifted wildly for a few moments more, then slowed again.

Desperate to avoid a similar fate, he hefted his axe and began pounding at the area surrounding him, seeking some target below. Wherever he spotted movement, Aryx struck. Unfortunately, the ground itself dulled his blows. Already the sand reached to his thighs. If he didn't do something quickly, the trapped minotaur would join his horse.

"Aryx!" a voice not Seph's called. "Aryx! Take the rope!"

He looked around and saw that the end of a thick rope, lying but a yard from him. The rope continued upward, rising over the edge of the ridge and disappearing beyond.

Still perched on the rock, Seph picked up the call. "Take it, Aryx, hurry!"

He clutched for the rope's end, barely missing. However, to his horror, the churning sand suddenly dragged him farther away, putting the rope yet another foot distant. Aryx cursed, kicking as best he could with his legs, trying to drive himself forward again.

Something snagged his ankle.

"Aryx!" Seph had the rope in his hands. He had seen that his brother could no longer reach the end and planned to toss it nearer.

Aryx wondered if he could. Whatever clutched his ankle tried to pull him deeper into the swirling sand. How much rope did Seph have to throw?

The younger minotaur tossed as hard as he could. For a moment, Aryx feared that the rope would land too far from him, but then it arced to the side, coming nearer. Kicking hard at whatever held him, Aryx managed to free his leg up to his ankle and, in doing so, pushed himself ahead a few inches. Those inches proved to be vital, and he barely managed to seize the frayed tip.

Holding on as tight as he could with one hand, Aryx shouted, "Pull me! Quick!"

"Pull! Now!" Seph called to the unseen rescuer.

The rope jerked, so much so that Aryx nearly lost his grip on it. Something grazed his leg, but before it could seize him, the minotaur felt himself tugged toward the rocky ridge. Aryx held tight with one hand, keeping the other gripped on the handle of his axe, fearing that any second something might reach out of the sand to pull him back.

Nothing did, and a few seconds later, he collided with the rock ledge. Aryx used the rope to pull him up above the treacherous sand, then began to scramble up the slope as best he could. Beside him, Seph also began to climb. The stench of musk continued to invade Aryx's senses, nearly sending him toppling at one point, but the image of what had befallen his mount kept the sand-encrusted warrior climbing.

At last he reached the top. Aryx sprawled on the edge of the ridge, gasping. After some seconds, he searched for Seph, only to discover his brother sitting beside him, his eyes filled with concern.

"By the Horned One!" a familiar feminine voice cried. "Aryx! Are you all right?"

He looked up, for the first time seeing his true rescuer. Delara, every muscle taut, knelt before him. Beyond her waited her mount, the other end of the rope tied to the saddle.

"Maybe . . ." he coughed up sand. "Maybe the gods do . . . do watch out for us now and then . . . or else . . . or else how would you be here now?"

She looked slightly flushed. "No god. Just luck. I was coming to see you when I noticed you and your brother riding off. I followed, but I lost you just outside of Nethosak. It took me several minutes to pick up your trail . . . partly due to my stupidity. I finally realized where you were going and—"

"And got here just in time to save my fool life." He smiled, finally reaching out a hand. "Thank you."

"Aryx! Come look at this!" Seph leaned over the edge, gazing down at the treacherous shoreline.

The pair followed his gaze. Aryx frowned at the site below him. All trace of what had happened had vanished. The sand now lay still and pristine. Had he not nearly been sucked under, Aryx might have thought that no one had walked the area for days. He couldn't even see a trace of where his mount had disappeared.

He noticed also that the fog had begun to drift back, almost as if by conscious choice. The musky odor, too, had faded, or perhaps Aryx could not smell it quite as well from the top of the ridge.

"Nothing," he murmured. "No evidence at all."

"But I still have the claw!" Seph responded. He looked around expectantly, then his expression darkened. "At least I did . . . I dropped it right here. . . ."

They searched the area but found nothing. "It must have fallen over the edge when we weren't paying attention." Aryx grunted. "That tears it, then! The Abyss take those creatures! I *know* this has to do with what Sargonnas said in the circus or what happened to the *Kraken's Eye*, but without even the claw, I've no proof!"

"But we saw everything that happened," Delara pointed out. However, her brow furrowed. "Although *what* we saw . . ."

Richard A. Knaak

"Exactly." Exasperated, Aryx kicked a large rock off the edge of the ridge. It landed with a thud in the middle of the beach. He almost expected it to sink beneath the sand, but it remained where it had fallen, further mocking his efforts. Aryx suspected that if someone walked along the shore now, he would face no risk. What lurked below attacked with cautious efficiency. Even if he brought Broedius, the emperor, and every officer of both races, Aryx doubted that anything would happen.

"We should still ride back and tell someone," his brother suggested. "They at least deserve to know."

Aryx snorted in disgust. "If Lord Broedius won't believe me after all he's already heard, then he won't believe this."

"What about Sargonnas?" Delara asked.

"What about him?"

His tone made her drop the question. Aryx felt some guilt, knowing that she still looked at the God of Vengeance with the eyes of one of the faithful. Yet Aryx himself saw no use in reporting this to the dark deity. Surely Sargonnas knew what stalked the shores. If he had done nothing so far, then why would he bother to act now?

The overcast sky rumbled and the wind picked up, swirling dust and leaves about. "There is someone who might listen, though," Aryx realized, Rand's face suddenly coming to mind. "And through him, I might just be able to convince one close to Lord Broedius himself."

Carnelia might listen to the cleric. Her affection for him was clear to the minotaur. If she listened, then at least Aryx could hope that perhaps the female knight could convince her uncle. A desperate plan, but the only one he had for now.

"We need to ride to the knighthood's headquarters immediately," he told the others. Rand tended to be there often, even when Carnelia had orders elsewhere. Aryx did not understand the blond human's position in the expedition yet, but perhaps Kiri-Jolith had somehow placed him with the Knights of Takhisis to balance the situation, or else why would both Sargonnas and Broedius accept him? "Seph, do you think your horse can carry both of us?"

"Mine will," Delara offered. Her animal stood a good two hands taller than his brother's, much of the additional weight pure muscle. The horse might not be as swift as the smaller one, but it should better carry two riders.

124

The rumbling grew stronger, closer, as they mounted. A storm brewed, one that Aryx found foreboding. Already a few large drops of rain fell, precursor, perhaps, to one of the violent storms the Blood Sea islands suffered now and then. He hoped the trio would at least reach Broedius's headquarters before the rain came down in earnest, but doubted it.

Lightning played in the sky as they hurried away from the site. Delara urged her massive steed on, the powerful beast swifter than Aryx could have hoped. As they raced toward Nethosak, though, his thoughts turned away from the dire threats he foresaw, instead focusing on the female he found his arms wrapped around. Despite her devotion to Sargonnas, Aryx found Delara's nearness enticing. Both a capable warrior and an attractive female, she somehow pulled him toward her as few in his past had done. He had known her only a short time, but he suspected that, as time passed, his infatuation might grow to something stronger.

That, of course, assumed that they all *had* a future. . . .

"Look there!" Seph shouted over the wind and thunder. "Do you see that?"

Aryx stirred, trying to look past Delara. The clouds had gathered particularly thick over the imperial capital, especially toward its center. That alone might have attracted no interest, but lightning flashed over and over again, seeming to concentrate above one area.

"A violent storm coming," Delara called.

"Violent, yes . . ." Aryx could not put his finger on it, but something about the concentration of elements over that part of the city disturbed him.

A massive bolt darted earthward, striking the heart of Nethosak.

"Did you see how that struck?" Seph shook his head. "I've never seen lightning hit like that! Do you think it did any damage?"

Before Aryx could answer, a second bolt shot down, a near perfect repetition of the first. He squinted, trying to estimate where they landed.

Delara leaned back slightly. "They must be hitting the very heart of the city! Do you think that the palace has been struck?"

As she asked that, Aryx felt the same sense of foreboding . . . and knew there and then that the palace of the emperor likely stood untouched. A third lightning strike hit the city, virtually a copy of the previous pair. Young he might be, but Aryx had sailed the world enough to understand that no storm could attack with such precision unless some power willed it to do so.

"Faster!" he shouted. "We need to ride faster!"

"Why?" Delara glanced back. "What is it?"

"They aren't striking the palace," Aryx roared back, "nor even the citadel of the Supreme Circle! If they're striking anywhere, then it's the temple that's their target . . . and I don't think the bolts will stop flying until it lies in ruins, Sargonnas himself with it!"

\* \* \* \* \*

And so at last it begins, Sargonnas thought, feeling the primal forces unleashed with each lightning bolt. That which had been hidden from him, that which served Father Chaos, now struck, knowing how weak the other battles the god continued to fight had made him. It knew also that he had expended much energy protecting the islands as well, keeping the insidious fog at bay.

No more. He could protect them no more. The only hope lay in what he and his ally had planned . . . and the luck that mortals sometimes benefited from.

The temple shook again. From without came the confused shouts of clerics. Sargonnas ignored the insignificant calls, all thought concentrated on the matter at hand. Grimacing with effort, he rose from his throne, drawing his jeweled sword. The enchanted blade gleamed, the great green stone seeming to eye him. The God of Vengeance felt the power coursing through the sword, power which he himself had granted it when he had forged it so long ago during the Age of Dreams.

"Are you ready?" he asked of the blade.

*I have always been ready . . . Master.*

"No tricks, now, for Father Chaos will have as much use for you as he does me."

The gem, which had flared brightly, now grew more subdued. *No tricks . . . Master.*

Again the temple shook. Sargonnas paled, turning momentarily transparent as he struggled on several planes of existence.

The servant of Father Chaos had chosen well the time of attack.

"Wait for him," he told the demon sword. "Guide him . . . but do not *devour* him."

*As you command . . . Master.*

Turning the blade point down, Sargonnas thrust the sword into the marble floor. It sank half its length before stopping, the stone flaring brightly once more.

Releasing his grip, the dark god looked to the ceiling, raising his hands high over his head. He smiled for his unseen foe.

"Very well, then," Sargonnas called. "Let us play in earnest now."

# Storm Over Nethosak

## Chapter Eight

They gathered beneath the sea, gathered in numbers so great they remained packed together for leagues on end. Although no light touched this deep world, they all looked up, awaiting the sign, awaiting the word of the most faithful servant. They would not move until that one spoke, until that one gave them permission. It had ever been the role of the Magori to obey, to perform as they were commanded, for that had been how they were created. They knew no other way.

In the darkness, they waited . . . but knew that soon their wait would be over.

\* \* \* \* \*

The bolts continued to strike even as the trio entered the capital. With each passing breath, the intensity of the assault grew stronger, now some three or four bolts at a time falling upon the center of the city. The very earth below them shook, the horses often having to steady themselves.

In Nethosak, the journey slowed as they fought past startled minotaurs, knights on horseback, and even a wagon whose animals had escaped their driver. Everyone seemed too stunned to do anything . . . and what *could* they do? Crowds gathered in the streets, some clearly believing that another quake had begun. Others looked up, wondering if the heavens would erupt over the rest of the capital.

"Clear the way!" Aryx roared. "Clear the way!"

Delara and Seph maneuvered the horses along, gradually

making progress. Another bolt arced down, shaking the entire area.

Seph eyed the wild sky. "Can the temple still be standing?"

"There is no power greater than the Blessed One!" Delara returned, but her voice wavered. She understood as well as Aryx that these were no normal bolts of lightning, that the power that wielded them might be as terrible as the God of Vengeance.

Again and again the bolts blazed, three, four, five and more at a time. They struck nowhere else. The clouds above the block where Sargonnas's temple stood had grown as black as pitch, but in their center swirled what looked like molten fire, and from there came the lightning. In addition, the rain began to pour in earnest, making the trek even more difficult.

Seph pointed ahead. "Look! A priest!"

The tall robed figure stumbled backward down the street, his eyes ever fixed on the direction from which he had come. So caught up was he by what he stared at, the priest almost collided with the horses.

"What's happening?" Delara shouted down to him. "Does the temple still stand?"

The cleric glanced up. Eyes wide and untrusting, he snapped, "Keep away from me!"

"We only want— Wait!"

Heedless of her words, the cleric rushed off, his gaze again fixed in the direction of the temple. Aryx watched him flee, wondering about the state of things if even the keepers of the temple were abandoning their sanctum.

Delara urged her mount on, Seph following a moment later. Aryx could feel the tension running through his companion. More than either of the brothers, she had to be wondering about Sargonnas. Aryx wanted to reassure her, but could think of nothing in the face of the fearsome storm.

On and on she urged the steed, paying little heed to those in her path. A second priest wandered past, followed by two grim acolytes. An officer of the State Guard tried to wave them back, but Delara stared him down, finally forcing the other minotaur to the side. The lightning continued relentlessly.

And then they came upon the temple.

"By the Blessed One!" Delara gasped, suddenly pulling hard on the reins.

Aryx swore. Next to them, Seph pulled up short, his mouth hanging open.

The Temple of Sargonnas stood seemingly untouched, but a frightening aura surrounded it, one that the dusky gray minotaur felt certain did not originate from the god. Every stone, every facet of the temple, shimmered with the unsettling green and blue light, a light that grew stronger with each bolt. Even more disturbing, when Aryx tried to peer close at any detail of the edifice, it seemed to waver, as if no longer quite real.

Scores of priests, acolytes, and temple guards surrounded the building, all but one standing at what might be a safe distance. The one contrary figure looked to be the high priest, Xarav, who stood midway up the great steps, beseeching the god to whom he had sworn his life.

"Hear me, Sargonnas!" he roared. "Your servants stand with you! Our strength is yours! Send back to the Abyss that which would dare confront you in your home, your domain! Hail to you, God of Vengeance—"

Lightning crackled. A harsh wind sent the high priest staggering, but he regained his balance, again imploring his god to unleash his wrath on the lesser power that dared touch his great temple.

"He's mad!" Aryx muttered, dismounting. "Mad!"

"No!" Delara wore a look almost as fanatical as that of the master cleric. "Sargonnas will hear him . . . will hear *us!* We're his chosen!"

"You'll be his dead chosen if you go any farther!" He pulled her back, fearing that she would attempt to join the mad priest.

One of the other clerics, perhaps a bit more level-headed than his master, sought to entice Xarav down from the steps. The elderly minotaur shook him off, almost sending the younger cleric tumbling. None of the others seemed inclined either to come to the high priest's aid or to try to convince him of the danger.

Xarav struggled his way up the steps, all the while calling out the praises of the conspicuously absent deity. He reached the top, then turned to face those below.

"Weak of faith!" the graying cleric roared. "Weak of will! If not for Sargonnas, there would be no minotaur race, and yet in this hour, you cannot stand fast, be strong in your belief!

There is no god greater than the Blessed One, no god stronger than the Horned One! Stand with him or be lost without him, for this is the hour of judgment! This is the hour in which the faithful will rise to victory with Sargonnas, and the faithless will be condemned to the Abyss!"

"He's ranting," Seph whispered to his brother. "He's insane!"

Aryx nodded, yet he saw that some around the temple had at last been affected by Xarav's determination. Not many of the other clerics, curiously enough, but some from among the throngs nearby.

"We *must* be stronger. . . ."

At first Aryx thought that the high priest had spoken, but then he realized it had been Delara. He glanced her way, saw that, like the others, she, too, had been affected by the master cleric's pontificating. Even as she spoke, she stepped forward.

Aryx would have none of that. While he granted Delara her faith, that did not, in his eyes, mean that she should commit suicide for Sargonnas, who still had not made his presence known. Too often in history, the gods had been more than willing to sacrifice their followers, and now seemed no different.

She glared at him when he seized her arm. "Let me go! He's right, Aryx! Sargonnas needs our faith, our will, behind him! We owe it to him!"

"Not for this! Better to fight in his name in battle than join Xarav in this madness! Look, Delara! Look closely at the temple! The high priest doesn't court his god; he simply courts death!"

True enough, more and more the temple seemed to waver from reality. Marble columns bent, twisted. The roof of the vast edifice shook, turned as if it were soft clay caught up in a whirlpool. Xarav appeared not to notice, still calling out for the glory of Sargonnas. Five or six other minotaurs had already begun to make their way up to him despite the obvious peril, true believers unwilling to see that they faced something more terrible than the storm.

Emboldened by these first few converts, Xarav called out again. "Let your faith guide you, my children! Now is the greatest test, and Sargonnas watches to see who will stand in his name! We are one in his glory or we are nothing! Come and add your strength!"

Two younger clerics broke from the ranks of the wary, joining their master. Several minotaurs from the general crowd cautiously stepped forward.

"This is insane!" Aryx could not believe how many climbed the steps. Perhaps if the Horned One joined them up there, Aryx might have even become one of the converts himself, but he had been around Sargonnas long enough to be wary.

Another series of bolts struck the roof. They did no apparent physical damage to the building, but each warped it, twisted it into something not in sync with this world.

Then what Aryx had feared all along happened. The winds around the temple grew more violent, whipping around and around as if forming a tornado. Those who had rejoined Xarav now struggled simply to stay in one place. Even the high priest had to clutch one of the twisted columns. Yet the winds swirled harder and harder, and as they did, the lightning poured down, a torrential rain of fearsome energy.

A bolt struck the roof and a piece finally cracked off. However, instead of collapsing, the fragment flew high into the air. A second fragment, larger than the first, flew off a moment later, spinning around in the giant whirlwind as if it were a tiny leaf.

The temple of Sargonnas shattered, walls, windows, columns, and roof flying up into the swirling winds, eventually vanishing into the fury above . . . and with them at last went the people.

Those gathered nearby scattered, fleeing for their lives. One of Xarav's converts tried to stumble back down the steps, but the wind suddenly pulled her into the air, and she went, screaming, into the black heavens. The high priest clutched the handles of the great doors, the entrance to the temple, the only part of the front still remaining. Xarav continued to shout to the sky, as if oblivious to the fact that his god's sanctum had been all but destroyed.

Even away from the temple, the winds proved treacherous. Aryx had to struggle against nearly impossible winds to pull Delara back away from the temple. Seph struggled to them, and the trio fought against forces that seized one unsteady warrior nearby, dragging him up into the vortex above the shattered building.

At last even the high priest could not maintain his hold.

Xarav's grip slipped, and with a roar, the elderly cleric flew off helplessly into the maw of the ungodly storm.

Several more bolts struck the remains of the temple. A few last fragments of the once proud structure soared into the air, vanishing.

Abruptly the lightning ceased. The storm continued to rage, but no longer did it assault the area. The fearsome fire in the sky faded into the black clouds, leaving only torrential rain, strong yet earthly winds, and the distant rumble of thunder.

Attempting to catch their breath, the three weary minotaurs paused to stare at the temple. Almost everywhere, the roof and walls had been completely torn away. For the most part, only the floor and a few of the bases of the marble columns remained. The one curious feature to survive the ruin of Sargonnas's sanctum was the doorway. Both the arch and the huge bronze doors still stood, guardians to a place that no longer existed. The doors remained shut.

"It's gone!" Delara shouted. "It's all gone!"

"What do you think happened to Sargonnas, Aryx?" Seph asked.

If the temple itself were any indication, then the god had been torn from Krynn, a victim of the power behind the lightning storm. Still, with gods, one could never be certain. "I don't know." A sudden, intense urge to investigate the site came over him. Aryx sought to overcome it, but it proved superior to his will. "Let's . . . let's take a look."

There were few other minotaurs in sight, most having wisely retreated far from the terrible destruction. Aryx himself wondered what drew him to the ruined structure when common sense dictated that he should turn and never look back. Whatever had assaulted the city center had not finished with the minotaurs yet, of that he remained certain. The terrible trials of which Sargonnas had spoken in the Great Circus had only just begun.

Yet, knowing that, he climbed the ravaged steps, then approached the towering doors. Why he did not simply go around them, the wary minotaur could not say. Somehow, even with the god's citadel little more than a memory, Aryx felt he had to enter as he always had.

As he reached out for them, the doors creaked open.

Seph reached for his axe. "Be careful, Aryx!"

The doors swung wide, inviting entry. Beyond, marble floors soaked by rain welcomed them to rooms that no longer existed. Drenched though he was, Aryx accepted the invitation and entered. "Wait here."

With Seph and Delara taking what refuge they could under the doorway, Aryx moved along cautiously. The storm made it hard to see more than a few yards, but he thought he saw something glisten where Sargonnas's chamber had once stood. Did the god yet sit in the ruins of his sanctum? An absurd notion, but not out of the question.

Something *did* glisten, despite the gloom and storm. Aryx started to reach for his own axe, wondering if the awesome power that had destroyed the temple had left behind some force intended to deal with intrusive warriors.

Lightning, this time far away, illuminated the area briefly. Aryx caught a flash of steel, a glimmer of emerald, and the familiar outline of a weapon of war.

Sargonnas's sword, the same wailing beast that had so readily put an end to the councillor, Garith, stood, hilt up, before him, the bottom half of its shining blade buried somehow in the marble floor.

Aryx cautiously approached it, wondering why the god would leave the sword behind. With such a blade, there were few foes who could stand against the wielder, yet the gray minotaur also suspected that not everyone could safely use it. The sword seemed to have a life of its own, a life that—

The green stone in the hilt flared brightly.

A life that Aryx suddenly realized had been responsible for the undeniable urge that had forced him to enter the ruined temple.

"Ancestors preserve me!" he snarled under his breath. Aryx began to retreat, wanting nothing to do with demon blades. He recalled only too well the legends of enchanted weapons, how for every loyal tool such as Kaz Dragonslayer's venerable Honor's Face, there had also existed those weapons that had readily turned on their wielders. The warrior had no doubt that what stood before him better suited the latter category.

*Be not afraid, O Master. . . .*

The words echoed in his head, a sly, powerful voice somehow reminiscent of Sargonnas. Aryx glanced around, seeking the speaker. Finding no one else, his eyes at last returned to the sinister sword, whose emerald gem continued to flare brightly.

*You have nothing to fear from me, Master. . . .*

"Nothing to fear?" The wary minotaur snorted. "Nothing to fear from such as you?"

*I am here for you, Aryximaraki,* the voice declared. *I am yours to wield in this struggle with the Chaos. . . .*

"Where's your master? Where's Sargonnas?"

*Sargonnas is where Sargonnas is . . . and you are here as you must be. . . .*

Aryx swore. He should have known better than to expect a straightforward answer from such a weapon. Had Sargonnas abandoned it here, no longer able to tolerate it? Had it turned on its master, betraying the God of Vengeance to the power behind the chaotic lightning storm?

"I'll have nothing to do with you," he declared. "You can stay here, a testimony to the insanity of the gods." Aryx turned about, heading back to his waiting companions.

*You would sacrifice your race, then?* came the mocking voice. *You would refuse that which could lead you to victory?*

The minotaur turned back, wiping rain from his muzzle. "One sword, however powerful, can't ensure victory . . . and against what? Do you know what we face? Do you know when and where it will come? Answer me that!"

*The Chaos comes sooner than you think. and if I cannot give you victory, then surely I can give you guidance . . . for that is what he commanded me to do. . . .*

Aryx blinked, clearing his eyes. Despite the sword's enigmatic pattern of speech, he understood enough of what it said and therefore could not deny that, at the very least, it could aid his people's cause. Sargonnas had left it behind in the face of a titanic struggle; surely he had done so for the benefit of his chosen. Whatever Aryx thought of the god in general, he decided that the Horned One could have had no other reason for abandoning such a powerful tool. Yet, for a mortal to take up a blade wielded by gods . . .

"I'm to take you?"

*You and no other . . . Master.*

"You'll obey me?"

*I will fight for you. . . .*

Not exactly phrased the way he would have liked it, but Aryx accepted the weapon's promise. "Do you have a name?"

The question seemed a foolish one, but the demon blade answered readily enough, as if expecting it. *Men and gods have called me the Sword of Tears . . . Master.*

Aryx started to ask it why such an ominous title, then decided that he did not truly want to know. The Sword of Tears seemed to be a weapon he would wield only when necessary, and even then with some caution.

*Take me up . . . use me. The time draws near when darkness and light must join for a final time or be replaced by nothingness. . . .*

Thunder rolled. Lightning flashed, causing Aryx to look up briefly, but he immediately saw that no new assault began. He stared at the sword, and suddenly the images of his crew mates returned to him. Had he held such a weapon, perhaps Aryx might have saved some of them. Surely the sword of a god could have done that much. How many lives could he save now if he took up the Sword of Tears? How many?

Steeling himself, the minotaur reached for the hilt, twisting his hand to take a proper grip.

The stone blazed.

*Yesss . . .* came the gleeful voice of the sword.

Energy coursed through Aryx's every muscle, his every nerve. He felt more alive than he had in weeks. His fears and doubts melted, became minuscule things. He knew that, whoever the foe, he had the means to strike him down . . . in fact, to strike down any who threatened that which he held dear. Broedius, Carnelia, and the rest of the knights would bow to him or suffer the consequences. Rand might protest, especially if harm came to his precious Carnelia, and if so, Aryx would deal with him as well. Chot, too, for that matter, for clearly he had outlived his usefulness as emperor, having bowed so meekly to the intruders. Yes, Aryx would then rally his people, bringing about—

"Aryx?"

Snarling, he turned to see who dared interrupt him. His baleful gaze fell upon his whining brother and the female who constantly sang the praises of the useless Sargonnas. Aryx could not believe that he had tolerated their presences for so long. Best to be rid of them now, and with the sword in hand, he knew just what to—

"No!" With herculean effort, Aryx forced his arm down. He glared at the Sword of Tears and knew at last the malevolence it contained. Small wonder that only one such as

Sargonnas had wielded it before. The shock of what he had thought of doing to Seph and Delara fueled his efforts, enabling him to raise the demon blade high in preparation to hurl it far away.

*You need me!* the sword implored. *I am your only hope!*

"You're worse than the creatures that killed my friends! You'd turn me into a butcher for your own amusement!" Aryx hesitated, trying to think of where to throw the sword. If he left it where someone could find it, the monstrous blade might yet wreak havoc on the island.

*Wait, O Master!* it pleaded. *You need not fear me! You need not worry! I merely tested you . . . yes, tested you. . . .*

"Tested! You wanted me to kill my brother!"

Seph and Delara stared wide-eyed at him, entirely oblivious to the downpour. They couldn't hear the sword's end of the conversation, and Aryx did not doubt that they wondered at his sanity. Nevertheless, he dared not let up against the sinister artifact.

*I would never have let you do it. . . . Oh, Master . . . the Horned One chose you to wield me. I would not disobey. . . .*

"But you would manipulate me." Aryx prepared himself to hurl the blade away. "I won't be your puppet."

*You will not be. . . . By the Horned One himself, I will not usurp your freedom of choice. . . .*

For the first time since the sword had started to talk to him, Aryx sensed fear on its part. Sargonnas had given it a command, and if it failed, it feared punishment.

*The Chaos will not suffer this one to exist . . . Master. No need for a little sword when no world remains . . . Only if there is light and darkness can I survive. . . . Only then can I eat. . . .*

Aryx tried not to think about what the Sword of Tears ate, pondering instead the rest of what it said. He believed the demon blade when it said it wanted Krynn to exist . . . and if that were the case, then it would behoove the enchanted artifact to work *with* him.

"All right." The weary minotaur lowered the weapon. "I won't toss you aside."

*A wise, wise decision. . . .* The stone flared again.

Aryx suddenly raised it high once more. "But if I ever feel your foul presence in my thoughts again—"

*Never! Never, my master . . . so I swear by the Horned One himself. . . .*

"You'd better not." Aryx looked the blade over, admiring its craftsmanship despite its dark abilities. "You'd better not."

*Never. . . .* The light in the green stone faded to nearly nothing.

By no means entirely trusting the Sword of Tears, the dusky gray minotaur nonetheless thrust the blade through his belt. At first opportunity, he would find a proper sheath, one that would hide some of the rich and much too enticing qualities of the artifact from other eyes. Aryx did not want others becoming overly interested in Sargonnas's toy. He had been fortunate enough to break the sword's hold, but others might not.

Delara gently touched his shoulder. "Aryx, are you all right?"

"No." How could he be with this new responsibility? By passing on the sword to him, Sargonnas had once more forced Aryx into a situation that the warrior felt insufficient to face. "Not in the least."

"That's . . . that's the Blessed One's blade, isn't it?" She almost reached out to it, but the green stone suddenly flared, causing her to quickly withdraw.

"The Sword of Tears," Aryx returned, frowning at the mischievous artifact. "And whatever happens, don't try to touch it again. It . . . has a taste for tricks."

"I don't even want to stand near it. Does it know what happened to Sargonnas?"

He touched the hilt. "Do you, demon?"

The sword remained silent. If it knew, it had no intention of telling. Perhaps Sargonnas had even been destroyed, and the sword dared not admit that. Aryx distrusted the artifact's loyalties and knew that he would still have to be wary, especially if it came to using the weapon.

"It doesn't answer," he finally informed them. "Whether it knows or not, I can't say."

Seph bent over slightly to study it. "Does it really talk to you?"

"In my mind." The drenched minotaur shook his head, sending cascades of water flying at his equally soaked companions. "We've got to get out of this damned rain! I need to think! I need time to . . . to breathe. . . ."

"But where can we go?" Seph asked, glancing around them. "The temple's not exactly fit for occupation right now."

Aryx blinked, not having considered that part of their situation. His belongings, and even some of Seph's, had perished with Sargonnas's sanctum. They could return to their clan house, but Orilg did not exactly favor Aryx at the moment.

"I could find some room for you at my clan, I think," Delara offered, her eyes meeting Aryx's. A breath later, she pulled her gaze away, amending, "Both of you, of course."

*The human must know . . .* the sword suddenly interjected.

"Human?" Aryx ignored the other minotaurs' perplexed looks.

*He who wears the colors of the bison god,* it explained, a touch of loathing in its tone as it mentioned the last words.

Rand. The sword wanted him to go to the cleric and tell him what had happened. Aryx saw sense in that, although he wished that someone other than the demon blade had brought it to his attention. Rand knew more about Sargonnas than anyone else, the minotaur suspected. "Change of plans," he told the others. "We go to the humans' headquarters. I need to see the cleric of Kiri-Jolith."

They did not argue, for which Aryx felt grateful. Neither Seph nor Delara needed to be a part of this any longer, but both appeared prepared to follow him wherever he led. Seph, Aryx understood, since the two brothers were loyal to one another. Delara, on the other hand, presented more of a quandary, although he thought perhaps his growing feelings toward her mirrored her own.

With some effort, they retrieved the horses. Their timing proved fortuitous, too, for the first of the clerics began filtering back toward the ruined temple. Others also dared to return, as curious as they were wary.

"They'll probably use this as an excuse to build a bigger and better one," Aryx muttered as he joined Delara atop her mount. "That is, if they ever have the chance."

She turned, her face so very near that their muzzles almost touched. "They'll have the chance . . . if only because of you."

Before Aryx could gather his wits for a reply, she turned away, urging the massive horse forward. The rain continued to come down hard, thunder and lightning still accenting the storm. Fortunately, the weather also kept the streets more or less deserted. They passed a band of knights on horseback and a few hardy warriors clearly on their way to important destinations, but not many other travelers.

Already well worn from the earlier ride, their own animals moved slower than before, but soon the banners of the Knights of Takhisis came into sight. Aryx noted that, despite the humans' vaunted superiority, their flags hung just as limp in the oppressive rain. Some had even been torn off by the earlier winds. Curiously, the humans he saw nearby moved about unconcerned, as if they did not know what had happened to the temple.

At the gate, they paused before four cloaked but still sodden guards who looked them over with bitterness. Aryx thought that they might give the trio difficulties, but to his surprise, they let the minotaurs pass on to the stables. Thanking the absent gods for small favors, Aryx and his companions soon left the two bedraggled animals munching hay under a warm roof and went in search of the blond human.

"Could it be they do not know what happened?" Delara asked, incredulous. "None of them acts as if anything happened in the city center! Could they not have heard?"

"It certainly seems like it," Aryx returned. "The storm must have slowed the news, but it still seems odd. Perhaps Lord Broedius has other things on his mind." The knight commander seemed to have everything on his mind except the safety and security of the minotaur homeland. The very thought rankled Aryx, stirring up once more his displeasure of the Knights of Takhisis in general.

A courier charged past them as they entered the commandeered clan house. Seph was nearly shoved against the wall by the armored figure. Aryx's brother snorted and reached for his axe, but Aryx quickly stopped him. Their ordeal had set all their tempers on edge, and he didn't want the others to get in trouble because he had dragged them to Lord Broedius's stronghold.

"Keep a cool head, Seph. Any of them would be eager for an excuse to lock us away . . . or worse. We can't afford that."

The light brown minotaur glanced back at the door through which the courier had vanished, but acquiesced. "I'm sorry, Aryx."

I only hope that we can find Rand before I do something wrong, the older brother thought, knowing that he had been but a second behind Seph in attempting to chase down the arrogant knight. Curiously, only a slight touch in his mind by the Sword of Tears had awakened him to the danger of giving in to his temper. The sinister artifact had actually saved them from possible disaster.

Few torches or oil lamps lit the long halls, giving the knighthood's sanctum an oppressive feel during the horrendous storm. Now and then a cold-eyed guard watched them pass, but none ever spoke. Aryx refused to ask for the cleric's whereabouts, hoping instead that they might run across him.

That they eventually did . . . in a sense. Recalling some vague mention by the cleric about where he was quartered, Aryx led the others down a long, dark corridor that was surprisingly unguarded. He had just begun to wonder whether he was leading them down a dead end when Carnelia emerged from the shadows ahead.

In contrast to the many times he had seen her before, the warrior woman had this once discarded her armor. Instead, she came clad in a black and quite feminine gown belted at the waist and cut low in front. Much to Aryx's surprise. Carnelia's dark hair cascaded down past her shoulders, something he would not have thought possible, considering the helmet she generally wore.

She looked as stunned as he when they came across one another. To her credit, she gave him a stiff but courteous nod. "Out of the storm, eh, bull? A wise move this night."

"You, too, I see." After a moment's hesitation, Aryx added, "I come seeking Rand. Do you know where I might find him?"

A brief smile escaped her. Carnelia smothered it before answering. "As a matter fact, if you continue down this hall to the very end, you'll find his quarters. My uncle thought it better if Rand remained more . . . distant . . . from his men."

Understandable. Broedius probably assumed the cleric would attempt to corrupt his officers with the word of Kiri-Jolith. Of course, such corruption apparently did not worry the knight commander's niece. "I thank you for your assistance."

Carnelia merely nodded, then stepped past the minotaurs as if they no longer existed. Aryx glanced back at her retreating form, trying to understand the female. He wished Rand good luck with Carnelia, hoping the cleric's god would watch over his servant. Rand would need all the help he could get if the female knight desired him.

They followed Carnelia's directions, arriving but a minute or two later at the door to Rand's chambers. Aryx felt an urge to burst in but forced himself to knock. The cleric had so far proven the only human friend he had, and Aryx couldn't afford to offend him.

"Carnelia?" Rand called out in response to Aryx's knock. The door opened, and the cleric, looking slightly disheveled, peered at his visitors. "Aryx!"

"Forgive us for disturbing you at this hour, but—"

"No! No, your timing is perfect, Aryx!" Rand stepped aside. "Come in! I've been wondering about you! I felt some kind of a disturbance earlier."

"Cleric, the Temple of Sargonnas is in ruins."

The human's expression froze. "The temple?"

"You've heard nothing, then?"

"I have been . . . ensconced here for some time."

From the slight tinge of red in Rand's face, Aryx suspected that the blond human had not been ensconced alone. He wondered how much influence Rand had with Carnelia and if he dared at times to make use of that influence.

The cleric of Kiri-Jolith ushered them inside, closing the door tightly behind them. Rand's quarters were simple and very likely unchanged from what they had been when this had served as one of the clan elder's apartments. Small oil lamps near each corner of the room illuminated a carved wooden desk near the right side, a spartan bed, unmade, at the far wall, and a weapon rack along the left. The rack had been emptied save for the cleric's staff and mace.

In the center of the room, Rand had made one significant change. The wooden floor had been cleared, and in the center had been traced, very lightly, a pattern that Aryx finally realized was a representation of the stars that made up the constellation of the bison god. Just enough room existed in the center for the cleric to sit or kneel during prayer. A small urn sat near the pattern, along with a few items no doubt needed by one of Rand's rank during rituals.

"Forgive my makeshift temple. Lord Broedius does not care for the word of my patron to be spread among his men . . . although I must admit I believe I have made some inroads with a few of them." There were few chairs, but he offered what seating he could. Seph and Delara sat, but Aryx, too keyed up, remained standing. Seeing that the minotaur would refuse any further offer, the cleric sat down on the edge of the bed and pressed on. "Tell me what happened, Aryx . . . everything."

"I'll tell you everything, human, but I also have something to show you." The gray minotaur drew forth the enchanted blade.

"Kiri-Jolith, protect us from this foul evil!" the cleric uttered, leaping to his feet and seizing hold of the medallion hanging from his neck. "Aryx! Do you know what that is?"

He probably knew better than Rand. "The Sword of Tears, it calls itself. Sargonnas's sword."

The demon blade glistened brightly despite the limited illumination of Rand's chamber. The green stone flared especially brilliantly in the presence of the cleric. However, Rand, after his initial shock, confronted the Sword of Tears with determination. He held the medallion before him as he moved closer. "Play no games with me, spawn of the Abyss! I know your master and I know his desire! You will do nothing while I am near, understand? Think not that Sargonnas is the only god who has power over you, demon!"

To Aryx's surprise, the glow around the sword faded. He felt the presence within retreat, as if Rand's words had struck true. For the first time, the warrior found himself truly impressed by the human's skills. True, Rand had saved his life, but since then Aryx had seen little of the cleric's abilities. Yet any who could confront the sinister artifact and even command it had to wield great power.

"You carry the cursed sword . . ." Rand muttered, a changed person now. "Tell me quickly all that occurred, Aryx, for I fear that we have very little time left to us!"

Aryx related, as carefully but swiftly as he could, the details of the horrific storm, the terrible lightning and its precise strikes against the temple, the inferno in the sky, and the final fury when the winds took up both building and people into the crimson maw. Belatedly he added the tale of his struggle on the beach and, in the end, his confrontation with the sword.

"And it told you to come to me? Of course." Rand paced back and forth, shaking his head. "I have heard none of this. Oh, I knew the storm raged, and I sensed something out there, but to be truthful, I have sensed something out there since we arrived. I knew, though, that Sargonnas—despite your opinion, Aryx—protected the islands from intrusion. At least, he did before this."

"But what happens now, cleric? What happens now that the temple and Sargonnas have vanished?"

"That is the question foremost in my mind, followed closely by why Lord Broedius seems not to have heard about the destruction in the center of the capital." Rand smoothed his robe. "Come with me, all of you! If Broedius knows nothing about this, then he should hear your words, even if I am obliged to tie him to his chair!"

Startled somewhat by the normally placid man's tone, the minotaurs reacted slowly. Rand threw open the door and marched down the hall, Aryx and the others racing to catch up to him. That the cleric saw the situation so serious further stirred up Aryx. Were they already too late to stop the events set into motion?

"Broedius!" the tall robed figure roared as he charged the doors to the knight commander's chambers. The two sentries guarding it moved forward to meet him, but a glance from Rand sent both flat against the walls, where they struggled futilely against invisible bonds. Aryx bit back a gasp, for the first time hoping he never got on the human's bad side.

The doors flung open before Rand, who marched in without pause. A roomful of startled and not at all friendly knights clad for battle greeted them, knights who immediately drew their weapons and shielded their commander. Only one, Carnelia, seemed hesitant. She must have gone directly to her quarters after leaving the cleric and clad herself for this meeting. With her eyes, she clearly tried to plead with Rand to leave now before he did or said anything wrong.

"Stand aside," Broedius quietly commanded his faithful. The broad-shouldered warrior's gaze flickered to his niece, then returned to Rand. "What do you want, cleric?"

"Just now, these minotaurs related to me horrifying news from the center of the city."

The ebony eyes narrowed. "Yes . . . the temple of Sargonnas is no more, ripped from the ground by a storm of no natural origin. They should have reported such news to me first, but I excuse them this time."

Rand and the minotaurs were taken aback. "You know already?" the cleric blurted. "You know?"

"Of course. In every war, a network of information-gathering must be established early. I've known since the first bolts struck."

"And you told me nothing?"

Some of the reserve dwindled from Broedius's face. "I've better things to do than keep you informed, servant of Kiri-

Jolith. Your god can keep you informed"—his eyes again flickered briefly toward Carnelia—"or others."

"But—"

"You've wasted enough of my time, cleric!" Broedius snarled. "I've far more important matters to deal with, matters of which the disappearance of a fickle god are only the tip!"

"What could be more important than the Blessed One's vanishing?" demanded Delara. She would have said more, but Aryx quickly quieted her.

Despite her height, Broedius stared down at her, his thick mustache twitching. He eyed the minotaurs, fixing his gaze at last on Aryx. "You might know, Aryx. What might concern me more? Could it be the disappearance, and very likely the death, of another patrol? Could it be the fact that an officer of mine has gained a confession from one of your clan concerning treachery against the knighthood?"

"What?" Now it was Aryx who had to be restrained. The young warrior cast about, seeking who would create such a lie. He knew that none of his people had been a part in the deaths. "What confession? Who brings forth such madness, such *lies?*"

"No lies, I assure you," an officer in back smoothly replied. One of the other knights stepped out of his way, revealing to Aryx the sly face of Subcommander Drejjen. Drejjen's eyes fairly blazed with triumph. "You'll find all in order, I assure you . . ."

"Who is it, then? Who do you claim confessed? I demand to see him!"

The subcommander clearly enjoyed his moment. "Why, a warrior named Kamax, I believe . . . someone who claimed ties to you, as a matter of fact. Close ties." Drejjen shrugged. "But I'm sorry to say, during questioning he lost his temper, broke free of his bonds, and I was forced to have him killed."

"Killed?" Aryx had seen Kamax only the other day. How could he have come to the attention of Drejjen? The furious minotaur looked around, noticing that near the subcommander was the same officer who had nearly led the unordered attack on House Orilg during negotiations. He had seen the warriors talking and probably saw how much Kamax had trusted Aryx.

Without realizing what he did, Aryx effortlessly drew the Sword of Tears. Shouts went up among the Knights of Takhisis, and at least half a dozen swords fixed on the enraged warrior. Behind him, Seph and Delara pulled free their own weapons.

"Stop this!" Rand called, but no one paid him any mind.

"Hold!" Broedius commanded. As for Drejjen, he made no move to join those protecting his honor and his life, instead seeming to savor the moment.

The Sword of Tears blazed brightly. Aryx felt an immense urge to cut through the ranks before him, lay low each Stygian-armored figure with the enchanted blade.

"Aryx!" Rand pleaded. "Now is not the time!"

Carnelia had her uncle's arm. "Broedius, this isn't wise. . . ."

At that moment, a knight dripping from head to toe burst through the doors. "Lord Broedius! Sir!"

His abrupt appearance seized everyone's attention. The knight fought for breath, looking as if he had run from the very sea itself to tell them his dire news.

Broedius seized the interruption like a lifeline. "Speak, man! What ails you?"

"The fog, my lord! The fog moves in!"

Only Aryx truly took that as alarming. Rand glanced his way, seeing how he reacted.

Broedius frowned. "What of it, man? We've nothing to fear from a little fog."

"Let him go on," the horrified minotaur muttered. "Let him go on, Commander. . . ."

The knight slipped to one knee, his strength all but gone. He had grown deathly pale, yet somehow he forced himself on. "It moved in . . . the *Predator* . . . she's stationed near the port. . . ."

"I know that, you fool!" After the majority of the forces had disembarked from the three black ships, Broedius had set the *Predator* the task of guarding the port entrance, utilizing its normal crew. The massive ship had remained near the edge of the fog since then, watching for any unrecognized intruders.

And the fog had moved in. . . . Aryx swallowed. Images of the *Kraken's Eye* welled up in his mind.

"The fog . . . the fog moved in . . . covered the *Predator* . . . and we began to hear shouts, screams . . . horrible screams . . ."

*It begins* . . . the sword whispered in Aryx's head. As if on cue, horns blared in the distance. Those assembled in the room looked about, seeking verification of what they were hearing.

146

"It's the minotaurs!" Drejjen announced. "They betray their hand at last!"

"Fool!" Aryx looked to the knight commander. "Lord Broedius! You have to issue immediate orders to release the generals, the emperor, and the rest! We all have to band together or we're all dead! Hurry, before it's too late!"

From outside came shouting, confused shouting. Broedius finally signaled one of his men to open a window and peer out. The shouting grew in volume as the officer obeyed. The horns began anew, this time with more urgency.

"Well? What do you see?"

The knight turned, looking nearly as pale as the man who had entered. "Nothing, my lord! Nothing! The fog's spread over the port . . . but in the distance, there seems to be a battle going on, from the sound of it! Perhaps pirates in the harbor . . ."

"Closer than the harbor," declared another knight. "That sounds as if they're already attacking on shore!" Even as he spoke, they heard officers outside trying to organize their men, while farther away, cries of shock and pain arose.

"It's the minotaurs, I tell you!" Drejjen insisted. "Led by that one!"

Aryx almost gaped as the knight accused him. Of its own accord, the Sword of Tears rose to battle position. He fought the blade down, though, knowing that his feud with Drejjen would have to wait, providing both of them survived this night.

"Broedius! This is the way the *Kraken's Eye* perished! The fog, the cries—" he sniffed the air venting in through the open window—"and the musky smell of *death*." Aryx pointed the tip of the blade toward the window. "You think it any coincidence that Sargonnas has vanished this very night, his temple but a ruin?"

"No." Broedius signaled his officers to lower their weapons. "No, I don't, minotaur. I think you, of all of us, grasp the terrible truth best." He surveyed the others, many of whom still looked suspicious or confused, and at last uttered what even Aryx had not been able to bring himself to say: "Our Lady's fears may have come to pass, gentlemen! The forces of Chaos could at this very minute be attacking the islands. . . ."

# Warriors of the Deep

## Chapter Nine

From the dark sea bottom surrounding the minotaur isles, they rose. The servant had given word and the Magori would obey. As one, they flowed toward the surface, knowing that the protective fog, the fog that in no manner hindered their own eyesight, now spread forward, the traitorous little god who had held it back no longer their concern. The Magori swarmed, their weapons ready, their minds filled with one purpose: to fulfill the wishes of the servant, who spoke the will of Father Chaos.

And that most faithful servant watched as they moved, its endless serpentine segments intertwining in growing anticipation and glee. The betrayer Sargonnas—surely destroyed, despite a lack of absolute evidence of his passing—had failed to shield his little toys, his little mortals. They would soon join him in blessed oblivion, the gift that all upon this tiny bit of mud and water called Krynn would before long receive, including even the servant itself.

Thinking of that, the Coil urged the host on. Yes, the sooner the paltry little mortals were erased from existence, the sooner Father Chaos's most trusted servant would receive its own reward . . . sweet, eternal nothingness.

\* \* \* \* \*

"Landren!"

One of Broedius's officers snapped to attention.

"Send word out immediately! Alert all talon subcommanders that I want the shipping district fortified! Have Axus,

148

Basilisk, and Cobra talons stand by in reserve! Go, man! Tell them all we're in a crisis situation! The enemy is at the doorstep, heavily armored and hidden by the fog! Go now!"

"Yes, sir!" Landren barged past the minotaurs, nearly flying out the doorway.

Aryx pressed. "Lord Broedius! The minotaur generals! You must release them!"

"The minotaur forces will fight under my subcommanders, Aryx! Boroman, Drejjen, Carnelia, Tyco, Ulris!" Carnelia and the other summoned subcommanders gathered at attention. "In addition to your own men, take charge of the native talons that were to have been assigned to you for the expedition! Go!"

They saluted, then rushed off. Rand started after Carnelia, but Broedius summoned him back.

"You have no need of me," the cleric practically snapped. "I will make myself of use in the conflict."

"I've use for you, cleric! I want you and the Knights of the Thorn to see what you can do about this cursed fog! You know where to find the mages, don't you?"

"I do," Rand replied with much distaste, "and . . . your idea has merit. As you command, then . . ."

With the cleric and most of Broedius's officers now departed, Aryx attempted one last plea. "Lord Broedius, your people haven't had the chance to train with our warriors! Release the generals and let them command their own forces, making proper use of their skills!"

"My subcommanders know their duties, bull." Broedius adjusted his helmet. "You have two choices  Either come with me or join one of the talons."

He bounded out the doors, the last of the knights following closely. Seph and Delara stared at Aryx, awaiting his decision. Frustrated, Aryx stood where he was for a minute, trying to assess the situation. Then the horns blared again, this time much nearer, reminding the bitter minotaur that the time for contemplation had passed. A battle had begun, and now it was the duty of every minotaur to fight.

"Come on!" Sword in hand, Aryx raced out of the Knight Commander's chambers.

Outside, the storm had all but ended, but in its wake, the stifling mists had spread to the very gates of the clan house. The thick stench of musk permeated everything. Figures darted in and out of the fog—a knight on horseback, a talon of minotaur warriors under the guidance of a human commander, even a riderless mount, the last panic-stricken.

Several more minotaurs came into sight, none part of any organized force. Armed with axes, swords, and lances, they had come from their homes, knowing that the realm required their strong arms. Ahead, the horns blared again and again, on occasion cutting off with an abruptness that bespoke their wielder's fate. Such knowledge did not deter the defenders, however.

"The port!" Aryx called. "We'll head there!"

Many of the other minotaurs joined them as they ran, perhaps believing that Aryx knew something they did not. Countless generations of breeding and training had created a race prepared even for such sudden catastrophes. Order formed, and with it ranks, Aryx, without realizing it, had become commander by unspoken consensus. Seph followed close behind his brother, and whenever the elder sibling looked back, he ever saw the look of anticipation on his sibling's face. Seph carried some fear into his first battle, but he also carried determination. Aryx could ask for nothing more. He only prayed that Seph's first battle would not be his last. Delara, meanwhile, remained at the gray minotaur's side, a sword in her hand.

As thick as the fog had grown, on occasion it broke just enough for shadowy scenes to be glimpsed. In the distance, a ship, perhaps the *Predator*, lay burning in the harbor. Aryx wondered if one of the desperate crew had done as Feresi had, trying to drive the monstrous reavers back with flames. Closer to shore, the flickering lights of torches revealed shadowy forms that could be neither man nor minotaur. While he could not see enough to verify his suspicions, Aryx suspected that what he had feared had indeed come to pass.

Knights of Takhisis rode into and out of the mists, barking orders. Wave after wave of minotaurs poured into the port area, but in Aryx's eyes, they moved with stiffness and uncertainty, no doubt brought about by serving under unfamiliar commanders. In truth, Lord Broedius would have been better off to leave the island's inhabitants to their own devices, for preserving the empire remained the greatest of any warrior's duties. Forcing his own officers upon them would only lead to friction.

From out of the mists emerged a mustached knight who, upon seeing Aryx and his ragtag legion, attempted to seize control. "You there! Take that band of yours and report to the great smithy north of here!"

The others looked to Aryx, who shook his head. "We need to be down there, by the shoreline!"

"Lord Broedius wants a force built up over by the smithy, one that he'll send in when the time is right, minotaur! Obey your orders!"

Aryx hesitated but a moment. If they took the time to gather their forces at the smithy, the invaders would gain too great a foothold in the city. He could not wait that long. If these were the same monsters that had slaughtered his crew mates, they needed to be stopped now, right at the shore.

He charged past the knight.

The human drew his sword. "Halt!"

Too late. Aryx's action had caused a tidal wave. Delara, Seph, and the rest of the makeshift force poured in behind him, sweeping past the frustrated human. Aryx glanced back just long enough to locate his companions, then picked up his pace. His inner demons now possessed him, and only one thing would drive them away. He took a deep breath, readied the enchanted sword . . .

. . . and came upon a scene directly out of his nightmares.

They swarmed on the docks, along the shoreline, and already well into the port. Scythe swords and barbed lances cut a bloody swath everywhere. Maddening, inhuman eyes stared without pity at those cut down. Aryx watched a minotaur fall, his head lopped off, and remembered the *Kraken's Eye*. A barbed lance skewered not one but two warriors who happened to stand too close to one another.

"By the Blessed One!" Delara cried out, as stunned as all the rest. "What *are* those monsters?"

They were not, as some had suggested, sea elves in armor. Aryx would have welcomed such foes far more than the abominations before him. Crustacean they were, but like lobsters mutated by the Graygem of legend. As tall as, or even taller than, Aryx, horns and all, and nearly twice as wide, they moved about on a pair of clawed limbs with remarkable dexterity. Unlike the tiny crustaceans they vaguely resembled, though, these monsters had but one other set of limbs, ending in three-digited, clawed appendages. Their shells were crimson and brown and covered the horrors from head to foot, save for the face and the throat, which were the color of dead flesh.

The face. Aryx could not conceive such a face, not even seeing it clearly for the first time. The long, tapering snout, a thing almost with a life of its own, darted about, and from within the tiny yet sinister maw at the end, row upon row of sharp teeth displayed themselves. Worse yet, above the serpentine snout clustered not two but *five* bulbous red orbs with no discernible pupils. The stunned minotaur found it impossible to believe that even the Blood Sea, where so many strange creatures could be found, could spawn such impossible monstrosities. Yes, these were certainly creatures of Chaos, and now they sought to do to his home what they had done to his ship. Already the horrific jagged swords and barbed lances of the invaders were drenched in blood.

To Aryx's surprise, instead of mounting fear, a blood rage filled him. He could not let this happen again, not to his home and family.

*Now is the time to strike*, urged the demon blade. *Now, while the rage burns strong within you, Master. You know some of their weaknesses. You can lead the others. . . .*

Their weaknesses. Yes, Aryx recalled vividly the few fortunate strikes against the monstrous reavers. "Go for the gullet or the face!" Aryx cried, raising the Sword of Tears high. "The pale areas! Watch out for their blood; it burns!" The dusky gray minotaur scanned the battle, seeing where the defenders already fighting had the most trouble. "Spread out along the area to the right!" he added, command now seeming almost natural to him. "Fill in that gap there! Don't bunch up too much!"

His confidence in the face of such horror galvanized those around him. Fear and shock gave way to determination. What had started out a tattered mob now became an organized force.

With a bellowed war cry, Aryx leapt into the fray, his makeshift force at his heels.

Curiously, he saw few knights, and those few he saw mostly remained in the rear, riding horses and giving commands to minotaurs. Then Aryx lost all interest in what Lord Broedius's men did as he and his companions met the foe. Aryx did not hesitate even as one of the monstrous reavers focused on him, its wicked multibarbed lance fixed on his chest. The minotaur warrior cut a deadly swath with the demon blade, picturing in his mind everyone who had died on his ship. Their ghosts lent him strength, the Sword of Tears wailing as it struck the lower area of the crustacean's soft region, continuing down and slicing through the armor plating as well. He pulled the weapon back immediately, avoiding all but a few drops of the corrosive blood.

Others beside Aryx were not so fortunate. One minotaur immediately fell as twin swords crisscrossed through his chest. Another hesitated, clearly daunted by the horrific swarm surging through the fog, and that hesitation, however short, cost him first his leg, then his head.

The familiar thick, musky smell filled the area, originating, Aryx at last realized, from the horrors themselves. They virtually stank of the stuff, so much so he finally had to force himself to breathe through his mouth. The stench further dampened the efforts of the minotaurs for, this near, it even made the eyes water.

*Strike! Strike again!* the enchanted sword encouraged. *Strike or be struck down!*

Aryx obeyed, losing himself more and more in the struggle. His view again filled with the huge, armored form of a monstrous invader, this creature wielding a scythe sword like the one that had killed Hugar. Recalling the veteran mariner and how he had done his best to see that each member of the crew learned to adapt to every situation, Aryx bitterly drove the length of the blade through the fortified chest of the creature.

It hissed, spat, then tried to fall upon him as the wound took its toll, so close Aryx had to grapple with one hand. A fresh wave of musk invaded his senses, momentarily stunning him. He felt claws around his throat, the same type of claws such as he had felt around his ankle during his earlier search of the beach. The crustacean squeezed, choking off his air supply.

Acidic blood splattered his head, narrowly missing his eyes. Someone had thrust the tip of his sword through the unsettling eyes and into what passed for the horror's brain. The aquatic reaver shivered, then grew still. As Aryx struggled underneath its lifeless form, others dragged the gargantuan corpse from him.

Delara, her blade stained from acid, helped him up. "Are you hurt?" Her eyes quickly scanned him. "Can you stand?"

"I . . . I think I'm okay."

"You said to go for the throat areas, but I thought surely the eyes would be sensitive, too."

Aryx inhaled, then stood. "You were right."

A white-furred veteran warrior handed the Sword of Tears back to Aryx as if it were any other weapon. "Your blade, General!"

He almost argued with the veteran that of all of them, Aryx had the least reason to be mistaken for a general, but the look in the eyes of those around him forced his mouth shut.

*You must lead, Master. . . . There is no one else. The knights still keep your generals prisoner. . . .*

Aryx held the sword ready. "Regroup! We have to hold them, then push them back!"

They cheered at his words and returned to the fray, joining their companions in an attempt to repulse the horrific invasion. Aryx only wished he felt the confidence he apparently displayed. The Chaos creature's nearly successful attempt to kill him reminded the minotaur that even with the deadly artifact in his hand, he faced a force whose own master rivaled the gods.

Another warrior went down, cut literally in two by a pair of the ghoulish attackers. Roaring in anger, Aryx threw himself at the duo, forcing one back and cleanly slicing off one of the claws of the other. The wounded reaver stumbled back, thick, burning fluid dripping from its wound. The other recovered, charging at him with its blade. Determined not to fall prey to the invader's grasping claws, Aryx brought the wailing sword across, cutting through the creature's own blade. His adversary now disarmed, the minotaur thrust once, then twice, into its squat throat just below the sinewy muzzle.

The Chaos creature collapsed as Aryx leapt out of reach. He would have sent a third thrust into its head, but more of the crustaceans emerged through the fog. The docks and shoreline seemed to be filled with the horrific reavers, yet still more came. Aryx's line held, but numbers alone threatened to overwhelm them. How could there be so many of the beasts? Did they assault the other regions of the two islands with equally astonishing swarms?

At last he caught sight of a talon of knights, the first he had seen in the front lines. Not at all to his surprise, they were led by Carnelia. With the knights came a legion of minotaur warriors fighting side by side with the humans. In the murk, Carnelia failed to notice him, but Aryx saw that to her credit, she did not simply throw her minotaur troops forward, letting them take the brunt of the assault. Under Drejjen or many of the other subcommanders, Aryx had no doubt that his people would have been used more severely, wasted by officers who had no regard for them. Even Carnelia, though, failed to utilize the minotaurs as equals, causing her line to falter in places as almost contrary commands left holes here and packed together too many warriors there.

Gritting his teeth, Aryx steered his group toward Carnelia's band. If he could link up to her left side, then the minotaurs with him would be able to help those with her better organize . . . at least, so he hoped.

The female knight barely noticed him. Assured that he did nothing to disrupt her lines, she ignored him thereafter, her concern now on a new wave of attackers pressing against the knights.

If they had originally thought that they would fare better than the unarmored minotaurs, the knights had surely by now realized the truth of things. The pure physical power and weapons of the aquatic reavers made the armor of the knights only a partial defense. A scythe sword cleaved through the breastplate of one impetuous soldier, cutting halfway through his chest as well. Another knight attempting to slay the one who had killed his comrade instead ended up skewered at the end of one of the lances, his twitching body held high in the air before being tossed aside by the shelled attacker.

A few of the humans realized quickly that the most vulnerable spots of the attackers were the throat and the eyes, but too many first attempted to find weak links in the harsh, plated scales of their foes. Many of those knights died swiftly but horribly, often without their heads or some limb.

Aryx could do nothing to warn them, his concern for those with him most important. He kept Seph nearby, determined that nothing would happen to his young brother. So far, Seph had held his own, striking dead two of the crustaceans with his axe and receiving only minor acid burns in return.

The minotaurs still held . . . and the reavers continued to swarm.

"They keep coming!" Someone roared. "They keep coming!"

"Then we keep fighting!" Aryx called in return, knowing from the *Kraken's Eye* that the servants of Chaos would give no quarter, no mercy. "We keep fighting until they stop coming!"

Not even in the epics he had heard as a child had Aryx ever recalled such a battle. At one time, he would have thought it glorious, but now he simply hoped that they could keep the enemy at bay. Their foe gave no indication that anything other than the complete extermination of the minotaur race would satisfy them. The minotaurs had to be equally determined if they wanted to survive.

In some places, the shelled reavers pushed forward, a harvest of butchered bodies left in their wake. In others, especially where Aryx and his band fought, the warriors held and even pushed back the horde slightly. Yet still the armored leviathans continued to come, rising up, no doubt, from the depths of the harbor.

"Is there no end to them?" gasped Delara. She had become more proficient than most in striking at the weak points of the monsters, but her efforts involved more risk than Aryx preferred. Delara would duck below the guard of her foe, then plunge her sword upward into its throat or maw. Unfortunately, twice Aryx had been forced to come to her aid.

As if their swords, lances, and claws were not terrible enough, the Chaos creatures wielded still another deadly weapon. Aryx first noted it when a massive brown warrior to his left grappled with one of the crustaceans. At first the minotaur appeared to have the upper hand, but then suddenly he went limp, falling into the crushing arms of his adversary. His collapse made no sense until another who grappled with one of the horrors also fell . . . but not before Aryx noted the sinewy maw bite hard into the warrior's throat. Even though the bite did not look fatal, its victim collapsed only a moment later.

The creatures had a poisonous, fatal bite. Aryx swore. Yet another threat. All the minotaurs had were their strong arms, their willingness to fight for their home. Could they compete against creatures bred to kill?

The battle raged on without pause, at one point taking them to the buildings on the very edge of the port. The servants of Chaos had spread everywhere, their numbers so great that none who fought them had even the slightest chance to pause for breath. The Sword of Tears wailed each time Aryx struck down a foe, yet there always seemed to be another enemy to take the previous one's place. Carnelia's talon continued to fight at the side of Aryx's band, an impromptu alliance that, as time progressed, proved one of the strongest points of the city's defense. Unfortunately, despite any success on their part, Aryx noted too many mino- taur corpses already littering the streets and lying across the docks. Far too many in comparison to the number of dead knights he saw. Under the command of Lord Broedius's unfeeling officers, the warriors of the empire were being wasted, slaughtered because those in charge saw them only as brutes or slaves.

A warehouse ahead of them burst into flames, clearly an accident. Broedius would have brooked no wasting of the supplies he had been gathering for his grand expedition, and the aquatic reavers had no taste of their own for fire. Even now they shifted to avoid it just as they had aboard the *Kraken's Eye*.

"Torches!" the bedraggled warrior suddenly roared. "Bring torches! Seph! Get as many able bodies as you can to gather torches! The flames unsettle them!" Aryx did not know if the flames would actually drive the creatures away—they had stayed aboard his ship despite the fire—but if it unnerved them enough for the minotaurs to press the advantage, then the ploy would be well worth it.

Seph vanished, a handful of others retreating with him. The loss of even a few minotaurs put extra strain on the remaining defenders, and two warriors quickly fell, one man- aging to cut open his adversary first. Seph's departure actu- ally benefited the dusky gray minotaur; Aryx no longer had to watch over his brother as he fought. He pressed forward, driv- ing back a pair of the hideous beasts. Of Delara he could no longer see any sign. Aryx assumed that she had joined Seph in the effort to gather torches.

Then a surge of reinforcements enabled the underwater dwellers to counterattack, and Aryx suddenly found himself at the point, with only two other warriors beside him. One of the crustaceans brought its lance down on Aryx, catching the demon sword by the blade. The barbs snagged the weapon, and it became all the minotaur could do just to hold on to the handle. He expected the enchanted weapon to do something, but the Sword of Tears remained oddly still, reacting no more than a mortal tool. The behemoth leaned forward, and for the first time, Aryx beheld the long, tapering snout and maw at such close range. The mouth, filled with rows of teeth, snapped at him like a striking serpent, yellow, acidic venom dripping from the upper fangs. He tried to swat the crustacean's jaws aside, but only succeeded in nearly losing his remaining grip.

Moving almost with a life of its own, the sinewy snout got around his groping hand. Teeth came within less than an inch of sinking into his upper shoulder just below the vein in his neck. Aryx seized the muzzle, trying to turn it.

A shower of burning poison drenched his face, especially his left eye. Intense pain rocked the minotaur, and he cried out. Aryx's eye felt as if someone had plunged a freshly forged dagger into it. Stunned by the agony, he at last lost his grip on his weapon.

Aryx fell to one knee, clutching his wounded face. He waited for the creature to drive the lance through his heart, knowing that at least the torture in his eye would also end. However, a sword suddenly darted past the injured warrior, coming under the crustacean's defenses. The blade buried itself deep in the throat, and when the behemoth opened its maw to hiss, a steady hand pulled Aryx back out of reach. The crustacean collapsed, crushing the lance under its weight.

"Take this! I can't find the sword!" a familiar feminine voice shouted. A worn but still worthy battle-axe had been thrust into his hand. Aryx had just enough time to glance back through his remaining eye and recognize Delara. With her help, he rose, trying to turn his pain into strength.

The undersea dwellers surged forward again, threatening to swarm over Aryx and Delara. He tried to push her away. "Get back to safety!"

"I'm not leaving you!" She stood fast at his side, already prepared to meet the first creature, knowing it would be her last foe.

A blaze of light from behind Aryx suddenly brought the shelled abominations up short. Delara used their sudden hesitation to pull Aryx back a step or two. He glanced behind her to see the cause of the crustaceans' consternation and discovered that Seph had returned . . . with more than a few supporters.

Dozens and dozens of minotaurs bearing fiery torches hurried through the back ranks of the fighters, spreading out as far as the eye could see.

The flames flickered eerily in the bulbous orbs of the crustaceans. The behemoths hesitated but did not retreat. Several weaved uncertainly.

"Bring the torches to the forefront!" Aryx called, better able to fight his pain in the face of growing hope.

As one, the torchbearers thrust their brands forward. Aryx, Delara, and the other defenders shifted ranks to allow them gaps.

The crustaceans had been fighting in good order, but now they stirred uneasily, beginning to lose some semblance of an organized force. Although they still had not retreated, they no longer moved with much determination.

"Attack now!" Aryx ordered. He and Delara flanked Seph, who carried a huge torch, requiring both hands to hold it. "Now!"

Fire and steel lunged at the first ranks of the crustaceans. A few backed away, while others froze. Some attempted to fight, but without a cohesive effort on the part of all, the reavers were at last forced back. Aryx cut down one foe so easily he almost felt ashamed, but the memories of his ship urged him onward.

Raising his axe high and giving a loud war cry, Aryx plunged headfirst into the enemy. Those with him rallied to his cry. The minotaur line surged on, first where Aryx and his band stood, then farther and farther along each side.

Far to his right, he noted that even Carnelia's talon carried torches now, and the knights, utilizing a feint-and-lunge technique, had begun cutting their way through the enemy. Aryx tried to utilize the same technique, adjusting it for the use of his axe.

"I passed word along to any runners or riders!" Seph yelled. "They're gathering torches everywhere!"

Aryx nodded, saving his breath. His arms felt as if iron shackles ending in lead weights had been attached to them, but still he somehow found the strength to fight on. The crustaceans continued to try to return to some semblance of order, but those in front proved reluctant to be first to face the flames. For the first time, Aryx caught sight of what might have been one of the leaders. Taller and wider than those around him, the massive creature stood impassively among the rest, eyeing the oncoming minotaurs. The snout bore a series of crimson streaks that the others did not have. Aryx tried to fight his way toward the creature, but, noticing him, the crustacean vanished among its fellows.

Finally daunted, the monstrous reavers started an orderly retreat. One line kept the minotaurs at length, despite the flames. Aryx realized the fire did not disturb them as much as it initially had. A worrisome thought for the future. Tonight, though, it had proven enough.

A long line began to establish itself as other warriors joined the fray, some of them from pockets of trapped defenders now rescued by Aryx's band. Knights added their strength as well, although most formed new talons alongside Carnelia's. Of Broedius or Rand, Aryx had yet to see a sign, and he began to wonder if they had survived this attack.

Although the defenders now had the advantage, the thick fog made for much continued danger. From time to time, out of the mists there came horrific missiles, lances tossed by strong, accurate arms. That the crustaceans could see quite well, despite the thick fog, came as no surprise to Aryx. He recalled all too well the precision with which they had moved aboard the *Kraken's Eye*. He shouted out warnings, trying to keep the defenders low, but many paid no heed, often standing straight in an attempt to see farther ahead. A veteran female warrior clutched her throat as a barbed spear sank through it. A husky brown male carrying a massive torch grunted in pain as the edge of another lance tore away the flesh on the side of his leg. He staggered but held on to the torch long enough for someone else to take it from him.

The defenders had to divide up as they neared the docks. Aryx and a handful of others, including his brother and Delara, wended their way down to the end of one dock, trying to keep an eye out for stragglers. Already a few careless searchers, believing the abominations all ahead of them, had fallen prey to a few defiant invaders, who attacked from inside buildings, beneath platforms, and, where the ground proved most moist, under the very feet of their adversaries. Aryx quickly passed word along that any soft ground had to be watched, but he knew the warning would not spread fast enough to save some.

The lapping of the waves as the tide shifted created a sense of peace that masked the still-present danger of attack. Four of Aryx's party made their way across another dock, while Aryx and Delara, with Seph right behind, led three others along the shoreline. The going was slow, since every bit of ground had to be studied. Even the docks required inch-by-inch searching. The shallow water beneath provided perfect cover for lingering crustaceans.

Aryx's head throbbed, and pain coursed through his damaged eye, but he didn't let anyone know just how much it hurt. Unable to see anything on his left, the wounded minotaur constantly turned his head from side to side as he searched.

Those who did not know him paid his actions little mind, but Delara especially watched him, an expression of concern occasionally crossing her features. She said nothing, but he noted that she often stayed to his left, possibly to make up for his impairment.

The search for the enemy grew more treacherous as they treaded the shoreline. Some of the warriors who had joined them earlier began to grow careless, perhaps thinking the region was secure. Aryx, however, knew better.

"Be careful about that sandy region there!" he called to one of the newcomers. "They can pull you down in seconds! Watch for shifting sand!"

"Aye!"

"I wish this fog would lift," grumbled Delara. "I can barely see the pair of you, much less Neru back on the dock."

"The mists faded a bit in the city," Seph pointed out, "but here it seems even thicker than before!"

"Which is why we've got to be careful." Aryx took another step and found himself standing ankle deep in water. "We go no farther! If they've retreated into the sea, we can't do much about that."

"Will they come back?" asked a warrior unfamiliar to him. The tall, black-furred male, a silver stripe running across his shoulder, had the same look of trust that so many of the others who had joined Aryx wore. They eyed him as they would have someone like General Geryl, which made the weary young mariner not at all happy. Aryx claimed to be no Kaz or Geryl. They were known champions of the realm; he had done only what duty demanded of him. Unfortunately, no one else appeared to see it that way.

"I don't know. Probably. Until this fog breaks, we're likely going to—"

A shout from the direction where he had sent the other minotaurs silenced him.

"That was Neru!" Delara tried to peer through the fog. "I can't see him, but I think I hear weapons clashing!"

"Go, then!" The entire band started toward the mist-enshrouded docks, but Aryx managed only a few steps before the throbbing grew so intense that he nearly fell to his knees. The others, caught up in trying to reach those in trouble, vanished ahead of him into the fog.

For the first time, Aryx wished that he still had the Sword of Tears. He wondered where the sinister blade had fallen. At least the blade could have reassured him a little, perhaps even muted the throbbing in his head and the intense pain coursing through what remained of his burned eye. Still, Aryx should have known better than to trust the demon blade. Hadn't it been Sargonnas's weapon? Like the god, it had not proven up to the promises it had conveyed.

Blinking away the tears clouding his good eye, the exhausted warrior stumbled toward the others. He still couldn't make them out, but he could hear the cries and clangs of combat. Axe held tight, Aryx hoped he would not be too late to help.

An explosion of sand gave him the only warning he had. Aryx whirled toward his blind side, swinging his axe, as a huge shadow loomed over him. The underwater dweller wielded two swords, and with one of them, he readily parried the minotaur's strike. The force of the crustacean's counterattack ripped the war axe from Aryx's hand, sending it flying into the water.

The attack also threw the warrior back. Aryx lay sprawled on the shore, watching with dismay as the lumbering creature loomed over him, scythe swords raised high. Aryx grabbed at the sand, hoping to find a rock, a stick, anything he could use to defend himself.

His hand fell upon what felt like the hilt of a sword, perhaps one lost by an earlier defender. Unable to believe his luck, he reacted instinctively, bringing the blade around even as the crimson and white monstrosity attacked. Aryx's sword shattered one of the attacker's weapons, then sank into the creature's unprotected throat. His foe shivered, dropping the other weapon. Aryx and the crustacean stared at one another, neither initially able to believe what had just happened.

Recovering, the minotaur tried to raise himself up so that he could push the blade in deeper, but in doing so, Aryx brought himself within range of the creature's massive claws. Hissing, the wounded crustacean swatted him on the injured side of his face, unleashing waves of excruciating pain.

He heard someone, perhaps Delara, call out his name. A crushing force pushed every bit of air from his lungs. Unable to fight both the pain and the lack of breath, Aryx blacked out, not at all certain that he would ever awaken.

# An Eye for an Eye

## Chapter Ten

Subcommander Drejjen cursed the fog. He cursed the shelled horrors that had emerged from it, and in the process, he cursed the minotaur warriors under his command, who could not seem to fight the way he intended them to. The fact that the orders he had given had been at times contradictory or put the minotaurs into hard-pressed situations did not occur to him. The failure *had* to lie in the locals, who did everything they could to frustrate the Knights of Takhisis, even during a crisis.

Now they even argued against his orders to clear the area of bodies. Thanks in great part to someone's clever suggestion to use torches against the overgrown lobsters, Drejjen's talon had finally turned the tide in this sector. The minotaurs had played some small part, adding numbers to offset those of the monsters, but if they thought they could rest now, Drejjen assured them that they were mistaken.

For creatures claiming to be fastidious, their reluctance to clean up the mess seemed contradictory. Did they expect the knights to dirty themselves with such a task? Drejjen and his men had enough to do, what with patrolling the area and keeping the minotaurs in line. The stench rising from the hideous corpses should have been all the encouragement the natives needed, but some had already sneaked off, supposedly to attend to loved ones.

"Sloppy," he muttered. "Undisciplined beastmen!" Drejjen coughed, then coughed again. "Damned fog. . . ."

Some of the minotaurs coughed as well, but he paid no mind. A little cough meant nothing, not to a Knight of Takhisis.

One of the beastmen began gathering the shelled corpses into a pile, clearly with the intention of creating a pyre. Drejjen cursed. The fool minotaur would probably burn down the entire district! Drejjen spurred his weary mount toward the warrior, in the end nearly running the minotaur down.

"What in the Lady's name do you think you're doing, bull?"

A fresh scar crossed the dark brown minotaur's muzzle. Tired as he appeared, he still answered defiantly, "Getting ready to burn these foul bodies! What does it look like?"

The subcommander thought of striking the bull in the face for his arrogant attitude, but decided he had better things to do. "It looks like you're trying to burn the city to the ground!"

The minotaur looked at him as if he had gone mad. "The bodies are far from any wooden structure! I checked the direction and strength of the wind and even built up a ring around the mound! This is the best spot to burn them, human! What else would you have me do with them?"

"Throw them in the harbor, of course."

"All these corpses? They'll all rot and foul the water!" He coughed. "They smell bad enough now. What do you think they'd be like after a few days in the water?"

Drejjen had finally had enough. "That is an order! You know how to understand a simple order, don't you? Although judging by the battle, it's no wonder you can never win your wars!"

The vein in the minotaur's neck throbbed. Every muscle on the beastman grew taut. The subcommander put a hand on the hilt of his weapon just in case the creature tried to attack him. Drejjen almost wished the minotaur would attack. He wanted some excuse to punish the whole lot of them for their insubordination and carelessness during the battle.

Unfortunately, the beastman did not attack. Instead, he snorted and turned back to the pile of stinking corpses. "As you wish . . . sir."

A satisfied grin spread over the subcommander's narrow, lupine face. Once again he had cowed one of the bulls. The experience gave him tremendous satisfaction. He watched for a time as the once-defiant warrior summoned some of his fellows and began dismantling the makeshift pyre. One of them managed to find a cart and a pair of horses, and the rest of the minotaurs began loading the bodies onto it.

A coughing fit came over the subcommander, one that would not stop until he managed to take a sip of water from the sack on his mount's saddle. Drejjen dearly looked forward to leaving the minotaur isles, the sooner the better. The weather here might suit the smelly bulls, but it did nothing for him. Now that the knights had won the day—or rather, evening—perhaps Lord Broedius would see things his way by packing the minotaurs in ships like the cattle they were and sailing off for the mainland. No need to waste all this time training and gathering supplies. The minotaurs were foot soldiers, bodies to be put in the path of lances and arrows so they could weary the enemy for the Knights of Takhisis.

Another coughing fit overcame him. As he drank, Drejjen watched the first load of dead abominations roll off toward the harbor. No, he would not miss anything about this damnable realm, especially the climate. Once back on Ansalon, the subcommander could at least finally rid himself of this annoying cough. . . .

*     *     *     *     *

". . . nothing else I can do for him."

"What about the other eye? Is it also damaged?"

"I don't think so, but— He stirs!"

Pain wracked Aryx, pain that meant, for the second time, he had cheated death. A small part of him regretted that, for it meant living with his guilt. At least his head didn't throb so much, and his eyes . . . *eye* . . .

"Aryx? Can you hear me?"

Delara's voice. He thought he had recognized it a moment ago. Aryx started to open his good eye, then hesitated. Delara had feared that he had lost that one, too. What if the last of the crustaceans had left him entirely blind?

He had no choice. Holding his breath, Aryx forced open his eyelids. New pain jolted the left one, and he saw only darkness. But from the right eye, the wounded minotaur sensed light . . . light that gradually coalesced into first a room, then shapes, then at last into people.

The room looked vaguely familiar, but it took the wounded warrior several seconds to identify it as the one occupied by the human cleric. Not so great a surprise, since the only one who could have possibly helped him after his substantial injuries would have been Rand. Intending to thank him, Aryx looked around for the pale, blond human, but instead found Delara again.

"Aryx . . ." Noting that he could obviously see her, she reached down and hugged him.

"By Orilg's broken horn!" A second figure clutched him, this time Seph.

Aryx managed to get one arm around Delara, but when he tried to bring the other to Seph, he realized his hand still gripped something. Did he still hold on to the weapon that he had found by the docks?

*Welcome back from the Abyss, Master . . .* the mocking voice of the Sword of Tears remarked.

He should have known. Somehow it had returned to him just before it would have been too late. Aryx supposed he should be grateful to the enchanted artifact, but he also wondered why it had taken it so long. If the Sword of Tears could come to him of its own volition, it should have been able to do that right after he had lost it. Once again the weakened minotaur realized that he could not entirely trust Sargonnas's legacy.

A figure clad in the ebony armor of the Knights of Takhisis loomed over him. It took Aryx a moment to focus on the face of Carnelia. "How do you feel, bull?"

Aryx started to laugh at the insipid question, but pain wracked him again, especially in what remained of his left eye. "What you see should tell you, human."

"I thought as much." To his surprise, she reached out her hand. "Well fought out there, warrior."

He managed to briefly take the proffered hand. "Also you."

"Your force kept its lines intact and countered the invaders admirably. The notion of the torches worked well."

"I fought only for my land, as any would. As for the torches, the *Kraken's Eye* taught me something, I guess."

Rand came up beside Carnelia, placing his arm around her in a display so open that Aryx could only stare. Carnelia reddened slightly but did not push the arm away.

"Would that we had all learned from your ship," the cleric said. "Perhaps we could have prevented some of the slaughter."

Mention of the deaths stirred Aryx. "The underwater dwellers! Have they—are they still—"

"Have they been driven from Nethosak?" a brusque voice rumbled. The clatter of armor presaged none other than Lord Broedius himself. The ebony eyes looked not so dark now, as if the toll of the battle had taken something from the knight. He looked drawn in the rest of the face, too. "Not yet, but it seems hopeful. Someone"—he eyed Aryx—"found their weakness. Because of that, the city still stands, albeit with terrible damage."

"What about the rest of Mithas?"

"We've reports of heavy fighting in places, mostly in the more populated regions. There's been no contact with some of the settlements on the eastern side of your island. As for Kothas, the Knights of the Thorn finally made contact with their brethren there. Kalpethis—your Morthosak—suffered heavily in its western sector, especially the port."

"They've been concentrating on the major cities," Carnelia added. "Especially the capitals. With the fog still hovering over everything and the danger of more of them lurking in the waters of the harbor, we've not had time to assess the damage to the ships, but we suspect it's heavy."

Aryx frowned. "If they destroy all the ships, then they could keep us here and eventually starve us out."

"That's a concern we've considered, Aryx," the knight commander agreed, "but I suspect it's not likely. Whatever commands these creatures doesn't strike me as willing to wait so long."

The wounded minotaur had to agree. He also believed that the crustacean's master reveled in the carnage, even the deaths of its own warriors.

"At the moment, we've a stalemate," the mustached commander continued, "but the longer the fog holds, the worse our position becomes. They live within it, see through it as we see on a bright, clear day." He coughed slightly. "And they can probably breathe the damned stuff a sight easier."

Aryx at last attempted to rise to a sitting position. Rand had utilized his own bed for the minotaur, and while Aryx felt grateful, he wondered why everyone gathered around him as if he had been crowned emperor. Lord Broedius surely had more important tasks with which to deal than one minotaur warrior's wounds.

"I'm sorry about the eye," Rand finally said. "Too much of the creature's acidic blood got into it, and I suspect it had never fully healed after the battle on your ship."

"No matter. The pain's all but gone." Something of a lie, but the human had already done so much for him that he couldn't let Rand feel guilty. Aryx started to raise his hands to his face, then recalled that he still gripped the sword.

"None of us could pry it from you," Delara explained. "After we dragged the carcass of the monster off you, we tried, but unless we cut off your hand, too . . ."

"So you're sticking with me now?" he asked the demon blade, more than a hint of sarcasm in his tone.

No response came from the sword.

"Release my hand."

Immediately he felt his fingers relax. Aryx pulled his hand from the hilt, then flexed his fingers and wrist. Satisfied, he peered around at the others. "What's going on here?"

Rand responded first. "What do you mean?"

"Seph and Delara I understand. Perhaps even you, cleric. Why, though, are these two here?" The gray minotaur indicated the Knights of Takhisis. "Of what importance is one native warrior to you, Lord Broedius?"

"Normally . . . none," responded the knight commander. Some of the spark returned to his ebony eyes. "But my niece has given me a vivid description of a battle that might easily have been lost. Instead, it was salvaged by the efforts of one minotaur, a minotaur who also led a force with which she fought side by side."

"I did nothing but try to save my home, and there's no guarantee I did even that."

"But if you hadn't acted as you did, there wouldn't be the chance to yet do that, bull."

Aryx shook his head. "I didn't do anything. Chance put me where I was."

"Or the hand of Kiri-Jolith," suggested Rand.

"Maybe."

Carnelia stepped forward. "Aryx, I've had little love for your kind. As my uncle has pointed out, your people killed my father, something which I can never forgive. But you weren't one of those responsible. If not for your efforts, I will willingly admit, I suspect my lines wouldn't have held against those abominations."

"It might have held . . . especially if you'd been better at using those under your command." Aryx silently cursed his mouth when he saw the look that flashed over Carnelia's face.

Camaraderie gave way to burgeoning fury. The minotaur immediately explained. "Not through any fault of your own, human! Lord Broedius, your niece spoke of how our two forces fought side by side, pushing back the foe with more success than in most areas."

"So she did."

"And what were the losses for us, compared to those talons where the minotaurs took their orders directly from your subcommanders?"

Broedius stroked his dark mustache as he pondered. "For most talons, the casualties were considerably higher."

"Especially among the minotaurs?"

"I fail to see the relevance of—"

Aryx snorted. "Of course not! You knights never *have*, although maybe your niece has some inkling." When Carnelia said nothing, he added, "It's true there's no love lost between our two sides, Lord Broedius. We care little for being told that we're to follow the dictates of a human, someone who understands nothing of our kind. Yet for the most part, my people tried, and in return we were barely treated better than the cattle your race likes to think we're descended from."

"What is your point, bull?"

The knight commander's use of the last word only proved Aryx's case. "There it is. I'm only a young warrior, not even the captain of my own ship, and what I say I know Seph and Delara understand all too well, too, even if you don't. Lord Broedius, Sargonnas might have delivered us to you, but we'll not be slave soldiers again! Allies, yes, but not fodder for your overzealous subcommanders, most of whom, like Drejjen, see nothing wrong with throwing minotaurs haphazardly into battle."

"Drejjen's minotaurs suffered the highest casualties," Carnelia interjected quietly. Her fury at Aryx had abated.

"You fail to recall that we have been sanctioned by our Lady, minotaur! We are destined, as our great Vision shows, to be the saviors, then masters, of all Krynn!"

"A task made easier with allies, not slaves. Krynn is our world, too, and after this battle, I can promise you that my people won't rest until the threat of the Chaos creatures is at an end. But we'll fight more willingly if our chains are removed, and you should understand that, Lord Broedius."

The broad-shouldered knight crossed his arms. His set expression made it impossible for Aryx to judge whether or not he had reached Broedius. Even the eyes told nothing, only reflecting back the minotaur's disfigured face.

"I came here, minotaur, to congratulate the warrior who helped us fend off this assault. I might not have done even that if Carnelia had not spoken in your behalf. I underestimated your knowledge of what we faced, I'll admit that, and so I'll let you continue to talk, for the moment, without fear of punishment."

*Take me up,* the Sword of Tears suddenly urged, *and he will listen more willingly. . . .*

Aryx refused to even respond to the demon blade's suggestion. Instead, he met the knight's gaze with his own, making certain that Broedius could plainly see the minotaur's scars of war. "You no longer have any reason to hold the emperor, and especially the generals. By now you must see what truly happened to your missing sentries."

"We told him what nearly happened to you when you went to investigate," Delara added.

"Then there can't be any other reason to hold them."

"Insubordination, perhaps?" Broedius calmly suggested.

"They did nothing but protest wrongs against those under their commands, which even the Knights of Takhisis permit at times, I've noticed."

"Within limits."

Aryx grew more and more frustrated at Broedius's stubbornness. "All right! You want us to fight this war your queen has called your destiny! We want to fight this war for our survival! We outnumber you greatly, even if reinforcements arrive! Worse for you, the Blessed One has disappeared! Nothing binds us to you as servants anymore, Lord Broedius. Treat us as allies, and together not even the greatest host of Chaos's creatures will be able to overcome us!"

He had said it. At long last, he had said it. All the knight commander had to do was give the minotaurs their due and his expedition could continue on, this time with less chance of disaster fomenting from within. Aryx did not expect everyone on both sides to be satisfied, but both forces stood a far better chance with cooperation than with division.

"The notion has merit," Rand contributed.

Carnelia looked at her uncle, who remained silent, staring past Aryx. He knew that Broedius might possibly despise the minotaurs more than Carnelia ever had, but Aryx hoped that

Broedius's intelligence, combined with his determination to fulfill the wills of both the distant Lord Ariakan and the dread goddess Takhisis, would make him see reason. If not, then the knights and minotaurs would, in the long run, be doomed to failure.

"Carnelia," Broedius finally began, "issue orders for the release of Emperor Chot, the council of the Supreme Circle, and all generals of the minotaur legions currently under house arrest." She started to obey, but Broedius waved her to a halt. "The generals will report to me at first light—make that the fifth hour, since I doubt this fog'll lift enough to call it light—to discuss the distribution of native forces under native commanders subject to my ultimate control." When Carnelia hesitated, the senior knight frowned at her. "Go!"

"Yes, Broedius!" Saluting, she rushed from the chamber.

The knight commander gazed at Aryx once more. "Don't think that this gives you all you demanded, bull. Know, though, that I understand the need for less aggression between our forces, and so your suggestions have merit. I'll grant the minotaurs control of their own legions so long as those generals realize that final say in matters belongs to me. I'll not argue with a dozen different commanders on the correct course of action in the midst of a war."

"You may have some trouble convincing them on that last point."

The trace of a smile briefly formed on the face of Lord Broedius. "My task won't be to convince them. That will be yours."

"Mine?" Aryx stumbled out of the bed, almost ready to take up the Sword of Tears. "What do you mean?"

"When you stood beside Sargonnas and endangered yourself when the assassin struck, you created a certain myth about yourself. Now there is the growing legend of the minotaur hero who saved the imperial capital from the minions of Chaos. By the time you meet with the generals, I daresay even they will know of your accomplishments this day."

Much to his dismay, Seph substantiated the human's words. "It's true, Aryx! The ones who followed you into battle have spread the word to others! They all saw how you waded into the invaders with the sword, cutting through them like Orilg himself!"

"That was the sword, not I!"

"A sword can only do what its wielder bids it to do," Broedius remarked. "Lord Ariakan himself said something of that sort."

None of them understood just how alive and independent the sword truly was, and Aryx doubted that the sinister blade would reveal the truth about itself now. "I'm no Orilg!"

"Orilg probably made similar denials about earlier champions when he lived, bull. Understand me; you've no voice in this matter. I give you the opportunity to forge the alliance of which you spoke. Whether you choose to succeed is entirely up to you." The knight commander gave him a salute. "For your actions in the defense of her Lady's expedition, I commend you. The generals will be gathered here by the fifth hour. You'll have your chance to speak with them while I go over damage assessments."

"I won't do this, Broedius!"

"Then we may all perish on this island." With that said, the knight commander marched out of the room, leaving an angry and still unsteady warrior behind.

Delara put a comforting hand on his shoulder. "You need to rest, Aryx! Lie down."

"He's mad! Don't any of you see that?"

"Aryx . . ." Rand whispered.

He turned on the human, then hesitated. Standing, Aryx could at last see Rand up close, and what he saw disturbed him. Despite how the cleric had handled himself while the knights had been present, the injured minotaur saw that Rand had clearly been through some fierce trial. As pale as the human had always looked, he seemed nearly as white as snow now. At some point during Aryx's argument with Broedius, Rand had seized a nearby chair for support, and this he clutched now, almost seeming ready to collapse.

"What ails you, cleric?"

"Forgive me for revealing too much. I did not want Broedius to know how much my work has taxed me. It seems—it seems to take more effort lately to draw from my patron, perhaps because he, too, has other matters to deal with. Also, I find that working with mages can present great difficulties."

"What difficulties? What are you attempting, human?"

Rand shrugged. "Among other things, trying to rid the islands of this cursed fog. I feel that without it, we could deal with the crustaceans, but neither prayers nor incantations have accomplished much. We managed to cause it to thin a bit in some regions."

"It did disperse a bit during the last part of the battle," Seph offered.

"I can only hope it did. Two of the Knights of the Thorn will be unable to cast spells for a day . . . a day we likely do not have. There is no word from the south, and the only messages we get from Kothas are short ones through a sickly mage with a talent for such spells. I think there will be a second assault on Lacynos—Nethosak—before long, and that this one will be worse than the first."

Aryx agreed. "And fire won't help us nearly as much as it did the first time. You know that."

"I do. That which controls them will not permit the same trick twice, not on this scale. That is why I feel we must remove this fog. It is an essential part of our adversaries. Without it, I believe these creatures will rout." He shook his head. "But some other spell must be utilized, something that hasn't been tried before. I have some thoughts . . . wild ones, I admit."

The injured minotaur's guilt increased. "And you've been attending me as well. Get some sleep, cleric. You need it more than I."

"I supposed I must," Rand agreed ruefully.

"Seph . . . Delara . . . I might need your assistance. My thanks for the use of your chambers, human, but by rights, you should be sleeping here. I'll return to . . ." Aryx hesitated, not at all certain where he should go now that Sargonnas's temple lay in ruins. Delara had offered refuge at her clan house if he did not care to return to his own, but . . .

Rand prevented them from leaving. "Aryx, Broedius wants you to speak with the minotaur generals at the fifth hour. If you leave here, you won't manage more than an hour or two of sleep. Stay here. There are other rooms in this quarter. The Knights of Takhisis prefer to live among company other than mine. Perhaps you and your friends would be interested. . . ."

A sound suggestion, and one that Aryx, who could feel his legs wanting to buckle, readily took up. "All right, then. Thank you, cleric."

"My name is Rand, Aryx."

"Thank you . . . *Rand*."

The thin, pale human led them to the doorway. "Let me show you the way, so you can all get some rest." His face darkened. "I suspect we will get very little rest from here on."

He led them to some empty rooms just a few yards from his own chambers. Clearly these, too, had belonged to elders of the clan. The finely crafted furniture, flowing drapes, and elaborate displays where once prized weapons had hung were unmistakable signs of their owners' high status. Aryx, though, cared little about status at the moment, seeing only that the bed, while more extravagant than his preferences, would serve well for sleeping.

Seph and Delara were given similar rooms adjacent to Aryx's. The minotaurs, more used to sharing quarters with family and comrades, felt a little guilty with so much room for each of them, but Rand pointed out that the entire hall remained empty. Had they desired so, they could have chosen any room. While the knights maintained control of the house, the clan elders would not return.

"Think of these bedrooms as the price of war," the cleric commented with a ghost of humor in his tone.

The others left Aryx. The minotaur fell onto the bed, twinges of pain still causing him to twitch now and then. He had kept his true condition secret from the others, not wanting them to worry. Given time and rest, he knew that much of the pain would fade. His eye might never heal completely, but the warrior hoped that someday he would become used to it.

The Sword of Tears hung from his scabbard, which in turn hung on a hook near the bed. The demon blade had said nothing, which disturbed Aryx. He felt that it kept secrets from him, secrets that might endanger not only him but also his companions. What could they be, though?

Aryx never got the opportunity to think the question through, for exhaustion at last caught up with him and he fell into a deep sleep.

And in that deep, deep sleep, he dreamed. . . .

* * * * *

A hand the size of a dragon plucked him from the bed, catching him just as he opened his eye. Aryx tried to cry out, but no words came from his mouth. The hand raised him high into the air, so high that he could see all of the fog-enshrouded minotaur isles and then all of Ansalon. Higher and higher he went, so that soon he could make out the entire disk of Krynn as seen from one side.

And then a voice boomed, "You don't have to frighten him half to death!"

A second voice, more fluent than the first, rumbled, "I hardly think I've frightened him, old comrade! He is one your grandchildren, after all, is he not?"

"He has the temper, all right. I just hope he doesn't make the same sort of mistakes. . . ."

Standing on the open palm of the great hand, Aryx turned about, trying to see the faces of the giants. Instead, he first made out a set of stars formed into a familiar pattern. The dusky gray minotaur wracked his brain, then cursed himself for not immediately recognizing the constellation of Kiri-Jolith.

As if recognition had been all it needed, the constellation suddenly transformed. Golden eyes stared out from a majestic bison head, eyes that seemed to find favor with Aryx. It made the minotaur calm . . . somewhat.

The bison spoke. "Hail to you, Aryximaraki de-Orilg! Hail to you, warrior!"

"You'll deafen him, you will," grunted the other, still unseen, speaker.

The god ignored his companion. Bringing Aryx up closer to his golden eyes, Kiri-Jolith seemed fascinated by what he saw. A twinkle of amusement in the divine warrior's gaze unsettled the young minotaur. Kaz Dragonslayer had once said that when a god had his eye on you, it's time to start praying. Aryx felt like doing so now, if he could only think of someone else to whom to pray.

"Aryximaraki," Kiri-Jolith began, all traces of humor gone. "Circumstance chose you . . . circumstance or fate, matters which even we gods cannot always control."

The invisible speaker snorted. "Bad luck, he means."

"But although you were beaten back, you returned to the fray even stronger than before. . . ."

"Spare the rehashing of old sayings! You all talk too much! Show him and be done with it!"

The bison-headed god glanced at the darkness where the other should have been, now at last a little annoyed. "As you wish, old comrade."

The god began to fold his hand into a fist. With nowhere to run, Aryx knelt with his arms over his head, awaiting the inevitable. The gargantuan fingers folded in on him, cutting off all light.

"Behold . . ." Kiri-Jolith uttered.

Aryx found himself floating in emptiness so dark, so desperate, that immediately he knew it could only be one place . . . the Abyss. Unable to prevent it, Aryx felt himself drawn deeper into that terrible place. All perspective went awry. Everything he had always known to be true about the physical world suddenly turned false in his head. The laws that governed this place had been created elsewhere, using entirely different guidelines. He knew all of this in a rush and knew that the source of this knowledge had to be Kiri-Jolith.

Then a great force scattered the darkness, bringing about a kaleidoscope of maddening colors and sounds, and in the center of it all, Aryx beheld several astonishing figures locked in mortal combat.

The battle of the gods . . .

Aryx knew this also, without even trying. He saw each of them as he had been raised to think of them. Brave, majestic Paladine, the platinum dragon and the armored knight both. From his maw, the glittering dragon let forth a shower of silver, and from his sword, the knight cut an electrifying arc. Aryx tried to focus on one form or another of the god, only to find instead that knight and dragon became what looked to be the most befuddled old human wizard he could have imagined . . . and yet somehow this form comforted him most.

A war cry tore his attention from Paladine, and there, with his back to the minotaur, stood his own patron, Kiri-Jolith. The bison-headed god carried a sword in one hand and a war axe in the other. Bringing both together with a tremendous crash, the God of Just Causes released a torrent of blue rain that sparkled with energy.

One after another, gods, most bearing human forms, flickered into and out of existence. Gilean, a tall, gray, thin figure, held a tome-shaped shield up before him, his expression unreadable. Near him stood Mishakal, a look of extreme sadness upon her delicate yet determined face. Even Reorx fought, his great war hammer striking some invisible surface again and again. Of all of them, the dwarf looked the most frustrated, the most upset, as if he took some personal blame for the struggle.

Of Takhisis, there was no sign.

She did not appear to be alone in her absence either. Very few of those termed the darker gods seemed to be in evidence, although one long, slim robed figure did grow to prominence for a time. By his ebony robes, he most resembled the wizards, and so Aryx assumed him to be Nuitari. Near the robed deity seemed to be a wild, watery female with eyes much like the one next to her, save that a savage passion ruled them. The warrior swallowed, for along with Sargonnas and Kiri-Jolith, what seafaring minotaur did not recognize turbulent Zeboim?

Aryx understood that these images were of his own design, that any of the gods could wear a thousand shapes a day if they so chose. It did not surprise him, then, when he saw Sargonnas just as he had seen him in the temple. Now, however, the pallid figure wore a complete suit of armor, including a visored and horned helm of frightening design. The visor bore the distorted image of a raging minotaur warrior, and Sargonnas fought like one, raising a weapon much like the Sword of Tears high and unleashing its power . . .

. . . but against what? Against what did the gods unleash their combined might?

In the blinding flashes of power, Aryx at last thought he glimpsed something. With his one good eye, he tried to focus on it, this time noting what seemed to be a form of Promethean proportions. It never remained in focus long, but more and more he thought it resembled some fiery giant. The visage, barely viewed, could only be described as chaotic, mad. To stare too long into even that partially seen countenance threatened to drive the minotaur mad as well, and so he quickly tore his gaze from it.

Father Chaos . . . the Father of All and of Nothing. He had heard the names from Sargonnas, and now he understood some of what they meant. A god more powerful than any of the gods, an elder god who, from the looks of him, might very well be the creator of Krynn's deities.

Aryx looked again at the figure in crimson and black armor, saw the strain beneath the fury, and knew that Sargonnas and the others were tiring. He recalled the Horned One's words about fighting on more than one plane and at last realized how much of a burden these few must be putting on themselves, Sargonnas especially. Did Kiri-Jolith also wage other battles at the same time? Was that why he could protect his children no better than his darker counterpart had?

Then, just as abruptly as he had been thrust into the battle, Aryx found himself again perched on the vast palm of Kiri-Jolith. He looked up at the god, for the first time seeing the great weariness, the lines of effort, in the majestic warrior's face.

"That which has been," the God of Just Causes explained. "The war still rages, but we who defend are fewer."

The remark instigated a question from Aryx, who had not thought of even daring to speak before now. "Sargonnas?"

"Probably run off with that harridan of his," muttered the unseen one. "So much for the honorable and brave God of Vengeance!"

"Sargonnas is not Takhisis," Kiri-Jolith replied to his companion. To Aryx, he answered, "Where the Horned One is, even I cannot say, but if he has not fallen to the Father of All and of Nothing, then he fights. Somehow, somewhere, he fights."

His first question resolved, the mortal dared to ask a second, more important one. "What do you want of me? What *more* do you want from me?"

"Nothing that you will not give freely, warrior."

"Finish it, Kiri," interrupted the unnamed other, sounding more and more impatient. "Finish with him. Give him the blasted eye."

Eye? Aryx cared little for the sound of that.

His fears grew stronger as the god's expression turned troubling. "Yes . . . the eye."

Another gigantic hand appeared, and with it, the bison-headed god reached up among the other stars, plucking at last a faint jade one from an obscure corner of the heavens. He brought the star down, and as the other hand neared, Aryx saw that the god had not seized a star after all, but rather a tiny emerald stone carved into a narrow oval shape.

"Would that I could give you something more in place of that which you lost, but time is short. Even this would have been more than I dared, but someone—" Kiri-Jolith glanced toward the direction from which the other voice ever came "—someone insisted that you were owed."

Again the other broke in. "Owed something other than that eye!"

"But it is all I can give for now. Hear me, Aryximaraki, I have saved this, not knowing for certain what to do with it until now. Perhaps Gilean or frustrating Zivilyn, who cannot point to us one proper future, although our very existences might depend upon it, could have told me why . . . if he cared. Now, though, I find purpose for my ancient act. This was meant for you, minotaur, for readily taking on a mantle that you did not choose, for becoming one of those who shape the course of action."

Aryx wanted to point out that he would not have had to do so if the gods had been of greater use to those they claimed to watch over. Clearly, although they wore mortal forms, the gods did not always think in mortal terms. So much could have been avoided if they had acted with more honor, more responsibility. For all that Aryx had been through, the gods wanted to reward Aryx with a single jewel. The notion actually stirred fresh the embers of the minotaur's ire. What good was a jewel during these times of crisis? If Mithas and Kothas were destroyed, not all the gold and gems in Ansalon would bring it back. "Spare me your rewards, Kiri-Jolith! I'll have little to spend them on if my family, my people, are destroyed by these monsters of Chaos!" He straightened, secretly marveling that he had the courage to stand up against the gods. "Is that all your kind think we mortals care about? Treasures and trifles? I've lost one brother so far, and possibly more, and you offer me some paltry treasure?"

"No . . . I offer you an eye for an eye."

The minotaur frowned. "What do you mean?"

The god held the emerald jewel so that Aryx could study it. "An eye for an eye. What the Coil's Magori warriors stole, I can return . . . albeit in somewhat different form."

The Coil? The Magori? Aryx started to ask the God of Just Causes about the names, but then at last the intricate details of the gem seized his attention. No simple stone this, after all. An eye of finest crystal stared back at the warrior, but not an eye with which a minotaur or even a human or elf would have been born. No, this eye had a reptilian cast to it, and more. The artisan who had carved it had imbued it with a sense of masterful guile and fiery life so startlingly real that Aryx almost thought that the eye appraised him in turn.

A false eye was still a false eye, though, however elaborate. His interest in it faded. "What do you expect me to do with that?"

"See things for what they are. Come closer, Aryximaraki."

The minotaur thought to decline the god's offer but found his body moving of its own accord across the vast palm. A swift glance at Kiri-Jolith quickly verified that the deity had decided to encourage the mortal's progress. Aryx would receive his unsettling gift whether the warrior truly wanted to or not.

"You will see as others see, but you will also see as others cannot. This is a gift with many sides, Aryximaraki. Learn to use them wisely."

"I don't want your—" was as far as Aryx got.

Kiri-Jolith did not throw the eye at him, but rather the gem flew from his huge fingers. Held in thrall by the god, Aryx could do nothing as the reptilian eye shot unerringly at his ruined socket. The minotaur braced himself, knowing that this would not be an easy acceptance.

"You'll need it, grandson," the other voice insisted, not without a little regret.

The emerald orb reached its target.

The minotaur roared in pain. However, instead of fire, ice coursed through him. A great chill shook Aryx, nearly sending him into a fit. He felt something moving, shifting in the damaged socket, something so cold his entire head felt almost numb.

"The pain will pass soon," the bison-headed god promised.

Suddenly he could see something with his left eye. The something remained only a dark blur for a time, then gradually solidified into the overwhelming head of Kiri-Jolith. The god, seemingly oblivious to what Aryx suffered, watched as his gift became a part of the minotaur.

The chilling pain at last began to fade, and as it did, Aryx's vision grew sharper. More and more he could see as he had before—no, even better, if he concentrated only on the left eye. The only unsettling thing about the view seemed to be a slight emerald cast to the world. Aryx shut his right eye and discovered that the world did indeed take on a greenish tint. Definitely unsettling, but he could become used to it. He would have to become used to it.

The God of Just Causes had indeed granted him a greater

gift than Aryx had initially supposed. The emerald coloring aside, the eye proved in every way superior to his old one. He had supposed that the new eye would only be cosmetic, that it would serve no true function. Knowing the gods, Aryx admitted to himself that he should have expected more. Gods did not give out useless trinkets. Dangerous ones, yes, but not useless.

Of course, Kaz Dragonslayer had been quoted more than once as saying that every gift of the gods had a price.

"When you wish to see beyond the surface, use only the dragon eye. It will reveal to you much more."

Aryx did not hear the rest, having focused on two words. "You said . . . 'dragon eye'?"

"From the eye of the ancient leviathan, Tyrannus Blood-bane, Aryximaraki, slain in the Age of Dreams."

Bloodbane. The dusky gray minotaur had heard that draconian surname in bard tales, something concerning the elves during the War of the Lance. He cared little for the thought of bearing any part of a dragon, much less from one called Tyrannus Bloodbane, but what choice did he have now? Besides, surely this dragon must be long dead if Kiri-Jolith had taken his eye.

"I don't like this!" the other voice warned. "You haven't even told him about—"

"He will know what he must know; I can do no more," Kiri-Jolith replied. "Time runs short, Aryximaraki. You must return now."

Return? Aryx did not know if this dream had any merit in reality, but his dream self could not return to the waking world without more from the god. Not for himself, no, but for all the others, his family and friends . . .

He turned on Kiri-Jolith, his fear for the others pushing him yet again to dare the bison-headed god's wrath. "You've given me an eye back, for which I thank you, but while we stand here, your children die all around you! We battle for our home, but the magic of gods battles against us, too! Those abominations from the sea have slaughtered far too many already! You claim some of my people as your own, yet we've been nothing but pawns of the Dark Queen for so long! If you are at all our god, then save your children!"

"You have the sword and you have the eye, and that is more than you think." Kiri-Jolith looked sad indeed. "I am doing what I can, Aryximaraki. Am I not sending you back to them?"

The massive bison head faded again into a constellation, and as it did, the hand upon which Aryx stood tilted, sending the helpless mortal plunging.

Caught between shock and fear, Aryx roared as he dropped toward the distant disk of Krynn. . . .

# Fragile Alliances

## Chapter Eleven

The Magori did not like the flames, perhaps because fire reminded them of that place from which they had come, a place to which they had no burning desire to return. Dismembering a few had convinced the rest that facing flame and foe would be better than earning the wrath of Father Chaos's most loyal and trusted servant. The Magori feared the most loyal servant more than they feared any flames. They would fight and slaughter, their endless numbers overwhelming the betrayer Sargonnas's children.

The serpentine segments writhed and slid about one another, some in agitation. There still existed for the Coil the annoyance that the betrayer Sargonnas had left no sign of his ending, no hint as to whether he had truly ceased to be. The Father of All and of Nothing would expect his most faithful servant to know the truth. Not knowing disturbed its otherwise intact sense of imminent triumph.

The betrayer had to be nonexistent; he *had* to be.

No matter. Whether or not the betrayer still existed, in but a short time, his so-called children would not. The Magori had already regrouped, this time urged to advance even if the defenders set both islands completely ablaze. All they needed to do was wait but a little longer, wait and let the very fog that protected the Magori weaken those upon the islands further. By this time, the enchanted mists had permeated everything, and that would soon make the daunting task of the insipid defenders yet more impossible.

One defender in particular interested the most faithful servant. One of the mortal creatures wielded a toy of the gods, a little pin that pricked too well. Why the little mortal had been granted this artifact of power, the Coil desired to know. Some last trick of Sargonnas's, perhaps, although in the end, a thousand little toys would not defeat the Father of All and of Nothing. Still, if the Coil seized this mortal and the weapon he wielded, it would surely please Father Chaos. Perhaps then he would grant the Coil blissful nothingness.

Yes, the servant of Chaos wanted this little mortal with the pin that pricked, wanted him very much. . . .

\* \* \* \* \*

Aryx bolted upright in bed, sweating. In his mind, he could still see himself falling, falling, falling. . . .

"A dream!" he muttered to himself. "A blasted dream!"

That helped calm him a bit. Aryx took a deep breath, relaxing himself even more. That he had dreamed of the gods did not surprise him; they had been in his thoughts much more than he had let the others know. Would that they were as evident in the waking world as they had been in his nightmares.

Aryx rose, wondering what hour it was. Perhaps only a few minutes after he had drifted off to sleep. The minotaur listened for activity but heard nothing. The best thing would be to search for a sentry and ask him. Of course, as tightly wound as Aryx now felt, he doubted he could have fallen asleep again anyway.

Arranging his kilt and harness, the dusky gray warrior debated taking with him the Sword of Tears. True, the journey might last only a few minutes there and back, but if the fifth hour approached, Aryx might not have time to return for his weapon. The demon blade could come to him of its own accord, but he did not want to count on that property. In fact, he did not want to count on any ability of the artifact save its skill at readily cutting through the armored shells of the Magori.

Magori? Aryx frowned, momentarily wondering where he had heard the curious name. The dream, of course. Kiri-Jolith had called the abominations the Magori and mentioned also that they were controlled by something known as the Coil, a servant of the Chaos. The former title somehow fit the crustaceans, but to think that Kiri-Jolith had actually imparted the information to Aryx would mean that the astonishing gift he had given to the minotaur also . . .

Suddenly he realized that he had been seeing out of both eyes.

Aryx stared at his left hand, shifting it farther to that direction. Not until he had stretched it back beyond his side did it disappear from view. Stunned, the minotaur shut his right lid. The world instantly took on an emerald hue, as if Aryx stared through the stone on the Sword of Tears.

Turning about, the troubled warrior searched for a mirror, any reflective surface in which he could inspect his appearance. He raced over to a small looking glass hanging near a weapons case and almost thrust his muzzle into it.

The scars from his blinding still remained, but the brown orb the dying reaver's acidic venom had ruined had now been replaced by one completely green, even the parts that were normally white. Even more startling, Aryx's left eye now had a different slant to it, one identical to that of a reptile or . . . or a dragon.

*From the eye of the ancient leviathan, Tyrannus Bloodbane, Aryximaraki, slain in the Age of Dreams . . .*

All true . . . the dream had been no dream, but a summons before the gods . . . or simply one god. Aryx realized he still did not know the identity of Kiri-Jolith's invisible companion, but surely it had to have been Habbakuk or some similar deity. That hardly mattered now, though. Aryx gingerly touched the bottom lid of the new eye, surprised to feel no pain.

The gifts of the gods generally had a price. He had thought such in the dream and did not change his mind now, seeing how the emerald eye glittered as he stared. Concentrating on his natural eye, Aryx uneasily noted how on his right he looked his old self, while on the left, it was as if another person—another creature, even—stared at him. He shivered, at last turning away from the mirror lest he be tempted to tear the god's gift from its socket.

What would the others say when they saw him? How could he answer their questions when they sought to know about the orb? Aryx cursed the gods in general. His ancestor, Kaz Dragonslayer, had spoken true: Trust in the gods to interfere in your life any way they could. Recalling more of the dream that had not been a dream, Aryx realized that in addition to Lord Broedius, Clan Orilg, and the minotaur generals, now two, and possibly more, gods had chosen him as their pawn in this war, again for no good reason that he could discern.

The worst part was that his own sense of honor would not let him shirk the roles thrust upon him even if Aryx knew himself inadequate.

His gaze fell upon the Sword of Tears. The minotaur's eyes went wide as he noted a dark aura around the sword, even those parts hidden by the sheath. He concentrated with his emerald eye and saw that the aura took on more solidity, as if some shield surrounded the artifact.

Aryx reached for the sheath. "Do you know anything about this gift? And what's this foul glow you've acquired?"

The Sword of Tears made no answer. Aryx snorted, having assumed such a response. He would gain nothing trying to question the sinister blade; it told him only what it intended to tell him. Switching eyes, the minotaur also noticed that the aura vanished. No one other than he could see it.

Opening both eyes now, Aryx relaxed . . . and as he did, the aura remained invisible. So only by concentrating with the emerald eye could he see such things with some sort of consistency. Of what use such a trick might be, Aryx could not say. Useful for a magical creature such as a dragon, but hardly for a warrior.

Buckling the sheath in place, he at last abandoned the room. Whether or not the time neared, Aryx could no longer stay where he was. The silence, the emptiness, reminded him too much of the Abyss and the images that Kiri-Jolith had revealed to him.

Krynn did indeed face destruction . . . no, worse than that. Somehow he knew that if the fiery giant succeeded, it would be as if Aryx's world had never existed. The gods did what they could to prevent that from happening—well, *some* did— but they needed also to rely on mortals to stand against the Father of All and of Nothing's own servants, the beings of Chaos. Wherever mortals won, they weakened Chaos. Where they failed . . . Krynn moved nearer and nearer to oblivion.

The minotaurs had been trained since their creation to fight. Each time they had been enslaved, they had risen again, stronger than before. Sargonnas had spoken the truth when he had indicated that the mortal forces of Ansalon, of all Krynn, needed the strong arm, the determination, of Aryx's people.

Apparently the servants of the Chaos had realized that also.

Aryx marched down the hall, careful not to disturb any of his companions. To his annoyance, he did not spot a sentry until he had reached the end of the one corridor and marched halfway down the next. Aryx still did not know how others would react to his "gift," but he could not hide it forever. Better to reveal the truth as soon as possible in the hope that those he confronted would see that behind the emerald orb still existed a simple warrior who wanted nothing more than the survival of his world.

The sentry remained in position as Aryx approached, eyes straight ahead. The minotaur stepped in front of the knight, looking down at him. "You there. What hour do we approach?"

The knight did not look him directly in the face. "We're just past the fourth hour."

He did not elaborate, nor even pay any attention to Aryx. The warrior snorted. His first contact with another had hardly turned out as he had expected. Aryx thought of drawing the sword just to get the guard to pay more attention, but he realized the folly of such an act. "How far past?"

At last the human glanced up, impatience and disregard evident in his own eyes. However, the moment he met Aryx's own gaze, the knight stiffened. The human's mouth hung open and he stared at the draconian orb.

"How far past?" Aryx repeated.

"Just . . . just a few minutes . . . no more." The sentry continued to stare, as if ensnared by Aryx's emerald eye.

"Thank you." The minotaur warrior quickly walked off in the direction of Lord Broedius's chambers. Behind him, Aryx could sense the Knight of Takhisis still watching him, no doubt his mouth yet hanging open. He hoped not everyone would react so. Aryx did not like the thought of leaving a trail of gawking spectators wherever he went.

Too soon, though, the minotaur suspected he would do just that. Each guard he passed broke from his duties to openly stare at the unsettling eye. One even followed him a few steps. If the trained warriors of Takhisis could not accept the eye, what would those such as Seph or Delara think? Would Kiri-Jolith's gift turn everyone away from him? Did he even dare to attempt to speak with the generals?

What choice did he have? Everyone had already lain the responsibility for cooperation on his shoulders. He would have to make his people listen despite the distraction of the emerald orb.

As he neared Broedius's chambers, he heard the rumble of talk from within—minotaur voices, none whose tone hinted at pleasure. Aryx paused several yards from the doors, composing himself. Two human sentries by the entrance glanced his way, then clutched their weapons more tightly the moment they noticed his left eye.

Seeing no reason to delay, Aryx marched toward the guards. "I'm Aryximaraki of Clan Orilg, sent by Lord Broedius himself to speak with the minotaur generals."

One guard could not even find his voice. The second managed to nod his head before belatedly adding, "You . . . Lord Broedius said you were . . . you were to have permission to enter as soon as you arrived."

"Then if you'll stop gawking and let me pass, I'll be out of your sight." His annoyance began to turn to anger. Aryx had been given no choice in accepting the god's gift.

The second knight opened the door. As Aryx barged through, he saw that only a few of the generals had arrived. Hojak stood there, an unfamiliar, tawny warrior next to him. Beyond them, General Geryl spoke with two others, one a short, muscular elder and the other the same size as Geryl, only with a girth nearly twice the circumference. Aryx's fellow clan member carried in one hand his axe, as did two of the others. The remaining duo, Hojak one of them, wielded long swords. Clearly the generals had not come to this meeting expecting much in the way of good news, although he doubted that they intended to do literal battle with Broedius and his officers.

They had all looked his way as the door had opened, no doubt expecting one of their own. Aryx's gaze darted from one officer to the next, quickly reading their reactions. In most, he read surprise, then further shock as they focused on the dragon eye. Hojak snorted, glaring at Aryx as if he saw one of the shelled reavers. Only Geryl reacted with a modicum of respect, but even he could not help gaping briefly at the figure before him.

"Some of you know me," Aryx began, attempting to pretend he had not changed in any way. "To you others, I'm Aryximaraki de-Orilg, warrior of the empire, crew member and survivor of the *Kraken's Eye* and—"

"We all know who you are, Aryx," Geryl quietly interjected, his eyes never leaving the dusky gray minotaur's own. "I think we do, at least."

"By the whims of Zeboim . . ." Hojak muttered. "Look at his eye!" The general next to him nodded wordlessly.

Geryl took a step forward. "Aryx . . . Aryximaraki . . . your part in the battle has been told and retold already in the few short hours since then." He took hold of his axe just below the head, then, with the weapon perpendicular to the floor, thrust it toward the younger warrior in a salute. "I honor you and honor your blade."

The act served to break much of the tension. The other generals, even Hojak, repeated the salute with their own weapons. Aryx acknowledged each, then stepped to the center of the room. "I merely fought for the empire, as any warrior would."

"But despite these foolish humans, you managed to bring order to the ranks," insisted the short elder. "We should have slaughtered the bunch the moment they docked! This battle would have gone differently if they'd not been there to interfere!"

Hojak snorted. "You weren't at the docks when Sargonnas made his appearance, Selkin! I dared do nothing!"

"I never intimated—"

"Generals!" To his horror, Aryx's voice boomed through the chamber. "Generals . . . it's the Knights of Takhisis I would talk to you about."

The doors opened behind him, and two more senior officers entered, officers who paused to stare the moment they noticed Aryx's eye. He swore under his breath. If the orb proved so distracting, Aryx might never gain their complete attention, and if that happened, how could he convince them of the need to cooperate with the humans?

You got me into this, Kiri-Jolith. At least make them listen, Aryx thought. Yet, deep down, Aryx knew that the task would be up to him. The gods had too great a battle of their own to wage.

More generals arrived. How many yet might still come, he could not say, but Aryx couldn't hesitate any longer. Broedius would enter precisely at the fifth hour, of that the uneasy warrior had no doubt.

Perhaps seeing the daunting test awaiting Aryx, Geryl spoke

up. "You say you came to speak to us about the humans, Aryx. What do you have to say?"

He surveyed the assembled officers, this time purposely displaying the draconian orb. Perhaps instead of distracting them, it might instead draw the generals to his words. "Lord Broedius has released all of you."

"That seems pretty obvious," Hojak grumbled. "But for what new dishonor?"

"Not for dishonor, but for alliance."

They grumbled, all of them. Even Geryl found Aryx's words suspicious. Only when the young warrior stared at each did they falter. The dragon eye cowed the generals, at least enough to make them listen. Perhaps Kiri-Jolith had known that, perhaps not, but Aryx now took full advantage of the effect. With the minotaur command still silent, he began to tell them what Lord Broedius had offered.

Most remained neutral in their expressions as Aryx outlined his discussions with the knight commander. Admittedly he embellished on some points, but Aryx hoped that if he could make the generals agree to the offer, Broedius would acquiesce on the lesser aspects. He tried to make them see that this stood as the best hope for the survival of the empire and their very race. In his heart, he believed this, and that firm belief aided him now.

While Aryx talked, he kept the emerald eye on each. Perhaps because of that, no one interrupted, no one stalked out of the chamber. As he concluded, Aryx felt that at least some of them saw his reasoning.

One who did not was Hojak. The gruff officer, a member of the Supreme Circle, snorted when Aryx reached the end of his argument. "So we're supposedly granted command of our forces, but still we bow to the one with the eyes like the Abyss! What difference, then, does it make? We will still be treated as fodder rather than allies! We're no better off!"

"I disagree," interrupted Geryl. "There must be an overall commander and while a human might not be to my liking, either, Hojak, Broedius is an experienced commander. Moreover, he knows the situation in Ansalon, which surely affects us, too."

"The knights don't understand about defending an island," argued another general.

"Against the underdwellers, we know as little as they."

Aryx surveyed the room, trying to judge the mood of the generals. He counted at least three against any such alliance and four in favor. Of the remaining generals, he could tell nothing.

Hojak remained adamant. "We're free enough now! We shouldn't have come here at all! If we rallied our forces, we could be rid of the humans and their problems in a matter of hours!"

Geryl laughed harshly. "And while we cleansed our realm of the humans, the reavers would be upon us, slaughtering our people in turn! Excellent strategy, Hojak!"

The other general grasped his weapon. "Do you mock me?"

"Of course not, but even you should see how dangerous your notion is!"

Hojak snorted, eyes turning red with anger. In another moment, he would reach a berserker fury from which only his death or that of his rival would free him. Aryx seized the enraged officer's weapon arm. Hojak turned on him, ready to do battle with the younger warrior instead.

"No!" Aryx leaned forward, practically planting his snout against the elder minotaur's own. He met the furious gaze, staring unblinking at General Hojak. In his present stage, Hojak might kill him, but Aryx refused to step back.

"Release me!"

"No!" Aryx's eyes narrowed. "No. We can't afford to fight one another, General! If we do, we dishonor those who depend on us! We dishonor all those who will die because we couldn't overcome our own distrust!" He grew tired of the constant bickering and fighting among his own kind. No wonder they had been enslaved so often. "You'll end this *now.*"

General Hojak glared at him. Then something he saw drained him of his fury. An almost fearful look spread across his face. Aryx had never seen such an expression save on that of some of his shipmates as the Magori's weapons had cut them down.

"Let go of me," whispered the older minotaur in an almost plaintive voice. "Let go . . ."

"Hojak!" called one of the others. "Are you—"

The outer doors burst open, and Lord Broedius himself charged into the room. He looked as if he hadn't slept at all since Aryx had last spoken with him. The knight commander surveyed the room almost absently until his gaze drifted to Aryx. Broedius started to say something, then noticed the dragon eye. After some hesitation, the Knight of Takhisis finally uttered, "Well, it's one surprise after another from you, Aryx!"

"Lord Broedius, I've spoken with the generals, and—"

"A moot point at the moment! It's you I seek, but they can come as well!"

Geryl stepped forward. "What is it, Knight Commander? Have the underdwellers returned?"

"In a manner of speaking, perhaps." The senior knight strode up to Aryx. "An offer's been made . . . an offer to parley."

Aryx could hardly believe that. "From the crustaceans?"

"No, from a voice—or maybe voices; I can't tell—from somewhere in the mist. Curiously, it's asked for you, Aryx."

"Me?" He shook his head. "That can't be, Lord Broedius! Why would any—"

The knight cut him off with the wave of a hand. "I care not the reason 'why' at the moment, minotaur, only that you're wanted. Will you come?"

Part of his mind screamed for him to say no. The images of all those who had died aboard the *Kraken's Eye* returned, reinforcing that desire. Yet Aryx could not, in his heart, answer so. Even if a thousand Magori armed with lances awaited him, honor demanded he face them. "I'll go with you, human, if only in the hopes that it might mean something."

"Very good." Broedius glanced back at the generals. "Come or stay, the choice is yours."

Geryl glanced at the others before speaking. "We've heard the offer through Aryx, Knight Commander, and if it still stands, we'll take it . . . for now. If need be, we'll fight alongside you and yours. This is not the time for differences."

The knight nodded slightly. "Agreed. Come!"

Broedius led them out of the clan house to where a number of riders waited. Rand and Carnelia sat among them, but of Seph and Delara, he saw no sign. Realizing that they had not been told, Aryx sought to go back, but a look from the ebony-eyed commander changed his mind. He could not hesitate now. Perhaps by leaving them behind, Aryx might keep them safe.

Reaction to the dragon eye proved predictable, with only the cleric of Kiri-Jolith holding his expression steady. Rand did not look at all pleased by Aryx's newfound orb, but neither did he gape as Carnelia and several of the others did. Their reaction only hardened the uncertain minotaur, making him appear perhaps emotionless, even cold, to the others.

A knight handed him the reins of a great brown charger who, upon sighting his new rider, nearly pulled the reins loose in sudden anxiety. Cursing, Aryx stared the animal down, which only brought new muttering from both minotaurs and humans.

He mounted quickly and, frowning at their obvious attention, snarled, "Let's get on with this. . . ."

Without waiting for them, he turned the charger and headed toward the docks.

* * * * *

As they neared their destination, Aryx could not help thinking of the sight those with him must present to any who could see them in the thick fog. Humans and minotaurs side by side, clearly riding more as allies than masters and servants. He only hoped the fragile alliance would hold, for now they surely needed it most.

The combined force rushed toward the shoreline, Aryx expecting each second to encounter the enemy by the swarms. However, as they arrived, Aryx could find no foe, even taking the thick fog into consideration. Talons of knights and legions of minotaurs stood waiting for commands, but of the foe, he could see no sign. So where had the source of this voice that had demanded his presence gone? Even with the dragon eye he could see nothing but the waves and, in the distance, derelict ships and boats. He saw that most of his companions shared his confusion. Broedius, however, seemed to take things in stride, reining his horse to a halt, then peering out at the seemingly empty seascape, as if seeing what even Aryx could not.

"Well?" the knight called out to the empty harbor. "We're here. *All* of us, including him!"

The horses suddenly stirred, more than one trying to turn. A knight shouted something, pointing at the nearby shore.

From beneath the sand, a single crustacean arose. In each

hand, it held one of the horrible scythe swords, yet it did nothing.

"Hold your positions!" Broedius called as some of the assembled defenders stirred. Behind him, General Geryl shouted a similar order, much to the sudden interest of the minotaur legions. Geryl looked at the knight commander as if daring him to reprimand the minotaur general, but Broedius only nodded.

A second shelled terror rose from the sand some distance from the first, and moments later a third emerged, in perfect line with the first two. Beyond them, Aryx could see two or three others. He suddenly imagined the entire island being ringed by this strange line of monstrous invaders.

They spoke then, in one disconcerting voice that rippled and echoed, setting the nerves on edge. As Broedius had said, though, the one voice also sounded like many, a puzzling contradiction.

"You are offered peace . . ." the strange voice began.

At first no one could believe his ears. The foe had come to offer terms of peace? The final battle had been won even before it had been fought? A murmur arose among the defenders.

"Silence in the ranks!" Geryl immediately shouted. The murmuring died.

"The peace of oblivion . . ." the voice finally added.

A sensation of shock ripped across the defenders. After a moment, Broedius urged his unwilling steed forward several paces. "Who are you? Who commands?"

Again silence. Then: "The Coil commands; the Magori obey . . ."

It might have been Aryx's imagination, or perhaps a trick of the growing mist, but he thought he saw the nearest of the creatures shiver. Obviously the Magori greatly feared this Coil.

Lord Broedius did not seem at all impressed by the answer. "Hear this, Coil! We'll not be conquered by you! So I swear by my Lady Takhisis, great Queen of the Heavens!"

A ripple of laughter, so inhuman that the hair on Aryx's neck actually stood on end. Several warriors took a step back. "Foolish little mortals . . . do you think gods may resist the father of gods?"

Only Rand and Aryx showed any signs of understanding

the enigmatic question, but before Aryx could ask the cleric what he might know, the Magori's master spoke again . . . to him.

"Warrior of Sargonnas, chosen of the betrayer, wielder of the demon sword, do you hear me?"

Steeling himself, Aryx urged his mount a couple of steps toward the still Magori. "I hear you! What do you want of me?"

"Where is the Horned One? Where is your Sargonnas?"

So it wanted to know where the god had gone. . . . Aryx's brow furrowed as he tried to think quickly. Surely this servant of Chaos must know what had befallen Sargonnas! If it controlled these aquatic abominations and the fog, then surely it had controlled the storm as well. It should certainly know that the temple had been ripped into the sky and with it had gone . . .

Aryx sensed an abrupt chill near his leg where the sheath containing the Sword of Tears hung.

A warning?

He stared beyond the Magori, trying somehow to meet the gaze of the creatures' invisible master. "He stands ready with his chosen!" the minotaur shouted. "He is everywhere!"

His words encouraged the minotaurs but had little effect on the unseen Coil, for once again it laughed.

"Then he will see his pets die. Father Chaos has decreed this little world not to be, and his most loyal servant, the Coil, will obey. You may still choose the peace of oblivion." As an apparent example of what the Coil meant, the crustacean nearest Aryx and his band suddenly hissed in outright terror. Tendrils of the fog twisted around it, and as they did, the Magori shivered and grew transparent. It struggled madly, trying to free itself, but all to no avail. At last the crustacean emitted a final, high-pitched hiss . . . then faded away, weapons and all. Silence reigned for a time as the unseen Coil allowed the defenders to digest the creature's fate before concluding. "A fate most fair and painless, would you not agree?'"

Someone did not. From the ranks, there flew an expertly aimed axe.

It struck one of the Magori directly in the throat, spraying fluids everywhere as the monstrous crustacean collapsed, a shrill hiss its dying cry. The other Magori remained where they were, weapons poised but unmoving.

A brief cheer rose up from both minotaurs and humans, one that swiftly died as a new monster rose from the earth to replace the first. Again the inhuman laughter wreaked havoc on Aryx's nervous system. He felt no better that others reacted as he did, some even worse.

The sea and sand suddenly boiled with Magori as far as the eye could see.

"Sound the call!" Broedius shouted, turning his mount.

More of the aquatic reavers burst forth, so many that the creatures packed against one another. They burrowed up from the sandy shoreline, bubbled up from the dimly seen harbor, and clambered over the farthest docks. Everywhere there were more than Aryx suspected anyone had seen during the first attack. The fog thickened noticeably, and the musky scent that still recalled for Aryx the nightmare aboard his ship grew so strong that he thought he might choke.

"You have rejected the peace of oblivion"—the voice of the Coil seemed to come from all around—"and so it shall be the peace of the *slaughter*, then. . . ."

The Magori advanced.

# Armageddon
## Chapter Twelve

Rand forced his steed back as the Magori approached. He hated leaving the others, especially Carnelia, but it remained essential for him to keep out of harm's reach. The reason for which he had joined Broedius's expedition required that he not risk himself, not until contact with those he waited for had been made.

The vision had come to him from Kiri-Jolith himself. Rand remained the link by which others of the faithful kept aware of what happened even while they made their own preparations. The blond cleric knew that by now the faithful must be drawing near, but until he actually sighted them, he dared not risk losing touch. That he did not know who they were did not matter, only that his god had sent them. Not even Broedius understood the extent of Rand's mission, although the knight commander had been told just enough aboard the *Kraken's Eye* by Sargonnas to keep Broedius from throwing the cleric overboard. Carnelia knew nothing, which had made Rand's burden worse.

He rode away from the impending battle wishing he could do something for the warriors about to give their lives. Every effort to push back the fog had failed. For a time, his hope that he could aid in clearing the air of the cursed mists had made him feel better, but as each attempt had failed, Rand had felt more and more useless. Sitting and waiting for others who might not come in time did not suit him, even if that task had been sanctioned by his patron.

Frustrated, the cleric suddenly pulled the reins tight, bringing his mount up short. He looked over his shoulder at the barely visible figures of the knights and minotaurs. Why should he return to the Knights of the Thorn, whose assistance so far in the task of destroying the fog had mostly consisted of bickering and backstabbing? Perhaps . . . perhaps with a mind uncluttered by their foul darkness, Rand could better touch upon the power of Kiri-Jolith. It had been difficult of late to even sense his patron's presence, but surely that was because of the cleric's nearness to the black mages.

Rand looked around and found a building that would give him ample view of the battle. Yes, he would do his best to push back the deadly fog without the Knights of the Thorn, but if that failed and he saw that the defenders needed him, Rand would abandon his task . . . *all* of his tasks . . . and come to their aid.

And if the gods, especially Kiri-Jolith, found fault in him for that, then so be it. Rand had taken up the mantle of a cleric to help his fellow creatures; if necessary, he would leave that role behind him in order to do the same thing.

\* \* \* \* \*

Knights on horseback began shouting out orders as the Magori approached. Aryx watched as minotaur legions were forced forward to indefensible positions while the knights formed tight ranks in higher, more secure locations. He cursed, knowing that if things began the same as they had the first battle, far too many of his people's lives would again be wasted.

"Broedius! Do as promised and give the generals their warriors back! Let them command our people before your officers lose half our numbers!"

The senior knight glared at him. "At the beginning of battle? Are you mad, minotaur? This is no time to rearrange the ranks!"

General Geryl rode up next to Broedius. "Give us the right, Knight Commander, and we'll adjust matters without tearing defenses apart! We know our warriors and we know our home! Grant us our command back, and your talons and our legions will fight more smoothly!"

Aryx could see Broedius's mind racing. "Your archers are already in position. Leave them. I'll signal a short retreat. Take command of the minotaur legions in an orderly manner and follow my direction! Understood?"

Geryl looked at the other generals, most of whom nodded immediately. Only a few, such as Hojak, showed any reservations, but they said nothing. "We agree, Knight Commander!"

Broedius's gaze shifted back to the approaching line of Magori passing through the mist. "Then go." He signaled one of his men. "Sound orderly retreat!"

The man looked aghast. "Sir?"

"You heard me!"

The knight put the horn to his lips. The blare sounded, and Aryx saw a sudden stiffness in the ranks. Drejjen and some of the nearest officers stared in the direction of the knight commander, but they nonetheless obeyed, summoning both men and minotaurs back.

The pace of the Magori increased, several lances flying toward the retreating ranks. Two minotaurs fell, one wounded in the leg. A pair of his compatriots rushed forward, dragging him to safety.

"They're moving faster than I thought they could," snarled the commander.

Aryx concentrated with his emerald eye. "And there's more directly behind the first rows!"

"How well can you see with that . . . that thing?"

"I can see what looks to be the masts of the *Predator* sticking out of the water. . . ."

Broedius's fists clenched at mention of the sunken ship, but he said, "I'll bear that little gift in mind. We may need it with this blasted fog."

Aryx saw something else. "Magori are swarming over some of the other vessels docked out there."

"I was afraid of that." The dark-eyed human stood in the saddle. "The first of those beasts are in range. I only hope your people have as good an eye as you." To the knight with the horn, he commanded, "Signal the archers!"

The man put the instrument to his lips, sending out a signal that cut through the fog like a well-sharpened axe blade.

A loud hiss filled the air as a torrent of arrows rained down on the monstrous horde. The Magori ignored the oncoming deluge of death, possibly not even knowing what the shafts were, for Aryx had never seen them use any sort of bow.

The volley struck. Arrows pierced throats, snouts, and eyes, and crustacean after crustacean fell, writhing. Yet more arrows uselessly struck armored hides, bouncing off and even breaking. For all the shafts fired, too many were wasted, and every gap left by a fallen Magori was immediately filled with another of the horrific invaders. The swarm had been barely slowed by the rain of missiles. Too few of the foe had perished.

"Again!"

The second volley struck with more force, the archers miraculously finding their mark even through the thick fog. Magori after Magori fell, to be trampled by its fellows. The deaths of so many seemed to mean nothing to the crustaceans. Perhaps they did not even understand the concept as the peoples of Krynn did, or perhaps their fear of the unseen Coil overwhelmed all else. Whichever the case, they continued to advance, a silent, monstrous horde, ever increasing.

Far too many shafts went wide of the mark, a sight which worried the young minotaur. He could understand a few wild shots here and there, but too many flew as if a number of the archers lacked full concentration.

"What's with those archers? I thought your people were proficient, Aryx!"

"They are. Something's wrong."

He noticed, too, that both the human and minotaur ranks moved in a slightly ragged manner, as if not all the warriors had their full wits about them. Aryx heard coughing . . . more coughing than normal.

Rand had feared the fog, wondering if it had something to do with the sickness that had struck down Torvak and so many others. If the cleric had spoken true, were they all doomed to suffer from it?

Aryx said nothing to Lord Broedius about his suspicions. To suggest as he thought would only provoke panic. Besides, what could be done about it? The foul mists enshrouded everything.

"Broedius," Carnelia muttered. "They're getting too close."

"Agreed." The knight commander glanced at his trumpeter. "Give the archers one last call, then we ride off."

At the sound of the horn, a new volley swept down over the Magori. Sloppier than the previous ones, it nonetheless brought down several of the abominations in the front. As Aryx joined his fellows in the rear, he looked back and saw that even those deaths had not deterred the creatures.

"Blast it!" Lord Broedius glared toward where the archers had to be. "I gave orders earlier to the officer in charge that they should use flaming shafts on that volley! What, by our Lady, is he doing?"

Aryx paid him no mind. Already the Magori had too much of a foothold on the island. The minotaur and human forces had at last shaped themselves into something cohesive, though, and all they needed was a signal. Aryx felt the Sword of Tears tingle by his side, as if urging him to act. He needed no encouragement, though, already having had enough of simply watching.

Broedius evidently thought much the same thing. "They've been given enough ground. We stand here. Give the signal."

At sound of the new note, the minotaurs roared and knights held high their blades. Moving as one, they at last advanced on the approaching horde.

Unwilling to stay behind, Aryx urged his steed forward. Broedius saw him and ordered the warrior back to his place. Aryx ignored him, drawing the Sword of Tears. As he neared the lines, minotaurs who saw him pointed excitedly, and many moved to allow him room, then formed ranks around him. The reluctant champion found himself leading a force into the fray, but by this time, he could do nothing. The enemy was too near for him to attempt to convince his followers that they had made a dreadful mistake.

The opposing lines collided. Cries of pain or death began to resound throughout the area.

Aryx met the first foe without hesitation, dodging his lance and coming up over the enemy's weapon with his sword. He cut open the Magori and immediately pulled back, avoiding its burning fluids. To his right, he caught a glimpse of General Geryl swinging his massive axe with such force that it nearly split its victim in twain. One of Broedius's officers plunged his blade through the clustered orbs of a Magori who had just lanced a knight on foot.

With each victory, however, there were also heavy losses. A young and too eager minotaur thrust his way forward. His blade bounced off the huge crustacean's armored hide, and in the process, the warrior stumbled. Immediately a host of swords slashed down, dismembering the hapless victim in a sight that Aryx suspected would be forever burned into his memory.

An ambitious Magori seized Aryx's right leg. Already

fending off another foe to his left, the minotaur could only kick, which did not serve to deter his second adversary.

Suddenly a familiar figure darted in to take on the Magori to Aryx's right. The fearsome reaver turned to defend itself, and as the two came together, Aryx saw with some surprise that his rescuer was again none other than Delara.

She parried the savage swipe of the Magori's blade, then literally disarmed her opponent. The crustacean hissed in pain, its ragged stump splattering corrosive blood everywhere. Shielding her eyes, Delara closed in. Before the crustacean could recover, she finished it with a thrust into the throat.

"I left you back in the knights' headquarters!"

"Well, you'll never leave me behind again!" she called back with a smile that, despite their predicament, made him flush.

"Where's Seph?" If Delara had made it here, had his brother, too?

She did not have to answer, for Aryx immediately spotted Seph. The younger minotaur held his own against a large foe, fending off attack after attack by his adversary until he jostled the Magori out of its position. Seph killed the reaver before it could regain its balance, then barely jumped back as a barbed lance struck the ground on which he had just stood.

Fear for his brother overwhelmed Aryx. "Seph! Get back behind the lines!"

"And leave them all for—" The other paused, seeing Aryx's eye for the first time. "What in the—"

Delara leapt toward Seph. "Watch out!"

An abomination wielding a sword slashed for the younger warrior's neck and likely would have decapitated Seph if not for Delara. She knocked into him, pushing him back. Unfortunately, in doing so, Delara caught the blow on her shoulder, the jagged scythe sword ripping away a small but bloody portion of her flesh. She cried out in pain.

Aryx maneuvered his horse closer, sweeping an arc with the Sword of Tears. The wailing blade severed both weapon arm and muzzle from the Magori warrior, who fell back, dying.

"Seph! For the last time, go back!"

"Too late!" his brother shouted.

Indeed, he had the right of it. The Magori pressed harder, beginning to create some holes regardless of the efforts of the defenders. From his vantage point, Aryx noted that many of his companions, be they human or minotaur, moved sluggishly and, even in the midst of deadly combat, coughed without control.

The fog, he realized. *The fog may defeat us before the Magori get the opportunity!*

Broedius rode back and forth, shouting commands to all. "Fill that gap! Keep those swords high! Blast it, watch that hole!"

A Magori burst through, a minotaur still pinned to the end of its lance. It shook the corpse free, but as it did, Broedius rode down on it, bringing his blade down hard against the blood-red, bulbous eyes. The blade sank in, spewing yellowish fluid over the knight's armor. The horse stumbled, shocked by the acidic splash, but recovered in time for Broedius to finish the task.

For all the underdwellers that they had killed, the defenders seemed not to have made any impact. Thick as the fog had grown, Aryx could still see the Magori numbers swelling. Those ever-increasing numbers continued to take their toll. The line of defense began to shift, retreating in some areas and causing even more pockets.

Another Magori broke through. One knight tried to stop him, but the wicked scythe sword severed his head from his body despite the human's armor. Two minotaurs with axes leapt onto the huge crustacean. One managed to get his weapon and arms around the snout of the reaver. With herculean effort, he pulled the axe head through the soft white flesh underneath.

The lines grew more and more uneven. Aryx's anxiety increased. If the lines here were not holding, how did they fare in other regions of the empire?

"Sound the horns!"

A blare went up, one that Aryx did not at first recognize. When he did, his heart dropped. Broedius had already called for a second cautious retreat. The defenders had been forced to give up more ground.

They could not retreat far without moving into the city itself. Aryx silently cursed Lord Broedius for his quick decision. Surely it would have been better to hold out longer than to retreat into the city. How could they hope to maintain order amid so many buildings?

The Magori moved in to take advantage. Horns sounded, calling for the line to hold again. Aryx gritted his teeth, thinking that by now it might be too late.

Thunder rolled even though Aryx did not recall seeing storm clouds. Belatedly he realized that the thunder had a distinctive beat to it, a familiar beat. Horses.

Far to his right, a gap opened in the lines, but this time for a purpose. Through it poured mounted lancers, Broedius's own plus some minotaurs, in numbers so great Aryx wondered if any had been left to support the rest of the island. Among them, Aryx identified one of the generals he had spoken to in the knight commander's chamber, which meant that this plan had been very hastily arranged. However, despite clearly being slapped together, the trick proved successful. The lancers charged through, and the Magori, still moving forward, became easy targets. Polished, sharpened lances skewered the crustaceans. For once, the monstrous invaders sought to escape, but by doing so, they collided with others behind them, creating further havoc.

As quickly as they had come, the lancers retreated back behind the lines. A few were brought down before they could do so, but the trick had probably worked even better than Broedius and the minotaur generals had hoped. For the first time, the Magori left small gaps. Seizing the moment, Aryx and the rest pushed forward again, regaining some of the ground lost.

"We've got them now!" Seph yelled, eyes bright.

"Not yet!" Aryx returned. "Not yet! They might push back again!"

Too soon his words proved prophetic. Despite surmounting losses, there seemed no end to the Magori. Not only did they finally fill the gaps, but in minutes the horde also threatened to overrun the defenders. This time the minotaurs and knights were forced to retreat under more dire circumstances.

Aryx watched in horror as first one, then another of the minotaurs who had followed him died by sword or lance. No one came forward to fill the gaps left by the dead defenders. As yet another warrior perished at the end of a barbed lance, Aryx realized that his mount now stood on the edge of one of the streets. The defenders had been pushed all the way from the shoreline to the city.

His horse shrieked as a barbed lance thrust through its

midsection. The animal pitched to the side, taking Aryx with it. He rolled off, barely avoiding two slashing swords. Landing in a crouched position, Aryx thrust, the Sword of Tears easily penetrating the nearest Magori's shell. The other creature sought to chop his sword arm off but missed by inches. The demon blade countered on its own, twisting around so that it went over the crustacean's weapon and cut a smooth line across what served as the monster's neck.

Aryx glared at the enchanted artifact, uncertain whether to be grateful or annoyed. "Perhaps you'd like to fight this war without me?"

No reply came from the Sword of Tears. Frustrated, the minotaur returned to the task at hand, hoping the demon blade would not at some critical moment make a choice of its own that would endanger rather than help its reluctant wielder. As with any minotaur warrior, Aryx preferred that his hand guided the weapon, not the other way around. That could cause one to grow lax, which in turn could cause one to grow very, very dead.

Broedius's voice suddenly rose high above the lines. "Sound for fire!"

The horns blared a different note. The weary minotaur heard the hiss of arrows and wondered how the knight expected the archers to find their mark under such circumstances. Then Aryx noted the glow above his head and a second later watched in wonder as fire rained down from the heavens. The knight commander had finally managed to get the archers to let loose a volley of burning shafts.

Caught up in the attack, the underdwellers failed to register the flight until the flames landed among them. A few fortunate shafts struck home, but most simply hit the earth. However, the appearance of the flames had almost as great an effect as if the arrows had found their targets, for the Magori hesitated, even stumbled, at sight of the flickering shafts. Unlike the previous time, however, they did not retreat.

With confusion once more in the invader ranks, the knights and minotaurs pressed forward. Magori backing up found themselves treading on fire, while those behind the flames hesitated to advance. Scores of the aquatic reavers perished, although the defenders also suffered some casualties. Lancers rushed out, replaying the same trick as before with equal accuracy.

Hopes rose. Even Aryx thought that surely now the invaders would be on the run. With renewed energy, he and the others pushed on. If they could, they would drive the Magori back into the sea.

An unsettling thing happened then, but Aryx suspected that only he saw it. Out in the dim harbor, where even the dragon eye proved hard-pressed to make out detail, the water suddenly swelled. A vast serpentine form—no, several intermingled serpentine forms—rose above the surface, churning the harbor.

As suddenly as the murky forms had appeared, a shift came over the crustaceans. Despite heavy losses, they halted the defenders' drive, then began to push back with an almost frantic energy. The more the things in the harbor stirred, the harder the Magori pushed. Once more knights and minotaurs had to retreat. The invaders fought as if seeking to flee some terrible force in their rear, and Aryx suspected that such a notion was not far from the truth.

The serpentine shapes sank beneath the surface again, but although the water stilled, the reavers' latest rampage did not. Again the Magori broke through the front line, this time in great numbers. Taken aback by the intensity of the new assault, the defenders tried to seal the gap as best they could, but the line began to collapse even more. Now those on the edge had to defend from more than one direction.

Lord Broedius stood in the saddle. "Sound second strike!"

After a momentary hesitation, someone sounded two short notes. Aryx had no time to wonder what "second strike" meant, too caught up in trying to watch out for not only himself, but Seph and Delara as well. Aryx worried about both of them, his brother because of his inexperience and Delara because of her continued risk-taking. Twice since she had rescued him he had to save Delara from her own actions as she nearly cut herself off from the shifting line. Aryx feared losing her as much as he did Seph.

Delara glanced his way, favoring him with a look that made him want to blush even in the midst of combat. They fought virtually side by side, their weapons a lethal combination.

"What did Lord Broedius yell?" she called.

" 'Second strike'!"

"What does he mean by—" A scythe sword came perilously close to decapitating her, and by the time she dealt with its wielder, the answer arrived in force.

From every avenue, from every street, poured minotaur warriors, General Geryl at their head. Now the defenders' numbers swelled. Geryl's swift decision to lead them strengthened the blow they struck. The crustaceans who had broken through attempted to retreat, but what had been a break in the line turned into a box, with the attackers trapped inside. The reavers fought hard, sending many of their adversaries to the grave, but far more Magori perished.

When the last of the underdwellers who had broken through lay dead, the newcomers moved to the forefront. Aryx and the others found themselves pushed back toward the rear of the line. Delara seized the gray minotaur and pulled him back yet farther, well out of reach of the battle.

"Breathe, Aryx! Catch your breath! This may be our only chance!"

"Aryx!" Seph seized his arm. "You're bleeding!"

He looked down and saw that his brother was right. A long, vicious gash cut across his chest and another alongside his left arm. Only now did he feel the stinging pain of his wounds. Fortunately, for all their vividness, Aryx quickly discovered that neither ran very deep.

Delara nudged Seph aside. "Let me see that. I've trained in field surgery." Not always trustful of clerics, the minotaur race had over the centuries developed the science of field surgery to such a degree that even the Knights of Solamnia had occasionally sought out their knowledge. "You shouldn't go back into battle without a bandage over that chest wound."

Seph hooked his axe into its harness. "There's a well over there. I'll bring water for all of us."

Aryx stared at the fierce fighting just yards from them. "But you can't wait for me!"

"You'll fight better for the few minutes of rest and the bandage, Aryx. A good warrior knows that. Look around you. Others are doing the same. And if you go headlong back into battle without resting, you know that most of them will follow you, so think of them, if not yourself."

Although he saw truth in her words, the gray minotaur still cringed inside, thinking that others might die while he stood here. Nonetheless, he tolerated Delara's ministrations and gratefully accepted the portion of water that Seph passed to him.

A fearsome figure on horseback rode up to them. It was Lord Broedius checking on the wounded. He eyed Aryx and his companions. "Well fought, minotaurs! If only your damnable god would have stayed around and fought as well as his so-called chosen!"

"Sargonnas did as he must!" Delara snapped, momentarily forgoing her efforts on Aryx. "If he is not here, then he is elsewhere, working to save all of us!"

"Or he may be dead. My Lady Takhisis doesn't abandon her subjects, which is why when this is over, we, her warriors, are destined to be the masters of Krynn!"

"This is hardly the time for theological discussion," a weary Aryx pointed out. "Lord Broedius, shouldn't more reinforcements be brought forward? We can't keep doling them out in pieces."

The knight's ebony eyes narrowed. "We're nearly out of reserves. With so much area to defend, virtually every available minotaur is stationed somewhere, as are my own men. Unfortunately, the two ships of reinforcements didn't arrive in time, and I doubt they'll be able to get through now. There should have been more here in the city to use as reserves, but this cursed disease is spreading like wildfire. Since your patriarch's collapse, the number of cases has escalated, especially just prior to the battle! Worse, several from both our races have fallen since the start from the same illness!"

"Now, why do I find that particularly fascinating?"

"You and me both, minotaur! This plague's not natural. The cleric thought the fog or our shelled friends might be responsible, and I'm inclined to believe him now. Of course, if we can't get rid of the fog, there's no use even thinking about it," Broedius added, mirroring Aryx's earlier thoughts. "We just have to keep fighting and hoping!" The knight commander coughed. "And this damned fog is getting thicker again! If only those blasted mages could have come up with some way to push it back, I feel certain that we could—"

A tremor shook the area hard. Pieces of masonry fell from nearby buildings. The knight fought for control of his startled mount and might have fallen if Seph had not seized the animal by the bit. Someone screamed.

"Tremor!" Aryx shouted.

"Tremor?" Delara clutched the nearest wall. "This is no tremor. This is a full quake!"

The Knight of Takhisis got his mount under control. "And damn well timed, by my Lady! This is no natural disaster!"

Aryx had to agree. He recalled the earlier quake and knew that it, too, had been no act of nature. Recalling the gargantuan shapes he had noticed in the harbor, Aryx wondered if they could not only swim but burrow like the Magori.

A horn sounded.

The ebony-eyed knight looked in the direction of the battle. "They've broken through again!" Broedius forced his horse around and rode off toward the lines without a word. Several of those in the area followed suit.

The reavers had indeed broken through again . . . and in several locations. The Magori clearly had been less surprised by the quake than the defenders, fueling the possibility that the force behind them had been responsible for it. To their credit, a group of knights under the command of an officer Aryx suspected to be Drejjen tried to re-form their talon directly in front of the foremost invaders, but, sorely outnumbered, they were soon fighting for their lives. Aryx started to rise, intending to join them whether Delara had finished or not. He could not stand by idly now.

A new tremor rocked the area. Drejjen's talon fell apart.

The top of the building by which the minotaurs stood began to collapse.

Aryx saw it first. "Look out!"

Delara leapt out of the way. Aryx threw Seph to the side, but the action cost him his balance, and in order to save himself, he had to stumble backward as quickly as he could.

Delara watched in horror as tons of mortar and stone plummeted toward the hapless minotaur. "Aryx!"

His feet slipped out from under him, but Aryx immediately went into a roll, praying to whatever god who might listen that it would be enough. The sky above him darkened as the collapsing wall neared.

A torrent of dust and rubble bathed him as he rolled. Rocks pelted him again and again, stinging bites like those of a thousand bees.

When at last it seemed safe, Aryx rose to his knees. Thick clouds of dust mixed with the fog, making it virtually impossible for even him to see more than a few yards at first. Of the others he could find no trace, but from the direction of the battle lines he heard renewed fury. The Magori had stepped up their attack once more, attacking with a ferocity Aryx found hard to believe. Little could stand against the monstrous reavers.

Aryx tried to rise to his feet but found the ground beneath him still too unstable. He heard someone who sounded like Seph call his name, but the voice came from far away. When Aryx tried to shout back, dust caused him to choke.

The clamor from the battle lines continued to grow. Forgetting his companions for the moment, Aryx noticed many figures milling about nearby. If memory served him, the lines should have been farther ahead.

He heard more shouting, above the other voices one that the bedraggled warrior thought he knew. A moment later, General Geryl materialized in the fog, with a band of minotaurs and knights, Drejjen included, surrounding him. With them came a vision that horrified Aryx, a fresh swarm of the Magori, their weapons already bloodied.

He searched for the Sword of Tears, but at first he could not find it. Once again the demon blade had betrayed him at the most critical of moments. Aryx started to curse Sargonnas's gift, then noticed a faint gleam from under the rubble. Sure enough, the sword lay buried beneath it. The warrior dug frantically, knowing that each second of delay cost his people. At last he managed to free the enchanted artifact.

Aryx held the weapon high, staring at the great stone. "Why didn't you tell me where you were?"

As before, the Sword of Tears did not answer him. Forgoing any further attempts at questioning, Aryx instead looked around, scanning the area one last time for either Seph or Delara. Far from the battle, he spotted a sword lying in the streets, the feminine arm of its former wielder thrust out of a pile of masonry.

Delara? Despite the carnage around him, he had to know. Aryx started toward the arm, but no sooner had he taken the first few steps when a new tremor struck. He stumbled, only with effort finding support. Aryx found himself facing the desperate defenders just in time to see General Geryl's horse falter.

The young minotaur cursed himself for a fool. If the body beneath were Delara's, Aryx clearly could not be of any help to her. No one could have survived such a crush of stone. Geryl and the others, even Subcommander Drejjen, needed his strong arm.

He took a step toward them, but then the ground directly beneath him shifted, the tremors having already weakened it. One of Aryx's feet sank down as rubble poured over it. Cursing, the warrior tugged on his leg.

A lance hurtled past his shoulder, sinking into the loose stone.

Reacting instinctively, Aryx seized it, pulling it free from the grip of a startled Magori. Recovering, the massive crustacean reached for him, mouth snapping and claws ready to tear Aryx in half. The gray minotaur swung the barbed lance around and thrust. He caught the reaver full in the mouth, ramming the lance in as far as he could.

The clawed hands seized the weapon, trying to pull it free. Aryx suddenly pulled with it, removing the barbed end and catching the deadly reaver off guard. Claws groping empty air, the Magori froze, confused by the tactic. Aryx took advantage, jamming the lance into its throat and finishing off the creature.

As his adversary fell, Aryx saw General Geryl's horse, already unsteady on its hooves, tumble over, three lances protruding from its side. The minotaur commander fell from his steed but rolled to his feet with incredible dexterity.

One of the knights tried to shield him and received a slash across the back of his neck that nearly severed his head. He collapsed into Geryl's arms. Geryl put the unfortunate man aside and struck at his slayer, cutting through one eye of the murderous Magori. A scythe sword came perilously near the elderly warrior, but Geryl dodged it, then sunk the blade of his axe into his attacker.

With some effort, Aryx at last freed his leg. However, as he took up the Sword of Tears, yet another shock wave struck. A column of earth thrust upward, and with it went the hapless warrior. Aryx watched the tops of some buildings fall below him. The column abruptly sank again, losing half its height and much of its width. He barely clung on to safety.

If the unseen Coil had caused the quake, then clearly the servant of Chaos cared little whether it destroyed friend or foe in the process. From his unstable perch, Aryx saw three Magori fall through a crack that split open beneath their feet. Another column of earth threw a knight and his mount high into the air.

General Geryl managed to stay on his feet, but a crevice opened up next to him, separating the champion from most of his followers. One of the reavers moved in on Geryl, brandishing its lance. The minotaur officer deflected the weapon, not seeing a second Magori coming up from behind him.

"General Geryl! Behind you!" Aryx's shout went unheard by the officer. The young minotaur tried to scramble down the column of earth, which had momentarily stabilized. He still had a chance to possibly save Geryl.

He had nearly made it down when the column collapsed entirely, tossing him to the earth like a doll. Aryx struck the ground shoulder first, the wind knocked out of him. For a few precious seconds, the world spun round. The minotaur shook his head, trying to clear his eyes.

As his vision returned, Aryx saw the second Magori raise its sword. At last Geryl noticed his other foe and tried to turn to compensate. Unfortunately, he turned too slowly. The reaver's deadly blade moved as a blur, cutting through flesh and bone.

The general roared in pain, but despite his horrific wound, he did not immediately fall. Teetering, the veteran warrior threw himself at the Magori who had severed his limb and drove the head of his axe through the unarmored throat. The monstrous invader hissed, grasping futilely at the gaping wound.

A wave of acidic blood rushed over General Geryl, searing his face. He fell on top of the dying crustacean, clutching his burn-wracked features.

The first Magori drove its lance through his back.

Cursing, Aryx stumbled to his feet again. He had no thought but to kill as many of the foe as he could before they killed him. The defenders had failed; aided by the fog, the endless waves of Magori had proven too much even for the proud minotaur empire. Seph and Delara were probably already dead, or else he would have seen them by now. All that remained for him was an honorable death.

"Aryx?"

He whirled toward the sound of the voice, the Sword of Tears wailing. Only at the last second did Aryx recognize Rand, but a Rand such as he had never seen, for despite being disheveled and dirty, the cleric wore about him an aura of silver-blue, an aura that radiated from within the human. It covered him from head to toe, moving as he moved. The sight left Aryx speechless.

The glowing human stepped toward him. "Praise be you still live, Aryx!"

The Sword of Tears suddenly shifted in the minotaur's grip, pulling Aryx's hand with it as it sought to embed itself in Rand's chest.

# Secrets

## Chapter Thirteen

"No! Not him!" Aryx tried to pull the demon blade back, weariness hampering his effort.

The sword said nothing, straining to reach the human. Rand remained just beyond its reach. Perhaps something had warned him at the last moment. He stood frozen, narrowed eyes fixed on the struggling weapon. The great green stone flared as the Sword of Tears sought its victim.

"No!" Aryx roared again. "You'll obey me now, or I'll throw you into the Blood Sea when I get the chance!"

The insidious artifact abruptly ceased its struggle, sending him reeling. Rand, perhaps risking himself more than he knew, quickly reached out to prevent Aryx from stumbling over the rubble. The cleric pulled the minotaur to the side of a battered building, out of sight of the battle. As he touched Aryx, the silver-blue aura around him first flashed brighter, then dulled to nearly nothing.

"Praise be that you are well, Aryx," the pale cleric said. "And thank you for your effort with that . . . sword."

The minotaur glared at the blade, tempted to hurl it down a nearby crevice. Yet despite the sword's treachery, he knew all too well that he would need it again. Against the Magori, it had proven the most effective weapon so far, although as the struggle had progressed, Aryx had wondered at its occasional sluggishness.

Despite their present danger, he finally sheathed it, not wanting again to risk harming the cleric.

"Good to see you're well, too, human." He eyed Rand, still seeing the faint aura. "But what are you doing here?"

The thin blond man looked down, almost ashamed. "I have made vows to fulfill some tasks for my patron. They forced me to step back from the battle. In order to try to make up for my lack of participation, I attempted alone what I and the Knights of the Thorn could not accomplish together—ridding us of this choking fog before it weakens us even more." He rubbed his face with his hands. "And as with the black mages, I succeeded in nothing."

The clatter of battle continued around them, but although Aryx wanted to return to the fray, Rand's talk of ridding the islands of the cursed mists caught his attention. He, too, felt that the defenders' only chance at this point required dispersing the fog, but if neither clerics nor mages could do it, then how could he hope to? "There's nothing you can do? Not even with the power of Kiri-Jolith behind you?"

"I am not even certain if I can touch upon his power anymore," Rand replied, eyes hollow. "It has grown steadily worse these past couple days, almost as if he draws distant from his own followers. I have had enough trouble maintaining certain links to others of my faith. Now I fear the struggle the gods face requires all his will, which leaves me nothing more to use. I have no power save hope, and even that is dwindling."

"No power?" Aryx surreptitiously focused the emerald orb on the human. The silvery blue aura intensified somewhat, although not nearly as much as it had when the cleric had saved him from falling. Still, he wondered how Rand could speak so casually about his lack of power with such a clear indication otherwise. Surely the cleric had to sense the energy surrounding him. What else could it be but magic of some sort? "None at all?"

"None. Even the mages can barely cast spells anymore. All I have to offer now is a good strong arm, which is what I had intended before coming across you."

Aryx grimaced. One strong arm would serve the battered defenders little at this point. Rand's other abilities would have better suited the dire straits in which they now found themselves, but despite evidence to the contrary, the cleric insisted that they had vanished.

Then what force surrounded the human? If it did not originate from Kiri-Jolith, then from *where*?

A cry, a minotaur cry, made both of them start. Aryx peered

through the fog with the dragon eye. Far away, he could see a Magori shuffling by, its sword crimson. Aryx swore, almost tempted to go after the murderous abomination. If something did not turn the course of events soon, even the power of a hundred master clerics or wizards would be unable to save his people.

"Human . . . Rand . . . you've got to try again!"

Rand shook his head. He looked older than when Aryx had first met him, but the warrior supposed that the cleric saw similar changes in the minotaur. "What is the point? I pray to Kiri-Jolith, I ask him to channel his power through me . . . and little happens."

"Well, then, if the power won't come from him, draw it—" He stared, noticing how the energy always seemed to radiate outward from the human. A thought flashed through his mind. "Draw it from *yourself*." Aryx knew nothing about magic or divine spells, but surely the aura that permeated Rand had to be of some use. He had noticed it around no one else . . . not that Aryx had had much of an opportunity to look. Somehow the gray minotaur suspected that with the aura, the cleric could do *something*, however slight.

"Draw the power from myself? Without my patron, I have no power, Aryx! That is how my faith works!"

"And I tell you, you have power of your own!" Determined to convince his companion, Aryx pulled Rand close. As they touched, the aura flared stronger, nearly blinding the minotaur. "The gods might have abandoned us, Rand, but something still flows through you! This eye—my eye—sees something in you!"

"You are mad!" The human tore free. "I have nothing!"

Aryx tried a different tactic, thinking of his own choices. "Then if Carnelia still lives, she'll certainly die soon . . . and probably at the end of a lance."

Mention of the female knight had the desired effect. Rand's already pale visage turned chalky white. The cleric trembled, probably picturing in his mind the image of his love skewered by a savage Magori. "Carnelia . . ."

The aura flared brighter still. Aryx had to shield the emerald orb. Could Rand truly not see what evidently lurked within and around him? If not the power from a god or magic as most knew it, what *could* it be?

*A new magic that is very old,* a voice in his head replied.

Aryx glared at the sheathed blade, but the Sword of Tears remained suspiciously quiet. Yet if the demon blade had not spoken, then the voice he had heard must have been his own thoughts. The minotaur grunted. Perhaps Rand had the right of it; perhaps Aryx had gone mad after all.

"You are correct, of course," Rand blurted. "Kiri-Jolith would expect nothing less from me. The tenets of my faith insist on always believing in yourself as well, for how can all the power a god might grant be of any use if the vessel is insufficient to the task? I *must* believe that I can do it. . . ."

Aryx had no idea whether or not what his companion said made any sense, but if it at least made Rand try, that would be all the weary minotaur could ask.

"Look within you," he suggested to the human, thinking of how the aura seemed to radiate from inside Rand. The concept had some similarities with the basics of minotaur combat training. A warrior who did not have confidence in his abilities did not survive long. "Draw from within you."

The clatter of arms warned them that the fighting had spread in their direction. Aryx turned to face whatever might confront them, but he left the untrustworthy blade sheathed, hoping he could draw it quickly if danger threatened. "You'd better start now, cleric, while we still have time!"

"Yes . . ." Rand seemed caught up in his thoughts. "Yes."

To Aryx's dismay, he sat down among the rubble, almost as if planning to relax. Then the minotaur saw that the cleric muttered something under his breath, almost as if he sought to put himself into a trance.

This had better work! Aryx concentrated, seeing the aura increase slightly. Whether that meant hope, he could not say. At this point, everything depended on Rand's will.

A shadowy form stepped toward their position, a form too tall for a human in armor and too broad for a minotaur. The lance it held had wicked barbs and more than one tip. Even had Aryx not seen its wielder, the weapon alone would have warned him that here approached no friend.

Reluctantly he drew the Sword of Tears. The green stone remained dull. Aryx wondered if that meant that the blade's powers had faded, too. If so, he would have to treat the artifact like any other weapon and hope his own skills had not rusted from too much faith in magic.

Taking one last glance behind him, he saw that Rand had

stiffened. As seen through the dragon orb, the cleric blazed gloriously. Surely something had to come of all that energy, but would it be enough? If Rand could disperse the fog from the edges of Nethosak, it would give the defenders hope.

The next moment he had to forget about clerics and fog as the Magori warrior stepped into sight. To Aryx's dismay, a second shadow appeared. How many more were there?

Gritting his teeth, the battle-worn minotaur charged toward the first, crying out as he attacked.

The nearest Magori backed up at the sound, almost colliding with the second. Aryx thrust under its guard, but the sword struck the armored hide and bounced off. As he feared, he could not trust the artifact's power any longer.

Recovering, Aryx's nearest foe swung the lance like a staff, trying to bowl the minotaur over. Aryx ducked under the attack, then thrust for the throat. He nicked the snout instead, but the wound deterred the Magori long enough for the warrior to regain his ground.

The second reaver attempted to get by its companion, but the damage caused by the quake made the footing treacherous. The Magori slipped, dropping its sword and falling forward. The accident pushed the first attacker off center, opening him up to another thrust by Aryx.

This time the blade did its work, sinking into the soft throat. Retreating swiftly, Aryx managed to avoid all but a few drops of the acidic blood.

Out of the corner of his eye, he saw Rand still concentrating, but now the human raised his hands over his head. Unfortunately, the aura around him had grown dimmer, not brighter. He wondered if the cleric still attempted to receive his power from his deity despite the minotaur's insistence that Rand should look within himself. "Rand! You're doing something wrong! Kiri-Jolith can't help you! You've got to take it from your—"

Aryx cut off as the second Magori swung at him. He parried the toothy blade, but the two weapons got caught together. The crimson orbs of the Magori flashed, and the abomination tried to pull minotaur and blade toward him. Seeing the reaver's monstrous maw opening, Aryx knew that it intended to bite him as soon as he came within range. Knowing the potency of that poisonous bite, the minotaur warrior pulled as hard as he could.

The Sword of Tears slid free, but Aryx lost his balance, falling onto his back. The Magori, too, struggled with its balance, but it recovered quickly.

"Rand!"

No word came from the cleric. Aryx rolled to the side, trying to rise in time to defend both of them. He had been too hopeful when Kiri-Jolith's gift had revealed some sort of power inherent in the human. Aryx had hoped that, with his encouragement, Rand might be able to help them.

They would die, but not without the minotaur doing what he could to save the pair. In desperation, Aryx threw himself at the remaining Magori, hoping to ram one of his own horns into the invader's neck.

"*Yes!*"

The triumphant cry meant nothing to Aryx as his foe wrapped one massive arm around his waist. What followed made both combatants pause, for suddenly a blinding light spread across the immediate area. Aryx, with his back partly toward the source, managed to protect his eyes. The Magori, caught unaware, hissed in obvious consternation, releasing the minotaur and trying to cover its eye cluster.

Aryx made use of its confusion, bringing the tip of his sword through the creature's snout and into its head. The crustacean shuddered, then tipped backward, collapsing over the rubble.

"Rand! What did—" he stopped, unable to continue.

The cleric stood, arms outstretched. An expression of extreme calm had spread across his face. The silver and blue aura that had surrounded him now extended to envelop Aryx and the two dead Magori as well. The area covered by the aura continued to swell equally in all directions.

Aryx also noticed that wherever the light spread, the fog dissipated. In mere seconds, the street before them had been cleared of the treacherous mist, and now the aura ate away at the murkiness beyond. The minotaur looked around. With or without the use of the dragon orb, he could find no trace of the fog in any location that Rand's spell had touched.

A Magori stumbled as the blazing light ripped away the protective fog around it. To Aryx's surprise, the massive creature shook, then began to retreat to where the mists still offered cover. A second and third of the invaders joined it, stumbling around as if half-blind.

Could it be that they cannot see well in brightness? A hopeful thought, for that meant that without the fog, the enemy would lose all formation, be unable to defend themselves properly.

He glanced back at Rand, who had not moved, apparently not even breathed. Curiously, the cleric looked thinner, worn, yet still his expression remained one of peace.

Sunlight shone down on the patch of ground where Aryx stood. He blinked in mild surprise, having forgotten that the battle had begun only a short time before dawn. The fog had left things so dark his mind had never registered the fact that by now the sun had long risen.

The growing sunlight caused further consternation for those invaders caught in it. They hissed, even cringed from the daylight. Aryx did not think they did so because it physically hurt them, but because it somehow *scared* the aquatic creatures.

A groan warned him just before Rand slumped. The minotaur grabbed the human, barely keeping him from falling to the ground.

"I . . . I did it." The cleric managed a weak smile.

"You certainly did . . . but what did you do?"

The smile widened. "I do not . . . I do not know . . . but I did as you said . . . looked inside me . . . and found this. Praise be to Kiri-Jolith!"

Aryx could no longer see much of an aura about the human, which concerned him. "The light! Will it—"

"It will go on until it no longer needs to go on. I know that, even though I do not know how I know."

While Aryx did not quite follow the last part of Rand's reply, he understood that his fear that the fog would advance again had proven false. Whatever strange magic the cleric had unleashed, it would complete its task.

"Can you move, Rand?"

"With . . . with your help. My horse . . . might still be around the back . . . where I left it."

The horse did indeed remain where the exhausted cleric had said it would be. Returning to Rand, he helped the human mount, then led the animal out into the suddenly deserted street. To his good fortune, Aryx caught a second horse, a black female that had once belonged to a Knight of Takhisis. Bloodstains across the saddle and the mare's neck gave indication of what had happened to its master, yet the horse itself had escaped with only a number of shallow slashes, caused, no doubt, by a lance.

A battle horn blared, followed almost immediately by another. Mounting, Aryx looked again to make certain that Rand would be able to make the journey.

As pale as he had grown, Rand managed to sit straight. "Ride as fast as you can, Aryx. . . . I will manage. I promise."

Encouraged, the young warrior urged the animals forward, hoping to catch up to the other defenders.

Aryx would hear the story about the turning of the battle from others later on. Many a warrior would give his or her version of how the miraculous blaze of light had burst from within the city, spreading across Nethosak and beyond. The beleaguered defenders, minotaur and human alike, could only imagine that the gods had finally answered their prayers. How else to explain what had happened?

The Magori clearly did not share their relief. Wherever the fog burned away, the crustaceans abandoned the fight, even when only a few still stood against them. Some actually dropped their weapons and fell to the ground, shivering. A few of the generals attempted to take prisoners in the hope of learning more about the foe, but each time they discovered that the crustaceans died shortly thereafter.

The reavers who had not simply dropped dead continued to flee toward the water. Their flight was impeded by their fellows, who, not having seen the oncoming light, reacted with confusion. Magori milled around, trying to both fight and run. They made for easy prey for the revitalized defenders, especially those Knights and minotaurs on horseback.

Aryx and Rand arrived near the shore as the cleric's astonishing spell ate away the last of the fog that had enshrouded that part of the island. Scores of the crustaceans still remained, and a few even put up some token resistance, but Aryx could already see that nothing could prevent victory for the minotaurs and their allies.

He wanted desperately to join the rest, if only to strike a last blow in the name of all those who had perished, Seph and Delara likely among them. Aryx had seen no sign of either one, and that had been the only thing to darken his mood in this otherwise glorious moment.

Possibly seeing his horned companion's concern, Rand

said, "Go, Aryx! I'll be all right. I know you're thinking about your brother and the rest who might have died this day. Go and strike a blow for me!"

"I could never strike a blow as great as you did, Rand!"

The cleric shook his head. "But without your encouragement, I would have done nothing. Now, go, Aryx Dragoneye! Go!"

No longer able to restrain himself, the dusky gray minotaur paused only long enough to pick up a battered war axe that some other defender had lost. No more would Aryx trust the Sword of Tears, not even with victory eminent. The blade had tried to kill one of those he knew, the one who had, in Aryx's eyes, saved his people.

The mare proved well trained, racing fearlessly toward the remnants of the Magori horde. Aryx let loose a battle cry, heading toward where the abominations clustered thickest. There, at the very edge of the shoreline, several of the aquatic invaders finally chose to make a stand, perhaps fearing the price of failure even more than the unshrouded day. They moved uncertainly, clearly unable to see well in the bright light, but their armored bodies and savage strength still made them deadly.

The war axe might not have been magical, but Aryx already knew the least protected portions of the invaders. He charged past the other defenders, crying out again and swinging at the nearest invader. The Magori thrust its lance, but the sun took its toll, for the crustacean's lunge went well to the right. Aryx struck at the abomination's snout, striking down the creature with a single blow.

Outnumbered, disorganized, the Magori still claimed many victims. Attempting to sever the arm from one warrior, a massive crustacean instead decapitated an unfortunate minotaur who stood next to the intended victim. The Magori's original foe then lunged, plunging her blade through snout and throat.

Again and again Aryx cut through the remaining ranks of the invaders. A demon possessed, he struck at one, then even as that adversary fell, attacked the next. From time to time, Aryx noticed a strange thing. Some of the Magori who faced him hesitated when the minotaur glared at them. Gradually he came to realize that the crustaceans found his emerald eye even more disturbing than his companions had. Aryx did not argue with the added advantage that gave him, for each time he battled one of the crustaceans, he saw his own dead before him.

The Magori sought the waves for escape or even attempted to burrow into the sand, but the fury of the minotaurs and the knights did not let them retreat without cost. Several of the aquatic reavers died half-buried in the ground or floating in the harbor. Later, the carnage would stun even the hardiest veterans, but for now the only thing that mattered was the extermination of the savage invaders.

Then, at last, Aryx could find no new foe. He turned his war-horse about, trying to locate at least one more Magori, but only hundreds of corpses met his ferocious gaze. Around him, exhausted warriors from both races fell to their knees or held on to one another as they tried to catch their breath. A number clustered near him, and Aryx realized that, in the end, he had led yet another makeshift force against the last of the invaders.

Some of them looked to him for guidance, and more than a few paid special attention to Kiri-Jolith's gift. Aryx tried to look as normal as possible as he ordered them to seek out their friends and loved ones. A number of warriors remained behind to guard the shoreline in case the reavers changed their minds again. Aryx doubted there would be a third battle. The rout had been too complete.

Exhausted, Aryx nonetheless refused to rest until he located the others. He rode through the ravaged port, trying to guess where to find Seph, Delara, and even, if they lived, Lord Broedius and Carnelia. Any familiar face would do.

He found the knight commander first. Lord Broedius, helm in hand, stood wiping his forehead as he surveyed the damage. Several subcommanders and minotaur officers conversed with him, no doubt reporting the extent of the damage. Considering the recent formation of their alliance, the humans and Aryx's people had managed to put together a fairly cohesive force. While the Knights of Takhisis were not exactly the most desirable allies in Aryx's eyes, he conceded that they had been deserving of respect today.

"What about the emperor?" Broedius asked one of the generals as Aryx rode up.

"He survived," responded Hojak. "Led a contingent of the palace guards north of here. Arm wound, but Chot's okay. He—" Hojak cut off as he recognized the newcomer.

The knight commander looked Aryx's way. "Ah. Hail to you, Aryx Dragoneye! One of the heroes of the battle of . . . the battle of Nethosak!" Until now, Broedius had never used the minotaur name for the imperial capital. "According to reports, you must have been in twelve places at the same time, wielding swords and axes ten feet long!"

Uncertain whether the human praised or mocked him, the minotaur replied, "I fought just as everyone else did."

"And where you fought, others found the strength to fight on, despite the foul mist. An insidious thing, that fog. As we suspected, once it lifted, the damned illness began to fade, too. For the first time in days, I can breathe freely. Oh, there are some still beyond help, but those in the ranks with only the first symptoms claim that their lungs have already cleared up . . . and we've you to thank, it seems."

One of the generals raised his axe in salute. "Hail, Aryximaraki de-Orilg! Hail, Aryx Dragoneye!"

Others in the group, even some of the knights, raised their weapons in salute. Aryx felt perplexed. He had done nothing but try to survive the battle. His gaze drifted to the back, where he suddenly noticed Rand in deep conversation with Carnelia, whose arm hung in a sling. Suspicions formed. What had the cleric told them? If anyone deserved to be hailed as a hero, it was Rand.

"I did nothing," he insisted. "Others such as General Geryl are certainly more deserving."

Broedius waved off his protests. "Most think otherwise, Aryx, and those like General Geryl will not be forgotten. Victory might be ours, but the price proved heavy."

How heavy, Aryx finally learned. The casualties among both races had been high, more so, of course, among the more numerous minotaurs. In several areas, even noncombatants had perished, including the very young and very old. The soulless Magori had made no distinction between warrior and child. Any living creature not a part of their swarm had been marked for death. Reports filtered in from beyond the capital of mass deaths, areas completely overrun. In some places, the Magori had wiped out all resistance and had been on their way deeper into the island when the fog had been pushed back by the cleric's spell, which the young warrior later discovered Rand claimed had been a blessing of Kiri-Jolith. Still, no matter how far into Mithas the crustaceans had encroached, all had turned and fled when deprived of the cover of fog.

Among the dead lay many of the clan patriarchs and top-ranking warriors of the realm. Four members of the Supreme Circle had perished, General Geryl chief among them. Dying with Geryl in the desperate stand that had delayed much of the swarm during the last few crucial minutes had been Drej-jen. To Aryx's surprise, the subcommander had rallied what troops remained after the general's death, utilizing minotaur and human alike with respect. Two minotaurs and one knight had survived that stand, and both of the former had reported that Drejjen himself had died only because he had tried to fill in the gap left when one of their own had fallen. A Magori blade had ripped through the knight's breastplate, slaying the subcommander with a single blow.

Despite the many names Aryx heard, two failed to be mentioned. No one had seen or heard from either Seph or Delara. Most of the officers knew them only by sight, but Carnelia and Rand could offer no hope either.

Broedius showed him some sympathy, reminding Aryx that he had once lost a brother, but then the knight turned the conversation back to other reports. Most important was the vast damage to the port and the ships there. "The entire harbor, in fact, is strewn with wreckage and ravaged vessels. As you reported earlier, the *Predator* lies at the bottom, not only useless to us but also creating a navigational hazard. There are others, too. The crustaceans' master made certain that they destroyed as much as possible. So far, reports indicate that at least half, and possibly three-quarters, of the expeditionary ships are beyond saving!"

"Then even though we've won, we still might have lost," Aryx ventured. He looked out at the ruined harbor, studying it while he considered the knight commander's problem. With effort, it would be possible to make the way clear for some shipping. In fact, the southern half needed only to have a few of the worst vessels towed to port, where they could be stripped to repair others. Unfortunately, what Lord Broedius said was true. Few large, sturdy vessels remained. The *Vengeance* had survived with only minor damage, but the *Queen's Veil* might not prove seaworthy. Two of her masts had been shattered, one of which had collapsed onto the deck. She also listed, which made Aryx suspect that the Magori had ripped through some of the planks. She would likely need a complete refitting in dry dock, something they had no time for now.

"Too true, minotaur," Broedius replied to his earlier comment. The knight stared at him under thick brows. "What say you, Aryx? Will they return?"

"My opinion is only one," Aryx pointed out. Seeing that the human would not be satisfied with that, he grudgingly added, "No, I don't think they will, but this isn't over."

"I agree, but for now we must return to the most important matter at hand . . . preparing to get this expedition under way before anything else delays it."

Aryx felt glad to see that he was not the only one stunned by Broedius's almost casual statement. "What do you mean? We've barely survived this attack, and we still don't know how much damage there's been to Kothas! The dead must be properly bidden farewell and the wounded must be tended! As you yourself pointed out, Lord Broedius, we've hardly a good ship left!"

"The dead will be tended to properly, yours and ours, Aryx. The wounded, too. My scouts report that the capital's fared better than you might think. Most of the damage is toward this end. Some supplies were lost, but we can supplement what remains when we reach Ansalon." The knight commander paused, facing both minotaurs and humans, as if daring any to disbelieve his words. "And as for ships, if we must cobble together what we need, then so be it! I already have a number of men ready to inspect the damage to each vessel still afloat, and even if some of them have to be towed, I'll—"

"That will not be necessary, Lord Broedius."

Rand, Carnelia slightly behind him, faced the assembled officers. He smiled briefly at Aryx, then put on a look of calm determination. The young warrior marveled that the cleric could still stand after the effort of his odd spell. Aryx shut his true eye; the aura had again dulled to nearly nothing. Whatever energy the cleric had invoked, he had used almost all of it.

A peculiar magic, the minotaur thought. More a part of him than anything else . . .

Broedius frowned at Rand's interruption. "What do you mean by that, cleric?"

The pale figure cleared his throat. "Do what must be done to gather as many seaworthy craft as possible, Lord Broedius, but we must be under way in a few days."

"And to what do I owe this even greater miracle, my miraculous cleric? Between you and Aryx, perhaps I don't even need the might of the minotaur legions! Perhaps I should just send you two to Ansalon to sweep away the minions of Chaos!"

"Scoff if you like," Rand returned, more defiant now, "but know that in two days, they will be here."

"Ah, yes! Now I understand! But the *Queen's Champion* and the *Dragonwing*, as immense and proud as they are, cleric, will hardly replace what we've lost."

"I do not mean those ships, but if they come, so much the better." Rand glanced at Carnelia, who apparently shared his secret. "No, Lord Broedius, in two days, *others* will arrive."

"Others?" Now the knight commander frowned. "What others? Who? How many? What secret have you been hiding, Rand?"

"One of necessity." He shrugged. "I swore an oath. They felt it best to do under the circumstances, but now I can safely tell you. They will be here when I said, that I promise. Enough ships to enable this expedition to continue and additional warriors to aid in the cause of Krynn."

That said, Rand turned away. However, Broedius remained unsatisfied. "You've still not told me who our new allies are, cleric. Where do these ships come from?"

The thin blond man did not turn, but he did answer . . . to a point. "They come from the east . . . or maybe the southeast, Lord Broedius. I know no more than that. And as to who they are, well, we shall all see . . . in two days."

# The Kazelati

## Chapter Fourteen

On the day on which Rand had predicted the ships would arrive, Aryx found the cleric standing as a lone sentinel on a ridge overlooking the port. He had stood there since morning, never moving, always watching. From time to time, the patient cleric had reached into a small pouch at his side or for the waterskin sitting nearby, but never did he abandon his chosen post, not even when others began to wonder if perhaps his promise had been a false one.

Lord Broedius had questioned Carnelia about this, and to Aryx's surprise, she had defended Rand openly to her uncle, saying that the cleric's word of honor meant as much to him as Carnelia's did to her. Lord Broedius had quieted after that, but from time to time, he had men check the horizon for any sign.

While the cleric patiently waited, word came at last from Kothas and Pries Avondale, the knight commander's representative there. Curiously, the other island had suffered to a lesser degree than Mithas, perhaps because the imperial capital, the heart of the homeland, stood on the latter isle. As with past adversaries, the servants of Chaos had surely seen Nethosak as the prime target. That was not to say that losses had not been heavy on the other island, especially since no one had alerted Avondale as to the new alliance. On Kothas, subcommanders had organized all defenses, led all talons and legions. Half of Morthosak lay in ruins.

However, Pries Avondale had instigated a bit of diplomacy of his own, making certain that minotaurs commanded in some manner, albeit on a minor scale. He had also made certain not to waste their numbers, which Aryx appreciated, knowing that his parents and some of his siblings were there. The knight commander and his second were contrasts in many ways. Broedius carried a passion within him, a passion that had melded to a degree with that of the minotaurs. Pries Avondale, on the other hand, remained more reserved, less likely to reveal his inner self. After the debacle with the crowds at the imperial port, Aryx had feared for the stability of the other island, but Avondale had done his best to smooth matters over. The minotaurs who journeyed with him from Kothas on one of the few remaining ships spoke highly of his efforts during the battle.

More important to Aryx than anything, even the mysterious fleet that had still not arrived, was finding Delara and his brother. Separated from him and driven to another part of Nethosak by the Magori hordes, they had been forced to fight for their lives. Seph had somehow managed to come through nearly unscathed, although he now sported a long scar across his right shoulder, and the tip of his left horn had been cracked off, which caused Aryx to jest that his brother wanted to be the new Orilg.

Delara, however, had suffered a bad gash in her right forearm and a slightly less severe one in her left leg, both of which were now bandaged. Despite her wounds, though, she had leapt up at sight of Aryx, embracing him. Somewhere along the way, Seph had surreptitiously left the pair alone, something they only discovered much later.

Seph and Delara had joined him this morning, the trio forming part of an impatient throng gathered on the water's edge. Word of the mysterious fleet had spread, and many had come to watch, some with weapons, just in case the newcomers turned out to be more danger than aid. Several minotaurs continued to stare at Aryx's emerald orb, and more than once he heard his name whispered along with the unnerving appellation *Dragoneye*. Aryx had related to his companions the fantastic tale of how he had received the orb, but while they managed to treat him the same as before, few others did. Everywhere the warrior went, the whispers followed. *Dragoneye . . . Dragoneye . . .*

He continued to mull over this dismaying addition to his name as he rejoined Delara and Seph.

Delara put her arm around him. "You are back fast. Any change?"

"None. Rand stands up there all alone. I tried to approach him, but he didn't care to have anyone near."

Seph glanced in the direction of the ridge. "Did he say anything about the ships?"

"Nothing. He still acts as if he expects them to arrive, though."

"Perhaps they were delayed by weather . . . or worse," Delara suggested. "We've all heard the rumors about terrible happenings all over Ansalon."

"I'd still like to know who they are. Rand's not let slip any hint. I doubt that they're knights, or else Lord Broedius would've known about them first."

Seph squatted for a moment, trying to work tired muscles. Like the others, he had spent much of the day cleaning up the city, carrying or lifting heavy barrels and crates or shifting old rubble aside. "I just hope they come."

"He's leaving." Delara pointed toward the ridge. "Do you think he's given up?"

In the distance, the weary cleric slowly made his way down the ridge. The others watched, certain at first that Rand had given up his vigil. However, as the cleric descended, he turned toward the docks.

Aryx frowned. "He doesn't look like he's giving up. He looks like he's expecting company . . . and soon. I think we'd better go see."

It didn't take them long to catch up to Rand. He ignored the curious stares of knights and minotaurs as he calmly walked to the very edge of the Blood Sea. As the others approached, he raised both hands high and waited.

"What is it?" Seph called, unable to conceal his eagerness. "Do you see them?"

Rand did not turn his gaze from the sea. "They will be here."

His companions peered out across the water but did not see anything. A thin haze spread across the water, but not enough to prevent them from seeing for quite some distance. Still, no ships appeared. Rand remained stalwart, but Delara and Seph shifted uneasily. Aryx knew that they had come to like the cleric, despite his outward formality, and did not want him falling into disgrace for making such outrageous promises in a time of dire crisis.

Aryx squinted, using the dragon eye in the hope that

perhaps it could see more distant objects. Perhaps the ships were just at the horizon, too tiny for a normal eye to see.

He saw nothing but more open sea. Aryx squinted harder, not knowing if it would make any difference.

An immense shadow materialized in the haze.

Surprised, Aryx opened both eyes wide . . . only to have the shadow fade away. For a moment, he had thought he had glimpsed a fleet of ghost ships, shadowy forms not too distant from the waiting port. Now, however, the minotaur saw nothing.

He squinted again, utilizing only the emerald orb.

The shadow ships materialized again, even closer now. Tall, ominous vessels, reminiscent of minotaur ships save that they were sleeker in design, swifter in the water. As he watched, they cut the distance to the port by half again. Their sails billowed, making full use of the sea winds. Aryx tried to count them, but could not. Not only were there too many, but in the mist, they also seemed to mingle with one another.

"By Honor's Face . . ." he finally managed. "Rand, I think your ships have arrived. . . ."

"What?" Rand shifted position. "You may be right."

He lowered his arms just long enough to take hold of the mace hanging from his side. Raising the weapon above his head, Rand swung the heavy weapon back and forth almost like a flag. The others stood clear, not because they feared being struck, but because they were uncertain as to what the cleric intended.

Suddenly the sea filled with ships.

They materialized everywhere, an armada as great as any the minotaurs had ever assembled. Above each flew a flag both vaguely familiar and yet completely unknown. In a field of gold stood a silver, twin-edged battle-axe. In some way, it reminded Aryx of his own house's clan symbols, but clearly these were not vessels of Orilg nor of any other house. In fact, together the major houses of the empire would have been hard put to gather such a fleet, especially now.

Aboard the foremost ship, he spotted the crew, all minotaurs. To his surprise, they resembled him, being slimmer in appearance and slightly more angular in the face than most minotaurs of the empire. The majority wore kilts similar to his own, save that the garments were of darker hues. The newcomers moved with a supple grace, and from their swift work aboard ship he knew they had reflexes superior to many champions of the arenas.

"Who are they?" Delara whispered. "Where are they from?"

Rand's only reply was a shake of his head. He lowered the mace and watched quietly as the lead vessel maneuvered carefully through the treacherous, wreck-filled waters, at last coming into port.

A vast band of riders approached from the city, Lord Broedius, Carnelia, and several minotaur and human officers among them. The knight commander remained mounted, but Carnelia joined Rand and the minotaurs.

"You spoke the truth after all," the senior knight called. "What you didn't say was just how many ships were coming."

"I did not know a number, only that they would bring as many as possible. I did not even know that they would be minotaurs!" Rand grimaced. "I do know that they and I follow the same patron."

"Oh?" Lord Broedius stared out at the countless vessels. "Are you saying that they all follow Kiri-Jolith?"

"Either Kiri-Jolith or Paladine, my lord."

"Amounts to the same thing, cleric."

Rand shook his head slightly. "Not to some, Lord Broedius."

The ship finished docking. Aryx studied the vessel closer, noting that the name had been written in an old style of minotaur script. *Avenger's Axe*. A strong name.

A sleek brown male with a patch of black running down his muzzle marched toward Rand, followed by two sturdy female warriors who looked enough alike to be twins. All three stood slightly taller than the average minotaur. The male saluted Rand respectfully, ignoring the rest. "Captain Bracizyrni de-Kaz reporting, Revered—"

"I am not the High Cleric. You may simply call me Rand. Did you encounter any trouble en route?"

The captain shook his head. "Some storms, but nothing terrible. A clean voyage . . . Rand. The artifacts used by our robed ones were also able to keep the shielding spells active at all times. I don't think we were noted at all."

Rand shook his head. "We must go with the supposition that you were, Captain Brac. Better to be safe."

"Aye, I suppose you're right."

Aryx looked over the newcomers. On their garments, they wore badges with the same unfamiliar clan marking as the ships' flags. What had the captain said was his name? Bracizyrni . . . *de-Kaz?*

"Clan of Kaz?" he uttered without thinking.

Brac glanced at him, stone-faced. "I claim blood through his brother, Toron Griffonrider."

"And I claim blood directly through his first-born son, Kyris," Aryx immediately challenged, not liking the other's haughty tone.

At first he thought it was his eye that so unsettled the foreign captain, but then he realized that Brac had focused on his lineage. "Direct from Kyris?"

"Yes, direct from Kyris." The sudden increase in respect he sensed from the outsider surprised him.

The cleric interrupted. "Forgive me for interrupting this meeting of cousins, my friends, but we must move on to other matters."

Taking the cue, Carnelia stepped forward. The knight saluted Brac, who saluted back after some hesitation. "I am Carnelia, Knight Warrior of the Knights of Takhisis and representative of Lord Broedius, who sits yonder."

"I am Brac, captain of the *Avenger's Axe*, expedition commander and representative for the ruling council of the Kazelati minotaurs."

"Who are the Kazelati?" Carnelia demanded. "I've no information concerning your branch of the minotaur empire."

Brac almost looked insulted. "We are not a part of the empire. When—" He paused and looked to Rand, who nodded for him to continue. "When the champion, Kaz of the Axe, left the empire, along with him came his mate, Helati, her brother, several of his siblings, including my august ancestor, and countless other warriors who no longer desired their future to be guided by Nethosak. For some time they resided in a region south of the empire. However, finding this to be insufficient, Kaz sent out many to discover a better place where those who followed him could create a newer, superior minotaur society, one that did not prey on others but truly understood the significance of honor and loyalty!"

This last stirred some disgruntlement among the minotaur generals. Already suspicious, they now eyed the captain and his crew as potential enemies rather than allies.

"A shorter and simpler version, please, Brac," Rand tactfully suggested.

"Aye, cleric. Such a place was found in a small set of islands far to the southeast of Ansalon. There the first major settlement of the Kazelati was raised, Ganthysos, named after the Dragonslayer's father. Since then we've kept our existence secret, although from time to time some left to report on the activities of our unenlightened cousins."

Carnelia smirked. "You sent spies to keep an eye on the empire."

"We did not interfere unless absolutely necessary." The captain pointed at Aryx. "By your bloodline, you're descended from some of them, child of Kyris."

Aryx sought to discern some trickery in the stranger's words but could see no guile. He felt a little uneasy, though, as if he had spied on the empire himself.

"There must be a change from the original plan, Brac," Rand finally interjected.

"What change is that, cleric?"

"We need you for more now than simply support. You must act as transport for their forces as well."

"With all due respect, they'll be packed in like—"

The blond human quickly cut Brac off. "All the more important to see to it that we get this journey over quickly. The Knights of Takhisis have a landing point in northeastern Ansalon. This warrior, Carnelia, will no doubt be able to show you and your captains where it is. Meanwhile, we need to send some of the other ships off to the other designated ports, and that has to be done tonight."

Rand detailed the matter as if he had given it the utmost consideration for weeks. Aryx suspected that this had been what had concerned the cleric during his vigil. He had promised the ships without knowing if the newcomers would agree. Fortunately, the more Rand explained what he wanted, the more everyone around him seemed to take it for granted that it would be done. Even Carnelia raised no fuss, although Aryx did not envy her when she finally stepped back to relate everything to Lord Broedius. However, it appeared that even the knight commander saw merit in the cleric's plans, for after he listened to his niece, he made only a few mumbled remarks, then sent Carnelia back to the waiting minotaurs.

Her look of satisfaction said it all. "Let's get this started!"

Rand nodded. "Brac, if possible, please have the *Avenger's Axe* stripped of all nonessential items. You must make as much room as you can."

"He'd better," Carnelia added. "Lord Broedius said that if we can, we're going to pack every warrior available on these vessels."

"You still plan to take so many after all that's happened?" Aryx frowned. "Who will defend Kothas and Mithas if we do that?" He had visions of the old, young, and wounded being slaughtered like cattle by a wave of Magori simply waiting for the bulk of minotaur might to sail away.

The female knight's eyes narrowed as she turned to reply. "We're fighting for the whole world, Aryx, not simply the empire. If the islands have to be stripped to keep this threat from devouring Krynn, can you really argue against that?"

He could not and saw that even the generals remained silent. Aryx doubted that the opinion of the emperor would vary from theirs, too, although inwardly they all had to be anxious. They could not be pleased to leave the islands almost defenseless, but neither could they turn their backs on the war. Honor would not permit it. If the rest of Ansalon, the rest of Krynn, fell because the minotaurs had hesitated to commit themselves wholeheartedly . . .

There's no choice. . . . Aryx quietly watched as Captain Brac made arrangements with the Knights of Takhisis and the imperial command. With this new fleet, it would be only a matter of days before they were ready to sail, only a matter of days until the empire lay open to the world. To save others, the minotaurs risked sacrificing themselves.

The image of Sargonnas flashed in his head—Sargonnas in the Circus, praising his children, speaking of their destiny. Fine, moving words from the god who had, in the end, left them to fend for themselves.

And where are you, Sargonnas? That creature of Chaos, the thing that called itself the Coil, didn't know what had happened to you after the temple had been destroyed! Where have you gone?

Where indeed?

\* \* \* \* \*

The question continued to nag Aryx throughout the rest of the day and the next. Despite that all went well otherwise, that no hint of unnatural fog or sightings of monstrous serpents had been reported, he felt uneasy. It did not help at all that people constantly looked to him as one of the saviors of the capital, nay, the *empire*. Aryx feared the greatly exaggerated stories of his part in the battle of Nethosak might leave other warriors neglectful. From what he had gathered, most of the stories ended with the underdwellers being driven to the bottom of the sea, where they were sucked away by the Maelstrom, never to return.

His darkening mood made him poor company for Delara or his brother, although they remained by him regardless. However, clan activities at last forced Aryx's newfound love to return for a time to her own people, and Seph, exhausted from a day of arranging supplies and helping clear yet more rubble, had collapsed on his bed and fallen immediately to sleep. Aryx, unable to sleep even on the soft bed, at last abandoned the headquarters of the Knights of Takhisis and journeyed out into the evening, keeping his head low and eyes narrowed at all times in order to prevent recognition.

Even in the dark of night, Nethosak rumbled with activity, almost making it possible for one to forget that a fair portion of the city needed to be rebuilt. The crews from the port had already made much headway in clearing part of the harbor, and to everyone's surprise, a merchant ship from the southern part of the mainland, completely oblivious to the dire events going on, had sailed in shortly after that, ready to trade.

Yet despite the rising hopes of everyone else, Aryx couldn't forget that in a short time the harbor, Nethosak, and the rest of his homeland would again be wide open to attack once the armada departed. Somehow he always ended up blaming the gods for that, for had they not brought this terrible situation to Krynn in the first place?

The Temple of Sargonnas—what little remained of it— looked much as he had seen it before. The clerics had done nothing to rebuild it yet, not with the efforts of the empire focused on other matters. Aryx noticed that few people passed near it, most going well out of their way to avoid even glancing at the ruins. He, on the other hand, had no difficulty approaching it, even walking up the steps to the doorway, which still stood intact.

Where are you, O great Blessed One? Aryx silently mocked. Where are any of you now? Does Kiri-Jolith listen to Rand? Do any of you hear us?

On impulse, the minotaur drew the Sword of Tears, glaring at the dim stone in the hilt. If he could have avoided having anyone else fall prey to it, Aryx would have left the demon blade in the ruins, abandoning the sinister artifact the way the gods had abandoned the mortal races. No good would come of the sword, of that he knew for certain.

Aryx stood at the top of the steps for several minutes, but no great insight occurred to him. The wind blew strong and the doors, left ajar after his initial discovery of the demon blade, swung slightly, emitting a low but constant creaking sound that gradually frayed his nerves. Sheathing the sword, Aryx stepped forward and pulled the doors tightly shut.

He blinked. As the doors met, a flash of light from the other side startled him. Gritting his teeth, Aryx immediately shoved the doors back open again, preparing himself.

Wind, darkness, and the remnants of the marble floor greeted him.

"Kaz's Axe!" the gray minotaur muttered. He glanced quickly around, relieved that no one had seen him act the fool. Had he truly expected Sargonnas to reappear now and tell him that everything would be all right? The Horned One had left the sword behind for the very reason that he would not be returning. One demonic artifact had been supposed to make up for his vanishing.

Frustrated at himself, Aryx reached for the doors again.

A hand reached out from nowhere and seized his own, pulling the startled warrior through the doorway.

"You're never satisfied, are you?" asked a voice both familiar and unknown.

Aryx declined to answer, for at the moment, he stood at the edge of a precipice so very steep that he could not see the bottom through the cloud cover. Night had somehow turned into day, a bright, almost golden day, but the beauty remained lost on Aryx as he contemplated what would have happened if he had appeared just a few inches ahead.

"It must run in the blood. I could never be satisfied with my lot either. . . ."

Aryx forced his gaze from the staggering drop and glanced at the speaker, an act that nearly made him step off the ledge in surprise. Another minotaur, a battle-axe fastened to his back, stood next to him, taller, a little wider, and scarred in so many places the younger warrior could not count them all. Proud of muzzle and defiant of eye, the elder minotaur seemed made of silver save for two deep brown eyes. Aryx could not tell whether the coloring of the other's fur had to do with his great age or a force that radiated from him.

Something about the face reminded him of another profile. The snout appeared slightly longer and the horns were a little bent, but somewhere Aryx had met or seen this veteran champion before. He knew that he faced a champion, in fact faced one who had won the highest honors in the Great Circus itself, for a worn medallion still hung around his neck.

He focused with the emerald orb, wondering if perhaps that might help him learn some truth about the silver minotaur.

The elder warrior frowned. "Don't be turning that evil one's gaze on me, lad."

Aryx immediately ceased. "My apologies . . . Habbakuk?"

At first he thought he had offended the glistening figure, but then he realized that the other's expression had not shifted to anger but rather laughter. "Habbakuk? Me? That would be a good jest on Kiri-Jolith and that bunch! Ha!"

The axe, a twin-edged terror, shifted as the silver minotaur laughed. Aryx caught a glimpse of his own confused face in its mirrorlike finish.

The axe jarred another memory to life, but before he could fit the pieces together, his unearthly companion, sobering, looked him in the eyes. "Would that I could send you Habbakuk, lad. Would that I could send anyone other than myself."

Now Aryx at least remembered where he had heard the voice. It had been the one that had contended with the God of Just Causes, the one that had never revealed a face. Surely one of the gods, then, despite the comments to the contrary.

"I shouldn't be doing this, young Aryx, but what penalty could I pay now? They can't kill me again; it's been done too often! Never become a favorite of a god, lad. They'll keep on finding excuses to disturb your rest."

"I don't understand. . . ."

"And you're probably the better for it." The gleaming figure pointed beyond both of them. "We've much to do in very little time. Tell me, can you see that smoking peak over there?"

Distracted, Aryx turned to study the distant peak . . .

. . . only to find himself staring down into the mouth of a raging volcano. Incredible heat swept over Aryx and fiery light nearly blinded him. The minotaur stumbled back in shock, nearly sending himself over the edge of a precipice far steeper than the last.

A buffer of warm air restored his balance. The silver warrior watched him, a hint of amusement in his eyes. Aryx recalled that among Sargonnas's titles, the shadowy deity included Lord of Volcanoes, yet he knew that this figure could not be the Horned One.

"Why are we here?" Aryx finally roared, trying to be heard over the rumbling. The volcano below him was one of the four major fiery mountains found in Argon's Chain, the range which ran down nearly the entire eastern side of Mithas. Although none had erupted in recent memory, they constantly threatened to explode. Aryx still did not know whether the quakes Nethosak had suffered had been because of the invaders or had simply been due to the constant anger of these craters.

"You wanted the lands protected. We have come here to see to that."

The younger warrior was not at all certain that he wanted his people protected in any manner that involved volcanoes. Such protection might end up doing more damage than that against which it defended. He recalled stories of early minotaur settlements completely buried by ash.

His unsettling guide reached into a belt pouch, then held out his hand and revealed a tarnished minotaur horn more than two feet long. Without ceremony, he tossed the horn into the volcano. "Makel Ogrebane."

Aryx knew the name. Makel had been a legendary fighter who had helped free his people from the rule of the ogres . . . for a time, at least. Aryx watched as the horn vanished into the molten pit with a puff of smoke that fluttered skyward, almost as if with a life of its own.

The gleaming minotaur watched the smoke vanish, then turned unblinking brown eyes to Aryx. "Come, lad."

No sooner had he spoken than they stood upon the lip of another volcano. While this one did not smolder as much as the first, its mouth stretched twice as distant. With one sweep, Aryx's companion had taken the pair of them miles to the south.

Here the silver warrior removed a second horn, this one shorter and grayer. The tip looked as if it had been chewed off. He tossed it into the infernal depths with as much fanfare as the first. "Bos of the Blood."

Aryx did not recognize this name, but when the horn touched the molten earth below, a great column shot up, nearly spraying them. Before Aryx could recover from his surprise, the other had transported them to their third destination, where again he repeated his peculiar ritual. This horn, thinner, shorter, and more curved, proved to be that of Jarisi Longarm, a female archer of great renown during the minotaurs' struggle against the dwarves.

At the fourth and last of the volcanoes, the silver champion took more time. Now he removed what seemed the most unremarkable of horns, a plain, tan stick barely two feet long, with very little curve. The end had clearly been broken off long before. A few scratches gave the horn its only character.

The figure beside Aryx at last threw the horn into the sizzling pool far below. "Orilg."

With a gasp, Aryx reached after the artifact, but much too late. As the horn struck the lava, a great puff of steam rose. Aryx squinted to protect his eyes, only to see something unexpected. The steam spread swiftly upward, and as it did, it experienced a ghostly transformation. The vapor became a warrior, a minotaur warrior of unprepossessing yet determined features who rose toward the sky, a short war axe in one hand and a long sword in the other.

The steam dispersed then, and with it the brief if astonishing vision.

"Mithas and Kothas have their sentinels now. Let even dragons beware. . . ." The unearthly figure turned to face the younger minotaur. "The best I could do, lad. Don't worry about the homeland now."

"What did you do?"

"Made an agreement with some loyal friends." He reached out to Aryx. "Give me your hand."

"Why?"

"Don't be suspicious of me. Give me your hand."

Aryx reluctantly did as requested. The silver warrior

seized hold of his wrist. The blink of an eye later, they stood on the original peak.

"If not Habbakuk, then who are you?"

Still clutching Aryx by the wrist, the ethereal figure smiled, then pointed with his free hand at the axe strapped to his back. "If those statues back home don't look at all like me, lad, I would have thought you'd at least recognized him."

The younger warrior glanced again at the wondrous axe, his reflection in it mirroring his confusion.

Mirror . . . face . . .

"I can't help you beyond this. The Father of All and of Nothing is everywhere, and even the gods are hard-pressed. You're on your own now, Grandson. Luck be with you."

The tall, gleaming warrior released Aryx's wrist.

"No!" he shouted, desperate to get more answers. "Kazi—"

"—ganthi!" Aryx finished. "Wait!"

He clamped his mouth shut, looking around at the darkened ruins of Sargonnas's temple. His hand still stretched forward as if he intended to shut the doors. The mountains, the volcanoes, and ghostly figure who had spoken with him had vanished. Even staring with the dragon orb brought no change.

"Aryx?"

Turning quickly, the emerald-eyed warrior expected to see the silver minotaur, but instead none other than Seph awaited him at the bottom of the cracked steps. Seph had his axe drawn and watched his brother with tremendous concern.

"What are you doing here, Seph?"

"I woke and couldn't find you. For some reason, I thought you might be around this area . . . but I didn't expect to see you standing up there like that."

"Like what? What did you see?"

Seph shrugged. "Like you were deciding whether or not to close the doors, which made no sense, Aryx, since the temple doesn't even have any walls."

"That's it? That's all you saw?"

"Was there something I missed? Did Sargonnas come back?"

Aryx debated telling his brother about what he had experienced . . . or imagined . . . but held back. "No, Sargonnas didn't come back. I doubt he ever will."

"Mithas and Kothas will survive, Aryx. I heard General

Hojak point out that if Chaos attacks any of us, it'll be the armada, since it represents the bulk of resistance."

Aryx descended the steps. "He's probably right . . . which is why we should both get what rest we can. Sorry to worry you, Seph."

"Well, with everyone else in the family spread throughout the empire, the two of us have to keep together. I don't want anything happening to you."

"Nor I you." As they abandoned the ruins of the temple, the dusky gray warrior realized that, imagination or not, he felt more secure about the fate of the islands. They would survive . . . for now. What Hojak had said made sense; if a threat still existed, the fleet would be its target. The ships represented not only the minotaurs' greatest hope, but possibly the hope of a good portion of the rest of Krynn as well.

Yet even in the most peaceful of times, the Maelstrom ever sought to appease its great hunger, and to have any chance of reaching the mainland quickly, the ships would have to skirt close to it.

Very close . . .

# The Maelstrom

## Chapter Fifteen

Just when Aryx and so many others had believed it could never happen, the greatest fleet in the history of the minotaurs, and perhaps even in the history of all Krynn, prepared to set sail. The ships from Kothas left first, arriving in the waters just off Nethosak. They were soon followed by those from the lesser ports. When all had gathered, the *Vengeance* and the *Avenger's Axe*, looking like sister ships in both name and determination, set forth, flagships for the grand expedition that would bring unimaginable legions of minotaurs to fight for glory and the survival of the world.

They could not, of course, fit every able warrior aboard the fleet. Even at its peak, the minotaur empire could never have done so. Lord Broedius had finally settled on transporting an armed force to the knights' command point, then immediately sending the ships back in order to load and transport a second army. With the threat to the islands apparently over, the commander felt the way clear for full-scale efforts in every aspect of the expedition. His intentions were obvious to most. He planned to present Lord Ariakan with the full might of the minotaur empire as soon as possible, whatever the cost.

To Aryx, it seemed only he doubted the clear destiny of the armada. However, as he stood on the deck of the *Vengeance*, watching the other ships follow, he could not help but admire the effort. Granted, much of the fleet consisted of the slim ships the Kazelati had provided, but the Kazelati were minotaurs, too, after all. Their triumphs were triumphs for the entire race.

He still had reservations about them, as did many from the empire. It was incredible to think that a society such as theirs had existed in secret all these centuries, watching the movements of the empire. Still, the Kazelati followed a noble lineage, and none of them looked ready to shirk their duty. They would fight beside their cousins against the Chaos creatures, as willing to die for the cause as any.

Clouds covered the heavens, but out in the open sea that often proved the case, especially the nearer one sailed toward the Maelstrom. No one knew for certain whether the vestiges of the Magori horde would attack at all, but Lord Broedius still insisted on the utmost precautions, which had been why their course lay so near the titanic whirlpool. Even the Magori would be at risk in the turbulent waters there.

The winds increased the farther out they got, another effect of the Maelstrom. Shouting made Aryx turn to watch the *Vengeance*'s crew, the humans having to work harder to compensate for the shifting sea. Fortunately several minotaurs rode aboard the vessel, their knowledge of the Blood Sea invaluable now. Slightly ahead of the *Vengeance*, the *Avenger's Axe* sailed a smoother course, its minotaur crew more adept at dealing with the wild waves.

Aryx could not say why, but he thought a change had come over the knights. Many of them had grown sullen, silent, and at times quite careless, despite the great victory won. Overall, he thought that they seemed distracted, as if a troublesome secret weighed heavily on the mind of each. Even Lord Broedius did not always act as himself, on occasion forgetting orders he had given or snapping at others for no good reason. Aryx had originally chalked it up to the humans' anxiety to return to the mainland, but now, after studying them up close aboard the ship, he wondered if perhaps they had another reason for their distraction.

Trying not to waste time puzzling out the minds of humans, he stared back along the route they had sailed. Mithas had finally vanished in the distance, but Aryx could not help but wonder how those left behind were faring. Some sections of the imperial port already functioned, while others had been left in such disarray that some questioned whether they would ever recover. To the surprise of many, additional foreign vessels had arrived in a few locations, most of their captains as unaware of the overall devastation wrought across parts of Krynn as the first merchant had been. In great need of the goods, those who could dealt with the newcomers, but few able minotaurs had been left behind to handle affairs. The emperor had reluctantly stayed behind to help coordinate the latest recovery efforts. Two of the surviving members of the Supreme Circle assisted him.

"You ought to come away from there," Delara whispered in his ears. "The Blood Sea looks extremely turbulent today."

He put his arm around her. Fate had thrown the pair of them together, and although they had barely had time to learn about each other, Aryx found himself thinking about the future . . . if the expedition succeeded. Delara did not stare at his emerald eye the way others still did. She saw only Aryx when she looked at him, not someone marked by the gods, and he very much appreciated that.

"Where's Seph?"

"Your brother's with the Kazelati volunteers who joined us from *Avenger's Axe*. Ever since he found out about these Kazelati, he's been pestering them with questions. He wants to discover all he can about these strange cousins of ours."

"And has he found out anything?"

"Hard to say. He seems in awe of them." Delara snorted, not entirely trusting the newcomers. "I find them arrogant."

A startling shift came over the weather. The wind intensified, the clouds thickened, and the waves rose higher and higher. The sudden change did not startle Aryx much, for now he could also hear a distant roaring, the Maelstrom's hungry call. Sailors on not only the *Vengeance* but every ship within sight darted about, tightening lines, loosening others, adjusting sails, and hoping that nothing would send them off course into the sea's voracious maw. Every minotaur respected the power of the Maelstrom.

Delara clutched the rail. "If the underdwellers try to swim in that, they'll be tossed all over the place."

"Maybe." Aryx tried not to underestimate the aquatic reavers and their sinister puppet master.

"And, of course, with you and the cleric aboard, they wouldn't dare attack in the first place . . . not after the way you drove them from the islands."

He wished he could believe her, he really did, but Aryx did not doubt that the crustaceans would try again, if only because they feared the Coil.

"You two had better go below." Rand, blond hair already soaked, stumbled toward them. He had not fully adjusted to the frantic rocking of the ship. "I know I will as soon as I can. The route we took to reach Mithas was nothing like this. I now know for certain that I prefer land to sea."

Aryx held back a chuckle. He liked the human cleric enough not to mock his troubles. Through the dragon eye, he saw that the aura had regained some intensity. "Don't say that too loud, or Zeboim might just take offense, human."

Thinking of the goddess, Aryx glanced out at the wild water. Had Sargonnas been with them, he could have perhaps persuaded his tempestuous daughter to bless their voyage, but then could they have trusted such a promise?

"I have the most humble respect for her as I do the rest of the gods, even—" Rand bit his lip. "Aryx, Delara, I must ask you something. Will you keep it to yourselves?" When they both nodded, he pressed on. "Have you noticed anything amiss among the Knights of Takhisis? Have you noticed a growing uncertainty?"

"They seem pretty certain to me," Delara interjected. "A haughty but capable bunch . . . for humans."

Aryx hesitated, not sure what he should admit to the cleric. Carefully he replied, "They seem distracted."

"Distracted . . . a delicate choice of words, my friend. I will be frank with you. You know that each of the Knights of Takhisis follows a Vision?"

Again Aryx nodded, but Delara added, "I've heard about it a couple of times, but I still don't quite understand."

Rand's expression darkened. "Her Infernal Majesty set upon each of her chosen knights a Vision in which they see their part in her eventual victory. The Vision spurs them on, makes them fanatical in their loyalty to her." The cleric hesitated, clearly looking as if he were about to betray someone. "Just a short time before the departure of the armada, Carnelia came to me and told me that she could no longer see the Vision Takhisis had cast for her. The Vision had simply ceased at some point. It was as if her goddess had severed any connection between the two of them."

"Was Carnelia being punished for something?"

"She thought as much herself, although for what crime, she could not say, but after she told me, I watched the others. I have come to the conclusion that not one of them, not even

247

Lord Broedius, although he hides it better, has any link to his patroness. For reasons I cannot fathom, Takhisis appears to have abandoned her knights. I believe they now go on mostly because of Lord Broedius's leadership."

Aryx tried to remain calm. Memories of the conversation he had heard through the temple doors returned. Sargonnas had been arguing with a female, one who had talked about deserting. "Why come to me?"

"Despite your faith in Kiri-Jolith, Sargonnas favored you. I wondered if he . . . but, no, it was a foolish thought. Why would even you know what occurs between the gods?"

Again Aryx thought about telling Rand his suspicions concerning the possible confrontation between Sargonnas and his mate, but in the end, he decided to hold back. To tell the knights that their goddess had truly abandoned both them and Krynn only served discord. Besides, did they really want the help of the dark gods at this juncture?

The cleric took his silence for his answer. "My apologies for even presenting such an absurd question, Aryx. I had hoped to give Carnelia some comfort."

A sudden jolt sent the human to the rail. Grimacing, Rand eyed the door leading to the cabins. With his rank as a cleric, he had been given a small private room. The human would have turned it down, but Broedius had insisted, pointing out that, as with the quarters provided in the capital, none of his officers cared to bunk with a nonbeliever.

"I think I've had enough of this for now. Would that I could calm this sea with the same power I used to push back the fog, but a second such miracle seems beyond me, perhaps forever. If you will excuse me . . ." Fighting the shifting deck, the cleric wended his way toward the door.

"Look there!" Delara whispered, suddenly pointing out to sea. "The Maelstrom!"

Even in the distance, the edge of the immense whirlpool could be seen. Water rose in swift, cascading waves, spiraling off farther in the distance. Bits of flotsam and jetsam, some pieces as big as small boats, floated helplessly toward the distant maw. The roar of the Maelstrom escalated with each passing moment.

The ships began to turn, the captains countering the Maelstrom's effect. Minotaurs knew better than anyone the idiosyncrasies of the titanic whirlpool and thereby understood where best to take advantage of its power. A good captain could actually speed up his journey by skirting the outer limits of the Maelstrom.

"All hands to stations!" somebody roared. If the crew had looked active before, they now moved with a fanatical pace. Everyone understood that a single error could send the ship on a course to the bottom of the Blood Sea.

As was typical, the clouds grew stormier the nearer they sailed. Thunder rolled, trying to compete with the roar from the vortex. Lightning played in the clouds. Rain began to add to the constant spray. The change proved more remarkable in that it took place in but a few minutes.

"We've got to get below!" Delara shouted.

"Go! I'll be there in a moment!" Despite a part of him that urged Aryx below, the minotaur did not move. He felt drawn to the Maelstrom, drawn to its fury. The whirlpool had been a part of his background since his birth. Since the Great Cataclysm that had destroyed Istar and created the minotaur isles, the Maelstrom had spun. It had become as certain a constant to his people as the sun and the moons.

A figure stepped near him. Thinking it was Delara, Aryx turned to insist that she go below without him.

Lord Broedius stood at the rail, the rain and spray seeming not to bother him one bit. Like Aryx, he, too, appeared fascinated by the Maelstrom.

"Will we have any trouble?" the minotaur shouted.

"The Maelstrom is the least of our worries," the knight commander replied. "I doubt we're alone out here."

"The Magori?"

"Perhaps. The servants of the Chaos come in many forms. The other ships are already being warned to be wary."

Aryx looked behind them. Far back, he could see one of the knights signaling with a covered lantern. From the *Avenger's Axe* came an answering flash, at which point the knight turned to signal another vessel. Meanwhile, someone aboard Captain Brac's ship began contacting yet others.

The ever-increasing rain swiftly threatened to turn into a full-fledged storm. Aryx gripped the rail, wondering at his own sanity for remaining on deck any longer.

Lightning crackled, and a bolt struck the sea near one of the other lead ships. Aryx tried to stop thinking about the Maelstrom by turning his gaze toward the direction of their eventual destination. The rain and seawater forced him to squint to try to keep the moisture out of his eyes.

A vast black ship rose high in the distance, seemingly completely at the mercy of the mad sea.

"By the sea goddess . . ." Aryx gripped the rail tighter as he tried to make out the storm-tossed vessel. It was a three-masted giant, almost identical to the *Vengeance* save that one of the masts had been torn completely away and the sails on the others were mere tatters. The ship listed to one side, and now and then a great wave would wash completely over the deck.

"Lord Broedius . . ."

The senior knight followed his gaze. Broedius cursed the moment he made out the ship. "One of ours . . ."

Although the other vessel remained distant, Aryx could just make out a few details now. "The rail's shattered in several places. That second mast will collapse soon. I think . . . I thought I saw a body, but I can't be certain."

"Never mind that, minotaur! Quick! Can you see any banners, any marks whatsoever to identify her?"

By this time, many others had noticed the battered vessel. Both men and minotaurs paused, trying to see it.

Aryx scanned the ship, searching for some identifying mark, but only spotted a tattered flag at the end with the skull and lily symbol of the Knights of Takhisis. He informed the knight commander of his failure.

"We've got to get nearer! I must know!"

"The Maelstrom's already got hold of her! If we go too near, it may pull us in with that ghost!"

Broedius would not hear him. The knight shouted orders. Although they clearly did not like them, the crew readily obeyed. Someone signaled from the *Avenger's Axe*, no doubt wanting to know the reason for the insane shift in course, but Broedius did not allow his signalman to answer it.

"Just tell them to remain on course!" he commanded.

Nearer and nearer they sailed, the water growing frothy. At one point, Aryx thought their attempt would end unfulfilled, for the other vessel suddenly listed more, almost lying on its side. However, another wave rocked it back upright, practically turning the ship toward its pursuers.

The crew worked frantically to keep the *Vengeance* from suffering a similar fate. Broedius ignored them, concerned only with seeing the other vessel up close. Others came on deck, including one of the Kazelati officers, a pretentious minotaur with sleek horns and almost golden fur.

"What is the meaning of this? I was just informed that we have altered course. Captain Brac will not—"

A single glance from the ebony-eyed knight silenced Brac's representative, who stepped back, still indignant.

Aryx tried to satisfy the knight commander's thirst for information before the two ships either collided or were both swept into the maw of the whirlpool. He shouted out descriptions of every bit of damage he could make out, but nothing would satisfy Broedius.

Then Aryx spotted a form tangled in the ropes and another impaled on a broken rail. Knights, both of them, although the second one had clearly not had time to armor himself. The dragon orb enabled Aryx to see that they had both been dead for some time. They were the only victims on deck, but from a ship this size, Aryx knew that countless more lay below or had been scattered to the sea.

At last the derelict came near enough so that the minotaur could read the name.

*Dragonwing.*

He pulled back from the rail, his worst fears justified. Lord Broedius noted his actions and turned on Aryx, awaiting word. Aryx first described the two figures he had seen and his suspicion that more lay below. Broedius nodded, but clearly understood that the minotaur had one last bit of information to impart.

"It's the *Dragonwing*, Knight Commander. Your reinforcements have arrived. . . ."

The veteran knight cursed the heavens, cursed the Chaos, and, to Aryx's surprise, even Takhisis. "You're certain that it could be no other ship, minotaur?"

"Any closer and even you'll be able to read the name yourself, Lord Broedius." In fact, if the two ships did get any closer, the *Vengeance* definitely risked a collision.

"Then we may assume that the *Queen's Champion* has also been lost." Broedius wore an expression of extreme weariness, causing the dusky gray warrior to wonder if the human had slept lately. Recalling the cleric's revelation concerning the knights and their goddess, he suspected not.

The *Dragonwing* drew perilously near as the current began

to shift both vessels. Aryx waited for Broedius to give the order to turn about, but the knight commander did nothing, still staring at the derelict. At last unwilling to risk matters any longer, the worried minotaur turned and shouted, "Turn her about! Quickly!"

Broedius looked at him, but did not countermand his orders. More than a little relieved, the crew immediately obeyed. Aryx watched with concern as, despite their efforts, the *Vengeance* initially made little headway. The *Dragonwing* drew closer, almost as if the specters of its dead warriors sought to take those aboard the other ship with them to the Abyss. Now anyone who looked close could see the two macabre corpses and read the name of the vessel.

Just as it seemed they would collide, the *Vengeance* pulled away, the skilled minotaur sailors having completely taken over for the humans. Beyond Aryx's ship, the *Dragonwing* suddenly shifted direction, a tremendous wave tossing her on a course almost directly toward the waiting Maelstrom.

"She promised them the future of Krynn," Broedius muttered. "She promised all of us the future of Krynn. . . ."

"Lord Broedius, they're beyond our help. You have this fleet to be concerned about."

The knight stiffened. "I've not forgotten myself, minotaur, but know that like your own *Kraken's Eye*, I knew many of those aboard the *Dragonwing* and her sister ship. I trained with some, trained others myself. They did not die in battle; they were slaughtered!"

Memories of his crew mates flashed before Aryx's eyes. "I know that, Knight Commander, and we may still face the same fates in these very waters."

"Yes, you're absolutely right." Broedius looked around. "I think perhaps I overestimated the safety this region would provide us."

Lightning again crackled. Another bolt struck the sea, a sight not uncommon around the Maelstrom but one that nonetheless Aryx found disturbing. Closing his mortal eye, Aryx stared carefully in the direction of the monstrous whirlpool. All seemed normal until he studied the very fringes. Through the emerald orb, the minotaur spotted what he thought appeared to be *sparks* flying out of the vortex. Many claimed the phenomenon to be in great part magical, its creation having come with the destruction of

Istar and the swallowing of much of the eastern side of old Ansalon, but now, for the first time, Aryx glimpsed some of that wild power. He wondered where such magic came from and if it could be harnessed. In some ways, it reminded him of the aura that had surrounded Rand, but more intense, untamed.

A shift in the clouds caught his attention. Something else besides lightning crackled up there as well. If the edges of the Maelstrom had teased him with brief glimpses of magic, the skies directly above abruptly swelled with raw power.

"Gods above and below!" he gasped. So much power, and all coming into play so near the ships. Another bolt struck the water, again close to one of the lead vessels. Aryx had experienced storms during sea voyages before, including some in the regions surrounding the Maelstrom, but something about this encroaching storm disturbed him as none other ever had. He did not think his concerns due simply to the possibility of attack; the very elements themselves unsettled him for reasons he could not explain.

Despite the danger, there could be no turning back for the *Vengeance*. This deep into the Blood Sea and with so many other vessels following its lead, the flagship could only press on. Planks groaned and sails fought desperately to contain the mad winds. Gradually they drew next to the *Avenger's Axe*, which struggled to maintain its course.

A flash of crimson enveloped the heavens, a flash that even without the dragon orb, Aryx would have had no trouble noticing.

A sense of foreboding swept over him.

Lord Broedius noticed. "What is it?" The knight commander wiped water from his eyes. "Was it that strange lightning flash?"

"Something's about to happen! I'm certain of it! We've got to get away! Alert the other ships of impending danger!"

The human looked at him, trying to gauge whether or not Aryx's warnings carried merit. Then, his expression growing still grimmer, the knight commander turned. "All ships to stand by for attack! Send the warning! Quickly!"

Frantic signalmen waved lanterns toward the nearest vessels. The Sword of Tears still hung sheathed at Aryx's side, but he reached instead for his war axe. The sword he would only use as a last desperate resort.

"The warning has already been passed on through half the fleet," Broedius said with some relief.

General Hojak and the Kazelati representative joined them. "What's the meaning of this?" Hojak rumbled. "Where's the threat?"

"What could possibly attack us in this violent—" began the Kazelati.

Out of the maw of the whirlpool shot a score and more crimson bolts, lightning from *below*, not above. They flew up high into the air, then arced downward, some of them dropping toward the fleeing armada.

A Kazelati ship in the distance burst into flying tinder as the first bolt touched down.

"By the axe of Kiri-Jolith!" Aryx gripped the rail, the blood draining from his face. How many minotaurs had just died? He looked at the others, seeing his own horror reflected there.

The other bolts rained down, but fortunately many missed direct targets. However, a few struck and struck well. A second vessel, one of the survivors of the siege of the empire, burst into flames. Several others caught fire simply by being grazed by the passing bolts.

"Find Rand!" Lord Broedius roared.

Aryx wondered if the knight commander thought that Rand could repeat his stunning spellwork. The minotaur had his doubts, but he understood that something had to be done or the fleet would face total devastation. Even as Aryx watched, a third vessel burst into flames. More close, the *Avenger's Axe* suffered a burning sail, one which Captain Brac's crew frantically sought to save.

One of the burning ships suddenly shifted direction, no longer able to keep free of the Maelstrom's lengthy grasp.

A thump caught Aryx's attention. Recalling the final seconds before the slaughter aboard the *Kraken's Eye*, he cautiously leaned over the railing and peered down. Too late, he recalled Hercal's sudden and terrible death, but no barbed lance shot up, only a violent wave that drenched the minotaur.

Looking through the dragon eye availed him no better at first, although it did give him a slightly better view under the surface. Aryx scanned the side of the ship. So far, he saw no Magori, but . . .

There. Only a glimpse, but the shelled back could not be mistaken for anything else.

Aryx straightened, shouting at the top of his lungs. "Magori near the hull!"

No sooner had he spoken than the first of the aquatic attackers rose out of the sea.

His earlier word of warning to Broedius had already set defenses into motion. Knights trotted to the rail, bows in hand. Aryx recognized few of them save that they were among the best archers the humans had to offer. Despite the storm, despite the waves, the archers did not move like men with a hopeless task. The minute they reached their destination, the knights immediately sought out targets, steadying their arms as best as possible.

The first of the monstrous reavers got a handhold on the ship's side. Despite their aquatic nature, the Magori appeared almost as uncomfortable with the raging sea as those aboard did. Had it been their own choice, Aryx suspected that the underdwellers would have chosen a different time and place to attack, but the sinister Coil clearly did not care.

A shaft buried itself in the throat of the initial attacker, sending the dead Magori falling back into the ocean. However, by that time, countless more crustaceans sought to clamber upward. Considering that they had to use one hand to hold their weapons, the Magori proved dexterous indeed, their feet acting almost as a second pair of climbing hands.

The archers let loose a steady rain of their own, and the first line of the foe died to a member. However, the shifting deck and the harsh spray slowed the humans' efforts more and more. The first opponent Aryx could reach pulled itself up over the rail, only to die from one swift blow of the minotaur's axe.

"Don't let them get aboard," a voice Aryx recognized belatedly as Delara's shouted. A moment later she reached the rail, arriving just in time to push one of the underdwellers back into the sea.

Stepping back, Aryx glanced at the nearest other ship, the *Avenger's Axe*. Although they had the fire under control, the other flagship now had attached to it more than twoscore crawling Magori . . . and that just on the side that he could see. Did all the other ships in the fleet have such numbers attacking? The legions of the Magori seemed endless.

More and more warriors, both human and minotaur, came on deck. Now a new problem arose, for although they had great numbers of their own, the defenders nearly tripped over one another. Everyone wanted to do his part to defend the ship, for without it they were all lost.

Delara pushed against him, sword already stained. "I thought I'd never reach you! This is madness! We're likely to strike one another down before the underdwellers even have the chance!"

"I know!" He looked back. "Form ranks! Take turns! Don't bunch up!"

Some seemed to hear his frantic shout, for lines did begin to form. Others, Lord Broedius's voice foremost among them, began crying further orders. The archers withdrew, now too close to remain effective. Knights and minotaurs with hand weapons moved up to fill the breaches, and when no gap remained, other warriors held their positions, awaiting their opportunity.

Aryx stepped back for a moment, again forced to wipe water from his eyes. However, as he looked up, the minotaur thought he saw huge tubular forms breaking through the surface of the water just at the very edge of the titanic whirlpool. As with the last time Aryx had seen them, they revealed no beginning or end, only gargantuan trunks that could crush or wrap around an entire ship. The shapes rose briefly above the sea, then sank out of sight again.

The Magori's master had come to see that they completed their bloody task.

He looked around to see if anyone else had noticed the monstrous serpentine forms, but the battle had seized the full attention of everyone else. By this time, all semblance of order had vanished in the fleet. Some vessels drifted helplessly toward the Maelstrom, while others did their best to either hold their positions or sail in the opposite direction from the terrible sea. Several were still on fire, and every ship that Aryx could make out had Magori attached to its hull.

A new danger loomed as Magori on one nearby vessel began trying to chop their way through the hull. Aryx glanced down at his own ship and saw one of the creatures attempting the same thing. Fortunately, as it raised its lance, a wave knocked the crustacean back into the water.

The treacherous sea worked with the fleet in this one instance. Many of the Magori could not hold on to the bottom of the hull for very long, not with the way the waves rocked and tossed each vessel. Still, the threat remained a real one, especially for those vessels trying to move to calmer waters.

"They're aboard ship!" someone suddenly cried.

Aryx whirled about, sighted three, then four of the Magori on the upper deck. To his horror, among the defenders up there he noted Seph. His younger brother wielded an axe beside Carnelia. More Magori pressed on, though, using the defenders' own numbers against them. The foremost creatures held barbed lances, forcing knights and minotaurs to either back up or be pierced.

Beyond them, arms upraised, stood Rand, who clearly had come back on deck with the hope of performing another spell, likely at the knight commander's behest. The cleric seemed to be beseeching the heavens for help, but Aryx noted that the aura remained almost dormant. Rand still thought that his miracle had been granted him through Kiri-Jolith, but the minotaur had by now become certain that the blond human drew his power from elsewhere, either himself, the world around him, or some combination. Seph and Carnelia did their best to protect the cleric as he tried to help the armada, but they were all doomed to failure unless someone made Rand see the truth.

Then a Magori blade nearly caught Seph in the throat, and all concern over the cleric's spells vanished as a more personal fear overwhelmed Aryx.

"Let me through!" He left his position, knowing full well that another eagerly waited to fill it. All he could think about was the danger to his brother. He had already lost one sibling to this war, possibly even more. Seph, though, had always been the closest to him. To lose Seph would be like losing his own arm.

However, a great flash caused him to pause in his tracks. Other fighters on both sides hesitated, trying to see the source. A fearsome display of elemental forces shot forth from the very center of the Maelstrom, turning the Blood Sea even more turbulent. Waves taller than the masts of the *Vengeance* crashed down on one of the ships already caught in the pull of the whirlpool, swamping it.

Knowing he could do nothing for those aboard the other vessels, Aryx renewed his efforts to reach his brother and Rand. Unfortunately, most of the other combatants recovered from their shock at nearly the same time, making his path difficult. A Knight of Takhisis fell in front of Aryx, his face ripped off by a lance. Before Aryx could reach the crustacean responsible, two minotaurs assaulted the creature, one chopping off its right hand, the other driving his axe into its head. Aryx took a breath, then pushed on.

Most of the original Magori had perished, but more climbed the sides to take their place. Several moved in on Seph and the others. Aryx's brother fought bravely, deflecting a Magori scythe sword and wounding the monster in the side of the throat. Aryx's hope rose; if Seph and the others maintained a united front, they would remain safe.

"Aryx!" Delara's voice came. "Drop!"

He obeyed immediately, trusting her urgency. A scythe sword buzzed past his horns exactly where his throat would have been. He rolled over, eyeing the monstrosity looming over him. However, the Magori no longer paid him any attention, Delara having already engaged it. Her swift sword darted past the crustacean's own blade again and again, although most of her attacks resulted only in superficial wounds. Aryx shifted to his knees, and as the underdweller stepped past him, he rose and jammed the sharp point of his axe into the creature's soft throat.

Acid burned his fingers, but Aryx gritted his teeth and shoved higher until at last he felt the creature shudder its last. The minotaur removed the axe, marveling that the damage to both his weapon and his fingers had not been more severe. Forced to pause again, Aryx glanced to the side and noticed an unsettling glow forming around the Maelstrom. He hoped that the fleet could escape before the whirlpool engulfed them, too.

In the time it had taken Aryx to kill his foe, still more of the foul crustaceans had swarmed over the rails of the upper deck. Even the storm could not wash away the musky stench surrounding them, and the clouds only served to let the Magori see well enough to attack their enemies with horrific precision. They harried the suddenly outnumbered defenders, dividing them. Rand remained well protected, but others were in desperate straits. Carnelia had Seph beside her, but he kept darting forward to strike, then quickly returning to the line. The female knight clearly wanted him to stay nearby, but Aryx's brother grew more and more reckless.

Only a few yards separated them now. Aryx shoved past a

knight who stood wiping acidic blood off his sword. Delara remained with Aryx, defending his flank.

"There's more of them coming over the side!" she called.

He saw exactly what she meant. To the harried defenders' right, half a dozen aquatic reavers poured over the rail, weapons at the ready. Two knights turned to meet them, a necessity that unfortunately divided the defenders' forces yet more. Carnelia's band, which consisted of another knight and three minotaurs, including Seph, tried to shift toward this new attack, but in doing so, the band fragmented further. Seph and Carnelia's sole knight found themselves separated from the rest.

A dying Magori stumbled into Aryx and Delara, sending all three back several paces. Aryx pushed the monster aside.

The knight alongside Seph fell to one knee, acid streaks across his tortured features. Seph reacted instinctively, trying to help the injured human up while still fighting. He did not see the Magori with the broken scythe sword coming up on his right.

"Seph! To your right!" Aryx leapt toward the two trapped combatants.

Aryx's younger brother looked up and saw the savage crustacean too late. He tried to deflect the blade with his axe but misjudged.

The broken sword tore a great gash in the young minotaur's chest. '

A cry erupted from Aryx's mouth, a horrible cry that startled more than one fighter on both sides. Axe raised high, the rage-filled minotaur cut down the Magori who had wounded his brother. The blade broke through the armored shell, sending an acidic spray across Aryx's chest. The physical pain only added to his mental anguish, turning him into a berserker. He tore into the next invader without hesitation. When that Magori fell, Aryx went after a third, beheading the creature as it futilely raised a lance to block the blow.

Again and again he tore into the aquatic reavers. Only at last, when none stood before him, did his rage abate enough for Aryx to realize what he had done. He looked around, his breath coming in ragged gulps, and saw those around him staring in both awe and fear.

"Aryx!" Delara nestled Seph in her arms. She had tried her best to bandage him, but too much blood had already seeped out, drenching the young warrior's body. Surprisingly, Seph remained conscious, although clearly pain wracked him.

"Seph!" Fighting continued on the lower deck, but Aryx abandoned his axe and went to his brother's side. Seph tried to greet him, but the effort proved too painful. "Seph! Don't move!"

"You were . . . Kaz of the Axe . . . there, Aryx. . . ." Seph coughed up blood. "Nothing could . . . could stand in your way. . . . You're a . . . a great warrior. . . ."

"Easy, Seph!" Aryx looked around for Rand. The cleric had saved him from grave wounds; surely he could do the same for Aryx's brother. Rand, however, stood in the midst of a blazing aura, somehow having at last rediscovered the path to his spells. Aryx ached to call the cleric to him, but if he did, then Rand might lose the one chance to save the fleet. Aryx did not even know if the human could repeat his earlier success, yet he had to be given the opportunity. Otherwise, more defenders than Seph would perish.

"The sails!" someone roared. "The sails are coming loose!"

The *Vengeance* lurched, no longer under even the remotest control of its crew. As the ship turned, Aryx saw two other ships in the distance collide, the bow of one completely demolishing the aft section of the other. As terrible as the sight was, however, the minotaur cared about only one thing: His brother lay dying, and he could do nothing. He gripped Seph tight as the flagship of Lord Broedius's armada began turning back toward the whirlpool.

The whirlpool continued to glow and swell, as if all the primal forces in the world had gathered there. It rocked the ships so violently that even the Magori could hold on no longer. By the scores, they plummeted back into Blood Sea. Even some of those aboard abandoned the attack, clearly sensing that some event both monumental and terrifying was about to take place.

The sinister glow within the Maelstrom flashed once, then again.

Then the Maelstrom *exploded*.

A spiraling column of water shot from the mouth of the whirlpool, rising so high in the sky that it nearly reached the clouds. A torrential downpour washed over the fleet. Crew and invaders clutched to whatever they could, but for some that proved not nearly enough. Aryx and Delara were fortunate;

crouching low to the deck, they and Seph slid against the rail. At least one knight fell overboard, his armor guaranteeing his death.

A rain of flotsam and jetsam pelted them, some objects that no doubt had been swallowed up by the Maelstrom hundreds of years before. Fish, bits of old wrecks, stones, broken statuary that perhaps had come from old Istar, even bones . . . everything the Maelstrom had swallowed over the centuries came flying up. A Magori staggered by, then collapsed, the broken spar of a ship having speared it like a lance. The rest of the Magori dived over the sides, clearly deciding that the surface was no place to be at this juncture.

And then a change came over the Blood Sea. The storm still raged and the waves still threatened to throw ships against one another, but no longer did any vessel float helplessly toward the embrace of the Maelstrom.

"By Zeboim's grace!" Delara gasped, rising and staring out at the Blood Sea. "It's . . . gone!"

The same mad cry echoed over the ship. Everyone who could stared out at the open sea, gaping at a sight both wondrous and frightening.

As weak as he had grown, Seph tried to rise. "What . . . what is it, Aryx?"

Aryx could not immediately answer. He stared at the sea, first with both eyes, then with the dragon orb, but still the astounding scene remained the same. He swallowed, unwilling to believe but forced to accept. "It's gone, Seph. . . . The Maelstrom's completely vanished."

# Sword's Betrayal

## Chapter Sixteen

No hint of the great fury that had so shaped the minotaurs' lives remained save the refuse that it had tossed up. Flotsam littered the wild sea wherever one looked. Judging by the size of the water column, Aryx suspected that even some of the shoreline had been showered with items.

"Vanished . . ." Seph murmured. He began to cough, softly in the beginning, then with more violence.

Aryx started to look down, then stiffened as the ship rocked violently, far more than the storm should have caused. He looked up toward Rand, but the cleric remained fixed in position, in the midst of some interminable trance.

"Look!" someone shouted.

Not far from the *Vengeance*, a massive shape broke the surface—the sinister serpentine trunk that Aryx had witnessed before. A second joined it, then another, all intertwining.

A smaller ship nearer to the massive coils could not avoid them. They twisted, wrapping around the hull of the minotaur vessel, ensnaring it. The coils tightened, crushing the hull of the ship.

Those aboard could do nothing to save their lives. A few sought to escape into the sea, but the waves took them under even as those aboard the *Vengeance* watched helplessly. Some tried to combat the scaled leviathans, chopping futilely at the cylindrical trunks even as their vessel collapsed around them. Those below had no chance to do anything but die, either killed by the destruction or drowned as the water rushed in.

But the human continued to stand there, a statue in tribute to delay.

"All hands to stations!" the captain roared. "Move it!"

A voice that Aryx had not heard for some time at last echoed in his head. *Draw me, Master. . . . Now is the time. Draw me. . . .*

The Sword of Tears. He had forgotten the foul weapon, wrapped up as he was in Seph's terrible wounds. "Never!" he muttered under his breath. "Never!"

*You must . . .*

He felt the urge to do so but fought it down. Only despair followed the demon blade. Even now, Aryx could not bring himself to use it.

The crew would get them out of reach. They *had* to succeed. Only one thing concerned Aryx now, and that was his brother.

"Seph! Take it easy! We'll get you below! Delara, help me get—"

He stopped when he saw Delara glance down at his brother. Her eyes widened, then her expression tightened.

Aryx shifted his gaze to the wounded minotaur, who had stopped coughing some moments ago. Suddenly even the absence of the gods and the destruction of the Maelstrom meant nothing to him. For all Aryx cared at that moment, the servants of Chaos could have taken the *Vengeance*, crew and all, and buried them at the bottom of the Blood Sea.

Seph was dead.

Holding his brother tightly, Aryx roared his pain to the world. He rocked Seph back and forth, oblivious to the frantic crew or the oncoming behemoth in the sea.

Delara tried to comfort him. "Aryx! He died in battle! He'll join your ancestors, fighting for honor and the glory of the empire forever!"

"Glory? Honor? Of what use are those to the dead?"

She pulled back, startled by his vehemence. Aryx felt guilty for snapping at her, but he couldn't help it. He wanted to strike out at something, anything, in order to assuage his misery and guilt. If he had only been a little swifter, a little stronger . . .

*You may still gain revenge. . . .*

The words of the Sword of Tears hit him hard, for they reflected exactly what he desired. Someone should pay, but those Magori who he had not killed had fled to the safety of the water. How, then, could he strike back?

As the ship rocked, he had his answer.

*Take me up . . .* urged the demon blade. *Take me up and strike at Chaos's servant. . . .*

Gently he lowered Seph, then stepped toward the rail, almost in a trance. Although Aryx carried his axe, his other hand stroked the hilt of the dark artifact. Ignoring the frantic pace of those around him, he leaned over the rail, staring at the scaled monster, moving ever nearer.

*Take me to it . . . plunge me into it. Together we will avenge all you have lost. Oh, Master . . .*

He imagined himself atop the Chaos creature, again and again cutting deep with the deadly blade. Aryx saw the creature writhing and dying under his terrible attack. His grip tightened on the hilt.

Another hand closed on his. "Aryx, what are you thinking?"

Delara's voice broke the sword's influence. Aryx exhaled. "No," he murmured, knowing that the weapon would nonetheless hear him. "Never again . . ."

The Sword of Tears did not reply, perhaps sulking. Aryx ignored it, instead glancing at Delara in gratitude. However, she looked past him, eyes fixed on the servant of Chaos. Aryx looked back and saw that the scaly abomination drew yet nearer, clearly after their ship in particular.

It wanted them, wanted the *Vengeance* in particular, and at the speed with which it moved, it would soon have . . .

The wind shifted with such an abruptness that it nearly threw Aryx over the rail. He gripped the rail tightly, looking up at the sails. They were filled with an intense wind that seemed so focused that the minotaur wondered whether it could be natural. He looked out at the Blood Sea and saw that the ships nearest theirs had also been caught up by the same wind . . . in fact, every vessel he looked at moved exactly the same, and all at an astonishing speed.

"Rand . . ." He looked up in time to see the cleric collapse into Carnelia's arms. As pale as ice, Rand had grown emaciated, almost as if what he had done had fed off his body. Of the aura that had surrounded him, Aryx could see but a faint trace. The cleric had drained himself completely.

The ships of the armada moved faster and faster, the crews scrambling to concentrate. No matter where they were, the various vessels all moved with the same precision, the same swiftness. Even the storm could not keep pace, and as for the horrendous abomination . . .

It moved still closer.

Aryx couldn't believe it. Despite Rand's spell, the serpentine forms edged ever closer toward the *Vengeance.*

He thought about drawing the Sword of Tears, thought about leaping into the sea, but again could not bring himself to trust the demon blade. It might just as easily sacrifice him in some insidious plot of its own. Aryx wondered if perhaps Sargonnas had been betrayed by it. Perhaps the fact that it alone had survived the destruction of the temple had been because the sword had planned it so.

Then the *Vengeance,* indeed the entire fleet, began to pull away. Aryx's hopes rose. "It can't keep up the pace! We're moving ahead of it!"

Delara said nothing, no doubt as transfixed as Aryx by the dwindling sight of the leviathan. He leaned forward, still feeling some guilt yet knowing that to have leapt off the ship to attack the creature would have been madness.

A hand drew the Sword of Tears from its sheath.

Aryx turned, startled. He had only a glimpse of Delara, eyes wide and unblinking, before she scrambled over the edge of the rail. The stone in the demonic weapon glared brightly, almost triumphantly.

"Delara! No!" The stunned warrior reached out for her, trying to grab her sword arm.

Delara let go of the rail, diving into the turbulent water.

"No!" Reacting instinctively, Aryx stepped over the rail, searching the water for her.

Lord Broedius's voice came from somewhere behind him. "Aryx! What do you think—"

He didn't hear the rest, for at that moment, Aryx caught sight of a greenish glimmer in the water and a soaked, brown form trying to make its way toward the pursuing abomination. Somehow, despite the waves, Delara held fast to the sword . . . or it held fast to her.

"Aryx!"

Aryx replaced his axe in its sling and leapt into the sea after her.

A wave caught him, nearly throwing the hapless minotaur against the hull. Struggling, Aryx pushed forward, muscles aching as he battled his way against the water. He did not question his sanity, only concentrated on trying to reach Delara. What he hoped to do after that, Aryx did not know.

The only thing that concerned him was reaching her.

Yet despite his best efforts, the Blood Sea fought back. Although Delara made headway, the best Aryx could do was stay in place. If he paused at all to rest, the waves pushed him back. By now the *Vengeance* and most of the rest of the fleet had passed him by, Rand's incredible and selective spell pushing them along at a tremendous rate.

Then a spark of emerald light caused him to stop and stare. He looked with astonishment, with horror, as Delara, at last having reached the monstrous servant of Chaos, managed a glancing strike. However, a wave caused by one of the colossal segments threw her back, tossing her about like a tiny bit of wood.

Aryx cried out to her . . . a dreadful mistake. Another wave caught him, forcing him under with his mouth still open. Water filled the gray minotaur's lungs, and he started to choke. Aryx desperately swam for the surface, but it evaded his weakening strokes.

Unable to breathe anymore, he blacked out, awaiting the cold caresses of the sea goddess, Zeboim.

\* \* \* \* \*

*Enough rest. It would be better if you woke before the world ended.*

The insistent voice stirred Aryx to life. The bedraggled minotaur coughed up water, his eyes stinging from the sea. Aryx struggled to raise himself but collapsed, burying his face in sand. He managed to spit the grit out, then tried to push himself up on one elbow, succeeding this time.

Blinking away seawater from his eyes, Aryx tried to focus on his surroundings. For a time, he could only make out blurred shapes, most of them likely rocks. Gradually the shapes defined themselves, proving to be, to his disappointment, exactly what he had thought they were . . . rocks. Aryx had hoped to find Delara or at least some trace of her. Daring to roll over, the weakened minotaur studied the rest of the area. He lay on the shore of some vast land, probably an island, but he recalled none from the charts. Some plants lined the inner edge, but beyond them, a high ridge prevented Aryx from getting a better idea where he might have ended up.

That he had survived at all surprised him. Even supposing that he hadn't swallowed half the Blood Sea, Aryx couldn't imagine how he had kept alive, especially unconscious, long enough to wash up on some distant shore.

A heavy, awkward weight on his back assured him of another miracle, the fact that his axe had remained hooked into its harness. At one time in his life, Aryx might have thanked the gods, but if any of them had been responsible, he doubted it had been for good reasons. Still, he unhooked the weapon and, after some debate, headed to the southwest, along the shore. The ridge there looked less steep, giving him hope of climbing it in order to identify his location.

Of Delara, he still saw no sign. A part of him feared that she had drowned, but another part recalled the sinister power of the Sword of Tears, which clearly needed a wielder, willing or otherwise, in order to act. For all Aryx knew, she still fought the Chaos creature.

As he climbed, Aryx also wondered about the voice that he thought had awakened him. It had reminded him of the sword, but surely the demonic blade could not speak to him from so far away. He also doubted that any of the gods, even Kiri-Jolith, paid much mind to him now. Certainly Aryx had made a poor pawn for their games. Perhaps a certain silver warrior guided him now, but even that Aryx found unlikely. His ancestor had made it quite clear he would be on his own.

He abandoned the hopeless train of thought as he reached the top and got his first good look at the landscape. To his surprise, forest and plains, with a smattering of hills mixed in, stretched ahead as far as the eye could see, even the dragon orb. While this might have been an island, Aryx had his doubts. As he scanned the area, more and more the frustrated minotaur suspected that he had somehow ended up on some part of the mainland . . . but where?

They had been too far south for him to end up on the island of Saifhum and far too north for the sea to take him to Kendermore. If anywhere on Ansalon, this had to be a part of the great peninsula, possibly Kern. He saw no sign of habitation, but then, few had ever made use of its great expanses. There had been some talk about the empire at last expanding here, for the forests offered strong timber for shipbuilding, but this war had put aside such a notion. Perhaps if the minotaur race survived . . .

Aryx pushed on, trying to keep the shoreline in sight while he looked for the best possible place to turn inland. He had no idea what to do or even if the fleet survived. The cleric's unorthodox spell, which surely had not come from Kiri-Jolith, might have sent them anywhere, but . . .

The gray minotaur froze as he noticed a figure wending its way over the plains northwest of him. Just a tiny figure, but one that looked vaguely like a minotaur.

Delara?

Picking up his pace, Aryx scrambled down the other side of the ridge, all the while trying to get a better view of the distant figure. Even the god's gift failed to enable him to see it very clearly. It *looked* like another minotaur, but he couldn't be certain.

Then, from the tiny figure's right side, came an emerald gleam.

"The Sword of Tears . . ." Aryx whispered. No other blade could have glittered with such life. Despite the impossibility of it all, he had found Delara, almost as if the two of them had somehow been drawn together.

Aryx dared not call to her, suspecting that the demon blade still kept her in thrall. He wanted to wait until he got closer and could possibly even snatch the sword from her. At worst, Aryx intended to offer himself to the artifact as a more suitable host. His only fear lay in the question of whether or not the blade might turn Delara against him and force her to attack. Aryx would not, *could* not, kill her.

What was she doing here? What had brought her all the way from the middle of the Blood Sea to this remote part of the mainland?

Those questions the sword could answer once Aryx caught up. One way or another, he would find out the truth from the insidious weapon. . . .

Delara maintained a strong but steady pace, never wavering from her path. Nonetheless, Aryx slowly cut the distance between them, enough so that he could at last make out her face. Delara looked worn, her expression almost strained. Her body bore a number of small wounds, but he could make out little more. Aryx wondered if she knew what the sword had done to her and struggled against it. He wished he had warned her about the blade.

A glimmer on the horizon caught his attention. Aryx had

sailed the sea long enough to recognize water. It was very distant, but if his calculations had been correct and this was the peninsula of Kern, then what he had noticed had to be the first glimpse of the Bay of Miremier, which continued far north until it opened into the Northern Courrain Ocean. It comforted him some to better know his position, but again the question of why the sword had brought Delara so far escaped him.

Despite his earlier progress, Delara now outpaced him. Try as he might, Aryx could gain no more ground. She moved as one possessed, probably an apt image. He wondered if she, or more likely the Sword of Tears, knew that he pursued.

The ground beneath his feet suddenly trembled. Memories of the quakes striking Nethosak returned. Aryx instinctively fell to the ground, riding the great tremor out. The ground shook for several minutes, but in a manner somewhat peculiar. The earth buckled in strange waves, as if a vast river flowed beneath it. Still, Aryx dared take no chances, for in the previously pastoral landscape, there now appeared cracks and crevices, more than one sufficient to swallow a foolish minotaur.

Then at last the tremor passed—or rather, seemed to flow on, for Aryx saw that in the distance, the grasslands continued to shake for a time, breaking apart in many places.

He rose, immediately looking for Delara, but the other minotaur had vanished. Aryx continued to search, certain that she, too, would have had to wait the tremor out even with the sword guiding her. Yet as precious minutes passed, Delara did not rise from cove,. nor did she appear in the distance.

Anxious, Aryx ran toward the location where he had last seen her. He avoided one minor crevice, then nearly fell into another still covered by a thin layer of soil. The tall grass made his path deceptive. The tremor had created cracks everywhere, but he could not see most until he had nearly stepped into them. His anxiety grew as he approached Delara's last location, for the ground seemed even more unstable. He marveled that the plains looked so innocent from a distance and yet hid so much threat.

And where Delara had stood, Aryx found the worst of the ravines, a gaping, jagged hole running for several yards. It looked bottomless. He paused, trying to convince himself that the sword would have prevented Delara from falling in. Yet as he stared into the darkness, Aryx grew suspicious, for as the hole descended, it spread, becoming so large one could nearly walk upright in it. He took a few tentative steps.

A few yards in, he found a footprint.

Aryx hesitated but a breath or two before descending farther. He could not ignore the track nor the possibility that Delara might lie at the bottom, leg, or worse, broken, perhaps even unconscious.

With no torch nor anything else to burn, Aryx moved on. For a time, the light behind him gave the minotaur hope. If Delara had fallen only a short distance, then he could still find her without too much trouble. If she had fallen deeper . . .

However, as Aryx continued, he found no further trace. Deeper and deeper he descended, still hoping. Curiously, long past the point when it should have, the light never quite faded, instead taking on an almost greenish tinge. Realizing that, Aryx thought at first that the Sword of Tears might be somewhere nearby, Delara with it. However, he eventually noticed that he could see far better with the left eye than the right. Once more, Kiri-Jolith's unsettling gift had come to his aid, yet Aryx took no joy from it, for still he could not find Delara. Only finding her—alive and unharmed—would satisfy him.

How deep did this fissure go? He had expected it to level out, but it continued to descend. Surely it could go little farther.

At that moment, the ground gave way beneath his feet.

With a gasp, Aryx fell through, the axe slipping from his grasp as he tried to find some purchase. However, the earth he groped for crumbled easily, not even slowing his fall. Aryx reached out for anything, fearing that he had escaped drowning only to be buried alive.

A stone half-buried in the side gave him momentary pause before slipping free. His descent slowed, Aryx managed to direct his path some, avoiding an abrupt drop that would have certainly spelled his doom. Unfortunately he could not completely stop himself, and with each second, the minotaur plummeted deeper into the earth. Aryx cursed, wondering if he would somehow end up in the Abyss when his journey finally ended.

When at last it did come to a halt, his first glance almost made him think that he had indeed fallen into the Abyss, for before Aryx there opened up a tremendous cavern vast enough to swallow the imperial palace and much more. He looked up, and even with the dragon orb he could not locate the ceiling. Small wonder that the quake had left the plains above so riddled with dangerous crevices. Something had already eaten away the earth beneath. He was amazed that the entire region had not already collapsed.

Such a thought did nothing to ease his worries, for even if he managed to locate Delara, the frustrated warrior had no idea how he might lead the pair of them to the surface. Worse, Aryx no longer even had a war axe with which to defend himself, which meant that the only weapon he and Delara would have between them would be the Sword of Tears.

Aryx picked up a large, sharp rock, aware that it would likely do little for him but not liking to go completely empty-handed, then stumbled along the great expanse, hoping it wouldn't run the entire width of the peninsula. The eye gave him something of a view, but even Kiri-Jolith's gift proved limited this deep beneath the earth. Aryx could see several yards ahead, but in a cavern so extensive, that meant little.

As he walked, he noticed that much of the ground lay strewn with recent rubble, no doubt from the tremor. In fact, the air itself remained so filled with dust that Aryx finally had to cover his nostrils and mouth with a piece of cloth from one of his belt pouches. Aryx wondered whether he might suffocate before he reached the end of his trek, but he could not go back. Even if an opening did offer itself, the determined warrior would not leave without Delara.

He wondered again how the others had fared. Were they safe in some harbor or on their way to Lord Ariakan? Had Rand recovered? The last spell had taken a great deal out of him. It might even be that Rand would never be able to perform any sort of spell again, be it one granted through his patron or of his own innate power.

Rumbling echoed from the darkness ahead, rumbling that set the walls to shaking and loosened more earth. Aryx planted himself against the nearest side. He paused, waiting for the entire ceiling to fall in, but after a few shakes, the area again stabilized.

Even then Aryx could hear continued rumbling, an almost orderly noise, as if some great beast moved beneath the earth. Pressing on, the minotaur clutched the stone tightly. The deeper he journeyed, the more Aryx suspected that no ordinary quake had formed all this.

Then, in the midst of the rumbling, he heard voices, voices of those who could not possibly be down here.

"Prepare to disembark!" Lord Broedius called.

"He's still not opened his eyes!" shouted a frustrated Carnelia.

"We will not risk our vessels for this," Captain Brac argued.

Other voices, many of them intermingling, rose from the cavern ahead. Curious despite everything, Aryx slowly wended his way toward them, listening as each rose and fell, seemingly in conversations in which each participant paid no mind to what the other said.

"Undo that line!" an unknown speaker cried.

"No one's seen the *Seahawk*. The poor girl must've gone down back near the Maelstrom," commented another.

"We've no choice but to drag him with us or leave him on the ship," Broedius replied.

On and on the nonsensical conversation ran. Now and then Aryx recognized some speaker, generally the knight commander or his niece, and from them he gathered a questionable scenario in which the surviving ships of the fleet had been blown toward some shore, damaged, it seemed, by the very spell Rand had cast to save them. The spell now raged out of control, and the cleric appeared to be unconscious, unable to cancel its effects.

Yet none of that explained why their voices came to him in this vast dark cavern.

Needing to know more, Aryx crept closer. A dim light suddenly greeted him as he turned around a bend, a light that increased as he neared.

The chamber before him not only rose to tremendous heights but also descended just as far. It looked to Aryx almost as if all the dwarves in the world had taken a year out of their lives to mine this area out. Perhaps such a notion even had merit, for what the minotaur could see of the far walls revealed a uniformity that did not seem the work of nature. Rounded ridges formed much of the sides of the vast chamber, ridges with diameters three or four times the warrior's height. Had he the time, Aryx might have studied them in detail, but more important to the minotaur was that which stood at the very center of the chamber's deep floor.

There an immense sphere of white fire blazed brightly, its light having appeared dim earlier only because of the immensity of its dark surroundings. More startling than the sphere itself, though, were the images floating within it, for as Aryx approached, he suddenly found Lord Broedius staring at him.

No . . . not at him, but rather beyond the minotaur. Broedius stood as if seizing the rail of a ship tightly. Pale, weary, he nonetheless continued to shout out orders to someone unseen.

"I don't care if they've got to go three at a time! We're not leaving any of the horses behind, not—"

Before he could finish, his image rippled, twisted, and transformed into one of the minotaur generals Aryx had met in Broedius's headquarters. For reasons that immediately became apparent once he spoke, the veteran warrior seemed to be standing at an angle. "Then swim if you have to! This ship's beyond help! If it lists any more than it has, it's going to sink! Make ready—"

The minotaur general transformed, becoming Carnelia, who knelt somewhere, her arms cradling an invisible burden. "Damn you, wake up! We need you again—I need you again!"

Her image twisted upward, regrew the horns it had lost during its previous transformation, once more shed the ebony armor, and at last became a taller, slimmer minotaur warrior, the Kazelati representative aboard the *Vengeance*. He leaned near somebody, whispering, but the words sounded loud to Aryx. "I warned against this madness! See if you can talk sense to Brac if we make it to shore! That we should risk our lives for the empire and these vermin of Takhisis—"

Other minotaurs and humans flashed before Aryx, each talking or in the midst of some action. Yet throughout it all, a few specific individuals reoccurred most: Broedius, Carnelia, Brac, the minotaur generals, and the senior Kazelati captains. The pattern repeated itself over and over. Aryx found himself so caught up in it he had even forgotten his search for Delara.

What had he discovered? Who had created this? They seemed terribly interested in the fleet, which did not bode well. Had he uncovered the Magori's home? Doubtful, for even they would require more than this empty cavern, which he also suspected had been recently created. Who, then? Did someone else watch?

Broedius reappeared. Now he stood at what might have been the edge of a gangplank, seeming to force some great object forward. The knight commander said nothing, working silently as if time had nearly run out. The *Vengeance* had surely run aground; Aryx could see no other reason for the knight's desperate actions.

Suddenly Broedius transformed once more, but not to any of the others that Aryx had seen earlier. Instead, the human shed his armored hide, shrank a little, and collapsed. The limp form refined itself in seconds, becoming a familiar sight that turned the watching warrior's curiosity into despair.

Seph. His lifeless body shifted slightly, gently rocking back and forth, the motions a ship at sea might cause. Eyes closed, Seph seemed to be contemplating something, most likely the ugly pale slash across his body. Moisture had washed away most of the blood, leaving only a dark pink stain.

Aryx felt an intense desire to cradle his body. He reached out, not expecting to touch his brother's body but wanting desperately to do so.

Seph suddenly faded, and as he did, laughter echoed throughout the chamber, laughter loud and mocking. Loose rocks fell everywhere, forcing Aryx to press himself against the nearest wall. He looked around, trying to find the source and already suspecting that he knew it.

The laughter grew, and as it did, a pale, sickly light spread throughout the cavern, a pale light that originated from the sides of the vast chamber. As the minotaur stared, parts of the walls began to move, to slide back and forth along one another. Now, even without the aid of Kiri-Jolith's gift, Aryx could make out hundreds of glowing, coiling, writhing serpentine forms, all interconnected and all seemingly without beginning or end. To his horror, Aryx realized that each of the rounded ridges had actually been one of the massive serpentine shapes.

He was surrounded. They were everywhere . . . *everywhere*.

"A shame," came the voice that he had heard through the Magori, the cold, mocking voice of the underdwellers' master. Sometimes it sounded like one creature, other times like a chorus. "A shame that the Father of All and of Nothing will not preserve a few of you for memory's sake! You are so entertaining, so amusing, so pathetic! Would that his most loyal servant could play with you forever and ever, little one, but the father has dictated that this little ball of mud must cease, as punishment to the betrayers, and his most loyal servant yearns to obey!"

The serpentine forms writhed in what only could be described as great satisfaction. Aryx had found the Coil, and now *it* had *him*.

# The Coils of Chaos

## Chapter Seventeen

The winds, the same winds that had swept them away from the dangers near the Maelstrom, now pounded the ships relentlessly. No longer simply filling the sails, the winds hurled vessels together, creating havoc and destruction. Two ships, both Kazelati, had already been sunk, the pair having collided with such speed that they had splintered one another.

Many of those aboard had perished, but others had survived, for the terrible winds had swept the ships near enough to land for some to swim ashore. However, those same winds had also caused three other vessels to wash up on the rocks. One had already begun to sink. The other pair, including the *Vengeance,* listed terribly, some of the lower decks already flooded. No aid came from the rest of the fleet; they had their hands full simply keeping their own vessels from ending up like the others, a much too likely prospect. Another of the survivors of the empire's once grand armada already moved helplessly toward the shoals, despite the crew's valiant attempts. Only the fact that the minotaurs, whether of the empire or the Kazelati realm, maintained oars aboard had kept the rest from beaching or sinking.

That would not last long, Carnelia knew, for already she had seen the oars on the nearest ships snap off as the desperate minotaurs rowed for their lives. The winds had the strength of magic behind them, and only magic could end their threat. Unfortunately the one seemingly responsible for it lay cradled in her arms, still unconscious.

"Come on, Rand, come on . . ." She rocked him back and forth, trying to revive him. He had collapsed after completing his stunning spell, a spell that had taken even more out of him than the last one had. She feared that he might never wake up.

Her uncle had ordered her to get the cleric off the ship, but Carnelia could not do it herself, and all the other knights had their hands full. She had tried to move him, but despite her training, the battle had sapped her strength too much.

The *Vengeance* listed more, causing Carnelia and her love to slide toward the rail. She held tight, letting her armored body take the brunt of the blow. The rail cracked under the weight but did not break.

Somewhere she could hear Broedius shouting orders. The last she had seen of her uncle, he had been trying to get the horses off the doomed vessel. The rocks upon which the *Vengeance* had grounded itself connected to the main shore, and with some effort and sufficient time, they would likely save most of the crew. However, while the knights could provide the effort, the sorcerous winds and the turbulent sea seemed eager not to provide the time.

A groan made her stiffen. Carnelia looked down to see Rand's eyes flutter open. "What . . . what . . ."

He said no more but simply stared at her. "Rand! Do you understand me?" After a long pause, he nodded. "Rand, that spell you cast . . . you've got to stop it! It's tossing the fleet against the rocks! You saved us from the attack, but—"

Carnelia broke off as the blond figure suddenly shook his head. "Not . . . not mine . . ."

"Not yours? What do you mean?"

He coughed. "My spell . . . gone . . . can feel it . . . not mine, but another . . ."

"But—but how can that be?"

The *Vengeance* suddenly shivered, a great groaning sound that sent chills through the female knight. The waves were knocking the ship loose from the reef, and if that happened, she would sink.

"Not mine," Rand continued, unaware of the danger. "I can feel . . . feel it. Something . . . someone else . . . controls it now."

All this time they had assumed that Rand's spell had simply gone awry because he had been unconscious. Now Carnelia realized that the battle in the Blood Sea had never ended, that the force that had unleashed the Magori upon them had simply continued its attack in a different manner.

Only it could have seized control of so great a spell.

"Can you do anything to stop it?"

He shook his head. "No . . . there is nothing left. Nothing. Kiri-Jolith could not . . . could not help me, so I followed Aryx's lead and drew from myself . . . and now there is nothing left. . . ."

He coughed again, nearly losing consciousness. A minotaur, the arrogant Kazelati representative, saw Carnelia and, to her surprise, bent close. "The ship will break apart soon! Come! Let me help you move him to safety!"

Carnelia gratefully thanked him for his aid. Yet as they gently lifted Rand up and carried him toward the gangplank, she wondered if they should have even bothered. The servant of Chaos had trapped them at last, and even if everyone made it to shore, would it mean anything at all in the long run? Takhisis had abandoned them. Sargonnas had abandoned them. Did they have any hope at all?

Rand groaned. Carnelia abandoned her dark thoughts. Hope or no hope, gods or no gods, she and the others would fight to the end. They had to.

What other choice did they have?

\* \* \* \* \*

The Coil quivered once, the many serpentine forms shivering as one. Aryx had some slight hope that something had happened to the horrific creature, but a moment later the thing—or things; Aryx had been unable to decide which term struck nearer the truth—recovered, once again laughing.

"So you have come! This most loyal one thought it had lost the little mortals for a time, but here one of you comes to it instead! Entertaining, yes! Entertaining little creatures, considering so finite a span of existence! You thought that you would yet escape oblivion, but you are nothing to this most loyal servant, no matter how clever you think yourself!"

Everywhere the Coil writhed in obvious pleasure. Aryx dropped the rock he had been holding, knowing how futile and foolish it would be to throw it at so gargantuan a monster.

"Soon, soon . . ." crooned the Coil from all around him. "Soon this ball of mud you call your world will be returned to the emptiness from which it came, and then the Father of All and of Nothing will reward his most loyal servant with the oblivion his servant so dearly desires! How could you little ones be so arrogant as to reject this most precious gift of Father Chaos?"

"We value existence," snarled Aryx, refusing to surrender, even against seemingly insurmountable odds. "We value the chance to do something, to be something, to experience things!"

"But for what purpose? In the end, all things return to the Father of All and of Nothing! He is the only existence that matters! You would do better to embrace his gifts, to end what surely is a futile path!"

The weary yet defiant warrior shook his head. "Not having truly lived, you'd never understand."

The Coil writhed, but this time not in satisfaction. "This most loyal servant need not understand, for Father Chaos has given a command, and the Coil shall obey!"

Aryx straightened, staring at the nearest segments of the vile creature. Had he still possessed a weapon, he would have brandished it. Instead, the minotaur could only shake his fist. "As long as we can, we'll fight!"

The Coil laughed again, and as it did, new segments sprouted from the earth, rising all around Aryx. The minotaur held his ground, watching as they neared him. If he died, he would die fighting.

An emerald flash caught his gaze, and as Aryx turned, a figure leapt from hiding, swinging a familiar blade in a savage arc. Caught unaware, the nearest segments of the Chaos creature did not move fast enough, and the Sword of Tears, wailing, sliced through them as if they had no substance at all.

The Coil shivered as the blade sank deep, a resounding, high-pitched noise that sounded like a cry of pain coming from all directions. What seemed like lightning crackled forth from each wound, followed by a thick stream of some putrid brown ichor. The entire area shook, and parts of the ceiling collapsed, threatening to bury both Aryx and his would-be rescuer: Delara.

She looked even more strained than when he had last seen her. Her features were pulled tight, her eyes wide and unblinking. Scratches and slight wounds decorated her arms and legs, legacies of her incredible, unwilling journey to reach this place. At her side, the stone in the demon blade's hilt glowed as Aryx had never seen it.

The Sword of Tears had forced her along, saving her from death in the Blood Sea in order to drag her to the peninsula, in pursuit, it seemed, of the creature who had commanded the Magori. Aryx realized that such a fate would have been his if he had fallen victim to its will. Looking at Delara now, he wished he had obeyed the artifact, if only to have saved her from this.

Despite the wounds, the Coil reacted, many of its segments converging on Delara. She leapt aside from some, ducked below others, all the while swinging the blade. Each time it sank into the thick, scaled skin, the Sword of Tears wailed, but to Aryx's ears, those cries seemed not as triumphant as in times past.

He looked around, seeking a blade or axe, but found nothing. Delara continued to evade the searching coils, but with less and less ease. She also missed more often as the seconds passed, as if the Chaos creature's individual parts had begun to take her measure.

Aryx silently cursed, feeling useless. A weapon . . . he needed a weapon.

A great green-gold segment struck Delara full in the body. She went flying across a large portion of the chamber, the sword falling from her hand. The demon blade bounced once, twice, then rolled several feet, landing but a few yards from Aryx.

Despite the loathing he felt for it, he lunged for the weapon, but as he did, a part of the creature wrapped around his legs, pulling him back. Aryx tried to push himself free, but smaller segments looped around his arms and chest, dragging him away from the Sword of Tears.

More segments seized Delara, who seemed to be coming to her senses. She tried one feeble attempt to escape them, but they wrapped her even tighter than the others had Aryx.

The Coil drew them both toward the fiery sphere, turning the pair so that they faced one another.

"Aryx! It took my mind, buried me within myself! I couldn't stop no matter how much I wanted to!"

He remembered how the artifact had tried to usurp his own mind. "I know, Delara. I know."

The Coil suddenly raised both of them high, dangling the two helpless minotaurs above the rocky floor. "Little mortals with little pins that prick," it hissed. "Do you think even that bothers this loyal servant? Even the many, many pinpricks the betrayer, Sargonnas, inflicted when his sanctum was attacked troubled this one little! It will be amusing to watch you as your strength ebbs and your wits scatter. You will make for a pleasant pastime while this ball of dirt fades away. . . ."

Without warning, it brought them down hard, stopping just before either of the minotaurs would have struck the ground. "And as you suffer, so, too, will the other little mortals! Would you like to see?"

Not waiting for a reply, it twisted them toward the sphere, which now pulsated. As they watched, the great sphere expanded, swelling to twice its previous diameter. Intense heat radiated from it, enough to make Aryx sweat.

At first the image within remained indistinct, murky. Then it gradually defined, although never with the precision of the prior visions. Lumpy shadows rippled along the bottom half of the picture, flowing forward at a constant rate. Something fairly large darted by in the middle. It took a moment for Aryx to realize that the reason for the murky image lay in the fact that what he saw before him took place underwater.

It took another moment to realize what caused the endless shadows rippling along the seabed.

"Magori . . ." Aryx muttered. And as he spoke, they drew into focus. Underwater, their bulbous eyes glowed faintly, and their mouths opened and closed like fish breathing. The monstrous crustaceans bore their weapons as if battle was imminent.

Battle . . .

Delara saw his darkening countenance. "Aryx! What is it? Where are they going?"

He started to answer, but the Coil spoke first, clearly delighted to explain such dire events to its victims. "The shelled ones have gone to redeem themselves, stupid creatures! This loyal servant has taken the curious spell of the human and made it my own!"

"The fleet's been blown toward this peninsula," Aryx explained. "Some of the ships have run aground, and others are in danger! Broedius and the others are trying to get everyone ashore so they can—"

"But they won't have time," Delara finished. "The Magori are coming after them from below. . . ."

The Coil's harsh laughter rocked the mighty cavern. More loose earth and stone tumbled from above. A glimmer of sunlight cut through at last. Aryx eyed the light with yearning.

"Oh, clever little mortals! Such delightful toys you make! Soon, yes, the others will know the wonder of Father Chaos's gift of oblivion! When the Magori are done here, they will attack what remains on your pitiful islets. They will suspect nothing until their blood flows, for did not their precious gods long ago promise their safety? All trace of your kind will be eradicated . . . but have heart! Soon there will exist no one who will remember your shameful defeat, no one at all!"

"The gods will stop it!" Delara declared. "Sargonnas will not permit it!"

Aryx wished he could convince Delara to forget her god. Like the others, Sargonnas had probably fled. The minotaurs and humans had only themselves to rely on now.

Curiously, though, her mention of Sargonnas caused a reaction in the Chaos creature. Some of the tubular segments pulled back, while others were obviously in an agitated state. The Coil said nothing for a time, not even bothering to mock their hopes.

At last, in voices a bit too interested, it asked, "And do you know this to be true?"

"He would never let you destroy us! Never!"

"But your god is gone . . . fled or destroyed! The betrayer Sargonnas is no more! He must be!" A segment looped around the Sword of Tears, bringing the demon blade close. The green stone did not glow at all. "Even his toy is no more!" It flung the deadly artifact far aside.

Aryx watched the blade clatter against one wall of the cavern. As the weapon tumbled to the floor, he thought the stone glowed faintly for a moment, but the image could also have been a product of his own imagination.

The Coil pulled Delara closer to the sphere. She squinted, the fiery ball's illumination nearly blinding her. "Where, then, is he? Where?"

The serpentine segments around her tightened. "I—I don't know," she finally gasped.

"You do not know because there is nothing to know!" the servant of Chaos declared triumphantly.

Aryx thought he heard a little quiver in that declaration. To his own surprise, the minotaur warrior found himself twisting toward Delara and saying, "You know, I think our friend's more uncertain than it would like us to think."

"There is no uncertainty!" the Chaos creature roared. The echoing sound caused a new cascade of rocks and dirt everywhere, threatening to bring down the entire ceiling. Curiously, it was the Coil itself who protected them from the rocks. "And for you, no hope at all! Your gods, the betrayers, have abandoned you all! They have fled or they have hidden, licking their wounds. They do not dare to show themselves, no matter—"

"Ah . . ." Aryx muttered, "but you don't know for certain, do you?"

The multitude of serpents coiled around one another in a much more agitated state, clearly affected by the minotaur's words. Aryx could only guess at the emotions of such an unsettling behemoth, but he suspected that he had come close to the truth. Not only did the Coil not know what had happened to its adversary, but that lack of knowledge disturbed it greatly.

"Can't find a god?" he asked it with overexaggerated astonishment. "How can you misplace a god?" Had the Coil been any mortal creature, Aryx's theatrical mannerisms would have been seen as just that, but the Chaos monster had no basis on which to judge them . . . or so the gray minotaur hoped.

"He will be found!" the voice hissed from everywhere. "The betrayer will be found hiding in some little corner of the all, hoping that Father Chaos will not punish him as he deserves! But punish him the Father of All and of Nothing will do, perhaps even giving him to the Coil to play with!"

"Or," Aryx interjected, "Sargonnas may be lurking around here even now, waiting for the time when you least expect his attack, prepared to cut each and every one of your segments into little twitching pieces."

"No!" Again the various segments of the Coil writhed, many in seemingly independent fashion. The more agitated the horror became, the less control it seemed to have over its individual parts.

"He could be watching you even now," Delara suggested.

The Coil laughed. This time the sound was a little forced. "Little mortal creatures, so cunning, so transparent! This loyal servant does not fear your words! The Coil is great! The Coil is powerful! At this most loyal servant's command, the Magori die and die again, until by their numbers they will crush the life from your friends! At the Coil's command, dragons of Father Chaos will soon wreak carnage on your little islets! This most loyal servant need not fear the so-called God of Vengeance! Sargonnas must fear the Coil instead! Yessss, the God of Vengeance *fears* the Coil!"

"If it talks long enough, it just might convince itself, Delara," Aryx returned, trying to hide the fact that the Coil's mention of friends dying had reminded him of Seph, Hecar, and who knew how many others who had perished in this divine war. "It fights from behind, only taking on the enemy when they're otherwise occupied. I think it perhaps fears having to fight Sargonnas face-to-face. That must have been some battle in the temple."

"Sargonnas does not forget his enemies." Delara's eyes brightened in devotion as they often did when she spoke of her god. "Nor do they forget his vengeance . . . for as long as they live, that is."

"You should be crushed," the Coil abruptly declared. "Yesss, you should be crushed or torn apart or tossed from the sky! Yesss, you should be taken one by one and in most interesting ways be given the gift of oblivion! Let us see if your Sargonnas will protect his chosen, his little mortal pets! Let us see that!"

Fortunately, before it could attempt to fulfill its threat, something in the sphere caught its attention. The Coil shifted, its many parts rolling over one another in what Aryx decided represented interest. He peered at the sphere, trying to see what would so please the servant of Chaos.

"They're attacking!" Delara gasped.

The Magori had reached the stricken fleet. While the image did not reveal what happened on individual vessels, it did show the crustaceans rising from the water even as the first of those who had made it to shore began to recover.

The view shifted, and with it came voices and sounds: Minotaurs and knights gathering what weapons they could. Horses being pulled into service. Officers of both races shouting orders.

Lord Broedius flashed into view. "Form ranks! Archers at attention! Buy us some time! Get fires going! Use torches against them if you can, but don't depend entirely on them!"

Broedius became a Kazelati captain. "Double ranks on the right! Defend that position, or the others will never get off the ship!"

Shifting again, the image retreated, showing a long stretch of wind-tossed shore. The Magori swarmed from the waters, pushing on as if their very lives depended upon it.

"They will not be turned back this time," the Coil explained. "The Magori, good for nothing but death, know that to fail now would be to suffer! They will fight and yours will die!"

As they watched, Aryx saw that what the foul creature had said apparently was true. Nothing the Magori had feared in the past seemed to disturb them now. Fire did not daunt them. They did not shun the day, although perhaps the cloud cover proved helpful. Still, they moved without any protection from the mists of past battle. Even the slowest-witted warrior could see these differences and wondered at them. The crustaceans seemed to have adapted to nearly all their failings, even defending their softer regions better from adversaries. They were by no means invincible, but their changes, along with their endless numbers, promised that the battle would surely lean in their favor.

Nevertheless, Aryx took heart that no one panicked or retreated. Minotaurs did not retreat simply because a foe appeared superior. The knights, too, refused to bow their heads. Arrows downed the first rank with astonishing accuracy. When the Magori grew too near, lines consisting of both humans and minotaurs moved up to meet them, taking the battle to the enemy instead of the other way around.

The crustaceans swarmed as they never had even on Mithas. Unfortunately, despite its efforts, the first line of defense gave ground in only minutes, overwhelmed by sheer force. Minotaur commanders shouted, directing warriors to where the lines grew thinnest. At last one of Lord Broedius's elite talons, on horseback, trampled a momentary breakthrough, pushing back the Magori all the way to the Blood Sea.

Knights and minotaurs alike clearly knew that they could not move into the higher ground deeper inland. Magori lances flew far, as more than one officer shouting orders from higher up discovered. If the lines tried to move up, the Magori would bring them down, using throwing arms remarkable not only in strength but in agility. Even without weapons, some of the Magori charged forward, reaching with their claws or, if near enough, snapping at any unprotected throat or face with their poisonous jaws.

Lord Broedius did not remain in the rear of the battle, instead charging in again and again to repel advancing reavers. He forced himself to stay back only when necessary. The knight commander even dragged the wounded behind the lines when able, something his personal guard could not argue him out of doing.

Whatever their differences, the minotaurs of the empire fought alongside the Kazelati as if all had been trained in the same unit. The slimmer, quicker Kazelati often thrust ahead, relying on the solid lines of their cousins to protect them when they stepped back. The axes of the empire cleaved with deadly effect, leaving a pile of Magori dead in their wake. So great were the underdwellers' numbers, though, that still the minotaurs would face defeat and death. Yet all they and their human allies could do was fight and hope, and all Aryx could do from his present vantage point was pray.

"So fortunate they will be," the Coil crooned. "See? Another receives the Father of All and of Nothing's gift! Soon, so very soon . . ."

Caught up in the struggle, the servant of Chaos virtually ignored his two prisoners now . . . and why not? Neither Aryx nor Delara could free themselves from it. Aryx could move one hand well enough, but without any weapon, it did him no good whatsoever. Besides, he doubted that any weapon other than the Sword of Tears would have done much good against such a leviathan, and even it had proven wanting thus far.

Thinking of the enchanted artifact, he carefully twisted his head so that he could see it. The Sword of Tears lay where it had fallen, the stone in the hilt giving no sign of life.

Even as Aryx thought that, the stone suddenly flashed brightly. The flash lasted but a moment and went unnoticed by the Coil, but the minotaur felt certain that he had not imagined it. He peered at it with the dragon orb, trying to focus on the gem.

Another flash of green greeted his gaze.

The sword had come to him once before when he had been near the docks. It had come to him, but Aryx had used it only by reflex. He had never dared let it control his actions to the extent that it desired.

At that moment, the Sword of Tears broke its long silence, reaching in to his thoughts. *Master . . .*

Aryx almost spoke out loud, so surprised was he to hear the demon blade again.

*Will you give yourself to me?*

He stared at the cursed blade, which the minotaur felt certain even now sought only its own gain. Aryx glared at the sword, letting it decipher his response.

*Will you give yourself for Sargonnas?*

For the God of Vengeance? For the god who had abandoned his children? True, Sargonnas had power that might destroy the Coil, but Aryx hesitated to agree to something he did not understand, especially concerning a god and a sword with questionable definitions of honor.

Yet if Sargonnas could defeat the hellish leviathan, it might save all the others, including those friends and family he had aboard the fleet.

"The *Vengeance* is breaking away!" Delara shouted, interrupting his desperate thoughts.

Aryx looked and saw that the image of the great flagship filled the sphere. The *Vengeance* had broken off the rocks, and as it slipped back out to sea, it tipped to one side. To the minotaur's horror, he saw that there were still a few aboard her.

The *Vengeance*. She had unnerved him when he had seen first her in the fog, and then even more so when Aryx had awakened to find himself aboard. To see her now, though, shook the minotaur. The waves pushed the once great ship around, smashing the bottom of her hull against the rocks again. The wood gave way, allowing the sea to rush in even faster.

The *Vengeance* began to sink.

*So it will go,* interjected the sword in his head, *unless we act now. Will you give yourself?*

Aryx had no desire to feel the sorcerous tentacles of the demon blade invading his mind again, but he nonetheless nodded.

The Sword of Tears suddenly darted toward his free hand.

He gripped it tightly, but when the sword tried to control him, Aryx fought against it. If he died here, he would die his own warrior, not the puppet of this parasitic weapon.

*Fool . . . fool of a master!*

The minotaur paid its cries no mind, already acting. He brought the edge of the blade up against the segments imprisoning him, trusting to the magical edge. The Sword of Tears sliced into the thick coils, and as the Chaos creature howled in shock and pain, Aryx freed himself, then darted toward Delara.

Once more he brought the blade down, and once more it cut through his monstrous foe with little difficulty. However, the sword no longer wailed, a curious but, to Aryx, unimportant thing. He cared only that it would continue to cut so long as he struck.

Looping coils shot forth from every direction. They ranged in size from as slim as Aryx's arm to diameters twice, three times his height and more. Aryx thrust with the Sword of Tears and watched with some satisfaction as it bit into the serpentine body. Again energy flashed and the attacking segment withdrew.

Delara, unfortunately, had no weapon save a jagged piece of rock with which to defend herself, and therefore her few strikes made little impression on the attacking monster. Only Aryx saved her from being snared and pulled away. However, he couldn't watch so many sides for long. If they didn't come up with something quickly, the Coil would eventually take them again, no doubt fulfilling its earlier threats to the letter.

"That sword had a reason to come here," Delara muttered. "Surely it couldn't have been this!"

Aryx nodded, unwilling to spare his breath for anything else at the moment. The enchanted blade had sent them into this place, but what it had in mind, he could not say.

*Give in to me!* it demanded.

"Never!" the gray minotaur whispered, fighting back the darkness that had begun to creep inside his head.

"You see?" the Coil mocked. "Even with your lives so threatened, no Sargonnas comes to save you! The Coil watches in all directions! The betrayer of Father Chaos has betrayed you in turn . . . and so the least this loyal and most noble servant can do is crush your miserable little existences from the memory of this ball of mud!"

A segment shot forward, crashing into Delara, who in turn crashed into Aryx's back. They tumbled backward, Aryx managing to right himself just in time to defend them as another, larger segment looped toward the hapless pair.

On a hunch, Aryx used his draconian eye to study the oncoming trunk. Immediately his sharper vision detected a weak spot in the piece, perhaps where Delara had earlier scored a slight hit. Without hesitation, the minotaur swung the deadly blade, aiming for that exact location.

The Sword of Tears tore into the side of the Coil, burying itself so quickly that Aryx feared for a moment that he would be unable to pull the axe free. Raw energy exploded from the wound, sending the minotaur back a pace. At the same time, a shiver ran along every visible segment of the Chaos monstrosity. Before the wounded trunk could withdraw, Aryx again plunged his blade into the gaping wound, cutting away at the interior of his gargantuan adversary. More of the thick, putrid fluid poured forth, raising a stench even stronger than that which the Magori exuded.

At last the Coil managed to retract the badly wounded piece. Rage filled every word. "Little mite that bites! Little parasite that thinks itself worthy! This most loyal servant will crush you as it crushed your feeble guardian in his temple!"

Segments of the leviathan rolled at them from every side. Aryx tried to fend them off, but there were too many. It seemed impossible that they might survive. Aryx managed a lucky strike, but the Coil moved with much more caution now, evading his reach. Aryx began to feel helpless.

Once more the Sword of Tears derided him. *Mortal fool! Bull-headed bull . . . you would sacrifice the world instead of yourself?*

"All right!" Aryx muttered. "I'll give in, but you've got to protect Delara! She has no weapon!"

"What's that?" Delara asked, overhearing part of his reply. "What are you talking about?"

*What is one female to countless lives?*

"You heard me! Protect her!"

*I can promise nothing, Master. . . .*

The sword had him. Even he could not expect it to truly keep Delara from harm. "Do what you can."

*I can do nothing until you do. . . .*

Aryx nodded. Steeling himself, he opened up his mind, his thoughts, to the demon blade.

With what felt like triumphant glee, the malevolent entity of the sword filled him, seized control of his body. Aryx watched as his arm moved in incredible patterns, slicing at the Coil relentlessly. Under the sudden shift, the nearest segments retreated several feet.

To the minotaur's surprise, though, the Sword of Tears did

not try to lead them to safety. Instead, it pulled Aryx forward regardless of any desire on his part to avoid that direction. The towering sphere of white fire filled his gaze, the images within indistinct for the moment, although Aryx thought he saw Carnelia trying to drag a weakened Rand to safety. Then all concern for those battling the Magori vanished as the demon blade positioned him for a thrust . . . directly into the sphere!

"What are you doing?" Delara asked him.

Aryx would have asked the same question, but the sword answered first. *Saving his chosen . . .*

What it meant, he had no time to decipher, for already the Sword of Tears thrust toward the fiery sphere, and Aryx could only shut his eyes and hope that he died swiftly.

The enchanted blade wailed loud and long as it pierced the Coil's fearsome toy. Aryx felt the hair on his body stand on end. He opened his eyes and watched as the energy from the sphere flowed from it into the tip of the sword. In reality, it took no more than the blink of an eye for the sword to devour the entire globe, yet to the warrior, it seemed forever.

Then, as the Coil's segments surrounded him, snared Delara again, and squeezed tight, the Sword of Tears twisted downward, driving itself into the ground.

Aryx's world exploded. The earth shook, the ceiling of the cavern fell in, and the servant of Chaos roared, not in agony but in what seemed extreme surprise and . . . and a little *fear*. The force threw Aryx away from where the sphere had stood, sending him crashing against the rocks. His grip on the Sword of Tears, or perhaps its grip on him, failed, and the weapon rattled to the ground a few feet away.

The battered warrior struggled to rise, knowing his only hope lay in the treacherous blade. However, as he tried to reach for the hilt with fingers so stiff that they could barely even close, another hand clad in an ebony and crimson gauntlet took up the Sword of Tears. Aryx forced his neck to turn so that he could see who had stolen from him his one chance to save not only Delara but everyone else.

From head to toe, he wore ebony armor edged in crimson. Although human in general form, he stood taller than any minotaur, even the Kazelati. This ominous knight Aryx had seen but one time before, when he had been granted the infernal vision of the gods of Krynn battling against the ferocious mad giant who could only be the Father of All and of Nothing. This knight had stood fighting against Father Chaos regardless of the consequences, and even without the great stylized bird of prey upon the breastplate or the massive horned helmet, Aryx would have recognized him immediately.

"Sargonnas . . ."

# The Final Sacrifice

## Chapter Eighteen

"Sargonnas . . ." Aryx repeated, still not quite believing that the figure before him could be real. He had been so certain that the god had abandoned all of them.

Even though the name was little more than a whisper, the dark knight glanced at him. "Aryximaraki. A brave warrior of the empire you are, mortal. Would that you had been one of mine from the beginning." The Sword of Tears blazed again, now that its master wielded it. "My sorrow over the losses you have faced. They could not be helped."

Aryx managed to rise to his knees, once more furious at having been used by the god. "Damn you, Sargonnas! Where were you? Where were you when your people were being slaughtered again?"

"Planning. Plotting. Letting this wyrm think what it would so that it might leave itself open." Sargonnas surveyed the entire region, staring at the hundreds, perhaps thousands, of writhing segments. "Ensuring the ultimate survival of my children, my chosen." He held up the Sword of Tears so that Aryx could see the sinister green stone. "Physically, I have been with you whenever you held this treacherous servant of mine, this blade that would be a god. . . ."

*I sought to obey, Master! I sought to obey! Never would I betray you!*

Aryx thought that only he could hear the frantic, almost whining, voice, but Sargonnas replied, "You sought to obey and still hold me within, eh? Obey and gain all for yourself, as if such a thing could come to pass?"

*Never, Master! Never! See? I even sought to destroy your foe!*

*I could not release you because I lacked the power! The servants of Chaos I cannot feed from, only this sphere of magic!*

"No . . . they are an unappetizing lot, are they not? Especially their puppet master."

At this, the walls around them suddenly resounded with the Coil's long, mocking laughter. "The betrayer shows his craven little face at last," it crowed, "and thinks that he will go unpunished! Such a fool, such a fool! The Father of All and of Nothing will greatly reward his most loyal servant when you are removed from the game and your little playthings have been eradicated, Sargonnas!"

The Horned One looked unaffected by the threat. "The only thing to be removed is you and yours, wyrm. The trap you hoped to spring has been sprung on you instead . . . and now you shall know why I am the God of Vengeance."

Sargonnas raised both hands high, the Sword of Tears aglow in the left. A crimson aura formed around him, an aura from which there suddenly radiated a burst of magical force. Curiously, it completely bypassed the minotaurs, but whenever it touched some segment of the Coil, the aura crackled and that segment shimmered and writhed. Sargonnas clenched his fist, and the magical force radiating from him intensified, illuminating the entire area.

However, the Chaos creature did not stand idly by as the Horned One attacked. First it moved—moved everywhere—shaking what remained of the cavern apart and sending a hailstorm of rock plummeting down. Every one of the huge green-gold segments stirred, twisting and winding through stone and earth. Yet only the tiniest of the rocks struck Aryx and Delara. The rest were deflected off them as if they wore some invisible magical armor. Tons of earth fell all around them, and still Sargonnas protected the pair, although it seemed harder as time passed. Despite the dark deity's timely intervention, however, Aryx felt little gratitude. He felt that Sargonnas had saved them only because it had been convenient to do so.

His initial attack over, the God of Vengeance used the demon blade to slice a great arc through the air, the Sword of Tears wailing all the while. Where the blade struck, a glittering, razor-sharp curve of metal formed, a curve of metal that flew about the valley, cutting at the many parts of the Coil. Some it damaged, sending bursts of energy shooting from the wounds, but others it could not even scratch. The blade flew above, under, and at the various components of the behemoth until at last one segment crushed the flying arc beneath its weight.

Then the Coil countered in earnest. From every angle, massive looped segments shot out, focused on Sargonnas. With the demon blade, the god slashed again and again, sometimes scoring, sometimes missing. Yet at last his defenses wavered, for one of the great serpentine trunks battered him from the side, sending the dark deity flying. Another segment caught him before he hit the ground, tossing Sargonnas high into the air again. However, the Horned One did not plummet earthward, but rather righted in the sky, floating well above his monstrous adversary.

Aryx tore his gaze from the combatants, Delara now his only concern. "We've got to get away while we can!"

She looked stunned. "But we cannot leave him now!"

"What do you hope to do? We've no weapons! Sargonnas intended this final struggle, Delara! Our parts are over!"

At last she nodded. Had he been on his own, Aryx suspected that he would have stayed and tried to help the god, but Delara would leave only if he did. After Seph, he didn't want to lose Delara.

They tried to make their way to the tunnel through which Aryx had originally arrived. The Coil and Sargonnas appeared not to notice them, caught up in their duel. The earth shook, causing the two minotaurs to stumble. Some light shone into the cavern, but it in no way encouraged Aryx, for the walls were still too high and steep for them to climb. The tunnel remained the only way out.

"Not much farther!" he called to Delara. Once they escaped the ruined cavern, things would be better.

"I just hope we can— Aryx! Look out!"

She pushed him forward just as a rockfall started. Aryx rolled over and tried to stand, but some of the collapsing rock struck him, sending the minotaur reeling backward. He grunted as every bone in his body shook. Briefly he glimpsed Delara pressing herself against the wall. Then dust and more rubble obscured everything.

One of the mammoth segments of the Coil slid past, pushing Aryx into the very tunnel mouth he and Delara had been trying to reach. He kicked at the thick, scaled hide, but the minotaur might as well have been striking the rock face next to him. Unable to enter the shattered cavern until the Coil had passed by, Aryx waited in frustration as the gargantuan trunk slowly moved on.

"Delara!" He did not care if the Coil took notice of him. It only mattered that he reach her and make certain that she had escaped the avalanche.

She lay near where Aryx had last seen her, her body half-buried by rock. At first Aryx thought that she stirred in response to his voice, but then he realized that her body only shifted because of the Coil's earthshaking movements. He stumbled his way toward her, fearful of what he might find but unwilling to give up hope.

"Delara . . ." He called her name again, but she made no response. Aryx hoped that she was only unconscious, yet from this close, he could make out blood on her shoulder and head. Delara faced away from him, preventing Aryx from knowing for certain her fate.

All around him the cavern shook as Sargonnas and the Coil locked in magical combat. Mountains of rock and earth had been pushed up. Little of the ceiling had survived, turning the cavern into a tall, jagged valley. Despite the destruction, Aryx paid little mind to the cosmic duel.

He reached for Delara. Her body felt warm, very warm, and his hopes rose. Aryx gently turned her over, trying to be careful not to cause any further damage to her wounds.

His hopes shattered as he stared at her deathlike face. Hand shaking, he checked her heart.

"No . . . By the gods, no!" First Seph, now Delara. The servants of Chaos had taken both from him right before his very eyes, and he had been unable to do anything to save them. Aryx clutched her body close, unwilling to part with it. He would never have the opportunity to spend a good portion of his life with her, as he had begun to hope.

The earth thundered as the god and beast clashed. A shower of rock struck the minotaur and his lost love, stirring Aryx to life again.

*She had no chance. . . .* He turned his gaze skyward, to where Sargonnas fended off attacking segments of the Coil. Both great combatants flared with magical energy, some of which they released against one another at random intervals. Aryx didn't know whom he hated more, the Coil for killing Delara or Sargonnas for failing to protect her. Yet despite his hatred for the Horned One, the warrior still knew which of the two he had to focus his fury on. There would be no future for anyone if the servant of Chaos proved victorious.

Gently lowering Delara to the ground, he looked around for a weapon. His search seemed fruitless until he happened to glance at her belt pouch. There, still in place, despite Delara's terrible journey, hung a long dagger.

A dagger against such a leviathan. It made Aryx laugh bitterly, but he nonetheless took up the dagger, studying it. Good minotaur craftsmanship. The blade itself stretched the length of his hand, better than he could have hoped for. It would probably avail him little, but Aryx *had* to strike back, even if in the end it resulted only in his death.

He rose from Delara's side, gauging the most likely target. Aryx spotted a massive segment that flared bright red where one of Sargonnas's earlier spells had scorched it. The minotaur moved carefully. The serpentine shapes that formed the horrific behemoth writhed constantly, making it possible that the creature could crush him without even realizing it had ever been under assault.

Aryx raised the small blade, his gaze fixed on the wounded spot. His mind screamed that he courted madness, but he ignored it, thinking only of Delara and Seph.

The ground below him burst open. Aryx flew into the air and landed entwined in some of the lesser coils.

"No more play!" roared the Coil, somewhat less mocking than before. "The Father of All and of Nothing would grant you wondrous oblivion, and although you are not worthy of his generosity, you shall yet receive it!"

Aryx had managed to hold on to Delara's dagger, but now he could find no open wound, no cut where he thought the mortal blade might do some good.

*The eye will guide you.*

He recognized the voice in his head as the same one that had awakened him on the shore. Aryx had thought it somehow related to the Sword of Tears or even Sargonnas, but that no longer could be possible. Who, then? The only other item of magical origins he carried was . . . was . . .

*This is a gift with many sides, Aryximaraki,* Kiri-Jolith had said about the dragon orb.

He fixed the emerald eye upon the coil, seeking a weak

spot. His hand suddenly shifted, hovering over a tiny crack between scales. Aryx gritted his teeth, prayed to his ancestors, and thrust the dagger down.

The segment exploded open, in the process knocking Aryx from his perch. Aware of the height from which he fell, the young warrior awaited his death.

His flight paused abruptly. The voice of one he had come both to hate and respect said, "Aryximaraki, you must stop putting yourself in these straits. . . ."

If Sargonnas meant to inject some humor into the situation, it was lost upon Aryx. He hung there as the God of Vengeance seemed to contemplate what to do with him. The dark deity's almost cavalier manner frustrated him. Did Sargonnas still think this was a game?

"I thought you were going to end this once and for all!" he snapped, not caring in the least that the tall armored figure had just saved his life. "End it before we're all dead!"

"I fight on many planes, Aryx, against not only this servant but also his master." Although he spoke calmly, the god's eyes blazed as he glared at the ungrateful mortal.

"But if you divide yourself like that, you can't win either battle! What matter if you hold off both if you can't defeat either? You've claimed my people as your chosen. Now save your children! Every moment you waste, more perish!"

The Coil sent an avalanche down upon them, so many tons of rock that the sky briefly vanished. Yet nothing touched either Sargonnas or Aryx. The god's belated protection did nothing to appease the warrior, who watched helplessly as the new downpour buried Delara's already battered body.

"You are correct as always, Aryximaraki," the armored figure finally admitted, placing Aryx on the rubble-strewn ground. "The path to triumph has always been apparent to me, but I would not take it. I am as much a coward as my so-beloved mistress, my honor no better than hers." Sargonnas gripped the Sword of Tears in both hands. "Very well, mortal. Come. It is time we put an end to this wriggling wyrm."

The sword fairly screamed as a blaze of emerald light darted out from it toward the rocks surrounding the pair. Aryx recognized immediately that the enchanted artifact could not be the source of so much power. Sargonnas had to be channeling his own forces through it. The rocks blew away, each of them striking some segment of the Coil with amazing accuracy. The Chaos creature withdrew many of its parts, clearly taken aback by the vehemence of its adversary.

"Wyrm!" Sargonnas shouted. "I have come to grant you oblivion a little earlier than your master promised!"

Coils lashed out at them from all sides. Sargonnas simply remained where he stood, sword out. Aryx braced himself, certain that this time he would die whatever the outcome of the battle. He prayed that Seph and Delara would be there to greet him when he passed over.

The God of Vengeance turned suddenly, facing the swiftest of the deadly serpentine trunks. He made no move to avoid the oncoming terror, but rather leaned in its direction, the Sword of Tears held ready.

As they collided, Sargonnas plunged the wailing blade halfway into the thick, scaled hide of the Coil. The god's entire body flared crimson as pure magic flowed from him first into the demon blade and then into the Coil itself.

A thousand voices, all of them belonging to the hideous serpent, roared in agony.

As Aryx watched, Sargonnas pushed the blade deeper. The other segments froze where they were, saving the minotaur from being crushed. Now the nearly blinding aura covered not only god, sword, and segment, but every writhing part of the Chaos creature that Aryx could see. Fragments of the already battered landscape plummeted from every side, threatening the warrior, yet Aryx could not keep his eyes from the final struggle of the pair.

Sargonnas pushed the sword still deeper, and as he did, the Coil's fearsome cries grew louder. However, Sargonnas, too, visibly suffered. His armor grew looser, and what Aryx could see of his face looked more drawn and terrible than it ever had in the temple. At last Aryx knew what Sargonnas intended. The god sought to sacrifice every bit of his essence necessary in order to at last destroy his adversary.

Although three-fourths of the sword lay buried in the monster's body, Sargonnas continued to press, as if only by completely plunging the demon blade in could he vanquish his foe. However, more and more Aryx wondered whether the god could do that and still maintain the flow of energy.

The Coil continued to howl as Sargonnas fell to one knee. Aryx finally stirred, realizing that he had to see if he could aid the god. He came up behind the straining deity, braced himself, and threw every bit of strength he had remaining into pushing against the sword hilt.

The Sword of Tears sank up to the guard. The Coil shrieked a thousand times at once. The eyes of the dark god met those of Aryx for a moment, a moment in which the minotaur read far too many conflicting notions.

Sargonnas became pure power, power which fed into the sword and from the sword into the Chaos creature. Not knowing what else to do, Aryx continued holding the hilt down, although every fiber of his body tingled as vestiges of magic coursed through him. He prayed to every ancestor, every deity he could think of who might lend him the strength to hold on until the finish.

With one last high wail, the Coil exploded.

Rock, massive gobbets of reptilian flesh, and Aryx were flung all about the valley. The hapless minotaur tumbled onto something soft and moist, then rolled several yards. Rocks collided with him, one smashing into his shoulder. Explosions, caused by segments of the Coil bursting from the surge of magic, continued to shake the mountains.

Again and again the entire region shook. The makeshift valley collapsed. Aryx had a glimpse of the tunnel through which he had thought to escape caving in, extending the new valley on and on. Earth rose in some places and sank in others, creating mountains and deep gullies.

Another rock struck him on the back of the head. Aryx blacked out then, hoping that at least before he died he had played some minor part in saving the minotaurs from extinction.

\* \* \* \* \*

Rand felt it first—the change in not only the weather, but *everything*. Stumbling from the rocky hiding place Carnelia had dragged him to earlier, he surveyed the battle. The cleric felt as if an immense weight had been taken from his shoulders.

Carnelia ran to him. "Rand! Get back! You're in no condition to fight!"

"I will not have to! Neither will you soon, I think!" He looked at her, a tentative smile escaping his lips. Carnelia did not understand his sudden change until the winds abruptly died, the crashing waves lessened, and even the sky began to clear . . . all within a few brief moments.

"What—what's happening, Rand? Did you—"

"I did nothing . . . but someone did."

"What does it mean?"

The cleric shook his head. "We can only wait and see."

There were those, however, who would not wait and see, chief among them Lord Broedius. Carnelia's uncle surely had noticed the stunning changes at the same time as the rest, but he reacted swiftly. Even as the Magori paused, uncertain as to what had happened, the knight commander began reorganizing the defenders, turning them into the aggressors.

"Look alive, you louts! Archers! Your targets are standing there gaping! Fire! First line, regroup and prepare to advance!"

Minotaur and human commanders began shouting out orders, coordinating with those given by the ebony-eyed warrior. Seasoned troops of both races quickly adjusted even as the huge crustaceans lost order. Sunlight peeked out, then spread across the battlefield. Those Magori it touched cringed, repelled by its brightness.

Out at sea, the suddenly calm waters enabled the crews of the surviving vessels to regain control. Startled Magori slipped from the hulls, unable to compensate in time for the change in the Blood Sea. Those of the invaders aboard found themselves without reinforcements, and while many continued to fight, albeit with lessening eagerness, others turned to flee just as they had when the Maelstrom had vanished.

"This is the last time, by the Lady!" Lord Broedius roared. "Drive those blasted shellfish into the sea and make certain that they don't come back!"

He nearly lost his balance—and his life—as two desperate Magori charged through the lines directly in front of the knight commander's horse. Carnelia looked on with fear, but Broedius fended off both until help in the form of the Kazelati came. Outnumbered four to one, the two Magori fell quickly.

"I've got to get down there and help! There's still too much danger!"

Rand hobbled forward. "I agree. Let us descend,"

She looked at him, startled by his last words. "Rand! You've already done so much and it's weakened you badly! Stay behind! Let me do my part now!"

The blond cleric grimaced. She was right when she spoke of his weakness, yet Rand did not want her down there without him nearby. Still, he realized that in the long run, his presence would more than likely keep Carnelia from concentrating fully on the enemy. He would actually be risking her life if he tried to remain at her side.

"All right," he finally muttered. "Go . . . and may Kiri-Jolith watch over you."

She gave him a rueful smile. "At this point, I'd settle for *any* god watching over me!"

Rand watched her scramble almost eagerly down the hillside. He touched the medallion on his chest, feeling no link whatsoever to his patron. Rand had felt no link before his last spell either. The cleric had tried to convince himself that Aryx had not been correct, that it *had* been the God of Just Causes who had provided Rand with the power. Yet if Kiri-Jolith maintained no link with him, then the cleric had drawn the magic from elsewhere. Difficult as such a notion had been to accept, he saw no other choice.

If I could only draw upon it now . . . Rand felt drained, more drained than he had ever felt in his life. If once he had been able to draw magic forth from either himself or his surroundings, he doubted he could do it now even if his life depended upon it. No, best if Rand did as Carnelia had suggested and stay where the last vestiges of the battle would not touch him. Besides, from the look of things, it would not be long now.

To their credit, the Magori fought. Rand almost felt pity for the monstrous creatures, clearly slaves to the horrific thing that had called itself the Coil. Of course, he doubted that the crustaceans would have come in peace, even given the choice. They simply did not like having to battle under conditions not favorable to them.

Carnelia stumbled slightly as she reached the bottom. Rand bit back words of caution as she started along the moist sand toward her uncle and the others. She had changed much since they had been first thrown together, and if it turned out that both their gods had abandoned Krynn, he hoped to discover a new future alongside her.

The moist ground behind Carnelia suddenly burst open, and a Magori with a lance rose up. Rand recognized the same markings on the snout that had earlier indicated one of the swarm's possible leaders. Her attention focused on the battle ahead, Carnelia neither saw nor heard the crimson and white crustacean as it lumbered toward her back, lance already poised to throw.

"Carnelia!" Rand nearly fell down the hillside as he desperately tried to attract the female knight's attention. Much to his dismay, though, she could not hear him.

The Magori threw its lance.

"No!" The cleric's hands crackled with silver-blue energy. The ground around the crustacean suddenly swirled, becoming a thick, pasty soup that pulled the Chaos creature down. Hissing, the Magori struggled to free itself, but it might as well have been trying to fly, for all the good its efforts did it. Even as Rand recovered from his shocking spell, the ground swallowed the abomination, leaving no trace.

It nearly proved impossible for him to reach her, so exhausted, so ruined did Rand feel. Each second that passed seemed an eternity.

Heedless of his own wound, Rand dragged himself to Carnelia's side. He stared at her still form, the terrible lance rising from her back like some macabre flagpole. She still breathed, but in short, ragged breaths that said that her life had but moments left.

No! I will not permit it! Not when we are this close to victory! Yet what could he do? The one time that he had saved a life, that of the minotaur Aryx, he had done so under the secret guidance of Kiri-Jolith. Granted, Rand had performed other miracles these past few days, but they meant nothing to him compared with the effort he knew he would need to help Carnelia. Perhaps if he had used this strange magic sparingly before, Rand might have not worried, but the last and unexpected spell had nearly caused him to black out. Only the sudden rush of fear had actually enabled him to unleash the spell that had killed the Magori. Surely no more remained within him. . . .

Rand refused to accept that. He would do what he could for Carnelia whatever the cost to him. Let this one final spell take his own life if necessary, but the cleric would save her!

He removed the lance, then placed his hands on her wound. Tears fluttered down his cheeks, but he paid neither them nor the battle any mind. Only Carnelia mattered.

Heal her! Rand pleaded to the power within, beseeching it

as he would have his lost god. He put his hands over the terrible wound. Take from me what you must! Give my life for hers if necessary, but heal her!

Something within him seemed to answer. Rand felt a primal force rise up inside him, one that threatened to wrench his very being apart, yet gladly did he accept the sacrifice if only Carnelia could be saved.

More and more power flowed through him. Rand watched his love, saw that he had stemmed the tide but had not yet reversed it. He needed to give her more. He needed to give her everything.

Rand gritted his teeth, pushing his will to the limit and beyond. *Everything!*

The force within continued to well up until the cleric thought it would overwhelm him . . . and then it burst free, flowing like an uncontrollable river into Carnelia's quivering form.

Rand screamed.

# Aftermath

## Chapter Nineteen

Somehow Aryx had survived. He should not have, but he had. The realization did nothing to assuage him; Aryx almost would have preferred to die. He had failed both Seph and Delara. He did not deserve to live.

*But you will live. . . .*

He stirred at the voice in his head, fearing that somehow, through all of it, the Sword of Tears had yet come to claim him. Aryx pushed himself up, trying to locate the demon blade, and instead saw the feet of a tall and massive minotaur warrior.

No . . . no minotaur, for the face that met his gaze did not belong to one of his kind, although it had similarities and its owner had certainly meddled in the affairs of the race enough.

"Kiri-Jolith . . ." He almost spat the name out.

"Aryximaraki." The god inclined his head slightly. Unlike the last time the beaten and battered warrior had seen him, the bison-headed deity looked almost real, almost mortal. Aryx wondered if Kiri-Jolith would bleed if punched hard enough in the mouth. "You have a right to be angry."

"How gracious of you . . ." Aryx managed to get to his feet with no help from the god. He stared close at the other, for the first time noting that Kiri-Jolith looked tired . . . very tired.

"Nothing more could be done, Aryximaraki. The matter had moved beyond the grasp of either Sargonnas or myself. We had planned other—"

"Wait! Are you saying this was all part of a plan?"

"No. Working to protect the minotaurs while bringing them properly into the struggle, that was the plan. Sending my Kazelati to support you, that was the plan. Bringing

Sargonnas close enough to confront Father Chaos's pet wyrm, to ensure its destruction, that was the plan." Kiri-Jolith extended a hand, indicating the landscape around them. "This—and so much that happened both on the islands and in the Blood Sea—was *not* part of the plan."

Aryx looked around, at last seeing the region around him. He no longer lay at the bottom of the shattered cavern but now stood in the immense valley formed in the wake of its destruction. Jagged mountains thrust up everywhere, surrounding the shadowed valley. The incredible formation spread across the neck of the peninsula for as far as the eye could see, even the dragon orb.

Had Sargonnas and the Coil truly raised up the earth so much? Despite his anger, it again amazed the dusky gray minotaur that he had survived. "Did you save me?"

"I? I found you here, just awakening. A marvel to me, mortal. Perhaps a last gift from my erstwhile ally."

Last gift? "Are you saying that Sargonnas is dead?" Aryx gazed down into the mighty valley. Even from such a great height, he could see that the landscape below lay draped in dripping, foul-smelling bits of what had once been Father Chaos's most loyal and persistent servant. Massive, burnt segments still remained, some of them still smoldering. The stench they raised would have driven off even the Magori. Aryx wondered whether any scavengers who passed by the region in the future would want to touch such putrid morsels.

Kiri-Jolith shrugged. "Only Sargonnas can reveal the truth of that." The bison-headed warrior glanced down at the carnage. "As you surmised, sometimes death and gods can become a confusing matter . . . but not so the destruction of overzealous wyrms."

The god walked over to Aryx, put a hand on his shoulder. Aryx flinched but did not pull away. "I am truly sorry about your losses. They could not be helped. I did what I could, for it was the least I could do after choosing you for this venture."

That made the weary warrior turn. "You chose me? I thought *circumstance* did."

The god nodded somberly. "Aye, circumstance it was, but after you had fallen overboard in the Blood Sea, I steered them toward you. Sargonnas knew I would send him someone of your race whom I felt worthy to mark my part in this pact, and you happened along just then."

Richard A. Knaak

Aryx snorted. "A poor choice you made, I'd say."

"You proved yourself more than worthy, young one. And while I feel for your losses, be assured that they could not be prevented."

Aryx bitterly desired to argue that assumption, but he knew better than to try to convince a god, even one as good as this. "Is it at last over? Have we saved our world?"

An indecipherable expression crossed Kiri-Jolith's features. "The war is not yet over and Sargonnas's loss will be felt, for he has vanished on all other planes as well. I can swear to this, for I stand in those places even as I stand here." The bison-headed warrior's tone shifted. "But if you wish to know whether your people have been rescued, I can grant you that knowledge."

"Of course I want to know!" Aryx snapped, finally growing impatient with the god's manner.

"Ever the temper. Clearly a family trait . . ." Kiri-Jolith took one last look around. "Curious. I cannot find it."

Aryx tried to follow his gaze. "What?"

"His favored blade. The wailing sword. I thought it might still be of some use, but I cannot sense it anywhere."

The thought of seeing the Sword of Tears again unnerved Aryx. Even Sargonnas had not trusted the blade. "It was probably destroyed along with the Coil. Sargonnas . . . Sargonnas put his entire power through it."

The God of Just Causes nodded. "You may be correct. A small matter now, and besides, we must make haste."

He clapped his hands together, and before Aryx understood what the god intended, the air rippled. Suddenly the pair stood in a different place, a ridge overlooking the shoreline where Lord Broedius and the others had been forced to come ashore.

The battle had ended. The only Magori that Aryx could see lay in piles on the beach. Minotaur and human officers could be seen organizing talons and legions of troops, some of them now mixed. Aryx thought he spotted Lord Broedius talking to several minotaurs, including the Kazelati, their taller, slimmer forms unmistakable. Out at sea, the survivors of the fleet had dropped anchor. Several small boats had gone out to some not-so-fortunate vessels that either lay half-sunk or caught up on rocks, waiting for crews to salvage what they could from the wrecks.

Far from the growing pyres of crustaceans, the defenders' dead lay lined shoulder to shoulder, knights next to minotaurs. Aryx saw that a detail had already been set aside to make certain that those who had fallen to the enemy would receive proper honors. A sense of cooperation he would never had expected had grown between his people and the Knights of Takhisis. While in many ways he applauded it, Aryx wondered if such an alliance would be wise in the long run.

Seeing the dead so well cared for reminded Aryx that Delara, too, needed to be honored. Realizing that her body lay buried with the Coil, he turned to demand that the god bring her to him. However, even as he opened his mouth, Aryx saw that Delara already lay nearby, Kiri-Jolith having apparently anticipated his request. Near her lay another still form . . . Seph.

"I'm sorry that she was not one of mine. Either way, I could do nothing for her, my friend. The matters of gods are not so simple anymore." The bison-headed figure reached down to touch her closed eyes. "She has my blessing nonetheless, just as your brave brother always has."

"What happens now?" Aryx asked, glancing away from Delara's calm, almost serene expression.

"You return to your people and they go on to fight their battles. Watch them, Aryximaraki, for they will play a significant role in the future, I think. But some of their choices may not be the best." Kiri-Jolith gave him a fleeting smile. "You will do well, though, at least if you can keep some of that bitterness from overwhelming you. Fight hard, warrior, and watch that eye of yours. I have suspicions that it has a life of its own at times."

Aryx did not quite understand until he thought of the voice that had at least on two occasions stirred him to consciousness after disaster. He nodded, not knowing how else to respond.

Kiri-Jolith stared off to the heavens. "I must go now. I stretch myself too thin being here as well as there. This war is far from over, Aryximaraki. Remember well what I said. Your people will likely play a great role in the future of Krynn. This is their chance, for good or ill. Whatever you minotaurs do—and that includes the Kazelati—do not keep repeating the same mistakes you have made in the past."

"We'll try not to."

"Kaz Dragonslayer would have been very proud of you," Kiri-Jolith added. "In fact, I know he must be, for he wished me to give you this."

From empty air, the warrior god produced a gleaming, single-edged axe that at first Aryx mistook for Honor's Face. Although he immediately realized his mistake, the minotaur nonetheless stood awed, for clearly if it was not that fabled weapon, it must be somehow related. While not quite a mirror finish, the side of the axe head reflected almost as well. The edge of the blade curved downward and looked to have been honed to such perfection that Aryx thought it must be capable of cutting through any material. As for the handle, it had been forged from some material with the appearance of platinum, although surely it could not be that rich metal.

"Aryximaraki, this is yours." Kiri-Jolith held out the new axe. Aryx could make out runes carved in the handle. "It is called Truth's Guardian."

Aryx took the axe with reverence. Originating from his grandfather, the axe must have incredible value.

"Wield it proudly, Aryx Dragoneye."

And with that, Kiri-Jolith vanished.

Aryx stood there for a time, almost expecting the god to return. The emptiness the warrior had felt after Seph's death had grown with Delara's, and now even Kiri-Jolith's departure, although far different, had turned that emptiness into a chasm as great as the Abyss.

He stared one last time at Truth's Guardian. Then, harnessing it to his back, Aryx went over to Delara. He caressed the side of her face once, then, steeling himself, began to make plans.

\*   \*   \*   \*   \*

"He said I'd find you here, and of course he was correct."

Aryx turned around to see Carnelia. She wobbled as she walked, at times almost like a puppet with some strings cut. Her left arm dangled loosely.

"Who?"

"Rand . . . he said that Kiri-Jolith told him before the god wished him farewell." The knight looked perplexed by what Rand had told her, almost as if she wondered whether he had gone mad.

"It wouldn't surprise me if it happened just as he said." The minotaur returned to work. He had almost enough rocks in place. Out here, a pyre would have taken too much time and might have set the entire area ablaze. Aryx had been forced to settle on two simple but well-stacked mounds. Fortunately the grieving warrior had managed to find a depression in which to lay the bodies, aiding his efforts immensely.

"Lord Broedius wishes to speak with you."

"When I'm done."

She hesitated before adding, "I'm sorry, Aryx. Rand also said that Delara died . . . and I see he was right about that, too." Carnelia did not ask him about the second mound where Seph lay, instead looking beyond him toward the distant but unmistakable mountains. It seemed a strain for her to use her neck. "There *are* mountains there! My uncle thought the scouts had imagined them. He's been in this region in the past and said that there were only forests and plains here."

Aryx stood, the last rock in place. "I'll explain them later."

"I don't understand. Explain the mountains?"

The minotaur waved Carnelia off. He started to walk past her, then eyed the female warrior closely. She looked pale, very pale. "You were wounded."

She laughed, a humorless sound. "I was *dead,* Aryx. Worse than you when we found you adrift in the Blood Sea. An underdweller lance in my back. Rand . . . Rand saved me, although I don't know how. It cost him, though."

"How?"

"He's aged. He looks twenty years older, and he says that a part of him is gone forever. He says he's no longer a cleric of Kiri-Jolith . . . that his path will be a different one from now on." She shook her head. "I don't know what that means, and I don't think Rand does either, at least not entirely."

Aryx, who felt he had suffered far more of the gods' ambiguous words than anyone, could not help her. "The gods don't like to make themselves clear. I think it spoils their games."

"You may be right," she returned, perhaps thinking of her own missing goddess. "Oh . . . and he's blind. Whatever he did to save me seemed to burn out his eyes. Rand didn't seem surprised, however. . . ." She exhaled sharply. "Rand and I are leaving the rest of you at first chance. Neither of us are any good to the effort now, and . . . and we're going to help each other heal as best we can, without swords or magic."

The weary minotaur snorted. More casualties of the gods. While he respected some of the deities, it would not have displeased him if they all simply left Krynn alone, as they had once before. Of course, not until the threat to the world had been vanquished.

"You'll probably be better off than any of us," he finally told her. Then he added, "Well, Broedius is waiting. We might as well go to him. He's probably already trying to get the fleet moving. He wouldn't want to keep his precious Lord Ariakan waiting." He could not hide some lingering bitterness.

Aryx had to help the human along, the effort to find him having taxed her too much. Where once she had looked with scorn upon the minotaurs, now among them were some who had become close comrades. This war would make for many changes before it was finished. The minotaur felt some certainty that Krynn did have a future, but what shape it would take remained a question.

In the distance, those on shore continued to gather together the dead, bind the wounded, and reorganize the expedition. A great victory had been won here, greater than even Lord Broedius and the human and minotaur commanders yet knew. It would be interesting to see what they thought of his tale, and even more interesting if they believed all of it.

As they neared the army, Aryx heard the knight commander and the minotaur generals talking about the surrounding landscape. Rand, leaning on a staff for support, stood next to Lord Broedius. The former cleric's eyes were shut as if in thought, but his expression seemed slightly troubled. Broedius spoke with animation and seemed especially interested in the area's capabilities as a potential jumping-off point for future campaigns . . . in conjunction with the empire.

"Once this expedition has reached a victorious conclusion, we will establish a better dialogue with your emperor. This area here, our present circumstance notwithstanding, would make an excellent point from which to launch our campaigns to the southern regions."

"The forest is healthy," General Hojak returned. "The trees would make strong ships." He nodded. "As the only surviving member of the Supreme Circle present, I think I can speak favorably to Chot . . . or his successor, if necessary. Your notion has merit, Lord Broedius."

"I have the power to make a binding agreement with you now, General. . . ."

Captain Brac, who had just arrived, stood next to the lead Kazelati representative from the *Vengeance*. Neither seemed at all pleased with the suggestions. Considering their attitudes toward the empire, Aryx did not find that at all surprising.

"It is obviously far too early for such concerns," the senior captain admonished. "Krynn is still at war."

"It's always wise to think about the future," the ebony-eyed knight remarked, his gaze flickering from Brac to Hojak. "It's always wise to build alliance for that future."

The two Kazelati said nothing, but Aryx knew that this discussion had not ended. If the Knights of Takhisis did forge an alliance with the empire, they might at the same time be breaking whatever fragile bond they had with the other minotaurs.

"The matter of a colony here was discussed not long ago, in fact," General Hojak continued, paying no mind to his irate cousins. "Had this war not come up, I suspect we would have sent ships here within a year, two at most. The empire desperately needs good timber and room for growth."

Rand suddenly stirred, turning his face in Aryx's direction. He seemed almost pleased at the interruption. "Hail, Aryx Dragoneye. I have been telling the knight commander that you have quite a tale to tell."

The others paused in their conversation to stare at him, many likely having assumed that he had been drowned at sea. Aryx read some awe among the minotaurs, especially the Kazelati, and even Broedius and Hojak eyed him with greater respect.

"Aye, I have a tale." He let Carnelia wend her way to Rand, happy at least to see the two of them together. For a recently blinded man, the blond human moved with remarkable precision. "Aye, an epic tale . . . and I would tell it now."

The ghosts of Seph, Delara, Hecar, the crew of the *Kraken's Eye*, and many others surrounded him as he spoke, but for now Aryx welcomed them. Tomorrow, he and the other warriors would move on to do their part to save Ansalon and the rest of Krynn from Chaos. The ghosts of those he had lost would stand behind him just as would his own ancestors, Kaz Dragonslayer included, all adding to his strength. Each of the other minotaurs in the army would be flanked by his own spirits, the legacy of hundreds of years of struggle and determination.

When Aryx had finished, Lord Broedius nodded. "A story to be retold once we've swept Chaos from Krynn. Your deeds will lend encouragement to both human and minotaur warriors!" He clapped one hand on the minotaur's shoulder. "And your name will be remembered for your part in strengthening the ties between our forces."

Aryx fought back a grimace, not at all certain if he wanted the honor.

Determined not to be outdone by an outsider, General Hojak came up and slapped him on the back. "A champion of the empire! You honor the memory of your cousin, the late lamented Geryl!" The general appeared to have forgotten his previous animosity toward his fellow officer. "And in honor of that, I say here and now that we name this new colony after you!"

With the exception of the Kazelati, those in attendance found the suggestion commendable. Aryx, however, fought hard to hide his dismay. He wanted no such honor, no such legacy. He had done nothing in this war for which he wanted to be remembered, not when so many he had known and cared for had perished.

An idea came to him, one that, under the circumstances, even the Kazelati could not argue against. None of them would have likely survived if not for his sacrifice.

"Not me. Don't name this new colony after me, but rather the one who defeated the master of the Magori."

Lord Broedius frowned. "Are you suggesting—"

"Sargonnas, yes. Call it Sargonath Ur Seeld." He looked around, daring them to find fault in the name. In the old style of the minotaur language, it meant "The Shield of Sargonnas." Or, more simply, just "Sargonath."

"Another admirable suggestion," the older minotaur commented. "Sargonath . . . yes, that might be more appropriate after all. . . ."

Aryx had suspected that Hojak would find merit in his recommendation. Better a missing god than a living hero, who might someday prove a thorn.

Brac and his companion held their expressions, but their eyes informed Aryx of what they thought of naming any site after the Horned One. No, the Kazelati would not long be a part of this alliance, and in some ways, Aryx could not blame them. He had managed to bring the Knights of Takhisis and his people together, but if it meant they once more took the ruinous path of conquest, the dusky gray minotaur doubted he wanted to be a part of it.

Of course, first they still had to win the war against Father Chaos's minions. As Broedius brought up plans for a march to the knighthood's post near Kernen, Aryx quietly stepped back from the assembly. He walked along until the Blood Sea would permit him to go no farther, then stared out at the now calm waters.

They would win, Aryx felt certain of that, and then, as Kiri-Jolith had hinted, the minotaurs would take a greater role in the affairs of all Krynn. Their alliance with the Knights of Takhisis promised that much of their new role would involve conflict, but he hoped it might also eventually involve a change for the better.

*We have been enslaved but have always thrown off our shackles,* so the litany began. Aryx drew Truth's Guardian from its harness, feeling comfort in its weight, the way it fit his hand. *We have been driven back, but always returned to the fray stronger than before. We have risen to new heights when all other races have fallen into decay. We are the future of Krynn, the fated masters of the entire world. We are the children of destiny.*

Indeed, the minotaurs' day of destiny was at hand. If not tomorrow, then soon . . . very soon. Aryx hoped only that his people would be prepared when it happened . . . or else their day would quickly be followed by a long, long night from which they might never rise again.

# THE SOULFORGE
## MARGARET WEIS

The long-awaited prequel to the bestselling Chronicles Trilogy by the author who brought Raistlin to life!

Raistlin Majere is six years old when he is introduced to the archmage who enrolls him in a school for the study of magic. There the gifted and talented but tormented boy comes to see magic as his salvation. Mages in the magical Tower of High Sorcery watch him in secret, for they see shadows darkening over Raistlin even as the same shadows lengthen over all Ansalon.

Finally, Raistlin draws near his goal of becoming a wizard. But first he must take the Test in the Tower of High Sorcery— or die trying.

# THE CHRONICLES TRILOGY
## MARGARET WEIS AND
## TRACY HICKMAN

Fifteen years after publication and with more than three million copies in print, the story of the worldwide best-selling trilogy is as compelling as ever.

Dragons have returned to Krynn with a vengeance. An unlikely band of heroes embarks on a perilous quest for the legendary DRAGONLANCE!